LITTLE HUT OF LEAPING FISHES

LITTLE HUT OF LEAPING FISHES

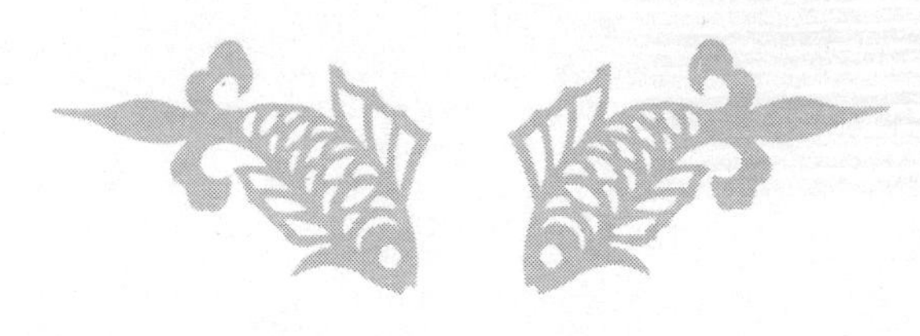

Chiew-Siah Tei

Picador

First published 2008 in Picador by
Pan Macmillan Australia Pty Limited, Sydney

First published in Great Britain 2008 by Picador
an imprint of Pan Macmillan Ltd
Pan Macmillan, 20 New Wharf Road, London N1 9RR
Basingstoke and Oxford
Associated companies throughout the world
www.panmacmillan.com

ISBN 978-0-330-45438-4 HB
ISBN 978-0-330-45619-7 TPB

The writer acknowledges support from the
Scottish Arts Council towards the writing of this title.

1 3 5 7 9 8 6 4 2

A CIP catalogue record for this book is available from
the British Library.

Printed and bound in the UK by
CPI Mackays, Chatham ME5 8TD

ONE

Chai Mansion, 1875

Autumn in Plum Blossom Village is a season of sweat and laughter. Of acres and acres of golden fields. Of paddy-reaping and threshing. Naked stalks and plump-eared rice. Smiling faces, exhausted bodies. Bare-footed children run wild in the open, chasing after dogs who chase them. Mothers prepare meals for fathers busy in the fields.

Crickets hide in the bushes; their noises crackle over the sky. Chrysanthemums smile a bright yellow. Snakes lurk in the mangroves, waiting patiently for toads and frogs that wait patiently for mosquitoes and flies.

At night, as soon as the last streaks of evening fade, chimneys stop smoking, doors are shut tight. Under the thatched roofs, contented children wander through dreamlands, smiles on their faces, saliva at the corners of their mouths. Mothers darn shoes and shirts for fathers who enjoy a last puff of the pipe before bed. Before the day starts again.

So it is tonight.

In the distance, dilapidated shacks are reduced to ambiguous specks, dotted around the western hillside, shadowed under a lingering canopy of clouds. The wind rises, sweeping the giant shelter eastward, past the highlands, the peasants' huts, past the winding Plum River and the paddy fields, before planting it right above the mansion by the eastern slope.

The Chai Mansion.

All of its four courtyards are engulfed in the dark shadow of the autumn cloud. During the day, activities centre on the east court where Master Chai resides, where servants wait reverently for orders, to fetch their demanding master this and that. To obey his endless requests. Opposite, in the west court, lives Likang, the master's eldest son, and his wives. Their rooms are carefully arranged: while Likang enjoys the comfort of the centre room, his first wife, Da Niang, is assigned to the chamber on the right, confirming her superior status over the second wife, Er Niang, who always grumbles about being placed in the less prestigious left. Likang's brother, Liwei, is content with the south court, which is as quiet as the vacant guest rooms in the north court.

Now all the courtyards rest in silence.

But not for long.

The first cries pierce the darkness, travel to the east court and drill into Master Chai's ears. He freezes to listen, then springs up, choking on the last puff of his pipe. He nods and nods, and grins. *There he comes, the eldest son of my eldest son.* Frightened by his sudden movement, his teenage maid steps back, and waits.

Butler Feng bursts in: 'A boy! It's a boy!'

His master glances up. Butler Feng stops and drops his smile. He bows and stands to one side.

Master Chai sits down, signals the servant girl to prepare his pipe, and howls: 'Go and get Likang!'

The girl drops the pipe. Butler Feng says yes and leaves.

He must be somewhere enjoying himself. Master Chai sighs, watching the young girl hurriedly pick up the pipe and light it.

Outside, the servants buzz with excitement, busily disseminating the news in the suddenly lit mansion. They trace the infant's cries to the west court, hushing each other to keep their voices down. Passing by, Butler Feng knits his brows tight, ordering the servants to disperse. Their whispers fill the courtyard as they leave.

Behind the closed door of Da Niang's room, the baby boy finally stops crying as he grows accustomed to his new world. Frail and pale, his mother takes a last look at him before the midwife takes him away.

After waiting so long, his sisters, Meilian, eight, and Meifong, five, spring forward, surround the midwife. Eager to look at him, their brother. They touch his little pink face, tiny fingers. Da Niang, too weak to intervene, watches him carried to the adjoining room. Her maid pours her a cup of warm ginger tea, but Da Niang sends her off to attend to her infant master instead. He starts crying again, missing the warmth of his mother's bosom.

Though tired, his mother struggles to stay awake, listens, and is glad when his cry ceases. *Sleep well, son.*

Moments later he wakes and cries again, but stops as soon as his hungry lips reach Mama Wang's nipple. Milk is plentiful from the enormous breasts of the nursemaid. Mama Wang, after being forced by her husband to sell her newborn baby for an ox to work the field, has seized the opportunity to serve this child. But she misses her own. *My Doggie*. She smiles, remembering the moment she first caught sight of him. *A lovely boy; naming him after an animal will blind the jealous evil spirits, will stop them from taking him away.* But then her smile turns bitter. *Yet he was taken*. The pain penetrates her heart, deepening, vibrating. Her body trembles. The infant's mouth loses hold of her nipple. He wails.

Now that the servant girl has left the room to take the two sisters to bed, Mama Wang is all by herself with the baby. *Someone else's.* She takes a closer look at the newborn as she guides him to her nipple again. Eyes closed, he enjoys his meal, sucking quietly, smelling the sweet scent of milk. *As lovely as my Doggie*. Mama Wang's eyes turn soft. She holds him closer to her, caresses his little arms, little legs and creased face. *Yes, you are my Doggie*.

Next door, his mother quietly listens to his yawns and breathings, so close yet distant, separated by the wooden wall. *If only I could feed him with my own milk.* All alone, she sighs, her tears well up.

'A girl factory no longer,' she murmurs.

Where is his father? Where is he? She stares up. A column of ants marches along the wooden beam, too busy to give an answer. And soon tiredness drowns her. She sleeps.

Two doors away, a teacup smashes to pieces on the floor. Er Niang stands, one hand on the table, the other on her protruding belly, puffing and trembling with rage.

'Why should she be first?' she cries, cupping the baby inside her. 'You will be a boy! You must be a boy! You will not lose out.'

Cowering in a corner, her maid presses her lean body hard against the wall, shivering as she stares into her mistress's blazing eyes.

At midnight, the newborn's father is dragged home by Butler Feng from a brothel in Pindong Town ten miles away. Half-drunk, Likang rushes through Da Niang's room to his child's bed, hurriedly pulls aside the white cotton covering the baby's tiny body. And he sees it, the little streak of manhood, resting quietly like the infant himself. *It's real.* He hums a snatch of opera as he leaves.

Awake since his return, Da Niang glances up as her husband passes by. Likang pauses, then forces a smile, nods, and retreats to his residence.

Da Niang shuts her eyes tight, tears streaming.

Early in the morning on the seventh day after the birth, Master Chai sends Butler Feng for Old Scholar Yan, the only scholar in Plum Blossom Village.

Arriving back at the threshold of the newborn's room in the west court, Butler Feng tugs aside a corner of the door curtain for Old Scholar Yan to peer in. Fed and content, and resting comfortably at Mama Wang's bosom, the baby seems to smile at the old man with umps and ahs: his eyes brighten, his cheeks flush pink, his forehead gleams in the morning rays that slip through the raised curtain. He smiles as if he knows him already, the scrawny old man. Squinting, Old Scholar Yan steps forward. Butler Feng holds out his hand.

'No.'

The curtain drops. Behind it the baby wails, loud and piercing.

Returning to Master Chai's study, Old Scholar Yan sits at the table before a piece of red paper and a plateful of ink, and frowns, for a long time. And writes nothing. Although there is more ink than needed, the scholar's teenage disciple keeps grinding the inkstick hard against the inkstone and peeping at Master Chai, who locks his wrinkled face tight. The young man watches, sweat streaming from his clean-shaven head. He tries to shut his ears, expecting a roar, but the master says nothing. The disciple is too young to know that Old Scholar Yan is the only person in Plum Blossom Village Master Chai would never roar at. He knows things the master does not know; he can read and write.

Still, there are many more things Master Chai does not know about Old Scholar Yan. He does not know the many nights the scholar has spent studying *I-Ching*, the Book of Changes, horoscopes and face-reading. He does not know that this most knowledgeable man in Plum Blossom Village sees something in his grandson's little face and eyes.

The scholar searches his old brain for names: to match that face, those eyes and the *something* inside them. Master Chai beckons to his maid to replace the untouched tea with a fresh cup of warm *o-long*.

Taking a sip of the tea, Old Scholar Yan finally writes on the red paper, boldly, in *lishu*, the ancient calligraphy of the Han Dynasty.

Holding the piece of writing, Master Chai rushes through the corridor to the ancestral hall. Butler Feng tags along and helps his master to set the precious names nicely on the prayer table in front of the ancestors' memorial plates. Master Chai throws a pair of *yao*, the half-moon-shape divinatory blocks, onto the floor. Both fall open, face up, smiling. *Approved.*

So Master Chai announces his grandson's name: Mingzhi; his scholar name is to be Ziwen, which means intelligent and knowledgeable. A literate man.

No more illiterates. The Master has decided. For generations his ancestors have spent their entire lives managing thousands of acres of land in and around Plum Blossom Village. None of them, except his second son, knows anything more than basic reading. This eldest son of the eldest son of Chai is to be different: an educated *shenshi*, a member of the gentry, who will be eligible for public office. His grandfather is determined; his father nods, and his mother smiles quietly.

Mama Wang provides sufficient milk for the baby's enormous appetite. Always, he buries his head in Mama Wang's breasts after his meal, dozes off soundly in the sweet and sour scents of milk and sweat. His mother watches, her heart contracting.

She is already weak from two earlier miscarriages, and the delivery drains her further. Taking care of her young son becomes impossible, as she is able to sit up only for meals in the first month after her confinement.

In the morning, when he is fed and dressed, Mama Wang takes him to his mother, lays him beside her. Pleased and thrilled, she caresses him and kisses him. Feels his delicate fingers, soft, chubby cheeks. Happy to hear his umps and ahs, to watch his lips twitching and his mouth opening as if talking to her, responding to her loving and caring words, which are only noises to him.

Sometimes she struggles to sit up, to cradle and hold him tight in her bosom. His pulse feels vibrant. *An active life*. She can almost see what lies ahead of him. Hope. That she has ceased to see in herself long before his birth.

His sisters come after breakfast. They gather round their mother's bed and play with their brother. Meilian pinches his cheeks and calls him little *bao* – steamed bun with filling – while Meifong holds his hands and sings the folk songs she has learned from their maid.

He shares smiles with them, giggles and gurgles as they sing and gesture.

—~—

His father sometimes visits, to see if he has grown. When he comes the two sisters crouch in a corner and watch their father looking down at the cradle, observing him.

'He is too weak. You should feed him more often.'

He always makes the same remarks. And Mama Wang always stares at the baby's well fleshed-out limbs and round body and nods in silence, not wishing to argue. Then Likang leaves, without holding the child or glancing at his daughters in the corner.

—~—

A month after Mingzhi's birth, Master Chai proudly holds a ceremony to celebrate his first grandson's Full Moon.

Early in the morning Mama Wang feeds Mingzhi his first meal of the day, bathes him and dresses him in his red shirt, red swaddling clothes, red gloves and red socks.

'May all good fortune fall on you,' Mama Wang whispers to the red baby in her arms.

His hands, enveloped in cotton gloves, move along his face, his nose and his mouth. His fingers fidget in the tightly tied gloves, unable to touch his face or his nose, and unable to taste his soft, delicious thumb. Frustrated, his face turns red too, and his legs keep kicking.

'Shh,' Mama Wang cradles him and calms him. 'This is the rule. You have to behave yourself from now on.'

In the ancestral hall Master Chai paces up and down tapping his dragonhead walking stick, giving orders to Butler Feng to give orders, checking the prayer table: a pair of red candles on glittering brass holders; a double lion brass joss-stick pot filled with sand, fresh with the green smell of Plum River; a full bunch of joss sticks and a pair of divinatory blocks. All must be in order. And the offerings are lined up: a whole roasted pig sits in the middle, surrounded by braised duck, boiled chicken, meaty spring rolls, mushroom and vegetable platters and herbal chicken soup. And the red rice cakes and red boiled eggs, of course. And seven small cups of rice wine and seven big bowls of plain rice with seven pairs of chopsticks and seven soup spoons for seven generations of ancestors.

Bracing himself with his brass stick, Master Chai stoops and counts carefully with his shrivelled fingers, making sure that no ancestor lacks anything. For if one place is mislaid, Master Chai will have to carry the sin of being disrespectful not only through the whole of this life, but also the next.

Finally candles and joss sticks are lit. Blazing flames dance high, burning red, flashing on the floor and pillars.

Smoke puffs up, joining the sweet and sour and herbal smells of the food, running wild between the beams and the pillars, brooding over the old man, his ancestors, his offerings and his servants.

Butler Feng drags Likang out of bed. Still yawning, Likang almost sleepwalks through the courtyard past the many servants shuffling around cleaning the floor and the pillars, or bringing in yet more offerings. He nearly collides with the prayer table.

Master Chai roars: 'Try to make yourself useful, will you?'

The sharp tail of the dragon stick points at Likang's face, and he is fully awake now. Butler Feng pulls him away instantly to avoid further rebukes.

Mama Wang, guarded by Meilian and Meifong, stops at the threshold of the ancestral hall. *Neither women nor other clans are allowed in the ancestral hall.* Likang goes to take Mingzhi from the nursemaid, holding him for the first time, awkwardly. In his father's arms the child fidgets and sneezes. His mouth twitches and his face crumples. The air is smelly and smoky and stuffy, the swaddling clothes too warm.

Grandfather Master Chai grins and welcomes his beloved grandson: 'Come here, my little precious pearl!'

Thunder howls in the baby's fragile eardrums, triggering his wails, an outburst only to be expected against the noise, the smoke, the flames, the heat and smells. He shifts in his red swaddling. Red-faced.

News of the crying eldest son of Master Chai's eldest son in the ancestral hall travels fast. In the west court, Er Niang sniggers in her room while Da Niang frowns in hers. *What an unlucky omen.* Da Niang repeatedly reads the lines from the *Dabei* scriptures, chants for the blessing of Buddha. *Please protect my Mingzhi from all evil spirits. Please.*

The divinatory blocks will not smile until the fifth fall. The ancestors seem to be displeased with their red-swaddled, wailing descendant. But Master Chai is pleased. He is pleased to see his grandson for the first time. Happy to touch his chubby cheeks. *He is a real Chai boy, the heir to the Chai clan.*

The kitchen has been busy since dawn. Thousands of rice cakes have been baked, thousands of eggs boiled and dyed red. Butler Feng instructs the servants to give them to the residents of Plum Blossom Village: three cakes and three eggs for each family. Taking the synonym pronunciation of 'three' (*san*) to represent 'life' (*sheng*), the master plants the good omens of 'alive' and 'active'.

Surprised peasants come from the village and nearby quarters, waiting patiently in two long queues at the main entrance. *Heavenly God has changed at last, beginning to take care of us.* For years they have almost forgotten the taste of rice cake. Grinning, they spread the word: 'He certainly is our lucky star.'

It is the first time Master Chai has given them such a treat.

At dusk, Liwei, Likang's younger brother, returns, exhausted from a two-month rent-collection trip to distant villages. Entering the village, he stares around in disbelief: merry faces everywhere, everyone holding a red handful, laughing and chattering excitedly.

A rare scene since the Taiping rebels' dream of a peasant-ruled China burst like a bubble. Years of war coupled with drought left the lands almost barren. Poverty and hunger long ago ripped the smiles off the peasants' faces. Land rents are high, can hardly be covered by the harvests. Liwei's rent-collecting trips always leave him feeling guilty; as if he is a bloodsucker, robbing every single *qian* from the poor peasants.

But today, they are smiling.

Liwei hurries towards the source of all this.

Finally, in front of the Chai mansion under the red banner, Liwei sees the last peasant receive his present. His heart thumps.

The child is born!

Leaving his luggage with Butler Feng, Liwei rushes to the west court to see the infant.

Mingzhi's mother stays in bed for another two months. Feeling stronger, she sits up and holds Mingzhi for longer periods. But her son needs more movement now. He searches around for Mama Wang and cries for her when he sees her standing to one side. Mama Wang lifts him and paces about the room to calm him down. His mother's eyes follow, her chest feels tight.

At dusk, after dinner, Uncle Liwei visits. He tells his little nephew stories that are only noises to him. But his uncle's gentle voice soothes Mingzhi. He stares up quietly and listens as though he understands the tales of monkey and pigsy, and the twenty-four dutiful children.

In the adjoining room Da Niang sits up, listening, imagining her child grabbing Uncle Liwei's fingers, smiling at him. And she smiles quietly, too.

—∞—

Happy faces are everywhere as the autumn harvest approaches. Working in the billowing paddy fields, chasing away sparrows and killing grasshoppers, the peasants say when they meet: 'Indeed, Heavenly God has changed at last.'

After years of poor harvests, a bumper crop is expected. Before their eyes are thousands of acres of golden fields, eye-catching, heart-warming.

—∞—

At six months old, Mingzhi is joined by his half-brother, Er Niang's son. This time Old Scholar Yan's face crumples and his hands tremble when he writes the names: Mingyuan, a wise person, and his scholar name is Haojie, which means an outstanding person, a hero. The scholar puts down his brush, his hands still shaking. The names are symbols rather than predictions, Old Scholar Yan knows deep inside himself. He has chosen them carefully to counter the fate he sees in the child, the possible future outcome of his unwise decisions, unheroic actions. The old man quietly reminds Master Chai to burn more joss sticks, light more oil lamps, not just in the ancestral hall but also in the temples.

—∞—

Rain starts pouring the night before Mingyuan's Full Moon. Thunderstorms howl. The Plum River seethes ferociously, pounding against its bank. A worried peasant checking the embankment that evening finds a fissure in its surface. He hurries for help but the embankment collapses before help arrives. Water runs wild in the fields, washing away the spring sprouts.

Master Chai sends Butler Feng and Liwei to lead the servants and peasants in containing the flood. The rain and thunderstorms stop after midnight, but the Plum River continues roaring. Sandbags are filled and stacked, cattle herded to higher ground, along with women, old and young, with armfuls of pots and pans and mattresses, dropping them along the way. There is little shelter. They crouch, soaking wet, in caves, between bushes, under trees.

Butler Feng and Liwei return at dawn covered in mud. Their lips are pale, their hands wrinkled, their eyes gloomy. *Everything's gone.*

Master Chai worries about his rents.

No rice cakes are baked, no red boiled eggs prepared for Mingyuan's Full Moon, despite Er Niang's angry stamping in her room, hard on her tiny feet and frustrated heart.

The next autumn on his birthday, Mingzhi is deemed to have turned two years old, having spent his first year inside his mother and the second in the outside world.

Early morning, and Mingzhi is seated on a table top in the centre hall of the east court, surrounded by a set of brushes for calligraphic writing, a pair of scissors, a couple of copper coins, books, a bowl with five grains, a ledger, a shovel, a set of mandarin costumes, and many other items, each representing a particular occupation.

Master Chai's eyes follow Mingzhi's hands as they move and touch the various objects. He grins when his little grandson lays his hands on the set of brushes but drops his smile when Mingzhi reaches for the handle of the shovel. *No!* Mingzhi moves away. The worried grandfather is relieved. The colourful mandarin costume catches Mingzhi's eyes. He grabs it. *Yes!* Master Chai holds his breath, but throws out a sigh when the infant drops the costume and snatches the ledger instead, observes it, opens it wide, tears it, giggles – and looks at nothing else.

Master Chai frowns, dismisses the ceremony as flawed. Mingzhi will be neither a businessman nor an accountant. He is predestined to be a scholar, a successful one.

A Mandarin.

Mingzhi totters in the courtyard, in small, careful steps, away from Mama Wang at one end and towards Da Niang at the other. He looks up, but is unable to see beyond the wall, and the hills and mountains that lie ahead.

Far away up north, where Mingzhi's young eyes can't reach, the white ghosts and the dwarf ghosts come rushing in: British, French, American, German, Russian, Italian, Austrian and Japanese, with watery mouths and glowing eyes. All hunger for a piece of the cake called China, sweet and soft and creamy, dying to gobble up their shares in a single bite.

And Mingzhi grows, in a small village ignorant of the threats that will change his life.

Two

Summer 1879

A glorious afternoon and Mingzhi wakes early from his nap, determined to make the most of his day. He grabs his kite, tugs at Mama Wang's sleeve and drags her with him.

Outside, the sun is blazing. Mama Wang stops the five-year-old from running to the courtyard. 'Stay here, you little precious pearl. It's too risky to play under the sun.'

Mingzhi pulls a face but does not argue. Mama Wang sits fanning herself on the wooden bench on the veranda, watching Mingzhi throw the kite skyward. The air is still. The kite twists above his head and falls.

He picks it up and tries again. Another quick fall, right on his head. He examines the joints of the kite and finds them all intact. He tries yet again, climbing on a stool this time, till the wind comes and the kite takes off. Mingzhi cheers as he pulls the string.

Mama Wang fans herself slower and slower, her eyes becoming smaller. Finally the fan drops as she dozes.

The kite crashes to the ground once more. Frustrated,

Mingzhi hurls the roll of thread away. There is a faint sound from the end of the courtyard. Squinting at Mama Wang, now asleep, Mingzhi steps down from the veranda and walks slowly toward the noise. It comes from a bush under a willow in a corner, gets louder as he approaches. He peers under the bush and a coil of reddish brown and black cord springs upright, hissing. The reptile flicks its forked tongue, toying with its prey. Petrified, Mingzhi stares into the pair of blazing eyes and cries out.

The mansion wakes. Mama Wang stands as rigid as a log, unable to take in the picture before her.

A figure runs past Mingzhi. A series of loud thumps follows. *What happened?* Mingzhi rubs away his tears and finds Uncle Liwei standing tall before him, holding a spade. The coral snake's body is just recognizable in the mess on the ground. Mingzhi clings tightly to his uncle's leg, feels its strength and knows he is safe.

'I'll protect you, wherever you are.'

He feels a hand on his head and hears Uncle Liwei's murmur, gradually drowned out by the voices of the fast gathering crowd.

At night Mingzhi's temperature rises: his body is burning hot, his eyeballs roll up. He tosses in bed, muttering senselessly, sobbing. Da Niang sits by the bedside, watching Mama Wang repeatedly wet a towel with cold water and press it to his forehead. It warms up in minutes. *The snake ghost has possessed my Doggie. It is taking him away!* Mama Wang keeps rubbing Mingzhi's face, limbs and body with the towel. She turns pale; her hands shaking.

'It's the snake ghost, madam. It is seeking revenge!'

'Stop that nonsense!' Da Niang's voice quavers. Her son's face is bursting red, an overripe persimmon waiting to explode. She helplessly sends her maid for Master Chai. The furious grandpa at once summons a doctor from Pin-dong Town.

Two doors away, Er Niang cranes her neck at the window for her servant, hoping for her to come back with the worst news possible. Mingyuan, now four years old, takes the opportunity of climbing onto the stool and reaching for the jar of sweets on top of the cabinet. *Too high.* He lifts his foot and stretches his arm, wobbling.

Thump! He falls and wails. Er Niang rushes forward, smacks him to stop him crying. 'You should be laughing now, not crying, you stupid child.'

Master Chai paces the room until midnight, until the doctor declares Mingzhi safe. Until Mingzhi's father, unaware of the incident, comes home after his satisfying trip to the brothel, happily chanting snatches of opera.

Next morning, Mingzhi wakes to find a stranger by his bedside.

'That's your new nanny.' His mother tries to calm him down.

'I want Mama Wang!'

He cries, shrinking into a corner of his bed, avoiding the new girl's touch, screaming for his lost nursemaid. But Master Chai does not yield.

Days, weeks and even months later, he still cries in his dreams at night, misses the warmth of Mama Wang's breasts, her husky yet tender voice. And when he wakes, he sucks his tasteless thumb in the darkness in tears.

—∾—

The ban on entering the courtyard is lifted a month after the incident with the snake. But now Mingzhi prefers to stay in his room. He has found himself a new world.

With the maid's help, Mingzhi curtains off the gap between his bed and the wardrobe in the corner with a sheet his mother has embroidered. This magic room slightly bigger than a two-door wardrobe is spacious enough for him to move around, for three persons to shelter inside.

Yes, it is a magic room. Every morning Mingzhi walks to the curtain as if approaching the entrance of the hidden paradise of Taohua Yuan, the legendary Peach Blossom Spring in the folklore of the Ming Dynasty: the only place on earth where peace, harmony and love are to be found, where everybody lives happily in perfect health. Concealed in a luxuriant peach-blossom grove by a stream, the village isolates itself from all the hustle and bustle of the outside world. Mingzhi has dreamed about it ever since Uncle Liwei told him the story.

Mingzhi touches the embroidery on the curtain. Peach flowers – ranging from as tiny as a copper coin to the size of a rice bowl, budding or blossoming in various tones of pink silk – shine in the morning rays, inviting him to his little Taohua Yuan. Mingzhi lifts up the curtain and slips into his secret kingdom.

On the stool in the corner sits a sandalwood box. Mingzhi opens it, and there are his treasures: a grasshopper and a dragonfly made of bamboo leaf, a carved wooden rabbit, a pair of copper turtles, a set of toy bricks and a white silk kerchief embroidered with his name.

Smoothing his kerchief on the floor, Mingzhi carefully arranges the family of insects and animals on top, as if they are racing. The rabbit cranes its neck at the backs of the turtles, which are well ahead of it. The dragonfly rests on the shell of one of the turtles with its tail raised high, as if cheering for its friend's triumph. And the grasshopper stands aside, watching, like a judge.

Mingzhi shhs: 'Be good, don't move. I'm making you a home.'

He piles up the bricks.

'Knock, knock, knock. Anybody there?' Uncle Liwei ducks in. 'Hey, how can the turtles win?' He shakes his head: 'They are slow. I told you that.'

'I know . . . But can't they win just for once?' Mingzhi looks up at him, hoping.

Uncle Liwei sighs and pats Mingzhi's head as he squats down level with the boy: 'You're just like your mother.'

'Is someone talking about me?'

Da Niang appears.

Mingzhi cheers and rushes to hold her hand, leading her to the stool.

Leaning against his mother, the boy urges Uncle Liwei to repeat his favourite story. His uncle protests, but yields later as always when Mingzhi insists. He clears his throat and the tale begins:

Once upon a time, a fisherman poling his boat along a stream suddenly saw ahead of him a mass of glowing peach blossoms: bright pink, cluster upon cluster. He gazed fascinated as the stream carried his little boat through the peach-blossom grove to a village he had never seen or heard of. The friendly villagers welcomed him with great hospitality, without asking where he came from, what he wanted . . .

Mingzhi feels Da Niang's hands around his shoulders, and he glances up. His mother's dreamy eyes look far away, as if she is wandering in the fairyland of Peach Blossom Spring. Uncle Liwei's voice envelops the three of them, fills the boy's little world behind the curtain.

. . . As he stayed on, the fisherman found the place a heaven: no quarrels, no disputes, only laughter and smiles on the healthy, gleaming faces of men and women, young and old. He lived there happily, enjoying talks over wine and chess after a day's farming with the villagers . . .

Mingzhi presses his body against his mother, feels the warmth she exudes, the calm Uncle Liwei's voice conveys.

The bed is warm and Mingzhi falls fast asleep. Outside the window, the night sky darkens. Mingzhi hears insects humming, close to his ears. He opens his eyes. His family of insects and animals, all as big as he is, marches in. The dragonfly leads; the turtles and rabbit follow while the grasshopper guards the rear. They stop by his bedside and gesture to him.

Mingzhi jumps off his bed and joins the parade behind the grasshopper. They march around the room, again and again. Then suddenly they are all riding on a flying dragon, round and round, higher and higher. Cheers and laughter fill the room. But moments later the old rivals, the rabbit and the turtles, begin pushing each other, shouting abuse, louder and louder. The dragon starts twisting violently, flips over and comes crashing down.

Mingzhi wakes to the sounds of clattering and banging, unsure if he is still in the dream. He turns to face the wall separating his room from his mother's. Through the chinks between the wooden planks, flickers of candlelight slip in, casting faint stripes on his bed, the wall and ceiling. *Mother.* He grasps the edges of his blanket tight. Waits. A door squeaks open. He hears his father's drunken muttering, along with Da Niang's pleadings, faint and helpless. Then there is heavy breathing, and moaning, like that of an animal.

The door squeaks again, closes with a bang. Mingzhi hears his mother sobbing, muffled yet audible in the silence of the night. He stares hard at the source of the unsettled stripes of light, imagines his mother burying her head under the pillow. But the young boy's heavy eyes soon droop, and he falls asleep again.

—~—

Likang always comes home early at the end of the month, when he has spent his allowance. A substantial dinner is prepared for the master of the west court. Boiled country chicken and braised duck are essential, and his favourite wine, *wu jiapi*, of course.

The dinner table is carefully arranged, too: first wife Da Niang to the right and second wife Er Niang to the left of the master's seat. The boys sit next to their mother, and the girls between their brothers.

Er Niang leans close to Likang, pours him a cup of *wu jiapi*, smiling brightly as he drains it.

'One more.' She refills his cup and squints over at the other side, only to find that Da Niang holds herself aloof, contemplating the bowl of rice in front of her.

The children watch their father tear a drumstick from the chicken. Grease oozes out between his fingers as he brings it to his mouth. Then, aware of the eyes on him, he pauses, puts the piece of chicken in Mingzhi's bowl and tears another for Mingyuan.

'Don't stare. Eat!' he orders, takes a stern look around, especially sharp at the girls.

So they quietly munch their food amid the sounds of their father's noisy gulping of meat and wine.

And the dinner ends with Er Niang supporting the drunken Likang to her room.

A peal of laughter breaks the quiet autumn morning. Mingzhi wakes. He kneels on his bed and peers through the window.

In the now bush-free courtyard, his half-brother Mingyuan is riding on the back of Er Niang's teenage servant girl, who is down on all fours.

'Faster, faster! You're too slow!' Mingyuan shouts, brandishing his bamboo cane.

The girl struggles over the leafy gravel, crushing the leaves, pressing the grit. Blood smears her palms and stains the dress under her knees. Tears fill her eyes.

'Be careful, son,' Er Niang calls from the veranda where she sits. 'Looks like I should get you a better horse.'

Mingyuan taps the girl's head with the cane: 'Did you hear that? I said faster.'

She inches forward.

Mingyuan croons:

'Little pony gallops,
Little pony gallops;
Takes me to the east,
Takes me to the south,
Takes me to the west,
Takes me to the north;
Takes me to the horizon.'

Mingzhi quietly sings along. Mingyuan looks around and sees him. He beckons to his Big Brother: 'Hey, here, join me for a ride!'

Mingzhi shakes his head.

'Come on, let's play hide and seek,' Mingyuan urges, but Er Niang chips in: 'Stop it, Mingyuan. Who do you think you are to play with him?'

A cricket leaps in front of the servant girl. She screams and winces. Mingyuan jumps off.

'It's only a cricket, silly!' He grinds the insect under his foot, then giggles.

Mingzhi's chest tightens. He cowers under the window, imagining the yellow and brown mess on Mingyuan's sole.

Er Niang's sharp voice penetrates his thoughts: 'Hey, what a brave boy you are, Mingyuan.'

Pale autumn sunlight slants in through the open window, falls on Mingzhi's head and shoulders. There is no heat in it, yet Mingzhi squints as he looks up.

He feels dizzy.

—∾—

. . . Days, weeks, months passed. Homesickness began to drown him. He bade farewell to his friends. Before the fisherman's departure, the head of Peach Blossom Spring reminded him to keep the place a secret . . .

Mingzhi does not understand the fisherman's decision to return home – a decision he later regretted, according to Uncle Liwei. *Even my little things enjoy living in their Taohua Yuan.* He builds a home with his wooden bricks: four pillars, four walls, a roof and a door, and houses his toy-pets in it: the stern-faced grasshopper, the sympathetic dragonfly, the arrogant rabbit and its rivals the turtles. All live in harmony under the same roof.

—∾—

Liwei concludes the year-end account: it's declining, though not a deficit.

Master Chai sits erect in his dragon chair, contemplates the open pages. His maid stands to one side, observing her master's taut face. He takes a sip of tea but spits it out at once, smashes the teacup on the floor and howls: 'Warm tea only, I said, stupid!'

The girl turns pale. *Another night without dinner.* She holds back her tears, quietly replaces the tea and clears the mess.

Spring comes and the women are busy plucking mulberry leaves from the trees that spiral up the eastern hillside. Setting out at dawn, the peasant women carry wicker baskets on their backs, exchanging gossip and household tips along the way. By early afternoon they struggle down the hill, hunched under full loads of fresh mulberry leaves. There is more chattering along the way as they head for the silkworm farm, passing the Chai Mansion.

Tossing in his bed during his afternoon-nap-hour, Mingzhi hears the commotion from beyond the wall that encloses the courtyard. A husky voice stands out among the others. *Mama Wang*. Mingzhi sits up, his heart pounding. The room is quiet; the maids have long since retreated to their naps. Mingzhi puts on his shoes, sneaks out of the room, walks across the courtyard and peeps through the gapped door.

In the street the women pass by in groups. Well wrapped up against the greedy mosquitoes and the burning sun, they all look alike: scarves on their heads, long-sleeved plain cotton shirts dotted with little flowery designs and dark-coloured trousers. But Mingzhi spots her as they pass. Mama Wang, plump as ever but even stronger-looking, is among the youngest and toughest women in the lead.

He calls out: 'Mama Wang!'

The clattering of the crowd drowns out his faint voice. Mama Wang's blue scarf moves further away, disappearing in the shuffle of blues, greens, greys and blacks.

He pushes the door open and darts out. The women are walking fast. Mingzhi lags behind with his shorter steps, passing an orchard, crossing a bridge. He speeds up, yet still the gap widens. Panting, he watches them turn right just after a farmhouse and disappear from view.

'No, wait!'

Almost crying, Mingzhi runs along the track. His feet are sore in his thin-soled cotton shoes, his heart burning. *I want Mama Wang!* He keeps running, past the farmhouse, turns the corner.

All is quiet.

The women and their chatter have left no trace in the afternoon air. Mingzhi glances around, panicked. Then he notices smoke puffing from the chimney of a farmhouse, twenty yards away. He spots the entrance and hurries towards it.

In the courtyard some women are unloading mulberry leaves, and their busyness blinds them to the little boy. Mingzhi moves between mounds of leaves, searching. But Mama Wang isn't there.

There is a row of four rooms behind the women. Mingzhi sneaks to the first door. Inside, there are more leaves; a storeroom apparently. He shifts to the next, peers through the wide-open window. Worms. Hundreds of thousands of them, round and white, wriggle in trays layered with mulberry leaves, laid out on the long wooden tables that fill the room.

Mingzhi feels as if they are burrowing through his stomach, in and out. Hundreds of thousands of them. He looks away, holds his breath and moves to the third room.

It is crowded with the same trays and tables, but the trays are filled with white silky balls. Tray by tray they are carried by some of the women into the adjoining room. Outside Mingzhi follows. And there he sees Mama Wang. Removing a tray from a table, she pours the cocoons into a big steaming cauldron. Mingzhi climbs onto the windowsill and looks down from the open window.

In the cauldron, the snowy balls surge about in the hot waves. Mingzhi imagines the hundreds of thousands of worms screaming in pain and then curling up dead in their silky homes.

Mama Wang sieves the floating silky balls from the surface, then goes for another tray.

And more are poured in.

More killings.

Mingzhi grasps the window frame. It squeaks noisily. Mama Wang glances up.

'My little precious pearl! What are you doing here?'

She hurries forward, reaching for Mingzhi's legs. Mingzhi steps back and down. He stares at Mama Wang through the window as though she is a stranger.

'Come over. Let me see if you've grown.'

Mama Wang holds out her hand. But Mingzhi shakes his head, turns and runs.

That night in Mingzhi's dreams, hundreds of thousands of worms wriggle over Mama Wang's broad, placid face. Soon they fade away altogether in a gush of steam.

Three

Paddy buds are sprouting and there is not much work for Liwei before his next rent-collection trip. He spends more time with Mingzhi, teaching him to recite from *Sanzi Jing*, the Three-Character Classic.

The small booklet of *Sanzi Jing* Uncle Liwei brings with him is mildewed and smells. The uncle and the six-year-old nephew squat in the middle of the courtyard, and spread the booklet wide page by page under the sun. Uncle Liwei reads aloud: 'Men are kind-natured when they are born. Their natures are similar; their habits become different . . .' Mingzhi follows, memorizing every single word his uncle utters without understanding their meaning, rattling them off, clear and apparently articulate.

In front of them are two shadows, inseparable, one big the other small; their rhythmic voices loud and vigorous, muffling the tiny voice that has been echoing them all morning.

It's Mingyuan.

Behind the window of Er Niang's room, he stands leaning

against the windowpane, cocks his ears, quietly reciting along.

~

Soon the Lunar New Year approaches. Like other children, Mingzhi now has only red good-luck envelopes, clattering firecrackers and mouth-watering rice cake in his dreams. He is eager to swirl in the whirling red paper flakes, the remains of spent firecrackers, eager to dig out the contents of red envelopes, to compare the amount of money collected with Mingyuan. And to enjoy a sweet mouthful of sticky tasty rice cake. *For a full fifteen days!* Mingzhi checks the calendar every morning as soon as he wakes, crossing off yesterdays.

'New Year is for the children,' the peasants say, and some add: 'Chai's children.'

There are new clothes, new shoes to prepare and red envelopes to fill for the young ones; also the silver paper and joss sticks – at the very least, if they leave out the rice cake – for the praying ritual. The peasants' smiles turn bitter. To some, celebrating the festival according to tradition means piling up their debts ever higher, slaving more for Master Chai.

Yet the festival comes and goes. Before the lucky ones have tasted enough rice cake or counted the harvest from their red envelopes, Old Scholar Yan's private school reopens on the sixteenth day of the new year.

The weather is good, so Old Scholar Yan instructs his disciple to set up the class under the old willow tree. With his hands locked tight behind him he strolls between rows of six- to twelve-year-old boys, reciting from *Sanzi Jing*:

'Men are kind-natured when they are born . . .' He pauses.

'. . . Their natures are similar; their habits become different . . .' Behind him a tiny voice continues, trembling but clear: '. . . If they are neglected, not properly taught, their nature will deteriorate . . .'

Old Scholar Yan turns back. Mingzhi meets his eyes and smiles shyly. His teacher nods, encouraging. The boy continues reciting the entire book. The old teacher looks on, smooths his beard and nods. He recognizes him: the eyes, the face. The look.

~

News of Mingzhi's performance on his first day at school reaches his grandfather. Master Chai takes a sip of tea. The refreshing taste of *o-long* lingers on his tongue, warms his throat and his chest. He can't contain his smile. Recent visits of Mandarin Liu from Pindong Town have made the old man thoughtful. A greedy fish he is, a hungry shark, asking more and more, threatening with even higher taxation if his appetite is not satisfied. Master Chai recognizes merely a few characters in the paper the mandarin raises before his face. A humiliation that is hard for him to swallow. *But not for much longer!* In his mind's eye Master Chai sees Mingzhi in his mandarin costume. He sees his grandson sitting at Mandarin Liu's desk before a roomful of officials while the proud grandfather watches from behind a curtain.

Master Chai takes another sip, not realizing the tea has

cooled off. When he finally notices, he quietly beckons his maid to replace it. The young girl is fortunate to escape punishment.

At dinner, Da Niang prepares her son's favourite salted-radish omelette. She is glad her husband is absent, so there is no family dinner for the west court. *Only Mingzhi and me.*

Da Niang sits close to her son, picks up a piece of omelette with her chopsticks and puts it in his bowl. She watches him stuffing it into his mouth, grinning at her while he munches. Cheeks bulging with food, his eyes narrow to tiny slits as he smiles, like the forever-cheerful Laughing Buddha. Da Niang giggles. *She is laughing!* Mingzhi keeps smiling and his eyes become even smaller. He picks up a piece of omelette for his mother in turn. Da Niang chews slowly, relishing the sweetness of the radish, the crunchiness of its fine fibre, and the buttery smell of egg. And watching her son watching her.

~

On rainy days Old Scholar Yan holds classes in his house. His students resent this, missing the warmth of the sunlight, the faint smell of plum blossoms in the air, the red dragonfly and splendid butterflies that colour the sky, and the humming of the cicada, an echo to their monotonous reading of *Sishu Wujing*, the Four Books and Five Classics – basic readings of Confucianism, and essentials for the civil-service examination.

Knowing this, Old Scholar Yan begins the class by telling a story of the Twenty-Four Dutiful Children. The students sit still, all eyes on their teacher, listening.

Except for Mingzhi.

He knows the stories well, having heard them more than once from Uncle Liwei. They are all similar: kind parents treating their child with much love and care, and the child paying them back by whatever means he can. And they live happily together forever after.

He looks out of the window. A curtain of rainwater falls from the eaves into the ditch. Behind it a family of mandarin ducks bathe in the pond in a corner of the courtyard, flapping their wings, quacking, the big ones pecking the little birds, helping to clean them.

Old Scholar Yan notices Mingzhi but says nothing. The boy looks far away. *A place beyond my knowledge.* Strolling between two rows of students, the old man trips on a desk leg, stumbles and nearly falls over.

—∞—

At home after school Mingzhi becomes his sisters' teacher. He smooths rice paper on his study desk and demonstrates his calligraphy skills.

The girls lean forward.

'Let's begin with the basics,' he lowers his voice, touches his beardless chin, mimicking Old Scholar Yan.

His sisters giggle. Meifong, the youngest, pats her brother's head. Mingzhi laughs, dodging. He writes, starting with a left slanting stroke, then one from the right, joined to the first line at the middle. Black ink seeps through the rice paper. The lines stand up: two legs supporting the body. *Ren*, 'people'. The girls study it, and try to associate the character with the word in their daily conversation.

Then they rush after Mingzhi's brush. He hides it behind him.

'Not yet.' Mingzhi adds a horizontal line across the first stroke. That gives *da*, 'big': a man with both his arms stretching out wide.

'One more.' He swiftly presses a dot in between the strokes, turning it into *tai*, 'greatest'.

The girls observe the changes. *Like magic.*

Ren – Da – Tai.

They read aloud after their brother.

Taking their turns, the sisters hold the brush for the first time. Though her hands tremble, Meilian, the eldest, manages to copy the strokes. Her lines are thin and shaky.

'Like chicken claws,' teases Meifong, her younger sister.

But she is not much better; the legs of her 'human' jumble to the left. And she is fond of dots, making hundreds of them on the paper.

'Stop it, what a waste.' Meilian reaches for the brush. Meifong dodges her, brandishing the brush, splashing the black ink about the room, onto her sister and her brother.

That's too much! Meilian and Mingzhi cup a handful of ink each, chase after Meifong.

The first lesson ends with three black faces laughing at each other, before the asthmatic Meifong flops into a chair, coughing. Mingzhi watches as Meilian massages Meifong's chest until her breathing eases. Mingzhi stares at the two smeared faces in front of him, almost unrecognizable, like strangers. A sudden fear rushes over him. *My sisters! I want my sisters! I want to see their smiles!* Panicked, he hurries for a moist cloth and rubs his sisters' cheeks with it despite their screams of protest, until the ink is wiped away and they appear clean again. And he feels safe.

—∞—

Master Chai has important visitors and Mingzhi is summoned to the east court, to recite poems of the Tang and Song Dynasties.

The centre hall seems too spacious and the guests, a dozen of them, are staring. Mingzhi is shy at first, aware of their gazes on him: Master Chai's critical under his tightly knitted brows and the guests' expectant. Mingzhi's body itches, his eyes fix on his feet and his voice quivers. Yet his pronunciation is clear and his words and rhythm accurate. The audience applaud, requesting more: Li Bai, Du Fu, Li Shangyin, Li Yi, Li Qingzhao, a long list of the greatest poets of the most glorious periods in the history of Chinese literature.

Mingzhi flushes, his eyes shine. He raises his voice, blurting out the poems, one after another.

Master Chai's brows loosen. He sits back, keeps knuckling the rhythms against his armrest. *That's my grandson.* He nods.

—∞—

Mingzhi's eldest sister, Meilian, waits for her brother to come home in the afternoons and asks him about his lessons for the day. The two hide behind the curtain in Mingzhi's secret world; Meilian listens to Mingzhi reading poems, telling tales as told by Old Scholar Yan, explaining the teachings of Confucianism as he has been taught.

Though starting late – at the age of fourteen – Meilian is certainly a fast learner. Before dinner she repeats the poems alongside her brother, and is able to explain the metaphors that are too difficult for a six-year-old: the solitude, the feelings of loss or resentment subtly wrapped under beautiful landscapes: the vast snowy land, the magnificent gorges, the borderless steppe, the roaring Yellow River or the quiet Yangzi Jiang. Mingzhi likes listening to his sister, her voice soft and comforting. He rests his head on her lap, his cheek against the smoothness of her silk dress.

At night, lying in his bed, Mingzhi stares hard at the light beams filtering through the seams of the planked wall, listening to his eldest sister's whispers from next door, vague, indistinct. Imagines her at her younger sister's bedside, telling her the story she has learned; imagines Meifong falling asleep before it ends.

Sometimes after the lights are put out, he hears his eldest sister reciting poems by Li Qingzhao, the greatest female poet of the Song Dynasty, and Meilian's favourite. Mingzhi remembers that Meilian once told him about the miserable life Li had led. It began happily, with an open-minded father who allowed her to learn reading and writing, and later a loving and caring husband. But everything changed when the Northern Song collapsed. First drifting with her husband during the war, later mourning for his early death, then a disastrous second marriage. What is marriage? What is war? Why did she have to marry again? He doesn't understand. And her sister always keeps quiet whenever he asks her questions. He thinks she doesn't understand, too.

But most of the time, Mingzhi falls asleep before Meilian stops. There is always a herd of sheep walking through his dream, dotted on the vast green steppe of Mongolia, exactly the way Meilian described it when they read the poems.

'It's beautiful, Eldest Sister,' he murmurs and rolls over, falling deep into his dreamland.

—∾—

Master Chai asks for a mid-year account for the first time. Liwei quietly lays the book on Master Chai's desk and leaves the room before his father notices it: the balance does not show even the slightest improvement.

—∾—

The village is swept by an anonymous plague. First the animals: pigs, cows, oxen, chicken, ducks, die with protruding bellies and foam spittle spewing from their mouths; then the weakest among the children. The unfortunate mothers cry their hearts out while the fathers have more worries: the living need to be fed.

Liwei, with Butler Feng's help, instructs the villagers to set up a crematorium, gather and burn the contaminated corpses. *Only the cattle, not my children.* The villagers are adamant: without the body as shelter, the young soul will be trapped at the edge of the underworld, wandering, unable to be reincarnated. Liwei has to yield to generations of belief in Daoism.

Unable to afford coffins, they wrap the bodies in swaddling bands and bury them by the marsh at the western hillside.

On Liwei's advice, Old Scholar Yan dismisses the children and announces the school closed until things improve. Mingzhi comes home early to the news that his youngest sister, Meifong, is ill. She lies unconscious in bed and occasionally vomits. Her body is burning hot and her face bursting red.

Mingzhi holds Meilian's hand tight, standing to one side with her, watching their mother hold open Meifong's jaw, force-feeding her herbal medicine. Excess liquid flows from the corners of Meifong's mouth, staining the pillow, spreading instantly, black against the white sheet. Mingzhi feels weak. He squeezes Meilian's fingers, and she lets him, does not yell.

By evening Da Niang starts wiping away spittle bubbles from Meifong. She asks Meilian to take Mingzhi to his room, and sends a maid to Master Chai, asking for a doctor.

The grandfather says nothing.

Late at night Mingzhi hears his mother's cry, long and tearing. He and Meilian cling tight together in bed, weeping under the blanket.

Master Chai gives the order to bury Meifong immediately. *Dying young, what a bad omen.* Worse still, dying of an unknown disease. *Feng Shui comes first.* Master Chai decides: the Chai clan's geomantic omen is not to be contaminated; the girl's body shall not enter the clan cemetery. Da Niang kneels in front of Master Chai and pleads. The old man turns his back on her and retreats to his room.

A crude wooden coffin takes Meifong to the mass cemetery on the eastern hillside, where orphans, loners and the unclaimed bodies of strangers are buried.

On the same night in Pindong Town, Likang has a row with a gang of local rascals over a singsong girl at the brothel. He is unlucky to be sent home on a stretcher with a broken leg and an asthma attack, but lucky, in a way, to be in time to see off his dead daughter.

—~—

When the school reopens, Master Chai allows Mingyuan to join his Big Brother. Anything may happen: a plague, a child's death, a father's injury, anything. Master Chai has been alerted. *Too risky to focus on just one.*

Er Niang cheers in her room. She orders her son's favourite roast pork for dinner. *A few more steps, son, and we shall get there.* She pours herself a cup of rice wine and drains it.

—~—

Mingzhi is delighted to have Mingyuan's company. The route to the school was too long, too quiet. Butler Feng, his escort, was quiet too, and unable to answer Mingzhi's questions about the poets and their poems, and the Confucian readings.

The two boys start with *Sanzi Jing* on the first day. Mingzhi reads it once for his half-brother, and is surprised that Mingyuan manages to remember half of it in minutes. A few days later they are able to recite the entire book together as they walk along, each ready to remind the other when there is a slip of memory: words missing, phrases jumbled. The journey becomes short, enjoyable.

Within two months Mingyuan has learned enough from Mingzhi to catch up with him. He becomes impatient. Slow walks and repeating the same poems and readings no longer interest him, but his surroundings do: he prods caterpillars with a twig, chases butterflies, catches dragonflies and tears their wings off. Butler Feng does nothing and Mingzhi's complaints are in vain.

Mingyuan starts running ahead of Mingzhi, challenging him to races. Mingzhi watches, and stays between his half-brother, rushing ahead, and Butler Feng, who guards behind.

—

Likang's broken leg and the relapse of asthma confine him to his room for two months. Despite his two wives' careful tending Likang is bored. He sends Butler Feng for the friends he had fun with at the Pindong Town brothel. They come with their fighter crickets, set the insects to fighting each other, and themselves to gambling over the results.

This does entertain Likang for a week, but no longer. On the eighth day, the humming of crickets begins to annoy him as much as his constant bleating and demands annoy his mates.

It is impossible to smuggle Likang's favourite singsong girl into the mansion, though Master Chai has always been tolerant with him because of his asthma. So these good friends of Likang finally work out the best solution: opium. It's so simple, just a bamboo pipe, a clay bowl and a candle, and the black gum, of course. That's all they need. The good friends shake their heads. *Should've thought about it much earlier; should've saved our time lingering at Likang's.* Yes, time is not to be wasted. So the candle is lit, the magic gum boiled and frothing, and magic smoke fills the pipe, finding its way to Likang's nostrils.

Likang's first puff of opium chokes him, but the second takes him to the ninth layer of sky, drifting: boneless, flesh-less, weightless. And he never steps down to earth again.

Master Chai falls ill on the evening of the Mid-Autumn Festival. The family dinner in the east court is cancelled, but the lanterns, which had been prepared in the morning, are left hanging on the boughs in the garden.

So are those in the west court. Mingzhi and Mingyuan watch Meilian hang a lantern on the branch and say it's for Meifong. Mingzhi looks at his sister's solemn face, knows she is still grieving for their sister's death.

They stand in silence. Moments later Meilian beckons them, organizes and leads a lantern parade around the courtyard. Candlelight, thin and soft, flickers within the colourful paper strips. The wind is strong. It clears the clouds and shakes their fragile lamps. They carefully bring them close to their bodies and shield the candles with their hands.

Before the first circuit ends Mingyuan shouts: 'Let me take the lead!'

As he rushes forward, Mingyuan stumbles over a stump and falls. He lands in a pool of mud and his paper lantern burns off in seconds. Mingzhi laughs pointing at Mingyuan and Meilian holds her brother's hand tight as she giggles. *She smiles!* Mingzhi sees that his eldest sister's face is clean and bright, like the moon above her.

The wind keeps blowing, sweeping a large cloud overhead.

In the east court, Master Chai lies awake in bed. His head aches. Outside the window the sky is gloomy. *Even the moon is against me, can't be at its fullest and clearest as it should be on this day.* Master Chai thinks about the preceding series of calamities: the declining revenue, the plague, the death and the injury.

And now, his own illness.

Something has to be done. The old man thinks hard.

The night is so quiet that the children's laughter – the boys' and the girl's – though some distance away, reaches their grandfather.

Yes, the girl.

Master Chai heaves a sigh of relief, closes his eyes and sleeps.

—∾—

Meilian's wedding is scheduled for the following month: to drive away all evils and restore good fortune. Master Chai happily announces the bridegroom-to-be: Mandarin Liu's eldest son, thirty-eight years old; Meilian is to be his second wife.

Da Niang hugs Meilian with all her might. Meilian feels her mother shiver, and herself sinking, emptying.

But Master Chai is so pleased with the arrangement that

he sends for the best tailor in Pindong Town, ordering a fine silk wedding gown to be made, to match the bridegroom's. *And I will be sitting at Mandarin Liu's family table, drinking with him.* Though not yet fully recovered, Master Chai feels his head lighter and his body energized.

Meilian stops coming to Mingzhi's room, and keeps herself to hers.

The boy asks his mother, 'What does "getting married" mean? Is Eldest Sister leaving us forever?'

Da Niang pats his head, sighs. There is a long silence.

'You will know later, son, you will know.'

On the wedding day Mingzhi sees his Eldest Sister being led into the red-curtained sedan. The autumn wind slaps her ferociously and the silk gown clings tight to her body, lean and trembling. Mingzhi can't see Meilian's face under her red headscarf, but remembers her look beneath the autumn moonlight. Smiling, clean and bright.

The sedan takes her away.

Four

For the first time Master Chai's eldest son comes up with a brilliant idea: to cultivate opium poppies. The market looks bright. Already, half the population of Pindong Town are enjoying this magic smoke, indulging themselves after a hard day's work, puffing the long pipe, leaving sweats and aches and all scolding and fault-finding behind. And more are expected to join them.

Master Chai praises Likang for his clever idea, and this eldest son of his smiles slyly: an uninterrupted free supply is guaranteed.

Recent harvests of paddy were poor, and the plague killed the cattle that might have brought extra income. Debts have piled up. The villagers have no choice but to accept Master Chai's suggestion. Furthermore, free seedlings will be provided, which is too good to resist.

And the timing is just right. Master Chai stands on a hillock in the late autumn wind, bracing himself with his dragon stick, watching the peasants sowing. *It won't be long.* Master Chai closes his eyes. He sees a valley full of red poppies in front of him and smells their exotic fragrance. The corners of his mouth gradually curl upwards, stretching the creased pair of lips.

As he opens his eyes again, Master Chai sees Liwei come through the pass, cross the river and enter the village, returning from his annual trip.

The old man's smile disappears. *Liwei.* He sighs, thinking about his younger son's reaction as he stares at the approaching figure. Then he thumps his dragon stick, turns and leaves.

The rent-collecting trip exhausts Liwei, and he is glad to come home, just in time to admire the green sprouts of paddy: eye-soothing, refreshing. His pace quickens as he approaches the fields, but there are only the dull-coloured soil and sacks of seedlings stacked by the fields.

'It's opium poppies.' A peasant points to the fields. 'All of them.'

Liwei holds his head with his hand, disbelieving. He remembers the stories he has heard: men made weak, families impoverished due to opium addiction. They are the plants of sin, the poppies, and the planters sinners. The planters –

My father . . . My family . . . Myself!

He drags his body on, his steps as heavy as his heart.

At home Mingzhi is waiting for his uncle. Two months seem so long, so much has happened. So much to tell.

—

When the news of Uncle Liwei's return reaches the west court, Mingzhi dashes into his secret world, wipes dust from the stool with his sleeve and sits on a cushion on the floor, with his arms around his bent knees – a good sitting posture for long hours of talking: Uncle Liwei's stories from afar and his own from home.

The cushion is soft and comfortable and Mingzhi dozes off. He has a big red persimmon in his dream. He takes a bite. It's sweet and juicy, and the sticky fluid drips down his chin.

'It's delicious, Uncle Liwei,' he murmurs, and his lips twitch. He opens his eyes gradually and wipes saliva from the corners of his mouth.

His uncle is not there.

In the ancestral hall, Liwei, who was summoned to the ceremony as soon as he set foot in the mansion, kneels with his brother Likang. Each holding a bunch of joss sticks in their hands, they kowtow after their father.

Later, Master Chai, with a pair of divinatory blocks in his hands, immerses himself in whispered prayer while his sons kneel in silence. Then he throws the blocks.

They fall face down. A bad omen.

Master Chai darts a solemn look at his sons.

'This is a difficult time and opium is our only chance.' He darts a sharp look at Liwei. 'The ancestors say, if we don't follow their instructions, the consequences will be dreadful.'

Liwei glances up, wanting to say something, but Master Chai immediately points at the blocks and raises his voice:

'This is a warning. The ancestors say the family has to work together in order to keep the Chai clan alive. Only undutiful scions would disregard the ancestors' will!' He stares at his sons. 'Have I made myself clear?'

Liwei lowers his head as soon as his eyes meet his father's. He knows he is trapped. Defying the elder, and worst of all, defying the ancestors, are sins too big to commit.

Liwei grasps the ground where he kneels, scratching the crude surface under him until his fingernails crack.

Later that night in the east court, Master Chai orders a dinner with his sons: to welcome Liwei's return, and to wish their new business well.

After his father has drained two cups of *wu jiapi*, Liwei carefully broaches his suggestion: to alternate the plantings of poppies and paddy: spring for paddy and autumn for poppies. A plan for self-sufficiency, says the second son.

Likang sneers but Master Chai seizes his chance: 'Since you know what's needed, you'd better manage the business for me.'

Speechless, Liwei watches his father gulp down another cup of *wu jiapi*, wipe his mouth and thump the cup on the table. *Clank!* Loud in the quiet hall. Liwei has nowhere to hide.

—∞—

The following day Mingzhi busily describes Meilian's wedding ceremony to his unusually quiet Uncle Liwei, filling his secret world with his childish voice.

Beyond the curtain, beyond his world, poppy plants raise

their heads, opening their eyes to their first glimpse of the blue sky. And soon they will stretch their arms and thrust their flowers upwards, releasing waves of pungent odour that will brood over the village, its surroundings, the nearby towns, and the unknown world beyond.

In his little space, leaning against Uncle Liwei's stout leg and staring up at him, Mingzhi smiles brightly, sweet and content.

School continues: outdoors on sunny mornings, indoors on gloomy days. Those unable to recite the readings are punished, standing in a corner for half a day, while able pupils are praised, occasionally presented with a new brush, an inkstick or a few pieces of rice paper. Mingyuan is fond of these awards, volunteers to recite, and accumulates prizes, showing them off. But Mingzhi is interested neither in the brushes nor the papers. An attentive glance or a gentle pat from his teacher leave him feeling warm, encouraged, and eager to learn more.

Still, Mingzhi receives more brushes than he needs. He shares them with those standing-in-a-corner-for-half-a-days, comforting them; but he keeps one for himself, the finest of all, made of goat's hair, inscribed in gold with 'Shanghai Fine Brush'.

During midday breaks, when Mingyuan and his schoolmates take their naps or play hide-and-seek, Mingzhi stays indoors, practising calligraphy with his precious brush. The rapid, cursive style of *caoshu* – the strength the strokes exude, the freedom of their movements – fascinates him, but Mingzhi is too young to wield the brush as he wishes. So he begins practising *kaishu*, the regular script, concentrates his energy in his arm, wrist and fingers, learns to control the brush: pressing down then withdrawing, a heavy dot followed by a soft twist, or a sharp tail after a powerful stroke.

Old Scholar Yan notices his quiet student, and spends time practising with him. Mingzhi watches his teacher write, noticing the slightest details: the way he holds the brush, the beginnings and endpoints of each stroke.

The samples of character radicals that Old Scholar Yan writes keep Mingzhi busy, trying to imitate the positioning of lines, strokes and dots, the exertion of strength: thickening the ink as he presses down, thinning it as he withdraws.

Mingzhi listens to his teacher's comments, recognizes when he has made a weak stroke, or lifted the brush away too quickly, or when a line is too long or too short, too high or too low, too far to the right or left, and corrects his mistakes.

Old Scholar Yan notices how fast Mingzhi has learned, and is pleased. *Not a master yet, but he will be one day*, the old man quietly remarks.

—∞—

At home, however, when not studying, Mingzhi sometimes likes to kick the shuttlecock with the young maid in the courtyard. He counts as he kicks, watching the duck feathers white against the blue sky, then against the green bushes as the shuttlecock falls. And then he kicks it up once more before it touches the ground. Mingzhi likes seeing the feathers spiralling in the air, like birds fluttering, flying away. *So free*. Its fall agitates him, his heart sinks, and he tries with all his might to stop the shuttlecock touching the earth.

Mingyuan never plays shuttlecock-kicking with Mingzhi. He despises it as a 'girl's trick' and prefers the eagle-preying-on-the-chicken game: he, the eagle, breaks his mother-hen's defence line, lunges at his prey – the unfortunate chick played by the maid – punching and pinching her.

But Da Niang joins Mingzhi occasionally, struggles to balance her lean body on her bound feet, kicking the shuttlecock upwards. Though teetering and breathless, she enjoys this little relaxed moment with her son. Mingzhi likes running to her, hugging her tight, so they both fall, laughing.

—~—

Spring again.

Mingzhi wakes to a sweet, pungent odour. He sneezes.

Outside, Master Chai's dragon stick thumps past, short and quick. Tuk, tuk, tuk . . . Like the old man's kicking heart. News of the first poppy blossoms excites the Master. He hurries to the fields with Liwei and Butler Feng.

From the same hillock where he stood three months ago, he sees a sea of pinkish-red opium poppies billowing in the morning breeze. *Red, the lucky colour.* Master Chai smooths his goatee, grins and nods. He looks northward, past the village, past the river, over the mountains.

Up north in the busy cities, hundreds of thousands of crates of opium are gathered, some shipped south-eastwards to Indochina, but mostly distributed inland: city – town – village.

Plum Blossom Village.

The Chai Mansion.

Likang.

In his room, Mingzhi keeps sneezing. He covers his nose with a kerchief and shuts all the windows, but the smell grows stronger.

—~—

After unloading its cargo along the river southward, on its return journey the salt boat collects grain and farm produce, and takes away the first harvest of opium, crudely dried under the sun without baking.

And it returns for the second, third, fourth harvests, and more.

Debts are settled and there is a balance after paying land rental. Contented peasants smile from their hearts: fathers proudly hold up their heads; mothers briskly prepare meat-meals; grandparents enjoy chewing mouthfuls of sticky rice cakes with their toothless gums; children run happily, playing with sparklers in their new clothes and new shoes in this and the many new years to come.

Mingzhi's interest in red good-luck envelopes is flagging, though, and the rice cakes now seem too sweet. There is something more important to anticipate in the New Year: Meilian.

Meilian comes home only once a year, on the second day of the New Year, like many other married daughters. Da Niang cranes her neck from Winter Day onwards, counting down until Meilian's return as she scoops out her dumplings; and she gets even edgier at the reunion dinner on New Year's Eve. *A reunion without my daughter.* The braised duck and the grease-dribbling chicken drumstick are tasteless to this anxious mother. Mingzhi keeps a jar of his eldest sister's favourite preserved plums in his room, waiting to share them with her when they look through his collection of calligraphic poems.

So much to tell, to do together, and so short a day.

When Meilian finally returns to her mother's arms, Da Niang notices that her already lean body is now thinner. She listens to her daughter's complaints: the opium-addict husband, the jealous first wife and third mistress, the stern-faced mother-in-law, begrudging Meilian's failure to produce a child . . . Da Niang can only hold her daughter tight, whispering into her ears, asking her to endure, to abide by the Three Rules of Obedience: be obedient to her father before marriage, to her husband after marriage and to her son after the death of her husband. She asks Meilian to hold on to the Four Virtues: to lead a life of perfect morality, to practise proper speech and modest manners, and to work diligently, as told by the greatest of scholars, Confucius. It's a woman's fate, and it's her duty to serve her man and his family, Da Niang says. Meilian listens quietly, her eyes full of tears.

Mingzhi notices his eldest sister's more prominent cheekbones, her paler face. And she is no longer interested in poems. What for? she says. Mingzhi sees emptiness in her eyes.

On her third trip home, Meilian carries a baby girl.

On her fourth, Meilian's husband comes visiting with her for the first time, bringing their newborn son.

And the new years come and go.

Spring 1890

After school Mingzhi walks along the path flanked by willow trees, alone. Butler Feng has stopped accompanying the brothers to and from school on Master Chai's order. They are teenagers now, the grandfather says, can make their own way. This suits Mingyuan well, and he always avoids walking together with his half-brother.

Mingzhi grows to enjoy this little freedom, the journey to and from school all by himself. Taking slow steps, admiring the view, relaxed. Above him, hanging leaves rustle in the afternoon breeze, catkins shower his head and shoulders. He stretches out a palm and catches a handful of the green flakes, soft against his flesh. The wind grows stronger, bringing with it a pungent smell. Mingzhi sneezes, and the catkins fall, whirling to the ground.

Opium.

Mingzhi frowns. He smells it even in the distance, so strong, engulfing the village, engulfing him. Ten years have passed since the outbuilding had been converted to a factory, ten years of reaping poppies and drying opium. Yet to him, the odour is still as unbearable as ever.

After spring harvest the fields flanking the path are bare, waiting to be ploughed and sowed again. *A break from the bloody scene of poppy blossoms, at least.* Hungry for a gasp of fresh air, he takes a deep breath, chokes, then coughs violently. As he has now crossed the bridge leading to the factory and the mansion, before him is a sea of raw opium blocks drying in an acre-wide open field.

Mingzhi clamps his nostrils shut, holds his breath and

moves quickly across the field. In the distance, he sees Mingyuan and his schoolmates running wild, chasing after each other, laughing and zigzagging in a dark maze of opium blocks.

Mingzhi's nose itches. He sneezes, again and again.

—‿‿—

The factory has been busy day and night. By the end of spring the salt boat will pass by, and it doesn't wait. Missing it will mean another four months of waiting, of sweet potatoes or plain porridge diets for the peasants, and the risk that the opium will be damp when the rainy season arrives.

Mingzhi takes his evening walk after dinner. His route has become a routine: past the open field and the factory, across the bridge, along the riverbank and up the hill slope, round the village and back.

That's his world.

Sometimes he stands on top of the hill and imagines what lies behind the mountain and the many mountains beyond: the people, their language, their food, their lives; the towns, the cities, the ocean, the gorges, the desert and the steppe. The many poems he has read creep into his head, luring him into painting mental pictures, colourful but vague: colourful as he thinks they should be; vague, as he hasn't witnessed any of them himself.

So most of the time he suppresses this restless desire, sitting for long periods near the bamboo groves by the river, listening to the symphony of the night: crickets chirping, frogs croaking, the owl's cries, the monkey's shrieks.

Admiring nature's greatest musicians, and thinking of nothing.

And the night passes.

But this evening as he steps out of the mansion, Mingzhi knows his musicians will be shy to perform. *Another busy night.* Light shines from the outbuilding not far away. Black shadows shuffle. Coming closer, Mingzhi sees Uncle Liwei at the entrance, instructing workers to pour raw opium into the vats and stir it. Behind him, the torch burns fiercely, casting a stooped, tired figure, his grey hair silver in the brightness of the fire, his forehead greasy from the heat.

He has aged.

Uncle Liwei glances up, sees him and beckons him over. Mingzhi hurries forward.

'It's ready, Second Young Master!' a worker shouts from inside the building.

Uncle Liwei immediately rushes in. Mingzhi knows his uncle has to oversee the workers as they pour liquid opium into the moulds to make opium blocks. He knows Uncle Liwei has to be there throughout the night.

He turns and walks away.

In the rustling evening wind, he hears the bustle of the workers and the clatters of the wooden stirrer against the clay vats. But there is other noise, coming from some nearby bushes. Mingzhi leaves the gravel path and crosses the grassland to the source of it.

He searches. Between the branches, a puppy whines, shivering. Its body, all black, is hidden in the dimness of the undergrowth. Mingzhi almost missed it. But its eyes, filled with fear, are bright against the surrounding dark. Mingzhi pats its head. It wags its tail.

Poor little thing.

'Where is your mother? And your father? Have they forgotten about you?'

The puppy keeps wagging, whining and squinting up at him from under its eyelids. Mingzhi picks it up and warms it in his arms.

'Charcoal, that's your name.'

—w—

On the fifth day of the fifth lunar month, Old Scholar Yan leads his students in a celebration of Poet's Day. To commemorate the patriotic poet of the Zhou Dynasty, Qu Yuan. Joss sticks in their hands, they stand in silence.

Later, Old Scholar Yan announces a competition for his students. They are to write about Qu Yuan, also an adviser to the emperor, who killed himself when his country fell into the enemy's hands.

How could a loyal official like him end by being accused of treachery? Mingzhi sits for a long time thinking: how Quan Yuan was framed by a jealous colleague; how the emperor misjudged him, ignored his sincere advice and ordered his exile; and how he drowned himself out of despair.

He murmurs a verse from *Lisao*, Encountering Sorrow, a record of Qu Yuan's noble ideal, written during his exile:

'I am the only clean soul in this muddy mess,
Staying awake among the drunks;
How could I let my body

Be contaminated by this filthy world?

I would rather float in the running stream,
Let the fishes clean my flesh . . .'

Outside, the sky is clear after the morning shower. Rainwater drips from the willows. Catkin flakes fall, whirling and ruffling the brimming surface of the pond. Mingzhi stares at the ripples. His eyes grow moist.

Did he make many ripples on the Nilo River when he jumped into it?

Silence.

Mingzhi remembers he once raised this question with Meilian when they read the poem together. Now he is able to see the lonely soul even without her explanation.

Eldest Sister. He feels a twinge in his heart.

Mingzhi looks around. His fellow classmates are busy writing. He grinds some ink, wets his brush, and begins.

Late at night. Engrossed in the poem in front of him, Old Scholar Yan does not realize that the candle is burning down. As the room gets darker, his head draws closer to the writing, so close it almost touches the pages.

His disciple quietly enters, brings in warm tea and replaces the candle with a new one. His master waves him away and asks him to take his rest.

Old Scholar Yan reads about a scarred and despondent soul in Mingzhi's poem, and sees how it alludes to the writer himself.

The boy. Old Scholar Yan sighs, remembering his first sight of Mingzhi.

But then, this thoughtful scholar suddenly realizes that Mingzhi is no longer a boy.

Mingzhi comes home with his winning prize, a book of *Lunyu*, The Analects of Confucius, which contains all the Confucian sayings. He hurries to his mother's room and opens the door.

Da Niang is sitting in front of an image of Buddha, with her back to Mingzhi, engrossed in chanting sutras. Her voice is soft, monotonous and calm. Straight-spined, she is so motionless that it seems an eternal posture. Smoke from the burning joss sticks fills the room, enveloping her like a shield.

Mingzhi stands outside the smoke shield, watching.

Moments later, he closes the door and leaves.

Returning to his room, Mingzhi drops his book on the desk and ducks into his secret world. Everything is there, as before. The stool, the sandalwood box with its inhabitants: the rabbit, grasshopper, dragonfly and turtles, and the kerchief and blocks. Mingzhi stoops, picks up the rabbit and examines it. Parts of its varnished outer layer have worn away, leaving it dull, lifeless.

Sitting down on the stool, he puts the rabbit back into the box, closes it and glances around.

Now that he is a well-built sixteen-year-old, this space between his bed and the wardrobe seems much smaller. But it feels empty: Da Niang has stopped coming here since Mingzhi's voice broke; Uncle Liwei hardly visits since

Master Chai put him in charge of the opium trade.

Eyes closed, Mingzhi remembers Da Niang's warm bosom, Uncle Liwei's calm voice, Meilian's soft whispers. *Like a dream.* Charcoal sneaks in, comes wagging and snufling to his side. Mingzhi opens his eyes, pats Charcoal's head, then holds a corner of the curtain tight and pulls it down.

A curtain of faded peach blossoms withers on the floor.

Five

Master Chai plans his sixtieth-birthday celebration: after the salt boat has taken away the biggest of the opium harvests. *Coincidentally, a double celebration.* Master Chai sits at his desk in front of the accounts. The figures are leaping, so is his heart. A good omen for a long and prosperous life.

Months ago he had ordered Butler Feng to contract the Northern Opera Troupe, the Master's favourite, to perform on seven consecutive nights.

It is everyone else's favourite too! Since the leaked news, the peasants have had nothing but the Northern Opera Troupe as their after-dinner subject, and, 'Is Golden Swallow, the troupe's leading artist, coming along?' becomes a speculation among them, and they bet on the result.

Their anticipation runs into the ploughing, sowing and reaping of the poppies, into the opium blocks, and it thickens as the opium dries. Then it bursts into the air – everything is revealed when the salt boat comes and loads away the opium, and another boat arrives, bringing with it the long-awaited troupe.

Arriving three days early, the troupe – a crew of eighteen artists, musicians, apprentices, their masters and the manager – along with nine colourfully flagged carts filled with costumes, props, musical instruments and make-up, forms a spectacular entourage. As soon as the procession enters the village, the peasant children crowd round, tailing the carts.

'Golden Swallow! Golden Swallow!'

The peasants stop ploughing and call to the group as it passes by the fields.

'There he is!' A peasant has spotted the pretty young leading artist.

'I told you he would come.'

'Certainly he would. The Northern Opera Troupe is nothing without him.'

'So, it's true – even without his make-up, he is still prettier than a woman!'

'Aiya, he looks just like a celestial goddess in his long white gown.'

'Eh, who's the boy next to him?'

'Must be Little Sparrow. They say he is training to be Golden Swallow's successor.'

The most popular opera troupe in the country and its most popular singer are here! The peasants buzz with excitement as they watch the troupe entering the Chai Mansion.

Seeing his fellow workers' behaviour, an old peasant sniffs: 'Hey, get back to work! What's so great about them? Only a bunch of depraved singsong actors.'

A big boo is the immediate response.

As soon as the main door thumps shut behind them, the children climb on top of each other to peep over the wall.

In the west court, Mingzhi hears the commotion. He also hears Er Niang and Mingyuan cheering in the courtyard. His mother remains silent in her room. He imagines her praying in front of the altar. *It must be a nuisance to her.*

'Can someone tell me what's going on?' Likang shouts from inside the master room. His midday nap has been interrupted.

But almost instantly Mingzhi hears him mutter: 'Where's my pipe?'

Mingzhi knows that moments later his father will be deaf to all noises.

—∞—

Likang lies sideways on his bed, smoking his pipe. He doesn't have to travel all the way to Pindong Town brothel for his lovely singsong girl. She is always there in the puffs of smoke, drifting with him through the ninth layer of the sky.

Master Chai is pleased to have his eldest son at home. *No more fights, no more broken limbs.* He sees no reason to stop him smoking. After all, it is Likang's idea that has opened the door to his family's wealth, which is growing as rapidly as Likang's appetite for opium.

—∞—

Butler Feng arranges for the troupe to settle in the north court. The all-male group has its first rehearsal almost immediately after the carts have been unloaded. Vague snatches of music can be heard wafting through the courtyards, and the servants are delighted.

'That must be *The Legend of Lady White Snake*! I can't wait to see that.'

'That's right. They say the head musician composed it himself.'

'Yes, what an achievement! That's why the Northern Opera stands out from the rest.'

'Exactly. Those old-fashioned companies, they only perform a few classic plays. I can name them with my five fingers: *Fifteen Strings of Cash*, *Si Lang Visits His Mother*, *The Butterfly Dreams*, and . . . what else . . . Oh, yes, *Longing for Worldly Pleasures* – not even five!'

The most eager among the servants make excuses from work and trace the vague snatches of music to the north court, but are disappointed to find that all the doors are locked and all the windows tightly sealed.

The secrets of the play are not to be revealed, not until it takes to the stage.

—∾—

Even Er Niang, the most enthusiastic of opera lovers, is not allowed into the troupe's compound.

At the dinner table in the west court, she nags Likang to help her gain access to the troupe, to learn singing from the artists. Annoyed at her badgering, Likang pushes away his unfinished bowl of rice and beckons to Da Niang: 'Come and massage my back.'

Er Niang stamps her feet under the table as Da Niang helps the half-drunken Likang leave the room.

Mingyuan puts some streaky pork into his mother's

bowl: 'Don't worry, Mother. I'll find a way. We will both learn singing together.'

Sitting at a corner of the dinner table, Mingzhi quietly finishes his dinner. Charcoal is waiting for him.

—w—

It is a quiet evening. The chirping of crickets lures Charcoal into the bushes. He pricks up his ears, darts here and there but catches nothing. Frogs croak from the riverbank. Charcoal jumps out of the foliage, looks at the riverbank and then back at the bushes, uncertain which to chase – the crickets or the frog.

Mingzhi laughs, whistles for the dog to come forward. It is a moonless night; they have to return home before dark.

Charcoal escorts his master down the slope. Suddenly, a sorrowful tune penetrates the night. The dog pricks up his ears again. Mingzhi follows the sound.

Down the hill, near the bamboo growth by the river, a figure sits, playing the flute. It appears lean and small, seems to be a woman. *A maid from the mansion, perhaps.* Mingzhi turns away at once, not wanting to be seen alone with a girl in a place like this.

'Wait! Don't go!'

Gentle and almost feminine, but it's a man's voice, no doubt.

Venturing closer, Mingzhi can see now a young face: trimmed eyebrows, sharp nose and delicate lips; could easily be mistaken for a girl's. The two men greet each other with a smile and exchange names.

Little Sparrow. Mingzhi repeats it in his mind, his eyes filled with questions.

'It's a given name, given by the troupe leader. Good for the stage,' his new friend explains. He shows the bamboo-leaf flute he's made for himself to Mingzhi. The green, refreshing smell of bamboo fills his nostrils. He places the folded leaf between his lips, tries to play it, but hears only a sharp and tearing noise, like scratching on metal.

Little Sparrow takes it from Mingzhi. 'A busker in Shaanxi taught me, this day two years ago.' He hesitates, smooths the edges of the flute and whispers: 'My birthday.'

Little Sparrow starts playing, and Mingzhi has to swallow back his Happy Birthday greeting.

Unlike the earlier piece, this tune is light and lively: a running stream, a splashing waterfall and cheeping birds, mingle in harmony.

Mingzhi applauds. Little Sparrow blushes, says it is a Shaanxi folk song.

Shaanxi. *The Mountainous West.* Mingzhi looks westwards. The western hill stands firm, blocking his view. *What is the world like behind it?* The hill remains silent.

Mingzhi tries but fails to visualize Little Sparrow's journeys: from the metropolis, Shanghai, in the east to the mountainous region, Shaanxi, in the west, also southwards to the mysterious Yunnan and, of course, north to the colourful but chaotic Imperial City.

Too far, too much. Too confusing. Mingzhi's mental pictures overlap and crumple together. He demands details and Little Sparrow does not disappoint him. His gentle voice takes Mingzhi on stormy days through the surging waves of the roaring Yellow River, trudging across the bare desert under the searing sun, struggling through the dense jungle in fear of cruel bandits, spiralling up and down narrow paths on land-sliding hills, stopping at the numerous cities, towns and villages, listening to folklore, stories and songs in different local accents.

Mingzhi's mental pictures become more vivid, more realistic.

The pair of new friends sit talking late into the night. Charcoal crouches between them, taking turns looking up at them as they take turns to talk. Left, right. Left, right. Sometimes slow, sometimes fast. Left, right. Left, right. It tires him and he yawns. His master and his friend laugh at his awkwardness.

Charcoal ignores them. His eyes droop, and he sleeps quietly in the warmth of their legs.

I have a friend. Mingzhi falls fast asleep, a smile hangs on his lips.

Little Sparrow's music swims into Mingzhi's dream, his pale face drifting in the river of sorrowful tunes. Then everything flows backwards, and Mingzhi sees Little Sparrow as a child: thin and frail, being left with the leader of the opera troupe, standing alone and watching his father walking away with fifty taels in his hands . . .

Mingzhi tosses about in bed. It is warm and he sweats, kicking away his blanket and slipping into his dream again.

The images come back swiftly, and have shifted a little forward in time: Little Sparrow practising body movements, struggling to keep his balance on a long bench . . . Little Sparrow learning the female role's acts, trying to hit the high notes but going out of tune . . . The troupe leader rushes forward and canes him violently . . .

Little Sparrow's muffled cry blends with the background music. Sad and helpless, and close to Mingzhi's ears.

Mingzhi opens his eyes to a whimpering Charcoal. The dog's forelegs rest on the bed and he leans close to Mingzhi, squinting at him. Mingzhi sits up and notices the blood-stains on the edge of the bed. He examines Charcoal's limbs carefully. On the dog's right foreleg there is a severe burn, a raw mess of hair and skin, flesh and blood, with some red paper flakes from a firecracker stuck to it. A red string is tied around the leg above the wound.

Outside, Mingyuan's laughter echoes amid the clattering of firecrackers. Mingzhi knows his half-brother has stolen them from the spare stocks meant for his grandfather's birthday celebration.

Mingyuan sneers, denying Mingzhi's allegation: 'I did not harm your stupid dog. It burnt itself.'

Mingzhi stands facing the morning sun. He watches as Mingyuan walks away through the courtyard, leaving a long shadow that falls over him.

—∞—

Mingzhi does not practise calligraphy during his midday break. He goes to the bamboo groves by the river. *Let's meet at noon*, he and Little Sparrow promised each other last night.

Mingzhi runs his fingers over the calligraphy set in his pocket, imagining his new friend's smiling face on receiving his belated birthday gift.

The noon sun stabs between the pointed leaves, falls sharp onto Mingzhi's head and shoulder. He sits closer to the clumps of bamboo, avoiding the sunlight.

Even the insects are wilting in the noon heat, preferring to rest in silence. Mingzhi plucks a bamboo leaf and tries to make a flute the way Little Sparrow did. He folds and unfolds it, and tries again. The sunlight gradually slants in through the leaves, quietly hunting him again.

There is no trace of Little Sparrow.

—∾—

Er Niang's voice carries from inside the north court. Shrill and high-pitched. Mingzhi stops, standing in front of the closed door.

Er Niang is singing a snatch from the nun's role in *Longing for Worldly Pleasures*:

'. . . Every day I burn incense and change the holy water in the temple;

I have seen several young men sporting by the temple gate.

One glanced at me and I glanced at him.

Ai, what suspense for us both!

How to be united as lovers! . . .'

There is applause, followed by another familiar voice: 'That's great, Mother!'

Mingzhi drops his hand, uncertain whether he should knock on the door.

The door squeaks open. Walking out, the middle-aged troupe leader nearly bumps into Mingzhi. His critical eyes run over Mingzhi from head to toe – his appearance, his demeanour – and he says: 'Are you here to learn Peking opera too, Eldest Grand Young Master?'

Mingzhi shakes his head and peers over the troupe leader's shoulder. In the courtyard, Little Sparrow is half-squatting on a wooden bench in a corner, holding a bowl of water in each outstretched hand and staring down at his shadow.

He is being punished. Mingzhi remembers the strict rules of the opera troupe Little Sparrow spelled out to him last night. All troupe members are to abide by them and there is no exception or excuse. Violation means punishment: caning, starving, scorching under the sweltering sun, and more. Little Sparrow said leaving the troupe without permission was a severe offence. He said it was his fourteenth birthday yesterday and he'd wanted to be away from the troupe, just for one night.

He said he was careful. He said . . .

Mingzhi quietly sneaks away, not wanting to be seen. Not by Er Niang or Mingyuan. And certainly not by Little Sparrow.

~

Mingzhi lies awake in bed, thinking about Little Sparrow: if he is still squatting in the courtyard, if he will get any dinner.

Outside the open window, the western hill sits gloomily

in the light of the waning moon. In the whirring wind, trees howl like lunatics, stretching their branches, twisting and extending them like tentacles. Mingzhi feels as though they have reached for him and bound him tight in his bed. He pulls his blanket away and takes a hungry gasp of air.

Then he hears the familiar notes. In long trembling waves they thread the night.

Mingzhi pictures Little Sparrow sitting alone in a corner of the north court, playing his flute.

Abruptly, the music stops.

The unfinished notes continue in Mingzhi's mind.

—∾—

Rumours roam around the mansion: Mingyuan is paying the troupe leader for him and his mother to learn Peking opera, and they have demanded to have Golden Swallow as their coach.

Likang sniffs in his bed when he hears the news and takes another puff of opium, making sure the flame has not gone out; Da Niang continues chanting sutras in front of her altar; while Liwei has been out in the field since dawn. And Master Chai, blinded and deafened by the excitement of his big day, is ignorant of the whispering maids in the corners, who disperse instantly like startled birds as his dragon stick thuds closer.

Gossip has it Er Niang is not the right material for Peking opera, and that Mingyuan only frolics away his afternoons with the martial actor's weapons, brandishing swords and spears in the courtyard.

These stories leap over the walls and plunge into the poppy fields. Passing the news on as they plough the field, by evening the peasants have a picture of Golden Swallow sitting with his hands over his ears while Er Niang sings briskly in front of him. This gives the hardworking labourers their best after-dinner entertainment for days. The elders among them, though, shake their heads: 'Master Chai's grandson and daughter-in-law learning opera singsong? Shame on him, shame on the Chai clan.'

Inside the mansion, the master of the Chai clan is proudly admiring his new gown, just completed and delivered by the Pindong Town tailor. Fine Suzhou silk. Soft and smooth and shiny. Elegant and prestigious. LONGEVITY. The character embroidered in gold on the front shines in the candlelight, as bright as Master Chai's smile.

Tomorrow.

Master Chai carefully lays down his precious gown and orders a cup of hot tea from his maid. The night is long.

In his room, Mingzhi blows out the candle and slips into his bed. It is a quiet night. The bamboo-leaf musician has been silent. Mingzhi's dream is quiet too. He pushes open the main door. It does not squeak. He sees fluttering birds and ducks, cocks fighting, pigs slouching in the mud, peasants working in the field, and the running stream, but hears nothing. Everything is soundless, and the air stagnant. *Where is Mother? Where is Uncle Liwei? And everyone else?* Shuddering, Mingzhi runs through the open field, fast, but no footsteps are heard. Silent wind slices his ears, and he feels as if he is drifting in the air. Now that he is panting, he feels only his beating heart and pounding pulse, thump, thump, thump, strong in his head.

Abruptly, he stops.

In front of him in the middle of the field, a stage suddenly lights up, bright and colourful. In the centre, the opera actors shuffle about waving their long flowing sleeves. Their mouths busily open and close, open and close, yet no sound comes out of them.

Mingzhi looks around, finds himself the only audience to this pantomimed Peking opera. He turns and runs again, across the field, past the bridge, up and down the hill. He keeps running in the silent darkness, and finally a familiar voice breaks through:

'Eldest Grand Young Master . . .'

Mingzhi heaves a long sigh, opening his eyes to the sunlit room. The maid has brought his breakfast.

'It's time to get ready, Eldest Grand Young Master.'

In the central hall all the servants gather, listening to Butler Feng's briefing: tea ceremony first thing in the morning followed by lunch and an opera performance. Duties are assigned, accompanied by a harsh warning: punishment, that'll be the only response to any mistakes, major or minor.

Master Chai, in his new gown, sits back in his dragon chair, waiting for his sons, daughters-in-law and grandchildren to serve tea, paying their respects in the traditional ritual.

The grandchildren take their turn after the adults. Eldest

Grandson Mingzhi, leading his half-brother Mingyuan, steps forward and kneels before his grandfather, holding out a cup of tea and declaring loud and clear:

'For the best of fortune, as deep as the Eastern Ocean;

For longevity, as sustainable as the Southern Mountain.'

Master Chai laughs, looking at the pair of handsome young men in front of him. *My lovely grandsons.* Taking a sip of tea, he returns the cup to Mingzhi and pats his head: 'You will recite to my guests later, show them how much you've learned. Be prepared for it, my dear grandson.'

Mingzhi frowns. The recent sessions have embarrassed him: standing alone, reading, and hearing his beloved poems drowned in the noise of the busily gobbling guests. A shame to the poets, a shame to himself. He is old enough to recognize the flatteries that follow: half-hearted, only to please his grandfather who uses him to feed his pride.

No! Mingzhi's shoulders drop, and the cup in his hand falls, smashing to pieces on the floor.

Master Chai's smile freezes. *What a bad omen.* Da Niang turns pale. She cries out instantly: 'Breaking into a flowering future! Breaking into a flowering future!'

This cliché fails to soothe the angry old man, his face as hard as steel.

Standing to one side, Er Niang sniggers quietly. She waits for Master Chai to take action, but is disappointed when Butler Feng bursts in: 'Mandarin Liu is on his way!'

Mandarin Liu enters the village in his official sedan, escorted by his retinue, bustling along the way. Standing to the sides of the path, the villagers whisper their sympathy for the sedan-bearers, who grit their teeth, letting beads of sweat run down their faces, necks and naked upper bodies. The villagers imagine the well-fed mandarin with his round face and limbs and protruding belly sitting comfortably in the swaying sedan, munching streaky pork. *Definitely not the bearers' favourite passenger.* As they joke among themselves the villagers watch the entourage heading towards the Chai Mansion.

The most honourable guest of honour arrives first! The broken cup has been nudged out of Master Chai's mind. He taps his dragon stick, leading Mandarin Liu to the guest of honour's seat.

Mandarin Liu's gift is generous: a set of marble statues of Good Fortune, Prosperity and Longevity, the three silver-haired old men. Master Chai smooths his goatee, unable to contain his smile as he admires the fine craftsmanship. *Things did change.* The marriage. The precious only grandson Meilian gave to the Liu family. Association with Mandarin Liu has facilitated his opium trade. Content with a share of the revenue, this father-in-law of Meilian has conveniently left Master Chai out of his tax list.

Guests keep streaming in. Sitting back on his chair receiving greetings, Master Chai's mind spins fast. *This connection has to be strengthened.* His eyes scan the hall and catch Liwei, who, sitting next to Mandarin Liu, is whispering with him about the next payment of the mandarin's share.

Liwei, his second son. Master Chai sighs, does not understand Liwei's decision to refuse all marriage proposals after his wife's death, two years after his wedding.

An obedient and good helper, he follows his father's will (though Master Chai knows deep down that Liwei disapproves of the opium business) in everything but this. He is adamant, determined to be single. *A widower for eighteen years.* Master Chai shakes his head: Liwei must have a son of his own, one who is as smart as Mingzhi.

Mingzhi. Master Chai looks around. The hall is full. Guests of honour, close and distant relatives, eating and drinking, and exchanging pleasantries. Servants busy serving. His sons, his daughters-in-law, Mingyuan.

And Mingzhi?

The main door thumps shut, locking away all noises and faces behind Mingzhi. He takes a deep breath. Relieved. *Enough of those sweet-as-honey birthday greetings and forced smiles.* The sky is clear blue; Mingzhi squints. *And he wants me to recite to them.*

Not anymore!

Mingzhi knows he will be angry, the old man, his grandfather, the head of his family, the master of Plum Blossom Village, whom no one dares to offend.

And I am doing it for the first time.

For some moments Mingzhi stares at the closed door, imagining his grandfather's reaction. Then he shrugs and turns away, walking straight ahead.

Outside, it is quiet. The peasants are enjoying their precious day off, having lunch with their families, thanks to their landlord's own big day. The normally busy fields are empty, the paths silent. Mingzhi walks in this unusually tranquil midday, breathing the fresh soil of the newly ploughed land, feeling relaxed. *There's only me.* Charcoal barks, running close to Mingzhi's legs, as if protesting. His master smiles, stoops and caresses him: 'And my Charcoal, of course.'

The faithful dog wags his tail as he follows Mingzhi across the bridge, through the field and up the hill. *We have plenty of time today, and no one is watching us.* Mingzhi decides to explore further than his usual evening walk.

On the other side of the hill Mingzhi discovers an escarpment. An old pine tree stands alone; its twisted trunk hanging from the rock face, the green needles covering the outstretched branches seemingly engraved upon the blue sky.

Mingzhi touches the creased and cracked bark, mottled black and brown, like an old man's wrinkled face. Charcoal rubs his back on the trunk, the perfect treatment for his itchy skin. Mingzhi recalls Old Scholar Yan's saying: the older a pine tree is, the greater the energy it has gathered, and wherever it stands, it cultivates good *feng shui*. He walks around the tree and finds it rooted in a ledge with a wall of stone behind it, leaving a narrow space just enough for him to squeeze through. There he sees a cave, concealed by the exposed roots and trunk. Sunlight slants in from a crevice in a corner; the afternoon breeze sneaks inside. Bright and airy. *Like a fairyland in the poems I've read.* Mingzhi walks about in it and finds a hidden corner: a perfect place for a reed-bed. He imagines spending afternoon hours with his pet in this new-found land. He whistles for Charcoal: 'Hey, we have a secret home now!'

—∾—

Minyuan replaces Mingzhi to recite for the guests. Da Niang worriedly sends her maid to look for Mingzhi. *Not today, my dear son.* She knows he has got himself into big trouble. Her eyebrows are as tight as Master Chai's pursed lips. Er Niang watches the old man closely as he sits straight up, locking his eyes on Mingyuan, fearing that his second grandson might fail him.

Poem after poem Mingyuan recites, fluent and clear. Master Chai nods and sits back, grinning. Er Niang winks triumphantly at Mingyuan then smirks at the pale-faced Da Niang.

A loud gong marks the opening of the Peking opera: *The Legend of Lady White Snake* is unveiled.

Little White, the snake demon played by Golden Swallow, fights against Master Qinghai, the monk who is determined to separate this snake demon from her human husband. Golden Swallow waves and flaps his long flowing sleeves, and swirls, round and round. But Master Qinghai seems stronger. Little White is pushed to the floor, mourning.

All eyes are on the stage. Mingzhi quietly sneaks in, hiding himself among the crowd, Charcoal following him closely.

Master Qinghai steps forward. Little Green, the faithful maid of Little White, rushes to stop him from hurting her mistress.

Mingzhi strains his eyes. This green snake, Little Green, looks familiar. Her round eyes, sharp nose and delicate lips . . .

Little Sparrow? Mingzhi is stunned to see his friend, almost unrecognizable, in heavy make-up and the maid's costume. But Charcoal has spotted him; he barks joyfully, wags his tail, jumps onto the stage and runs to Little Sparrow.

The musicians drop their large and small gongs, drum and clapper, *yueqin* and *huqin*, *erhu* and *sanxian*, all fall clinking and clattering. Golden Swallow shrinks into a corner; the monk actor brandishes the spear in his hand; Little Sparrow stands still while Charcoal passionately rubs his back against the petrified actor's legs.

The crowd exchange queries, their voices droning in commotion.

A black dog on stage, on my birthday! Trembling with rage, Master Chai braces himself with his dragon stick. *Worse than a broken cup.* He watches Charcoal happily jump down from the stage, threading his way through the crowd, running towards the back of the hall.

To Mingzhi, the master's beloved eldest grandson.

Numbed to his feet, Mingzhi exchanges a quick glance with Little Sparrow on the stage. They look into each other's eyes, dull and lifeless.

For the first time, Mingzhi is punished: no dinner, and he is not allowed to leave his room until the opera troupe has completed all its performances. Likang and Da Niang are warned, too, to keep an eye on their son's behaviour, and a maid is assigned to keep track of and report on Mingzhi's whereabouts.

Worst of all, Mingzhi is forced to give up Charcoal. The master of the house insists: a black dog brings bad luck. Mingzhi begs: 'Let me keep Charcoal! I will keep him in my room; he won't get out again!'

Master Chai howls: 'I said no black dog in my house. Do you understand?' His chest feels tight, and he clutches at his heart with one hand.

Mingyuan steps forward and massages his grandfather's back and shoulders. Master Chai heaves a long sigh, feeling relieved. That he has a second grandson.

—~—

Little Sparrow disappears from the stage after the unfinished first performance – a cruel punishment for a budding actor.

Longing for Worldly Pleasure replaces *The Legend of Lady White Snake* on the following nights. Golden Swallow monopolizes the stage playing the nun, a solo performance. His most faithful fan, Er Niang, glues herself to her seat, the best in the front row, and fixes her eyes on her beloved actor.

Thinking about Mingzhi being punished, Er Niang smiles, echoing Shi Fan, the nun on the stage, and hums:

'. . . I want to go down the mountain and seek a lover.

I don't care if he beats me, scolds me, laughs at me, maligns me . . .'

From the stage Golden Swallow glances over, and their gazes meet.

—~—

Mingzhi stares at the blank paper, all night, and writes nothing. The opera music roams around the mansion and travels to the west court. Golden Swallow's singing, in crisp, clear, long and drawn-out words, is heard:

'. . . It is only because my father was fond of reading the Buddhist scriptures

And my mother liked to intone Buddha's name.

Every day they burned incense at the temple and worshipped Buddha.

After birth I was sickly,

So they dedicated me to the Buddhist faith

And made me live as a nun . . .'

Mingzhi imagines the unhappy, secluded nun sitting alone in her room in front of a set of *muyi*, tapping the wooden frog drums with a stick to give emphasis as she chants sutras. Her daily task as a nun. Like a prisoner, counting her days.

Like him.

Mingzhi wets his brush with abundant ink, pressing down forcefully on the paper, making a huge dot. Black. Hopeless. He flops in his chair and lays his face on the desk. His streaming tears soak the paper, blotching the ink, smearing his cheek.

The maid comes to check later and finds Mingzhi asleep in the chair. She pulls a blanket over him, puts out the candle and leaves.

Mingzhi drifts towards his cave-home. Little Sparrow stands smiling in the streak of sunlight, beckoning him to come closer, and Charcoal barks, running towards him. Mingzhi hurries forward. *Ouch!* He stumbles over a stone and falls.

Blank.

The world around him turns pitch-black. No Little

Sparrow, no Charcoal. Mingzhi blunders about looking for his friend and his dog, knocking into this and that, stumbling here and there. Then he stops as he hears the familiar tune of a bamboo-leaf flute, threading through the darkness.

Mingzhi rubs his eyes and shakes his head. He is fully awake now. The long trembling waves of sound continue. *He's out there!* Remembering his friend is leaving tomorrow, Mingzhi's heart tightens.

Outside the window there is no trace of movement. It's almost midnight, and the mansion is asleep. Mingzhi does not hesitate for long. He cleans the ink from his face and walks out.

In the bamboo grove by the river Little Sparrow sits waiting, eyes dark-ringed, cheeks hollow. Risking another punishment only to say goodbye to his friend. Mingzhi feels a twinge of guilt, and is speechless, as is Little Sparrow, knowing they may not see one another again. He takes out the calligraphy set he has been keeping for days.

'A late birthday present.'

Little Sparrow quietly runs his fingers on the fine brush and the exquisite ink-set. *I have nothing to offer him.* As he watches Mingzhi fiddling with his leaf-flute, Little Sparrow plucks a bamboo leaf then shows Mingzhi how to fold it into a flute. Mingzhi tries a few times and succeeds. His friend nods: 'At least I have something for you.'

Mingzhi smiles thank-you, demands more: to learn how to play. As he places the flute between his lips, he hears noises from the bushes close by. So does Little Sparrow. They turn pale: *Are they here for us?*

For some moments they remain silent but no one approaches. The noises in the bushes grow louder and clearer: the familiar voices of a man and woman flirting and laughing frivolously. Curious, the two friends move slowly forward, hiding themselves in the shadow of the bamboo grove, then the undergrowth. Peeping through the foliage, they see –

Er Niang and Golden Swallow.

The pair sit leaning against each other, Golden Swallow's arm around Er Niang's shoulders. In the faint moonlight, Er Niang's tilted face appears dazed, flushed; she is staring at her lover with dreamy gaze, listening closely to his tender murmurings.

They kiss.

Mingzhi and Little Sparrow shrink back, cheeks burning, staring at each other in disbelief. Mingzhi turns to leave. Fallen twigs crunch loudly under his feet, and he stops at once. Er Niang pulls herself away from Golden Sparrow, her face ashen.

From the bushes a stray cat meows as it darts in front of the lovers, noisily rustling through the bushes. Golden Swallow laughs and pulls Er Niang into his arms again: 'Hey, calm down. There's no one here this late.'

Slowly Mingzhi and Little Sparrow retreat, wordless, pretending nothing has happened. Mingzhi mimes 'follow me' to his friend and leads him up the hill. 'I have a secret to share with you,' he says, and speeds up. When they reach the ledge, something black darts out of the cave and lopes towards them. Charcoal! He jumps onto Mingzhi and licks his face. Little Sparrow pats the dog's head, and is glad for

Mingzhi that Uncle Liwei has helped to shelter Charcoal in the cave.

By dawn Mingzhi is able to play a couple of tunes on the flute. They leave the cave and part before the mansion awakes.

Mingzhi sneaks back into his room. Eyes closed, he imprints a lasting image of his friend in his mind: a fragile young man, with a sad, helpless look.

Opening his eyes, Mingzhi sees his own taut face in the mirror.

Is this how he will remember me too?

His nerves twitch behind his temples.

Six

Mingzhi spends longer hours in school now, reading and writing after the rest have gone home. The tranquil afternoons alone in the classroom comfort him, because *no one is watching*. Old Scholar Yan's disciple always brings Mingzhi lunch then retreats in silence, leaving him to his world of literature. He buries himself in it: from the ancient poems of the Xia, Shang and Zhou Dynasties to the verses of the Song Dynasty, hundreds of poems from the glorious Tang Dynasty and the prose of the later periods. School gives him the best excuse to keep away from the mansion with its many watchful eyes. He is safe under the umbrella of 'study', for which he is allowed as much time as he needs.

Taking advantage of this, on his way back from school Mingzhi makes secret trips to his cave, taking food for Charcoal. He plays with the dog, laughing and rolling on the ground. *The best part of the day.*

Mingzhi knows the uncertainty of this happiness. He knows it is only a matter of time before his secret is discovered. So he knows he must make the most of it while it lasts. When he leaves it is always painful to hear Charcoal whine, begging to go with him.

In the fields the poppy plants have grown into a sea of billowing green. It will be a couple of months before they blossom. Mingzhi likes the fresh smell of green leaves, likes breathing them in as much as he can before the flowering begins. It is also during this season that Uncle Liwei is able to join him in his evening walks.

On such evenings, uncle and nephew take slow strolls across the bridge, past the fields and down to the river. There they sit and talk of the day's events: school, Charcoal and the cave, Da Niang. Their roles have changed, though, as Uncle Liwei, now quieter, prefers to be a listener (the mansion and the opium trade, his only world, are not something he is proud of). And Mingzhi willingly shares his secrets and feelings with his uncle.

Sometimes they walk in silence, feeling the soothing breeze, listening to the crunch of gravel and twigs under their feet, the tiny movements of field mice, chirping crickets, running water, croaking frogs. The evening passes quickly.

Mingzhi values these comforting moments, the times he shares with his uncle. *Too short, too precious.* He knows these will end when the poppies bloom, when the field turns into a sea of pinkish red.

He yearns for them to stop growing, for time to be frozen.

~

Mandarin Liu visits again, this time to collect his share of the profits. For the entire morning he and Master Chai sit in the central hall. Gales of laughter penetrate the closed room. Two young maids standing outside waiting for orders press their ears to the door, determined to be the first to capture the latest news.

Abruptly the door is flung open. The girls dodge back, barely escaping a heavy blow. They are lucky, too, to escape punishment as their master keeps smiling as he smooths his goatee.

—∾—

By afternoon the rumour spreads through the mansion: Master Chai's second son, Liwei, is engaged to Mandarin Liu's youngest sister, and the wedding will follow soon.

Another convenient marriage. The servants sniff as they gossip amongst themselves: 'An unmarried maiden in her early thirties? There must be something wrong with her.'

In the west court Er Niang is more excited about her dear son, Mingyuan, being summoned for the first time to recite poems for his grandfather's most important guest. *Another big step forward.* Standing in the courtyard she raises her voice in the exaggerated drawn-out style of Peking opera in the direction of Da Niang's room: 'Heavenly God has opened His eyes at last, made the right judgement, giving Mingyuan his place on earth!'

Silence. Er Niang hears her high-pitched voice echo in the empty courtyard and her maid laughing under her sleeve. She rushes forward and slaps the girl: 'What is so funny? Silly girl.'

And she sends the maid off to prepare Mingyuan's favourite roast pork for dinner.

In her room Da Niang sits still, fixing her gaze at the altar. Strings of smoke sway upwards from the pot of burning joss sticks. Ascending. Dispersing.

She has heard the rumour and the provoking shout.

The burned incenses are now teetering columns of grey, crumbling into the pot. A gust of wind wafts through the open window, sweeping some ash into Da Niang's eyes. She squints in pain, her tears squeezing out. *Where is* he? *Does he know about this?*

In front of her the Buddha image is a blur.

—w—

Mingzhi lies in a corner of the cave on the mound of dried reeds collected during his visits. Against his legs Charcoal sleeps soundly. At the end of the bed stands the sandalwood box of his childhood toys – the grasshopper, dragonfly, rabbit and turtles – wrapped in the faded embroidered sheet.

Through the crevice the afternoon sun slips in, casting a long beam of light across Mingzhi's body and across the dog. Mingzhi feels the heat on his skin but stays still, not wanting to wake Charcoal. He feels it comforting though, the heat, as warm as Charcoal's soft, hairy body that rests against his bare feet.

My companion. Mingzhi gazes down. The dog's dark hair gleams in the sunlight. Suddenly the images of Er Niang's dreamy eyes and flushed cheeks in the moonlight creep into Mingzhi's mind. The lovers' murmurings. The hugging and kissing.

He feels his face burning.

—w—

The maids swear to the servants surrounding them: their quiet, obedient Second Young Master has had a big row with his father, the master of the house. The girls busily describe the episode, talking over each other.

'He said, "No, I'm not going to marry her," and our Master thumped his stick . . .' The older girl exclaims.

The younger girl butts in: 'Our Master was louder. He shouted: "I've decided! That's it. Just go and prepare for the wedding." '

'And then . . .' The older girl pauses. 'Guess what happened next?'

The servants urge: 'Hey, go on, tell us all about it.'

'You won't believe it . . . Our Second Young Master, our soft-spoken Second Young Master, banged the desk and roared: "I said NO! How many times have I told you, I will never marry again. That is final." '

'And he rushed out.'

'Are you kidding?'

The two girls say simultaneously: 'I swear to Heavenly God that every single word is nothing but the truth.'

'What a real man he is!' The servants chuckle as they imagine their master furiously trembling and thumping with his stick.

'Wish we had seen and heard that.' They sigh with regret.

Mingzhi comes home late, just in time for dinner.

'Aye, our Eldest Grand Young Master has been working hard lately,' Er Niang deliberately raises her voice in front of Likang. 'Surely that mandarin post is already in the bag for him.'

Mingzhi avoids looking at her, still embarrassed when he thinks about her intimacy with Golden Swallow. Ignoring her ridicule and his father's long face, Mingzhi sits down beside his mother.

Er Niang heaves an exaggerated sigh and continues her monologue: 'Unlike my Mingyuan. All he can do is recite to Mandarin Liu.'

'Did you, son?' Likang smiles and gazes at Mingyuan.

'Of course he did! The Master asked for him only this morning!' Er Niang answers before her son can.

Likang happily picks out some streaky pork for Mingyuan. Er Niang winks triumphantly at her son and helps him to even more of his favourite dish.

Mingzhi feels his mother's hand on his arm, and knows she is asking him to be tolerant. He nods: *I know, I know.*

Mingzhi finishes his dinner as quickly as he can, to make his time for a walk with his uncle. The days are counting, as the poppies are budding.

—∾—

It is a stifling evening. Uncle Liwei is silent, his face taut and his mind preoccupied. They cross the bridge, walk past the fields and head towards the river, wordlessly. Mingzhi is uncomfortable with his uncle's heavy air.

'Let's go and visit Charcoal. He will be happy to see us!' Mingzhi suggests, hoping to cheer his uncle up.

Uncle Liwei does not answer but turns onto the path that leads to the hill. Mingzhi follows.

Charcoal is overwhelmed. He barks, leaping and spinning in circles. Mingzhi throws a twig up. Charcoal jumps, catches it, struts around with his tail held high, as if announcing himself the winner. Uncle Liwei, sitting on a corner of the reed bed, laughs at the dog. Mingzhi laughs too, at his uncle's laughter.

Uncle Liwei throws another twig to the far end of the cave. Charcoal immediately drops the old and rushes for the new.

Mingzhi observes his uncle closely: his grey hair, stooped back and look of desolation. He bursts out: 'Why don't you remarry, Uncle? Don't you ever feel lonely without a wife and children?'

Uncle Liwei becomes very still. After some moments, he says: 'I don't need another woman or another son. I'm not alone. I have you.'

'But . . .'

'It's getting dark. Let's go home.'

He walks out of the cave, hurries away. *He is angry with me.* Mingzhi rushes to keep up with his uncle.

Behind him, Charcoal barks, drops his twig, cries and scratches at the rocky ground. Then he jumps to the bed, scattering the reeds, before darting out of the cave, running after his master for the first time since he was taken here.

—∞—

Mingzhi sees only his uncle moving away from him, ignoring his calls. He chases him, a tall figure shuffling into the bamboo grove. Charcoal follows. *Wait!* Struggling forward, Mingzhi slips and rolls down the slope. Gets up. Runs. Closes in. Reaches out and taps Uncle Liwei's shoulder.

The man turns round. A masked face! Shocked, Mingzhi steps back, stumbles and falls. Charcoal comes and licks his face. The masked man approaches, stands in front of Mingzhi and removes his mask –

A blank face without eyes, nose or mouth!

Charcoal howls, long and piercing . . .

What a nightmare. Mingzhi sits up panting, his heart still pounding in his chest. Charcoal's cry sounded so close, so real.

The dawn bells toll in the distant temple. Mingzhi rubs his eyes. *Time to get ready for school.* When the maid brings him his breakfast he catches her strange expression.

'Is there anything you want to tell me?'

She stammers: 'Eldest Grand Young Master . . . You . . . You'd better go to the main courtyard and . . . and . . . have a look for yourself.'

'What is it?'

She shakes her head, her lips pursed tight.

Mingzhi rushes out.

In the middle of the central court lies something black and still.

Charcoal. Covered in blood.

'They told me and I didn't believe it.' Mingyuan, who has just arrived, gives the body a kick. 'He really is dead!' His cheerful shout sounds especially sharp in the morning air. He turns to Mingzhi: 'Well, don't look at me. It wasn't me. You know who ordered it.'

Mingzhi hears nothing of Mingyuan's words. His grandfather's words buzz in his head: *I said no black dog in my house.* So loudly that he feels as if his skull will crack.

—∞—

Mingzhi slips and falls on the dewy grass, rises, struggles on up the slope and slips again. His limbs are scratched and he is wet and muddy all over. His eyes are blurred and his mouth tastes salt. *Is it mud or sweat or tears?* He doesn't know and doesn't care. The only thing in his mind is: *keep going*. He lets his blind feet blunder on.

Take me away, as far away as possible.

—w—

The whole mansion is shaken: the precious Eldest Grand Young Master is missing.

The first alarm is raised in the west court when Mingzhi is absent from the dinner table. Likang mutters about Mingzhi running wild and blames Da Niang for spoiling their son. He throws a deep sigh and retreats to his room. When there is still no trace of the boy at midnight, Da Niang, who has been waiting helplessly at the main door, sends her maid to Master Chai.

In minutes the mansion is awake. The grandfather scolds Da Niang for delaying, and all family members and servants are summoned to the central court. The enquiry begins.

According to the maid, Mingzhi left for school that morning as usual. But Mingyuan adds at once: his half-brother never arrived there. The furious Master Chai slaps Mingyuan loud on the face, angry with him for not saying so earlier. The boy holds his cheek, unsure of what has happened.

Er Niang's chuckles cease. Staring at the old man, who has locked both hands behind his back and is pacing the courtyard in agitation, she realizes: *The eldest is still the eldest.*

Master Chai organizes the servants into two teams, led by Liwei and Butler Feng, and warns: 'Do not come home without my grandson!'

It is dark and cold but the reeds keep Mingzhi warm. *How long have I slept? An hour, three, five or more?* He tries to get up but his body aches, no longer seems to belong to him. Weak, weary, he sleeps again.

The water is lukewarm and Mingzhi swims in it, up and down, back and forth, moving in circles, turning somersaults. And he breathes in it, like a fish. *So comfortable, so free.* He sees an object approaching – black, hairy – it's Charcoal! Mingzhi beckons, and the dog swims towards him. Reaching out, Charcoal's body feels cold, sending a chill into Mingzhi's veins. He shivers, gulps water, panics. Hands swinging, legs kicking.

But he is sinking fast, drowning.

Then there are beams of light and noises, loud, familiar.

Everything vanishes.

Liwei and his team find Mingzhi curled like a shrimp in a corner of the pitch-dark cave. The anxious uncle rushes forward, pats Mingzhi's cheeks and calls: 'Wake up! Wake up, Mingzhi.'

'Cold, cold . . .' Mingzhi murmurs, his eyes rolling up in

his head. Liwei lifts him and shakes him. *Be strong, wake up*. But Mingzhi's frail body hangs heavy in his uncle's arms. Liwei refuses the servants' help, but nearly falls as he staggers forwards. The servants exchange puzzled looks: *What's wrong with him? He has always been so calm and in control.*

—∞—

Mingzhi opens his eyes onto his mother's face: eyes red and swollen, cheeks hollow. *Where am I?* He takes a quick glance round: the same gauze net around the bed, the same walls, windows, chairs, desk and cupboards.

The same room.

Back again. He shuts his eyes tight, his face crumpling.

—∞—

After starving her for two days Master Chai sends Mingzhi's maid back to her home village: the ultimate punishment for negligence. Butler Feng is called upon: to pick the most capable among the servants to be the Master's eyes and ears, to watch over Mingzhi. Master Chai is cautious this time, and Butler Feng has only one obvious choice: Little Mouse. Quick-witted, agile, alert, this hyperactive teenager has always been impatient with the trivial chores in the kitchen. Always looks out for more important errands. With his mousy head and brain that earned him his name, Little Mouse seems to be the perfect answer to Master Chai's question.

There must be no more mistakes. The revelations about Charcoal and about the secret cave have proved too much for the old man. He knows he can't fully trust even Liwei.

Liwei, what has got into you? He sighs. *What am I going to tell Mandarin Liu?* After moments of careful thought, he decides to delay the wedding arrangements for as long as he can. And Mingzhi must be ready for his exam as soon as possible.

Before Butler Feng finishes his words, Little Mouse darts out of the kitchen and into Mingzhi's room. The rumour about Mingzhi going to Pindong to sit for the exam has been a hot topic in the kitchen, and the subsequent question is 'who will go with him?' A chance to step out of the busy and greasy kitchen has been every servant's dream. *So I could be the lucky one!* Little Mouse almost gallops into Mingzhi's room.

The young servant finds his equally young master at the desk, rice papers spread out in front of him, next to them an empty inkwell. Little Mouse scratches his head, then quietly gets the inkstick and starts grinding, without uttering a word. Mingzhi looks on, begins to like this mousy teenager.

Mingzhi has only one thing in mind now: his studies. His grandfather's emphatic desire that he become a mandarin has given him a hint about power, authority and control.

Yes, control. That's what I need.

Determined to excel in the civil-service exam, Mingzhi buries himself in the world of knowledge, keeping busy with the Four Books and the Five Classics.

He begins with *Daxue*, the Great Learning, and *Zhongrong*, the Doctrine of the Mean. While the former invites him into the virtual gate of the Confucian School, the latter teaches him the laws regulating all happenings and forms of being, the correct course to be pursued, directing him to distinguish right from wrong. These principles attach themselves to his young heart as wisteria vines cling to the crevices in walls; they are as clear as the purple blossoms that brighten under the spring sun, guiding his moral judgement.

And he knows:

To be cruel to animals (Charcoal) is wrong.

To be cruel to human beings (the maid) is wrong.

To neglect the responsibility of parenting (fathering) is wrong.

To indulge in opium is wrong.

To cultivate opium and encourage addiction to it are wrong.

He knows also, he has to make wrongs right.

I will, one day, Mingzhi promises himself.

In order to accomplish his wish Mingzhi knows he must learn more, must master knowledge.

Old Scholar Yan observes Mingzhi closely, delighted about his favourite student's soaring enthusiasm for study, but worrying too that Mingzhi may be over-pressuring himself: the first to come to school and the last to leave; studying late into the night, according to the servant boy; controlling the amount he eats to avoid after-meal tiredness that affects his learning. No games, no evening walks. Only books.

The old man sees changes in the youth: more prominent cheekbones, darkened eyes; inside them a sea of knowledge, still accumulating though already making waves, waiting for the right moment to pour forth.

He needs more. Old Scholar Yan scratches his head, drafting out a long list of essay topics, assigning one every other day to Mingzhi, marking the papers handed in, discussing them with the young writer. Comments are given and suggestions detailed in the master's fine calligraphy. Long paragraphs at first, reduced to a couple of lines as the days go by. Finding flaws seems to take some effort now. The old scholar is amazed though a little apprehensive. *Soon enough he won't need me any longer.*

Da Niang boils ginseng tea in the morning and bird's nest soup at night, brings them to her son, sitting quietly and watching him drain them.

Morning after morning.

Night after night.

Season

after

season.

Seven

Pindong Town, 1892

Morning in Pindong Town is a bright, colourful scene of noisy, crowded streets. With hurtling traffic of carts, cows, donkeys and horses. Pedestrians. Bustling hawkers. Haggling customers.

Singsong girls gesture to prospective clients from under the red lanterns at brothel doorways.

Caged magpies hang high in teahouses, above the heads of their boastful, spittle-showering masters. Their songs hover in the clear blue sky.

Hollering, gong-banging buskers: puppeteer, fire-eater, sword-eater, goldfish-swallower, tightrope-walker. Baring their upper bodies, letting their sweat run down. Their tanned skin gleams in the glorious spring sun.

Mingzhi walks into the picture. Little Mouse, his young servant, tags along.

Clink! Clink!

Behind Mingzhi a cart is pulled to a halt. Loud shrills of bells ring in his ears: 'Clink-clink! Clink-clink! Clink-clink-clink!'

From the driving seat a stout, swarthy peasant waves at

Mingzhi, as if herding cattle: 'Shoo-shoo! Shoo-shoo!' He brandishes a crop, urging his donkey forward.

Mingzhi watches as the donkey inches towards him. Little Mouse drags him away. Both stumble and fall onto a doorstep, panting.

'Aiya, young master, look at you . . . What a mess. Come in and let us massage you.'

Such a sweet voice. Mingzhi glances up.

Under a huge red lantern shine some colourful faces, looking down at Mingzhi, and their rouged lips move simultaneously: 'Yes, please come in, let us comfort you.'

Already there are hands on his sleeves, arms and face, like an octopus, seeking every opportunity to grip every inch of his skin. He blushes. *Strange women touching me!* He struggles to rise, wobbles a little and starts running. Little Mouse follows.

A storm of giggling bursts out behind them. Mingzhi glances back. The women flap their hands, beckoning and blinking coquettishly. Mingzhi speeds up, to another burst of chortling.

Taking refuge in a teahouse, Mingzhi dusts his clothes and collects himself. Little Mouse finds them a vacant table in a corner by the balcony on the first floor, overlooking the main street.

Mingzhi leans against the wooden balustrade, peering at the bustling scene below.

Pedestrians are still rushing. Horse or donkey or ox-carts push and jingle their way through the crowd, trot-trot-trot, clink-clink-clink, between the rows of stalls flanking the street.

The stalls.

Hungry eaters sit or squat around a big, steaming cauldron at the soybean and pancake stall, watching closely as the middle-aged hawker slips one piece of dough after another into the hot, golden oil. Their watery mouths hang open as the pieces frizzle and somersault in the sea of burning oil, swelling into bulging golden pancakes beneath whiffs of steam and smell. Ready to be eaten. And the smell lures more passers-by into joining the breakfast queue.

Women, young and old, gather round the textile stall, selecting their favourite materials: sky blue or ocean green or rosy red or soft yellow, plain or dotted or checked or flowery, every colour and pattern.

And men, lowering their heads, quietly squeeze in and hide among the on-lookers before the Magic Tonic for Men stall, trying their best not to be seen by their acquaintances. But the well-built stall owner is determined to make himself and the surrounding men the centre of attention. He bangs his gong and claps his clapper:

'After drinking my Magic Tonic,'
Clap-clap!
'You'll be as lively as a magic dragon!'
Gong!
'After drinking my Magic Tonic,'
Clap-clap!
'Your woman will be as tame as a kitten!'
Gong! Gong!
'After drinking my Magic Tonic,'
Clap-clap!

'The world is yours for the taking!'

Gong! Gong! Gong!

Mingzhi takes a deep breath.

Below him is a world of smell, colour and action.

Of real life.

Mingzhi's eyes brim with tears. *My first step out, after all these years.*

Watching his master, Little Mouse shakes his head. *Oh, poet.*

He is accustomed to these sudden solemnities. Although his young master is eighteen, only two years older than he is, he is always immersed in his own thoughts. A flash of rainbow after a downpour, or fallen leaves in the courtyard, or the carcass of a lizard between the door panels of a wardrobe, these small things can make Mingzhi tearful, contemplative for half a day. And there's always sadness in his eyes. *He has read too much about the autumn wind, withered flowers, whirling snow and the waning moon.* Little Mouse shakes his head once more.

Soon the gong bangs again in the street below, and Little Mouse happily sips his tea while tapping out the rhythm of the Magic Tonic ditty.

Mingzhi's hungry eyes drift about with the eddying crowd. One moment here, the next there. They stop suddenly, attracted to a patch of silky light blue shining in the morning sun. At the textile stall the customers part, as if making way for a dignitary, someone too sacred for them to get close to.

A girl in an exquisite blue dress threads through the impromptu path and goes to the stall front. She smiles and whispers to her companion, a teenager in a maid's attire. The servant holds out a bolt of turquoise material for her mistress, who brings it close to her face. Her clean, young face. Now reflecting the shiny hue of silk, the colour of the ocean that sinks deeply into her dimples. Mingzhi melts into them: the colour, her dimples, and sees nothing of the busy, noisy surroundings.

Only her.

Then she turns away, and the maid follows. Mingzhi cranes his neck, glimpses a corner of blue disappearing into a sea of dull, plain cotton.

Who is she?

Mingzhi's young heart ripples.

Night falls. All is quiet.

Mingzhi sits in his room in the teahouse-lodge, poring over his books. In a corner Little Mouse is curled on a straw mat, sleeping soundly. Outside the window, high in the sky, a lone star twinkles like a knowing eye. *Are you my lucky star?* The wise eye keeps blinking, now bright, now dim, as if to say: yes, no, yes, no.

His fate is a secret that the faraway star is forbidden to tell. Mingzhi must decode its signs for himself: yes or no, yes or no.

He frowns. *Tomorrow is the day.* His heart pounds.

'You will pass, I'm sure.' At their last meeting Old Scholar Yan had reassured Mingzhi; he had found out that the chief examiner was an old friend of his, Scholar Dai, a fourth-ranking Imperial Scholar.

'He is fair and kind. He will like your work, I know.' His teacher is confident.

Even so Mingzhi can't help worrying. The title of *xiucai*, 'intellectual', which he will attain on passing this first exam at district level will not grant him a position in the civil service, but it will qualify him for the provincial-level exam. At the provincial level, only half of the *xiucai* will be awarded the title of *juren*, 'recommended man', and these lucky ones will be eligible for low-ranking official positions.

I've still to get through the first stage. Mingzhi knows tomorrow is a decisive day. A fail means wasting another year and a half on a re-sit, and a diminution of his confidence.

So it is a big day, a big occasion, especially for grandfather Master Chai. *But for all the wrong reasons.* Mingzhi sighs lightly, shakes his head as he remembers yesterday's ceremony. The prayers in front of the ancestors' memorial plates at the ancestral hall. The throwing of *yao*, the divinatory blocks. And the smile on his grandfather's face later, as broad as the divinatory blocks on the floor.

'A good omen,' the old man had said. His laughter ran wild between the pillars and the beams, swirling in the airy hall.

Mingzhi shivers in a sudden gust of wind. He closes the window, returns to his books. In the corner Little Mouse turns over, muttering meaninglessly then falling deep into dreamlands again. Mingzhi does not understand how the boy can feel so much at home, can rest so comfortably. Master Chai insisted Mingzhi spend the night prior to the exam at Pindong Town, to save him from starting the journey at dawn and arriving at the examination hall tired. But Mingzhi knows sleep will evade him tonight.

The candle burns low. Mingzhi lights another and starts to leaf through a book.

In the flickering flame, his lonely shadow sways on the whitewashed wall, late into the night.

Early morning, and the examination hall is already full. Mingzhi sits at the back, behind hundreds of candidates. Noises buzz but subside moments later when a faint voice shouts for attention from the students. Mingzhi tries to catch a glimpse of Chief Examiner Scholar Dai, but sees only the many heads and bodies in front of him. He shifts from left to right, sees just a snatch of the silky black official gown at the far end of the room.

And soon the exam begins. Mingzhi buries himself in his paper.

It's not that difficult, really. He has completed the first round, the most important of all: the understanding and interpretation of the Four Books and Five Classics. As he has been memorizing them day and night, the sentences and passages and their definitions have engraved themselves in his mind. The second test, versatility in the command of various literary forms, doesn't take him much time either. Having completed a poem, Mingzhi concentrates on finishing the eight-legged styled essay, the most classical form of prose, in the final stage.

The plateful of ink dwindles as he repeatedly wets his brush and goes on writing, and empties when Mingzhi takes a final soak and marks a full stop.

Done.

He does a last check-through of his paper: nothing to add and nothing left out. Satisfied, Mingzhi looks up.

Above the many heads still bent over their papers, at the front of the hall, sitting at the desk in the middle, the man in his official gown, the chief examiner, is no stranger but Mandarin Liu.

Mingzhi freezes.

Mandarin Liu, glancing around the room, catches sight of Mingzhi.

Aye, so there he is, the old man's grandson. He rubs his jaw with his palm, then smiles a cold *wait-and-see* smile as he holds the gaze of the gawking young man.

Mingzhi shudders. He recalls Mandarin Liu's last visit to the mansion three months ago.

It was a quiet afternoon. In the same room where the most influential man of Plum Blossom Village and the most powerful man of Pindong Town had shared their laughter as they established a bond through a marriage plan, the two servant girls waiting outside the room heard not laughter but angry shouts, accompanied by sounds of banging and clattering through the room's closed doors.

Mandarin Liu had heard enough excuses: Liwei being busy with the poppies, or away on rent-collection trips, or there being a sudden illness of Master Chai or Likang or Liwei, or the coincidence of an inauspicious lunar year. Year after year, again and again the wedding delayed.

'Enough is enough!' Mandarin Liu flung open the door.

It was a humiliation too hard for the mandarin to swallow, the breach of a marital agreement. 'You'll not get away with this! Just wait and see!' were Mandarin Liu's last words before storming out of the mansion with his escorts.

And he hasn't had to wait long. Here is his chance. Mandarin Liu watches Mingzhi like a hunter weighing up its prey. Mingzhi feels himself being sliced into pieces, and his heart bleeds.

—∞—

'No, not him!'

Master Chai flops down into his chair.

'What terrible timing!' Back from his spying mission, Master Chai's resourceful servant narrates the story he has gathered from workers in the government office of Pindong Town. The respected Imperial Scholar Dai, worn out by the long journey from the Imperial City, fell ill upon his arrival at the official residence.

'He struggled to get up that morning but collapsed on the floor.'

The young servant mimics the motion, as if he had witnessed it on the spot. A natural performer he is, though not appreciated by his stern-faced master. The old man bellows: 'Get to the point!'

The young man drops his shoulders and blurts out in one breath: 'They said Scholar Dai asked Mandarin Liu to send for another fourth-ranking scholar from the capital; but Mandarin Liu insisted on taking his place, though he is only ranked seventh and not an imperial scholar.'

Master Chai heaves a long sigh, recalling how he had repeatedly told his former good friend and prospective in-law about Mingzhi's sitting the exam. *That cunning man must have taken note.*

Master Chai stares blankly ahead. On the sculptured pillars at the far end of the hall, his favourite green dragon stretches its head in high relief. Its bulbous eyes look up to the ceiling, as if yearning to leap into the sky. The promise of hope. Like his for Mingzhi.

Taking a deep breath, Master Chai lifts his stick and thumps it heavily to the floor. *Something has to be done.* The office will take a month to finalize the result. There's still time.

Master Chai scratches his silvery white head. The young maid quietly and deftly replaces the untouched *o-long* with a fresh cup. After three more cups of cold tea have been taken away, the Master smooths his goatee, sits back and takes a sip of the fourth, still warm. *That greedy shark, I know how to hunt him.*

As the maid leaves with orders to summon Liwei, Master Chai makes a mental calculation of the revenue from the last harvest, and is glad of the booming profits, and their usefulness.

~

Mingzhi lies in his bed, refusing dinner, not wanting a sip of tea.

Da Niang brings in bird's nest soup, and calls her son. Mingzhi turns his face to the wall, one wet cheek pressing against the tear-sodden pillow, cold against his burning eyes. Determined to hide his crying from his mother, he covers his head with his blanket, does not answer, knowing that his croaking voice will betray him.

He hears his mother's words, soft and gentle: 'It doesn't

matter. You can try again. It won't be him next time.'

You don't understand, Mother.

He has spent years waiting for this opportunity. Remembering the days and nights of ceaseless study, a sudden wave of exhaustion seizes Mingzhi. Soon Da Niang's sigh and her footsteps slowly drift out of the room. The door closes. And now there are other sounds, right outside. A man's voice, vague and distant, then his mother's. Soft whispers, muffled and unclear. Mingzhi thinks of sitting up, curious. But he is too tired: the sleepless night in Pindong, the exam, the journey and his worries have worn him out. He sleeps.

The man with the blank face returns to his dreams, his voice warm and soothing, whispering in Mingzhi's ears: 'Be patient, my dear.'

Mingzhi feels comforted, and is eager to speak to him, this strange yet seemingly familiar man. But he is walking away. Mingzhi lurches forward, grasps the man's shoulder. The man turns –

Oh, it's her, the girl in the blue dress. She smiles, clean and placid.

Mingzhi reaches for her, his fingers skim her delicate face, so soft, so smooth, but in seconds it grows distorted, like an image in the water that ripples away.

Blank. Nothing's left.

—~—

Liwei returns with the two chests of cash, two hundred taels in total. Still sealed; unopened. Mandarin Liu has refused to see him.

The tremulous Master Chai points his finger at Liwei: 'This is all your fault!'

He storms off to the ancestral hall. Servants are gathered and instructions given: they are to ensure candles are lit and joss sticks burnt constantly from morning till night. The Chai ancestors must feel warm, respected and cared for in the netherworld, so they will protect their descendants.

In the west court Liwei observes his nephew in the flickering candlelight, notices his prominent cheekbones and dark-ringed eyes, and feels sorry for him. Mingzhi pats his shoulder, forces a smile, his voice weak and tired: 'It's OK, Uncle. I'll try again.'

Walking Uncle Liwei to the door, Mingzhi hears his father, snoring in the next room. What he doesn't hear are the voices from two doors away.

Mingyuan and Er Niang.

'Serve them right, for not letting you take the exam along with him.'

'How could they say I'm not ready? Let's see how ready he is!'

The mother and son toast each other with cups of warm *wu jiapi*, having an early celebration late into the night.

In the ancestral hall the worried grandfather kneels in front of the altar, praying to the guardians of the Chai clan.

Ceaselessly.

Mingzhi is still in bed when the news arrives: his name came up first in the scoreboard.

Master Chai orders a ceremony to thank the Chai ancestors. First a round of ear-shattering firecrackers, then more joss sticks, silver papers and candles are burnt. And dishes of chicken and duck and pork, of course. The delighted grandfather cannot stop smiling: 'Let them have a big feast in the netherworld. They've worked hard to make the impossible possible.'

And they will have more to do. Master Chai knows Mandarin Liu must be furious, and will think of other ways to satisfy his rage. His revenge will come sooner or later. Only the mighty Chai ancestors can protect the family.

The old man suddenly realizes he needs to order even more joss sticks and silver paper.

In the kitchen, while the servants are building the fire on the hearth, chopping chicken and duck and pork, and mixing up spices and sauces, the most resourceful servant squeezes in and sniffs: 'As I say, the right person to thank is that Scholar Dai.'

Immediately everyone stops working and gathers round this garrulous spy.

'Everybody in the government office knows it: as soon as Scholar Dai got better, he demanded to read all the papers.'

'So what?'

'So what? He recovered our Eldest Grand Young Master's writing from the disqualified lot, fell in love with it and put him first.'

'How could Mandarin Liu allow this?'

'As I say, Mandarin Liu is only a seventh-ranking officer, three grades lower than the fourth-ranking Imperial Scholar. He has to do what he's told –'

He stops instantly as Butler Feng enters. 'Stop gossiping and get back to work! Everything must be ready by noon.'

At the dinner table, for the first time Likang pours a cup of *wu jiapi* for Mingzhi. Er Niang and Mingyuan look on: the roast pork, braised duck and boiled chicken seem tasteless, and too tough to swallow.

Mingzhi watches his father drain the wine before taking his first sip. The liquid slips in, burning his tongue and throat. Mingzhi keeps his mouth shut, keeps himself expressionless.

'That's my son.' His father grins and fills his cup. This time Mingzhi finds it more bearable, and downs it without hesitation.

Turning around, he catches his mother's worried eye.

Mingzhi tosses about in his bed, drifting in his dream and feeling hot, burning hot. His dream is noisy; he hears voices, familiar voices, but sees nothing. He is no longer a child, a man says. I'm worried, a woman whispers. Her voice is soft and gentle, and her face gradually surfaces –

The girl in the blue dress.

She is walking away; Mingzhi rushes after her but she is yards ahead. He keeps running and sweating.

Hot, burning hot. He feels as if some part of his body is bursting.

—w—

Old Scholar Yan, now shrunken and toothless, wobbles his way to the Chai Mansion.

'Your grandson needs to learn more,' he says, and his wheezing fills the spacious hall in the east court. 'He needs to attend an advanced institution.'

Master Chai contemplates the venerable scholar's suggestion: to send Mingzhi to the school in Pindong Town run by a former student, a *jinshi* holder, who has gained a reputation for his well-structured curriculum and team of experienced tutors.

Taking sips of tea, Old Scholar Yan rubs his back with one hand, and waits. But not for long. Before the tea turns cold, the Master concludes: this learned man knows best. He knows what's best for Mingzhi.

Old Scholar Yan leaves in a sedan ordered by the Master, in which the old man keeps smiling and nodding, while the sedan bearers exchange puzzled looks: *However wise he is, the old man is indeed too old now.*

—w—

When the news reaches the west court, the young servant Little Mouse capers about, delighted at the opportunity to get away from this remote village, this mansion with its stifling rules. A chance to be free.

His excitement is cut short when his young master, eager to leave too, orders Little Mouse to pack his clothes.

Outside, Mingyuan, just back from the east court, glances through the open window as he passes and sees his half-brother in a joyful trance. Some kind of sour fluid rises from the pit of Mingyuan's stomach and fills his chest.

Hearing footsteps Mingzhi glances up. When their eyes meet Mingyuan looks away instantly and hurries off with heavy footsteps.

Reaching his room he wrenches open the door, darts in and punches the wooden wall, hard.

Bang!

'Calm down, son.' Er Niang, who has been lagging behind, totters forward on her bound feet. She understands her son's fury: their request for Mingyuan to enrol in the town school has been rejected by his grandfather.

'This is unfair! Why can't I go to the school, too?'

Another *Bang!*

'You will have your chance, too. As the old man says, you just have to do well in the exam. And you will do better than him, I know.'

Mingyuan sits by the bedside, grasping the bedpost with both hands, so tightly that it shakes.

—ʌʌ—

Mingzhi pays a visit to Old Scholar Yan, to thank him.

The old man refuses the red envelope his student presents: 'Study hard and follow your destiny. That's what I want from you.'

Mingzhi kneels before his teacher and kowtows. Old Scholar Yan sighs: 'Your life is not here. You have a bigger world ahead of you.' His eyes glint under his drooping eyelids, as if hiding a secret. Mingzhi looks puzzled, but Old Scholar Yan stays silent and smiles a mysterious smile instead.

You will find out yourself. It won't be long.

—~—

They play a game of Chinese chess, uncle and nephew, on the eve of Mingzhi's departure for Pindong Town.

Begun just after dinner, the game takes longer than usual. Every strategy is thoughtfully planned and every step carefully considered. Silent moments pass between each move. Little Mouse, who waits at one side to refill their tea when needed, stands nodding his head as he dozes off.

After four brews of chrysanthemum tea, Mingzhi makes the final move and takes Uncle Liwei's last piece from the board. The silence breaks.

'You're playing much better than me now.' Liwei smiles at his nephew. He puts the jade-carved pieces and the chess-board back in their box, and passes it to Mingzhi. 'Take it with you.'

Mingzhi holds it in both hands and stares at the marble cover, with the *xiangqi* characters 'Chinese chess' gold-etched in the middle.

'It's meaningless to have a chess set without a partner to play with.'

'You will find one there, a new partner at your new place.'

Mingzhi runs his fingers over the inscription. 'Maybe. But it won't be the same,' he says.

As he looks into Mingzhi's misty eyes, Uncle Liwei grips the young man's shoulder. *You have to be strong, Mingzhi.*

Mingzhi holds the box tightly and feels it heavy in his hands.

In her room, Da Niang overhears the uncle and nephew, their voices filtering through the planked wall, like whispers, soft and gentle.

She remembers Mingzhi's birth: how she listened from the adjoining room, like now, to his infant cry, his yawns and sighs.

My son.

A wave of warmth surges through her. *Oh, the soup.* Da Niang hurries to the kitchen, decides to add some red dates to the bird's nest soup. Her son's last homemade nourishment before leaving the mansion. *Wish I could think of more ingredients to put in.*

Mingzhi notices the slices of red dates floating in the soup. He takes slow sips, rolls the dates on his tongue and savours their refreshing taste. Watching him, his mother smiles, but quickly turns solemn. She fiddles with the chess box on the table. *Liwei's.* Her fingers follow the characters inscribed on the surface.

'This looks like an elephant.' She points at *xiang*.

'You're a genius, Mother. That's the character for "elephant". It's pictography, the way our ancestors wrote five thousand years ago.'

Da Niang raises her eyebrows, curious.

Mingzhi smooths a piece of rice paper, grinds some ink and writes, showing his mother how the character was transformed, stage by stage, from the original shape of an elephant to the present written character.

Da Niang examines them, from the most modern form to the most ancient.

'This is amazing.' Her forefinger follows the curves of the original pictography and the wet ink stains the tip of it. 'The origin of the word,' she mumbles, as if in deep thought. 'The origin . . .' *of a human being. Of you.*

Mingzhi watches his mother. She raises her palm and contemplates her finger. A layer of black smudges the fair, delicate skin.

No, I can't tell him.

'Mother, you're tired. Please have an early night. I'll go to bed soon, too.'

'I'm fine. My son, though I've never known how to read and write, I know one proverb at least: *yinshui siyuan*.' Da Niang takes Mingzhi's hands. 'Well, my dear, you're a learned person, tell me what it means.'

'Literally, it means, "always keep in mind the source of water that gives you life", which also means "one should never forget one's origins".'

'That's right, son. Never forget your origins. That's what I want you to keep in mind.'

Mingzhi is confused. Feeling his mother's hands shake, he envelops her cold palm in his, trying to warm it up.

'I will, Mother. I'll always remember everything you say to me.'

EIGHT

Mandarin Liu sends his man, asking for twenty per cent of the opium revenue, overriding the previously agreed ten.

Master Chai frowns, can do nothing but grit his teeth and tell Liwei to comply with the demand.

Something has to be done. The old man's hands grasp the armrests tightly, his eyes fixed on the dragons on the pillars, on their angry stares.

—~—

Little Mouse unloads Mingzhi's luggage from the cart, a bundle of clothes and two heavy chests of books, and asks for instructions.

Taken aback at first, Mingzhi then realizes he is in *his* room, without Master Chai, without Likang, Liwei or Da Niang.

I am in charge!

He takes a glance around, clears his throat and gives a barrage of orders: clothes on the shelves of the wardrobe (outerwear on the top shelf; formal dress, *magua*, on the second; followed by casual wear, undergarments, socks and gloves); books in the bookcase, arranged by author, genre and period; rice paper stacked neatly on the left-hand corner of the desk, and on the right, the ink set and brush.

Everything is placed according to his instructions.

Mingzhi picks up his box of childhood toys, shakes it and listens to the clinking of his little things: the rabbit, the turtles, the dragonfly and the grasshopper. Yet his bamboo-leaf flute remains silent. He puts down the box, and tucks it away in the lowest drawer of the wardrobe.

Arranged by Butler Feng on Master Chai's orders, Mingzhi occupies a courtyard in a four-courtyard building: self-contained, with a separate entrance through the back garden. Quiet and secluded. *Just the right place for my studies!* And his meals are catered for, too, brought in by the maid from the main house. Mingzhi makes a mental note, reminding himself to reward Butler Feng with a handsome red envelope.

Determined to take the provincial-level exam next year, Mingzhi resolves to follow his routine as strictly as before: school in the morning and afternoon, revision at night.

He takes breaks in between, though, strolling around the back garden in the evening breeze. He lets the slivers of catkins from the fluttering willows shower his head and shoulders. Watches them ruffle the surface of the small pond in a corner. Squats to see the red carp darting around and blowing bubbles, pop-pop-pop, pop-pop-pop.

Evening, and sitting at his desk next to the open window, Mingzhi hears the sounds of water splashing. He imagines the fish playing hide-and-seek and chasing each other. The young man has the sudden urge to record this moment. He smooths out a piece of rice paper, grinds some ink and writes, swiftly:

Little Hut of Leaping Fishes

With Little Mouse's help, Mingzhi hangs the scroll on the wall above his desk, then steps back, fixes his gaze on it, grinning. The rapid, cursive strokes resemble the movements of fish: pushing themselves out of water, jumping high, turning their bodies this way and that, as free as their spirits.

As free as Mingzhi.

This is my world, my Taohua Yuan. My long-lost Peach Blossom Spring.

Little Mouse sees his master's eyes gleam in the yellow paraffin light, notices they are wet, brimming with tears. He retreats to his corner.

—~—

Mingzhi likes his little hut, likes spending time there, studying.

The longing for bird's nest soup subsides. Nightmares retreat. The faceless man, the drowning, climbing and running, become vague, unclear. And the girl in blue visits more often, with her deep dimples, in which Mingzhi sinks. When he wakes, a smile lingers on his face. The day grows brighter, and he is energized.

—~—

Mingzhi finds it difficult to keep to his routine. It's different, this school. Preparation for exams forms part of the curriculum, not all of it. Head Teacher Scholar Ning, a former student of Old Scholar Yan, encourages his students to discuss the issues of the day, to express their opinions in weekly reports. They are to observe the major happenings in the capital and other parts of the country, are told about the existence of foreign devils, and wars fought elsewhere with barbarians.

Mingzhi doesn't pay attention.

What have these to do with me? They are so far away. He is reluctant to know more, fearing that his studies are being side-tracked. He writes his commentaries half-heartedly, submits them only to fulfil the requirement, and directs far more effort on the study of literature and Confucian ethics, and on practising his classical prose.

Time is too precious to waste.

Sometimes, though, vague images of big, white, hairy, animal-like men drift through his mind. *What do they look like? Where are they from? Why are they here?* To find answers to his questions means spending time talking with people, something he avoids.

Mingzhi chooses to suppress his curiosity, to keep his mind on his books.

The town centre is a long street lined with shops. In between the shops, narrow alleys branch out. Both sides of the alleys are lined with houses, each with one, two, three or four courtyards.

In the morning, walking out of the alley into the street is like returning to the real world. At first Mingzhi is attracted to the colourful, lively scenes. Eyes strain for more: strange people – the various buskers and hawkers in outlandish clothes – from Yunnan, Shanxi, Sichuan, Mongolia, and other parts of the country; and ears are pricked to catch their unfamiliar accents: some high-pitched, some ranging across more than eight tones, some sounding like drunken gibberish. Mingzhi imagines the places these people come from, the *feng* and *shui*, the geometrical combinations that nurture their appearances, their speech.

He observes them from a distance, never approaching or stopping to ask questions, avoids getting too close. The flame from the fire-eater's burning torch seems too fierce, the heat too searing. The pectoral muscles of the martial-arts master dance like a pair of restless mice, and his scarred face looks intimidating, his kicks and punches too powerful, his movements too agile.

They are part of a picture from which Mingzhi is excluded, of which he is only a spectator.

Day in, day out, when the eyes and ears have captured enough, curiosity subsides. Everything becomes a nuisance: the hustle and bustle, the rich smell of boiling oil, the business of threading his way through the crowd. His pace quickens each day, though still he slows down when he passes the textile stall, searching for a glimpse of the blue dress that seems to have evaporated. Merged with the greasy air. Gone.

A corner of his heart is emptying out. He can feel it, the hole, bored right through, but he swiftly covers it up with an enormous sign which says 'EXAM'. Nothing must distract him.

—~—

Mingzhi spends his first Sunday in Pindong Town in his little hut, studying. On his second, he decides to explore the town and its surroundings, hungry for a breath of fresh air in the country.

He wakes Little Mouse, sets out early in the morning. Emerging from the alley, Mingzhi stands in the main street, deciding on his destination: eastwards to the serpentine country path or westwards, where more houses are to be seen. Facing west, he catches sight of tall, swaying reeds, and knows the river is close by. Immediately he gestures to his servant: 'Let's go.'

The morning breeze assails him with the smells of damp soil and green leaves, and Mingzhi's literature-sodden mind is baptized in the clean air, refreshed. Poems and prose in ancient calligraphy dart through his head as he walks, flitting one after another, vivid as on the original pages. Far from the traces of other pedestrians, he croons the tunes of the poems, and admires the echoes they make in the empty wilderness.

He strolls slowly at first, his footsteps as light as his heart. No more pointing fingers, no more gossip. *I am just an individual here in Pindong Town, like any other man in the street.* The burden of being the Eldest Grand Young Master of Landlord Chai lifts.

He smiles and his pace quickens. A bamboo container of drinking water in his arms and a bundle of books on his back, Little Mouse must jog now and then to keep up with his master, and is already panting heavily.

A hill is in sight, covered in dense woods. As he turns a corner, Mingzhi catches a glimpse of bright green at the summit: the tiled roof of a temple. Its red-painted walls and fine relief sculptures stand out among the luxuriant pines, cypresses and bamboo growths. In the misty air, two leaping dragons, one at each corner of the eaves, strive to thrust their wriggling bodies into the sky.

So fierce, so powerful.

Mingzhi stands for some moments, admiring the scene before him.

Later as he approaches the foot of the hill, he discovers a path, carefully paved with rock pieces to form steep steps that lead to the top, presumably the only way to the temple.

'That . . . must be . . . the Green Dragon Temple!' calls Little Mouse, who is puffing and lagging behind his master.

Mingzhi remembers the maid from the main house who told them once about this famous place of worship, about the Goddess of Mercy who grants the requests of Her pious worshippers, from an abundant harvest or a flourishing business, to getting the right bride or bridegroom or a son to continue the family line. The woman had mentioned that people came from all quarters just to get Her blessings. 'Go and burn some joss sticks, She'll bless you for your exam,' she'd said.

EXAM!

The word swells and grimaces in his mind like the

ferocious dragons on the temple roof. Mingzhi realizes that half the day is gone, and he should return to his books.

'Get out of there!'

A hoarse voice breaks the tranquillity. Two sedans are lurching towards Mingzhi, who dodges, stumbling into the bushes at the side of the footpath.

An outburst of laughter follows. The sedan-bearers turn and sneer at this fragile bookworm as they 'hi-yo' and 'hoo-ha' away.

The first sedan passes. The passenger, an elegant middle-aged woman, stares ahead without glancing at Mingzhi. He rises to his feet and brushes the dust and dirt off his clothes. The second sedan approaches. Mingzhi hears soft giggles. He turns to look.

The girl in blue!

She is not wearing blue now but silky pink, reflected in her cheeks, the lovely colour of a healthy young woman.

Mingzhi stands gawking: her eyes brighten as she laughs again, her lightly rouged lips stretch and curl upwards, and her dimples sink deeper.

Her smile . . .

Mingzhi keeps staring. But the young girl covers her mouth with a hand and looks away at once. Mingzhi catches a glimpse of the nape of her neck, a patch of milky white.

Her delicate skin.

Then she passes, leaving a whiff of fragrance in the air. The smell of jasmine. Gentle, feminine.

Her smell.

Mingzhi does not know how he got home, but once

there with a room full of books, he fixes his mind on only one thing: the exam.

Before bed, though, he promises himself a weekly Sunday morning walk, and maybe a visit to the temple at some point.

Later that night, the smell of jasmine lingers in his dreams.

~

There is a bigger crowd at the textile stall this morning. Mingzhi peers over the jostling heads. Bolts of material piled high on the display table. The stall owner, as tall and scrawny as a bamboo stick, shouts at the top of his voice:

'Cheap textiles from England!

Made by automatic machines!

Good value for money!'

His rusty voice breaks through the crowd, pulling in more curious passers-by for a glance at the so-called *yang-huo*, foreign merchandise.

A middle-aged woman blurts out: 'Hey, Old Bamboo Cane, what's so good about foreign textiles? I want the stuff from Nanchang district, excellent hand-made quality.'

'Aye, I offer you a good bargain and you ask for trouble. As I said, Mama Zhang, even if you're willing to pay me double there's no way I can get you any.'

'Have you been making too much money lately, Old Bamboo Cane? Does my cash mean nothing to you?'

'Don't get me wrong, Mama Zhang. The women in Nanchang have put away their spinning machines and stopped their weaving. How can they compete with the foreign devils' evil engines? Who would want to pay more if they can save a bit of money?'

The foreign devils' evil engines in a foreign land!

What do they look like and how do they work?

In Mingzhi's mind's eye there are giant steel frameworks operated by huge, hairy barbarians. Bolts of cloth spring from the machines every second, one after another, and are stacked on top of one another, piled high. Suddenly one of the bolts falls over, knocking against his shoulder.

'Ouch!'

Mingzhi rubs his shoulder and shakes his head. Only then does he realize that it's Little Mouse who has been prodding him.

'We're going to be late, Eldest Grand Young Master,' the young man grins and leads his dreamy master away.

On the third weekend, Butler Feng arrives early in the morning on Master Chai's orders, and finds both master and servant still in bed.

The dutiful butler passes on his old master's reminder to the young: he must come home once a fortnight, as instructed.

Home? Mingzhi sits at the edge of his bed, rubbing his eyes, trying to collect his memories.

Little Mouse, after getting a rap on the head from Butler Feng, slips away with a contorted face, and returns with a basin of water.

Mingzhi washes his face. The water sends a chill through him. The bleakness of the mansion slowly wriggles its way into his memory, crawling over him from head to toe. He is fully awake now.

Time passes so quickly.

Master Chai orders a dinner with his eldest grandson, to check on his progress. Mingzhi keeps his answers short and precise, keeping his eyes on his bowl of rice, avoiding the sharp stares being shot at him. When all questions have been asked and answers given, the spacious hall falls into a deep silence, broken only by the occasional sounds of munching and gulping, amplified in Mingzhi's ears.

Mingzhi finishes his food as quickly as he can. The maid pours a last round of hot tea. Eager to leave the room, Mingzhi hurriedly drains it, and is scalded.

It's been three weeks; such a long time.

Da Niang hurries to her son's room as soon as Mingzhi returns from the east court. To see if he has lost weight, or is suffering from malnutrition, or has not been keeping himself tidy.

Her clean-shaven son stands tall, bright-eyed, smiling: 'I'm fine, Mother.'

The maid brings in tea, preparing to pour as usual. Mingzhi waves her off. Da Niang reaches for the teapot but Mingzhi has got it. For the first time he pours a cupful for his mother.

Da Niang takes a slow sip. Warm. Their favourite *longjing*. Staring up, she sees calmness in Mingzhi's smile.

He's grown.

Her eyes are welling.

Uncle Liwei calls, and Mingzhi leaves with him for a game of chess. Da Niang sees them off. In the distance the two departing silhouettes are almost identical.

'I'm sure I'll get you this time.'

'No, you won't. Not even if I let you make five moves before me.'

'You'll regret saying that.'

'I mean it . . .'

Their voices gradually subside as they disappear into the courtyard. Da Niang sits staring into the darkness, until the maid comes to clear the table.

—∾—

Mingzhi's excellent result in his first monthly assessment has won him a scholarship of four taels.

He stares at the four pieces of silver on his palm, thinking about what they mean. Little Mouse counts on his fingers: 'Enough to pay for your tuition fees and daily meals, but not the rent. It's an expensive room, this one.'

Mingzhi carefully wraps the money in his kerchief and keeps it in his sandalwood box, promising himself that he will top his class from now on.

Soon enough I won't need money from home.

—∾—

'The foreign devil is in town!'

Little Mouse rushes in, his freckled face flushed and his eyes sparkling. He lays the dinner basket on the table. 'I wish I'd seen him myself!' He unloads the dishes. 'They say he came this afternoon.'

Mingzhi puts down his book and pours himself a cup of tea.

'I don't understand!' At the dinner table Little Mouse scratches his head and points his chopsticks in all directions: 'Apparently he said he is a messenger of God. How can he be a devil then?'

Mingzhi, who has insisted his servant eat with him since they moved here, gestures at the bowlful of fried pumpkin with dried shrimps and streaky pork: 'Your food is getting cold, it won't taste good that way.'

'Aren't you curious, Eldest Grand Young Master?' Little Mouse pokes the pumpkin with his chopsticks before picking a piece up.

'What an old pumpkin!' He raises it and examines its long, hair-like fibres. 'They say he has hair like this all over his face.'

Suddenly Mingzhi grabs the bowl: 'I'll have it if you're not eating.'

'Hey –'

Little Mouse lurches forward, stretches out his arm and aims his chopsticks at the dish in Mingzhi's hand. Mingzhi moves it away. Another attack is launched; this time Mingzhi leaves the table, and Little Mouse chases after him.

The game of tag ends with the servant clearing up a mess of broken ceramic and mashed pumpkin from the floor, before the two finish their plain rice by soaking it in hot tea. They are pleased with their newly invented recipe, though.

When night falls, Mingzhi is back at his desk. Only the sounds of leaping fish keep him company.

Along with the splashes of the leaping fish, a white, hairy man swims into his dreams. His face is deathly pale, his eyes dark and hollow, like two powerful whirlpools, spinning fast, pulling Mingzhi into them. Mingzhi struggles, legs kicking, hands waving, groping for something solid . . . Books, a pile of them! He frantically grabs and throws them into the holes, filling them up.

The waves subside. The hairy man is gone.

Beyond Mingzhi's books, beyond his knowledge, scholars from the Neo-Confucian School of Statecraft, led by Kang Yuwei and Liang Qichao, sow the seed of reformation. It sprouts swiftly, only waiting for the right moment to thrust northwards to the Imperial City.

Everything changes.

—~—

Returning from a fortnight's errand in the Provincial Capital, Head Teacher Scholar Ning hurries into the classroom. He flings a stack of papers onto the table, and they slip.

Seeing their weekly commentaries strewn across the floor, the students hold their breath, waiting. Scholar Ning glances at the half-shaven heads before him.

'Do you consider these texts to be social commentaries? These sweet and flowery phrases?'

Silence.

'Can someone tell me why you are here?'

Still, silence is his only answer. He flops into his chair, rests his elbows on the desk, and waits.

From a corner a tiny voice raises: 'To study and prepare for our exams.'

A tide of nodding heads washes across the room. And someone adds: 'To secure a post in the civil service.'

'You bunch of useless bookworms!'

Scholar Ning gets up, bracing himself against the desk, puffing.

'Are you still indulging yourselves in daydreams about the past, about the years of the glorious Qianlong period, when you bookworms could pore over classical literature day and night? That was once upon a time, when the Great Qing Empire stood firm as the centre of the world, when the foreign devils bowed and kowtowed to our emperor. But now . . .'

He looks his students in the eyes; they look away, uneasy.

'They are here, the white men, more and more of them, taking territory after territory, and hungering for more . . .'

Scholar Ning's words come faster, his voice louder: 'Listen to the screams and groans of our soldiers as their ships are bombed and burnt, and they're forced to surrender. Treaties are signed, lands handed over. The French landed in Annam, the British took Burma, the Russians grabbed the northern region, and the Japanese have joined the queue too, fixing their gaze on Korea!'

Bang!

The silent audience jump in their seats.

Scholar Ning, his hand still on the desk, continues: 'And you, the educated ones, our hopeful new generation, you bury yourselves in the old classics like ostriches with their heads in the sand . . .'

He pauses, and after a long silence, he asks: 'How are you going to sit your exams if China no longer exists?'

Looking up, Mingzhi sees that his teacher's eyes are brimming with tears. He sweats profusely, feels the heat inside his body, his veins, where his blood stirs, running wild. In his mind he sees the map of a mutilated China, bloodstained, broken into pieces and labelled with unknown characters.

That evening Mingzhi sits at his desk before the open pages. In the fading daylight, dotted lines of black ink swim before his eyes, like armies of ants, marching up and down. Jostling. Slithering. Accelerating. As he blinks, the columns double. Treble. Overlap.

How am I going to sit the exam if China doesn't exist?

Yet Mingzhi shakes his head and tries to shrug off his troubled thoughts. Little Mouse brings in a paraffin lamp. Mingzhi turns it to maximum brightness. A wash of clear yellow floods the room. Mingzhi wipes his face with a moist towel, then buries his head in his books.

That same night in the central hall of the Chai Mansion, shadows of dragons dance on whitewashed walls in flickering candlelight, flanking Master Chai and his two sons.

It is a rare tea-meeting after dinner. Master Chai relaxes in his chair, Likang slouches in his, while Liwei, arms folded, sits straight, trying to read the old man's thoughts. But the master of the house takes his time, sipping his favourite *o-long*. Warm, of course.

Finally he puts down his cup and broaches his plan: to have two seasons of poppies. No more paddy, the old man has decided.

Likang smiles broadly, and his brother frowns.

It's too risky!

Liwei knows his father is annoyed at Mandarin Liu for robbing him of a large proportion of his revenue, and is eager to recover the loss.

'We should grow our own grains,' he says hesitantly.

'Use your brains, Liwei! It's so much cheaper to buy from another province.'

'What if something happens, a drought, a famine? We'll all die of hunger if we don't have our own stock of crops.'

Thump!

The hand that holds the dragon stick trembles. The old man's face turns taut. 'Shut up! Watch your words and no more talking back!'

Liwei's mouth snaps shut; Likang, relaxing in his chair, says in his peculiar slow drawl: 'That's right. Don't you see it? The more we plant, the more money we get. That's the magic of opium . . .' He yawns. 'Ah-ha – excuse me, time to go . . . Oh, yes, definitely more poppies.'

Still yawning, Likang drags his lazy bones back to the west court for his magic pipe.

Master Chai throws out his last words: 'Do as I say. I'll expect a double harvest this year!' He thumps his stick all the way to his room.

Alone in the hall, Liwei feels the four walls detach themselves, drift about, and the dragons on the pillars lunge at him, their sinister faces swaying before him, their enormous mouths wide open . . .

Two huge holes, dark and bottomless. Where hope sinks quietly all the way down.

But then something strikes him. *Oh yes, there's one bright light, in this abyss, this gloomy mansion.*

Mingzhi.

Thinking of the young man, Liwei's pursed lips crack a little, tilting upwards. He longs for a game of chess; just the thing on a night like this.

Ten miles away, his chess partner holds his head with both hands, forcing his eyes to focus on the reading in front of him.

Sunday again and it's Vesak, the celebration of the birth and enlightenment of the Buddha. The temple is crowded. Worshippers fill the front courtyard and the main hall: buying joss sticks, burning them, and praying before the statue of the Goddess of Mercy. Smoke, thick and stifling, swirls inside and outside.

Mingzhi's eyes are blurred and watery, and he keeps sneezing. *Where on earth has he gone?* In the courtyard he stands on his toes, trying to peer over the shuffling heads for Little Mouse. A burly man blocks Mingzhi's view, and he is elbowed from the right and then pushed from behind. He stumbles, bumping into the burly man, who turns to stare at him with bulbous eyes. Mingzhi shrinks to one side, and squeezes his way out of the crowd.

The back garden is quiet; only a handful of people are walking about, appreciating the blooming flowers of spring. As he rushes in, Mingzhi wipes the sweat from his forehead with his sleeve and then looks up –

In the far corner, next to the ornamental landscape and pond, stands the girl in blue!

She is admiring the white jasmine blossom, growing in luxuriant abundance. Her fingers gently touch the flowers, and her face moves close to them. The soft petals seem to have sunk into the deep whirls of her dimples.

Mingzhi's heart throbs. He steps out but stops at once; his foot hovers in the air, and is pulled back immediately. *WhatshouldIsay?WhatcanIsay?WhatwillIsay?* He scratches his head, constructing phrases in his mind, but his scholarly eloquence seems to have vanished, and he is unable to form a single decent sentence.

'Young Mistress.' The maid he saw at the textile stall enters through the moon gate, calling to her mistress. 'Madam says it's time to go.'

No!

Mingzhi anxiously rubs his fingers. Seeing the girl coming towards him, Mingzhi edges to one side and bumps into a tree. Some blossom flutters to the ground. *Jasmine!* Swiftly he picks one up and as the girl passes by, holds it out to her. Instinctively she opens her palm, and the little blossom falls into it. She glances up to see an embarrassed young man, who mutters, 'For you,' then scuttles away.

The feeble bookworm on the hillside. She remembers.

The petals feel soft in her palm.

'What happened, Young Mistress?'

Without answering, she smiles quietly, blushing.

Mingzhi finds Little Mouse and rushes him out.

'What's going on?'

His master ignores him, hurrying ahead. Little Mouse skips a bit to keep up.

They run helter-skelter down the hill and are soon on the path by the river. Mingzhi slows down, panting heavily. Then he turns to beckon to Little Mouse, who lags behind.

'Watch out!'

Too late. Mingzhi's right foot misses the firm ground and steps into a puddle.

'Ahh!'

He lands heavily on the gravel, his right leg still in the

puddle, and pain shoots through his body. Little Mouse helps him up.

'Ouch!'

A tearing agony in his right ankle forces him to sit back. Little Mouse takes off Mingzhi's shoes and watches the gradual swelling of his ankle.

What to do? Little Mouse paces up and down, scratching his head, while Mingzhi massages his ankle, then stops as it aggravates the pain.

'Can I help you?'

What a strange accent . . . The young master and servant look for the source of the voice . . . *From a strange man!*

The man is tall but a little stooped, dressed in a long black gown. His face is pale – no, translucent, for his veins are visible. His short hair is oddly yellow, and his body hair flashes like gold in the afternoon sunlight.

Little Mouse shouts: 'The foreign devil!'

The man smiles and looks Mingzhi in the eyes, deep blue meeting dark brown. Mingzhi reads his gaze: *concern, sympathy*. He feels the warmth in it, and relaxes.

Father Terry carries Mingzhi to his house nearby, also a church. Behind them Little Mouse tags along in a fluster, unsure if he should stop them and rescue his master from the foreign devil or just follow them.

Before he can make up his mind, they are already settled in a small, cosy room.

The priest applies an ointment to Mingzhi's injured ankle and bandages it neatly. In his awkward Mandarin,

Father Terry tells Mingzhi not to disturb his foot. The young men look doubtfully at the thick layers of white cotton. For an injury like this, the traditional Chinese medical practitioners will twist and rub and massage. To keep the nerves in place, they say. Father Terry smiles, seems to have read their minds, and says they should let the torn muscle tissues recover by themselves and not damage them further. Tells them he studied medicine in England – where he comes from – before leaving for Rome and becoming a missionary. And that he learned Mandarin after arriving in China five years ago.

The places Father Terry mentioned sound alien to Mingzhi; he looks around to disguise his ignorance.

There are books, hundreds of them, displayed neatly on the shelves against the four walls. Some are in Chinese but more are in thin, cursive characters he doesn't recognize. He picks one up from the shelf next to him. Among the pages of this strangely lettered book there are illustrations: a man perched on a horizontal pole supported by two large metal wheels (why doesn't he fall?); linked compartments with wheels that run on tracks and puff smoke (a metal dragon?); and a huge boat that is also belching out smoke (it must be steaming hot in there) . . . Lines of captions crab-walk underneath the pictures.

Mingzhi wishes he could read about them, these strange things described in strange words.

A hairy hand reaches for the pages, a finger points at the pictures.

'A bicycle. A train. A steam ship.'

Names that Mingzhi has never heard. The priest goes

on speaking in smooth-toned unrecognizable syllables. Mingzhi stares blankly at him.

'It's English, my mother tongue.' His saviour smiles. 'Feel free to come round when you're better.'

He knows. He's a scholar too.

—~—

Little Mouse holds his palm up and grits his teeth to stop himself from chuckling: 'If I ever tell Master Chai or Butler Feng about your meeting with the foreign devil, may I be struck down by the Thunder God, and may my body burst into pieces and be scattered all over.'

Mingzhi asks his servant to repeat the words, leaving out the last line about his body bursting into pieces. Tells him to stop laughing, too. This time Little Mouse takes his pledge more seriously, and Mingzhi nods, satisfied. He knows Little Mouse will keep his promise, but does not know that his servant decided to do so after he had his first taste of foreign confectionary. The sweet, sticky, tongue-melting chocolate was too good to resist, and it would be too stupid not to have any more. There is a big jar full of it on Father Terry's desk.

Mingzhi checks his carefully bandaged ankle, and applies more ointment through the seams at the edges. The swelling is easing, he can feel that. *Grandfather will be furious if he finds out.* For him, traditional Chinese medical treatment has always been the only answer to any illness. *But this works.* He looks at the bottle of yellow liquid given by Father Terry.

Not a devil after all, the white man, both master and servant conclude.

—~—

Evening, and Mingzhi is revising the literature of the Song Dynasty. The poems of the famous Two Lis – Li Yi, the last emperor of the dynasty, and Li Qingzhao, a woman poet – are essential reading. Both were talented and shared similar fates: a happy beginning followed by a gloomy second part of life due to the outbreak of war.

How vulnerable human beings are, unable to decide their own fates.

Careful study of their poems allows Mingzhi to differentiate their earlier works from later ones, which are depressing. Autumn, fallen leaves, withered flowers. The waning moon, chill evenings, sleepless nights. Bleak corridors, empty courtyards, desolate gardens. Taking readers deep into their world of despair and hopelessness. *These are the best of their works,* Mingzhi recognizes: *the product of their suffering.* It is this pain that has made the poems immortal. But does that mean their suffering was worthwhile? Certainly they didn't choose to experience pain so as to be remembered. *But were they able to make choices at all?*

Mingzhi is confused. For the first time the young man feels reluctant to read on. He pushes his book away, and the pages flip over and open at Li Qingzhao's *Shengsheng Man*, 'Every Sound, Lentamente', Meilian's favourite piece.

Eldest sister. My once happy and careless eldest sister.

Mingzhi recalls those days when they read together in his secret world. His nerves twitch behind his temples, a gnawing pain. He wonders, if his sister were a poet, what her work would be like. As good but also as sad as Li Qingzhao's?

He has a sudden urge to see her, to talk to her, his eldest sister.

—∞—

Seeing Meilian has become difficult since Mandarin Liu and Master Chai fell out. Mandarin Liu rejected all visits from members of the Chai family. Mingzhi knows this well, does not wish to offend Mandarin Liu and embarrass himself.

The government office, where Mandarin Liu and his family live, is on the main street, not far from Mingzhi's school. Whenever he passes by, Mingzhi peers over the guards and through the open door, but is always disappointed. No trace of Meilian. Only corridors and walls, layer upon layer. Like a prison.

So near and yet so far. Mingzhi sighs and paces the room, limping slightly. Looking at his restless master, Little Mouse quietly sneaks away, picking at his ears as he tries to pick his mousy brain. It doesn't take him long to come up with an idea.

'Birds of a feather flock together,' that's his theory, from which he deduces that most servants, no matter who they work for, like making friends with one another. They like to get together and exchange gossip and cunning tricks. And they are always inclined to help each other out.

Despite his master's sneers, Little Mouse is soon proved right. The maid from the main house, who sometimes brings them meals, knows the servants of the government office well. As soon as his ankle is fully recovered, Mingzhi gets the maid to make arrangements.

—∞—

The moon is full. In a back lane, a door creaks open. Mingzhi sneaks through. The middle-aged maid who lets him in leads him to the pavilion at the far end of the garden.

Meilian, slender as ever, is waiting.

Mingzhi's eyes well up, and his sister weeps. Her face is as pale as the moonlight. Mingzhi remembers their last Mid-Autumn Festival together, her smiling face. He pats her shoulder. *I know, I know.* But this only aggravates her sobbing.

'Cousin sister-in-law!' a girl shouts from inside the house.

'Young Mistress, you can't see her now . . .' The maid standing guard at the gate tries in vain to stop the intruder.

The girl in blue!

Eyes wide, she stops at the threshold of the arched door, staring at them. Meilian rushes forward and grips her arm.

'It's not what you think, Sister Jasmine. He is my brother, Mingzhi.'

Very slowly the girl nods, seeming to trust Meilian. She looks closer, and recognizes him, the feeble bookworm from the hillside.

Cousin sister-in-law? So she's related to Mandarin Liu – his brother's daughter!

'I've made you this.' The girl hands Meilian a garland of jasmine. 'Don't worry. I won't tell anyone.'

She leaves, and a whiff of jasmine lingers behind her.

Meilian glances at the carefully threaded flowers in her hands. 'Jasmine, that's her name. She's the only one here who's nice to me.'

But her brother is not listening. He is standing stock-still, his gaze lost in the faraway darkness, taking his soul with it, along with his adolescent romantic fantasies.

—∞—

He weeps, curling up like a wounded animal under the blanket, stuffing one corner in his mouth to muffle his sobbing.

Why? Why must she be Mandarin Liu's niece?

He bites the cotton hem in his hand, and the fingers that hold it, but does not feel the pain. Numb, like his heart.

No more dreams. The smell of jasmine is dissipating, evaporating into the night sky.

—∞—

Mingzhi's Sunday morning walks now end with an afternoon in Father Terry's study. The timing is just right. When he and Little Mouse arrive at the priest's doorstep puffing and panting, hungry and thirsty, Sunday mass has just come to an end. There is always some leftover food set aside for them.

Food is the bait Father Terry uses to attract some participants to his service. Poor peasants from nearby villages willingly glue themselves to the pews for the entire morning, staring blankly at the priest with his babbling about God and Satan, waiting for the moment when he says lunch is ready. Then they leave, happily, not only with a full stomach but also a bagful of rice or flour or sugar.

'This foreign God is not so bad after all,' they say, on their way to the Green Dragon Temple to burn joss sticks for the Goddess of Mercy. To thank Her for granting them their wishes, getting them the meal and some rice or flour or sugar to take home.

Father Terry knows this but lets them.

'It's only a matter of time.' He is optimistic: 'God is patient with his children.'

And so he has never urged Mingzhi to attend mass. He knows he is different, this young man; knows he needs something else.

Mingzhi begins his English lessons.

'This is the only way,' his blue-eyed tutor explains, 'that you can learn from my books.'

Mingzhi can only agree. He is more than happy to learn something new, something most people around him do not have access to, know nothing about.

This is a challenge, he tells himself.

It's completely different, this language. The writing crab-walks from left to right, linking hands, joining one word to another; and with the speech, his tongue is twisted and curled and stretched and held, his mouth twitches, and he has to er and ssh and fi and ke and te.

And he returns home exhausted, with a maimed mouth and twisted tongue.

But Father Terry likes his student, praises him for learning fast and mastering the pronunciation. Assures Mingzhi that soon enough he will be able to read the books on the shelves, and discuss them in English. Mingzhi can only grimace, sticking out his tongue and panting like a dog. Glancing around, the four walls of books beckon and wink at him, luring him back to his elementary exercises, the checking of dictionaries and the memorizing of vocabulary.

~

With school, anyhow, Mingzhi has never been neglectful. Five months on, he has monopolized all the four-tael scholarships.

Head Teacher Scholar Ning brings them news: more factories are built, weapons in Hanyang, machinery in Kunming, and textile and iron mills in Guangdong. More railways are laid. They are invited in this time, the foreigners, he says, German, American, British, the so-called experts.

A Self-Strengthening Movement with the aid of foreign strength! Mingzhi smiles quietly. In his mind he busily translates, spells, pronounces. *Weapons. Machinery. Textiles. Iron. Railways.* And illustrates. Giant machines, rolling incessantly, and thump, thump, thumping fast, drowning out Scholar Ning's accounts of another form of invasion. Father Terry's voice surfaces: *This is the march of time.* Calm and steady, humming in Mingzhi's head.

Come autumn, school breaks for harvest. Mingzhi returns to the smell he hates. The familiar sights of paddy-threshing are replaced by the drying of opium. Pungent black blocks, hundreds of thousands of them, cover the fields, reconstructing the rural landscape. Gone is the golden grain, the flakes of chaff drifting in the morning rays, the smell of freshly flailed rice.

Mingzhi stays in his room. No chess, no evening walks. Keeps himself busy with his books: mostly Chinese texts but a couple in English, too, carefully hidden in the bottom of his chest, under layers of clothes. He takes them out in the quiet night and reads them into the small hours.

Always, there is another lighted window in the west court a few doors away from Mingzhi's. The yellow rays from the two windows thinly penetrate the darkness, like two sleepless eyes. In his room Mingyuan is studying hard, too, determined not to lose out to his half-brother.

During the day, though, Mingyuan takes to following Uncle Liwei, learning his trade. His mother orders: 'Get a grip on the business, you'll have control of it in the end.' Her son nods, agrees. Grandfather Master Chai is delighted, praises his second grandson for his initiative. Mingzhi says nothing, cares only for his books. Da Niang is silent, too, keeping herself in her room, chanting sutras, while Uncle Liwei, now even busier, is happy with Mingzhi's lack of interest in the family business. The young man will have a future outside the mansion, his uncle is certain.

The sowing starts again, and before it is completed, Mingzhi urges Little Mouse to pack his luggage. He gives an excuse to his grandfather: to complete the essays specially assigned by Head Teacher Scholar Ning, and leaves.

—∞—

Scholar Ning does have an assignment for Mingzhi. The school founded by reformers in the neighbouring Provincial Capital has become the head teacher's model: the culture of debating social and political issues, the details of their discussions, and the learning of Western knowledge from translated texts. The latter fascinates him most of all, opening his eyes to the outside world. When the first edition of a journal published by the reformers reaches him, Scholar Ning decides to start his own in-school quarterly journal.

His best student, Mingzhi, is designated editor-in-chief on the two-man editorial board. Teacher and student cut articles out of the journal from the reformative school and other publications, and invite contributions from reputable scholars. Write them down word by word; each manages five copies of a single twofold, four-page broadsheet paper a day. After a fortnight of hard work, a hundred of the first edition are produced, just in time to greet the students returning from their autumn break. The cost is covered with the minimum charges carefully calculated and imposed for this purpose. The journals sell out in half a day, and there is a demand for more. Scholar Ning gathers another ten of his favourite students with equally excellent calligraphic skills, working overnight, producing another hundred copies. All these sell out, too.

Without a second thought Scholar Ning buys printing

equipment in town with the extra income. An editorial committee consisting of five sub-editors, led by Mingzhi, is formally established. A free hand is given to Mingzhi, while the head teacher oversees his work.

Although he feels honoured, Mingzhi is not without worries. Extra responsibilities mean less time for study. But he is excited, too. Happy to be the first to read the journal from the reformers' school: Kang Yuwei's forceful, critical comments; Liang Qichao's outstanding literary style, his gentle yet persuasive debating skills; and the information contained in the translated Western articles. He learns swiftly as he searches through the pages for suitable extracts. His thirsty brain absorbs fast, filling up, saturated with knowledge.

He plans his time carefully: still studies at night, though cuts back to five nights a week, and spends the other two working on the journal; still goes to Father Terry's on Sunday, learning English. Still bags the scholarships.

With the use of printing blocks, the production of the journal becomes easier, faster. Now Mingzhi has time for other editorial plans. He begins to extract and translate from Father Terry's books. He is careful, though, pretending these pieces are from newspapers in the Provincial Capital, as he does not want to reveal his knowledge of English. *No point, and too risky if the news travels to the village.* He tries to avoid making himself too conspicuous; is content just to see them printed in black and white, and his fellow students reading them, gathering in groups and exchanging opinions about them excitedly.

Mingzhi quietly enjoys his little secret.

Scholar Ning trusts Mingzhi, says nothing, but signs and

approves every proof. Surprised at the high quality of the publication, he is proud of the editor-in-chief he has appointed.

—~—

Evening, and the editorial meeting has adjourned early. There is no trace of Little Mouse in the front square of the school where he usually waits for his young master. After waiting a while, Mingzhi decides to walk home alone.

The night screen swiftly rolls down. Arms folded on his chest against the chill winter wind, Mingzhi hurries along the quiet street, past the many tightly shut doors and the lighted windows through which the occasional aroma of meat soup wafts. Mingzhi sniffs, and his stomach begins to rumble. He looks up. The lane leading to his little hut is in sight; he quickens his pace and turns the corner.

A back alley, narrow and almost pitch-black. The only brightness comes from a curtained door at the far end, casting a pale yellow across the darkness. Like a tired eye, delivering a touch of bleakness. *Not the right lane.* Mingzhi is about to turn around when a figure bursts through the curtain, and blunders towards him. A man, apparently, as scrawny as a skeleton. He mutters: 'A magic puff after dinner, and you'll be as happy as the celestial beings!'

As he approaches Mingzhi, the man lifts his eyelids, and shouts: 'Hey, you should have a go, young man! Life is shit without it!'

He holds his hand out, reaching for Mingzhi, who instantly steps away. Stumbling forward, eyes rolling back, the man falls onto the ground and does not move. In an instant the sound of snoring is heard.

Mingzhi looks at the source of light, hesitates, and then walks to it. He peers through a corner of the stained curtain.

A smoke-shrouded room lit by the faint glow of a paraffin lamp. Cloudy, obscure. A seemingly unreal picture, where vague figures loom. Men, about ten of them, lie sideways in a row of wooden beds, each holding a long pipe, puffing. With their dreamy eyes half-closed, they seem to be wandering in fantasy lands.

Opium.

In the yellowish blur, the men share the same jaundiced faces, the same high cheekbones and sunken, dark-ringed eyes.

Like his father.

Abruptly someone bumps into him. A man is being thrown out.

'Clear your debts before you step in here again!'

A burly man, apparently the steward of this opium den, pulls at the collar of his defenceless victim, shouts abuse at him, pushes him to the ground. The poor man can do nothing but groan, as he drags himself to his feet.

'Let me have a puff, just one puff, please . . .'

'A puff? That's what you'd get!' The steward spits on him, then retreats into the smoky room. The curtain flaps behind him.

Opium.

Mingzhi feels his stomach twist and realizes he is very late for dinner now.

My dinner . . . is paid for with money from the opium harvest . . .

Very slowly he walks away, head lowered, weighed down with thought.

'Eldest Grand Young Master!' Little Mouse runs towards him, huffing and grumbling. 'I've been searching high and low!'

But his master keeps walking and hears nothing of Little Mouse's grievances.

—ʍ—

Mingzhi counts the money accumulated from his scholarships, knows nothing can be achieved with it yet. *The exam next spring.* That's the only way out.

It won't be long, he knows. Another harvest; he only has to bear it for another harvest, and all will be over soon after spring.

Nine

Plum Blossom Village, 1893

When a sea of pinkish red begins to billow in the early spring breeze, in the Chai Mansion the master's elated laughter echoes through the central hall. *A double harvest at last!* He strolls among the pillars, imagining the dragons hooray-hoorayed as they dance around him, and decides: a celebration is to be held, and a grand one, to mark this milestone.

—∞—

Lagging behind, Little Mouse scratches his head as he stares at the back of his master, hurrying ahead. For the first time Mingzhi is eager to get home! The month-long spring holiday to be spent at the mansion seems too long even to Little Mouse himself; it must be much worse for his master who has to sit his exam after the break. *Why has he changed?* Little Mouse keeps scratching, leaving not the clues he looks for but flakes of dandruff falling in the morning rays.

'Hey! You're so slow!'

Sweat streaming, puffing, panting, and frowning, Mingzhi anxiously beckons for his servant to speed up.

—~—

He isn't here.

Mingzhi searches every corner of the north court: underneath the huge banner of NORTHERN OPERA TROUPE, between the colourful flags and bunting and the many carts and trunks, and among the actors, musicians and apprentices who are busy unloading and unpacking. Apart from a couple of new apprentices there are familiar faces, but not *the one*.

Little Sparrow.

Lips sealed tight, gaze averted; all members of the troupe will only shake their heads when asked about the actor. As if he has never existed.

'Can I help you, Eldest Grand Young Master?' The troupe leader smiles a sly smile. 'But I think your grandfather will be of more help to you than I will.' He winks.

Grandpa? A huge question mark rises, occupying Mingzhi's mind, and soon his head is aching.

—~—

The peasants are overwhelmed: the Northern Opera Troupe will perform for them in the open field, for three days! Butler Feng makes an announcement: a special treat from Master Chai to mark the first double harvest.

While the workers are busy setting up the stage, the peasants are busy, too, tattling about it excitedly.

'I say, Old Chan, I've told you to stop grumbling, we can

buy rice and flour from the landlord anyway. And we get to see free opera!'

'Yes, I like to see opera too; but all these years – from my great-grandparents' great-grandparents to my parents – we've been growing our own food, it feels stupid to work on a piece of land without getting anything edible out of it.'

'You worry too much, Old Chan. Town people get their opium, Landlord Chai gets his money, we get our food from him – and now the opera, too! Isn't it wonderful?'

'Aye, we've been working hard from dawn to dusk day after day, shouldn't we get some entertainment?'

'That's right. What do you think the troupe is going to perform? Golden Swallow's favourite, *Longing for Worldly Pleasure*?'

'That I don't know, but I know I long to see him, that pretty, dainty singsong actor!'

The skinny peasant grimaces, stretches out both arms and mimics Golden Swallow waving his long, flowing sleeves, eliciting a burst of laughter from the crowd. Their laughter echoes through the valley, the fields, the hills and the Plum River, blending into a lively picture of joy and contentment.

—~—

Not everybody is as happy as the villagers, though. In her room Er Niang snorts as she stamps her feet, resenting Master Chai for his decision. Resenting the innocent peasants, too, for their enthusiasm for opera. Blames them for the fact that the performance exclusively for the mansion has been reduced to four days.

Only four days!

Imagining the delicate Golden Swallow performing for crude, shallow peasants who shout and whistle and yell and applaud in the wrong places, Er Niang feels as if something is scratching inside her, and she is unable to let it out.

—∞—

On the first three nights Mingzhi stays in his room, studying – preparing for an exam is always the best excuse – or pretending to do so, while Little Mouse paces the room, agitated. The music is too pleasant, the songs too seductive and the story intriguing. Little Mouse yearns to see the lead actor's performance, his facial expressions – the tilting of brows, the darting of eyes, the twitching of lips; the waving of his long, flowing sleeves; his flexible, skilful body movements; and his colourful, splendid costumes.

His young master does not budge, staying put at his desk; but the open pages before him are colonized by the tiny ants, dense black dots on yellowish paper, blurring his eyes, muddling his mind.

Where is Little Sparrow? What has it got to do with Grandpa?

Questions without any clues to possible answers. Mingzhi's head is cracking. Little Mouse, though as smart as his name, has been too distracted by the music and songs and stories and the scenes of opera he imagines, and so he becomes insensitive to his distraught master.

A real bookworm he is, ignoring such great performances from such a great opera troupe. Little Mouse keeps grumbling and bleating in silence as he paces the room, or cranes his neck at the door in the direction of all the enchanting sounds from beyond it.

Come the fourth night, when Mingzhi tells Little Mouse to go and enjoy the show, Little Mouse thinks nothing but leaves at once.

'Be careful. Remember to hide yourself at the back!'

Slipping away on his agile mousy legs, the servant disappears even before Mingzhi finishes his words.

Outside the window a full moon hangs high, clean against the dark blue sky, reminding Mingzhi of his eldest sister, and of his first meeting with Little Sparrow. He has a sudden urge to take a walk: across the bridge, to the river, by the bamboo grove.

The west court is empty. Mingzhi knows his mother has no excuse to escape the occasion though she would prefer to stay in her room. Likang has his pipe with him and a special seat with a slanting chair in the front row, determined not to miss this fascinating performance. In his smoke-shrouded hallucinations, colours and images onstage are intensified, as splendid as fairy tales. And Er Niang and Mingyuan, that pair of enthusiastic opera lovers, are always first in place, an eager audience.

All is quiet outside. Mingzhi picks up the leaf-flute given to him by Little Sparrow and heads for the path leading to the river. As he walks alone, the evenings he shared with Uncle Liwei creep into his mind. His uncle's gentle, caring words blend with the night breeze, the rustling leaves, the crunching of gravel and fallen branches beneath his feet, the running water. That familiar warm, calming voice, which he yearns to hear now. But Mingzhi knows his dutiful uncle is fulfilling the duty of a good son, accompanying his father to the show. After all, it is the result of his own hard work they are celebrating.

Is it a result he is happy with?

Mingzhi sits on the stump by the bamboo grove, fingering the leaf-flute. Thinking. He is confused: *Uncle Liwei could have made a different choice; he could have left.*

Mingzhi knows his uncle is more capable of being independent than anyone else. *But why didn't he go?* In his open palms, the flute that once was green and fresh is now dry and crumpled. Faded. Like Little Sparrow's life. *My friend . . . He might have escaped the troupe to live a new life.* Mingzhi feels relieved: if his conjecture is correct he should be happy for his friend. *Why doesn't Uncle Liwei do so, too?* Mingzhi thinks it over, again and again: the mansion, Grandfather Chai and the few people in it – what has held Uncle Liwei there? But no explanations are forthcoming, and the persistent droning croaks of the frogs add to his frustration.

He shakes his head, trying to clear his mind of the questions. The moon has slid to the western hill, half hidden behind the lush shade of the mulberry trees. And Mingzhi realizes he has been sitting there for a long time. *Too long!* He gets to his feet at once. The show must have ended a while ago, and Little Mouse must be worrying himself to death over his master's disappearance!

Mingzhi is about to head back to the mansion when he hears noises. Frivolous laughter. A man's and a woman's, familiar, coming from the bushes. *It's them again!* He remembers Er Niang and Golden Swallow's rendezvous on the night he last met Little Sparrow. The flirting, kissing and touching. Ashamed and disgusted, Mingzhi moves stealthily away, taking a big circuit to avoid the lovers.

In the dark silence Mingzhi sneaks into the house through the side door and closes it behind him.

'On a beautiful night like this, it's a shame to stay in your room. Isn't it, Eldest Brother?'

Mingyuan. Standing in the shadow of the overgrown willow.

Thinking about Er Niang, with Golden Swallow out there, Mingzhi becomes speechless. He tries to smile but only manages an awkward grimace. There is suspicion in Mingyuan's eyes.

'Thank God you're back!' Little Mouse darts out, still kneading his fingers. 'I'll be beaten to death if someone finds out you've been out alone!'

'So I'm here now.' Seizing the opportunity, Mingzhi hurries to his room with Little Mouse, ignoring Mingyuan's critical gaze that follows him as he leaves.

At midnight the mansion is wakened to startling news: Er Niang and Golden Swallow have been discovered. Adultery. The couple are tied up and locked in the storeroom, and will be punished in the morning according to the custom: *jin zhulong*, to be drowned in the river in separate pig cages.

Master Chai stands firm in the courtyard, while the troupe leader pleads: 'Golden Swallow is too precious to us. Didn't you admire his performance?'

Master Chai thumps his dragon stick, turns his back on the hook-nosed man. *No compromise. The rule must be followed.*

The troupe leader raises his voice: 'I did you a favour, dismissing Little Sparrow as you ordered. You owe me one!'

'I don't owe you anything; I paid you for what you did. That little rascal should never have entered my house and corrupted my grandson!'

Little Sparrow?

Mingzhi stares at his grandfather, whose face shows no expression. The troupe leader points his finger at Master Chai: 'You! Don't think you can do anything you like just because of all your money! Let's see how you end up!'

He storms away, and hurries his troupe to pack and leave at once.

The servants are shocked into gossiping in sibilant whispers. Likang lets out a loud humph and urges Da Niang, who is in tears, to return to the west court with him. Liwei lowers his head, wordless.

Awakened by his maid, Mingyuan rushes to the storeroom, tries to break the lock with an axe but is stopped by the servants on Master Chai's orders. Despite his grandson's yelling and howling, the old man does not yield, and Mingyuan is dragged away and locked in his room. His grudging eyes fall on Mingzhi as he passes by, and he screams: 'It's you, I know it's you!'

Mingzhi stands stock-still, feels the hatred in Mingyuan's gaze.

It wasn't me. I've done nothing!

Little Mouse holds his master's arm and leads him to his room. Mingzhi's face is pale: 'Grandpa's going to kill them . . . They're going to die!'

I should do something. He glances at his servant.

With Little Mouse's help, Mingzhi lets his half-brother out through the window, hands him a bulging cotton pouch of his scholarship money. Reminds him to return afterwards.

Mingyuan's voice is dry and cold: 'Don't you pretend. I won't thank you for this.'

Mingzhi shudders.

—~—

In the morning, stories about the runaway adulterers are exchanged among the villagers. The most convincing is that the troupe leader sneaked in later that night to rescue his precious actor. And in the gossipers' minds there is a picture of the furious Master Chai thumping his stick so hard on the ground that the dragon tail breaks off, detached from its head.

'Shame on Landlord Chai, shame on Chai's clan,' an elderly villager sighs. 'Who knows what else they've been covering up behind those high walls?'

A younger peasant chimes in: 'That I don't know; the only thing I know now is that the Northern Opera Troupe is gone!'

'Aye, this is predestined. If you're not meant to have something, you'll never get it. Poor people like us were never intended to enjoy the opera.'

'Hm, opera or no opera, life goes on. You still have to work, still have to feed all these hungry mouths at home!'

Immediately all resentment is reduced to silence, and the peasants can only shake their heads and sigh.

—∞—

Where is Little Sparrow now?

Mingzhi feels weak as he thinks about his friend. GRANDFATHER is an enormous shadow looming in the air that hangs heavily over the mansion, plunging down on Mingzhi's chest, pressing him flat.

In the dark there is a pair of eyes. Sharp. Piercing. Scanning him all over, looking for loopholes. Yet Mingzhi's worries for his friend have blinded him to the threat.

—∞—

Mingzhi notices how things have changed for Mingyuan. The angry grandfather's anger extends to the only son left by his adulterous daughter-in-law. Mingyuan is no longer asked to recite for Master Chai's guests, nor does his interest in the opium trade please the old man, and he is excluded from the family dinner on several occasions. Likang says nothing: that second wife of his has shamed him, and seeing Mingyuan reminds him of this shame. Da Niang, of course, is in no position to say anything, nor is Liwei. Mingyuan now keeps himself more to himself. The west court becomes quieter without his elated laughter, boastful talk and abusive shouts at the servants.

Mingzhi feels for his half-brother, takes the initiative to approach him and discusses their studies together.

The sharp edges between them seem to have softened. Mingyuan accepts his half-brother's overtures, practising calligraphy, revising texts with Mingzhi. A perfect combination of activities at a perfect time: he will take his first exam next month while Mingzhi sits his second.

When Mingyuan comes, Little Mouse crouches in a corner, waiting to serve tea or help grind ink. But he also watches Mingyuan closely with his mousy gaze fixed on Mingyuan's secretive eyes, scrutinizing the room or darting a warning stare at Little Mouse.

This faithful servant is glad that as days pass, his master shows no signs of wishing to share his knowledge of English with Mingyuan. Only revises his foreign readings in the small hours, alone.

Like spirits of the night they plunge in through the open window. Hovering in the middle of the room. Mingzhi counts and identifies: Mercury, Venus, Earth, Mars, Jupiter, Neptune, Saturn and its ring, Uranus. They take up their positions, rotating, and the moon revolves around the Earth. Then the fireball hurls itself in, blazing, lighting up the room, and the planets circle around it. Round and round and round, getting closer and closer and closer – and bang after bang they crash into the glowing flames, one after another. Explosion after explosion, blinding the eyes.

Splashing debris.

Drifting ashes.

Blank.

Mingzhi wakes at dawn with a stiff neck. He fell asleep at his desk last night, his face laid between the open pages of Father Terry's book of astronomy.

Crouching in a corner Little Mouse is still in dreamland. Mingzhi quietly pulls a blanket over his loyal servant.

Streaks of morning break through the clouds that wreathe the eastern hill. There are patches of red and orange and yellow against the ink-blue sky. Mingzhi watches as the dark grains gradually fade away and the landscape comes into focus.

An old pine tree stands alone on a ridge.

The cave. Charcoal. Little Sparrow.

Scenes of his past flit by, frame by frame.

Mama Wang. The secret world behind the curtain. Da Niang. Uncle Liwei. Meifong. Meilian. Old Scholar Yan.

Mingzhi's chest feels tight. He is desperately in need of fresh air, a walk in the country, and he does not hesitate.

As soon as Mingzhi leaves the west court, Mingyuan steps out of his room and sneaks into Mingzhi's.

He must have something, some secret, something from the town.

Mingyuan searches high and low, carefully to make no noise. And there on the desk, he sees it –

A foreign book!

Mingyuan can't believe his luck. He is about to grab it when Little Mouse stirs and murmurs: 'Go away! You little rascal!'

Panicked, Mingyuan retreats at once. Eyes still closed, Little Mouse mutters a few unintelligible words, then drifts off again. Through the window the sunlight has now slanted onto his blanketed body. He feels warm, too warm. In his dream the room is ablaze, the flames are reaching for him; and someone is watching, laughing, the voice sounds familiar –

Little Mouse sits up, panting heavily. The blanket slips, drops to the floor. He glances around –

Eldest Grand Young Master?

—∞—

A rare visitor to the west court, Master Chai's arrival creates a commotion. Curious servants lock their curious gazes on their master and his escort, Butler Feng, and Mingyuan who tails along. *A special-mission team on a special mission!* They busily whisper among themselves as the three hurry past, and look on, awaiting the next episode.

Thump, thump, thump . . . Master Chai and his stick find their way to Mingzhi's room. The door is flung open.

Mingzhi, who returned from his walk just moments ago, turns pale as he remembers the foreign book he left on the table when he went out.

Mingyuan darts forward: 'Here, on the desk!'

Rice paper, brush and ink-set lie in the right-hand corner, the Four Books and Five Classics sit on the left.

'It was there, the foreign book!' Mingyuan insists. 'He must have hidden it!'

My half-brother. Mingzhi heaves a sigh, his heart twitching.

Half leaning against the door, Da Niang watches. Worry creeps over her face, carving deep creases between her brows. Mingzhi's heart twitches again. He is worried about his mother's worry for him.

Master Chai signals Butler Feng to search. The drawers; in and out and on top of the wardrobe; under the bed, the blanket, the pillow.

The chest.

Mingzhi holds his breath.

The first drawer. Gowns are pulled out, thrown to one side.

The second.

Third.

Butler Feng slides out the last drawer. Mingzhi's heart leaps into his throat.

The contents are emptied onto the floor.

Mingzhi closes his eyes, expecting a heavy blow from his grandfather.

Moments pass; nothing happens. He opens his eyes, sees only the mess of his undergarments strewn about, and the three searchers scanning the room for possible locations they might have missed. In a corner Little Mouse stoops to pick up his master's clothing. Behind Master Chai, Butler Feng and Mingyuan, he winks at Mingzhi and smiles a mousy smile: *Relax, I've taken care of everything!*

Mingzhi breathes, relieved. But Mingyuan does not; his voice trembles, the tone shrill and flustered: 'It was here, it must be here somewhere . . .'

Mingyuan's sudden fear now makes him forget that the master of the house is there mastering the situation. He hurries forward, sweeps the desk, the top of the wardrobe and the chest with both hands. Brushes, paper, inkstick, inkstone and bowls, the Four Books and Five Classics fall to the ground. There is a cracking of inks and bowls, a scattering of paper. And nothing more.

Mingyuan rushes to the wardrobe –

THUMP!

Mingyuan freezes. His grandfather's face is taut, his body rigid.

Master Chai storms off without uttering a word or taking another look at Mingyuan. An embarrassment. That he has taken a jealous boy's accusation seriously. Has acted too hastily. For a man of his age, and the master of the Chai family, this is beyond a joke. He can see the maids sniggering and whispering behind the doors and windows. It is the son of that adulterous, runaway woman who has caused him this embarrassment.

An abject liar. Like mother like son.

The angry old man thumps out his anger all the way back to the east court with his new stick, a new dragonhead, made of brass. Every thump is a heavy blow to Mingyuan's heart.

Mingzhi watches Mingyuan leave the room. Head lowered, shoulders drooping, wordless. Just as he reaches the threshold, Mingyuan shoots a fierce glare at Mingzhi.

You better watch out!

Mingzhi reads his half-brother's thought, a chill crawling up his spine. The brittle bridge between them breaks to pieces like the ceramic ink bowls on the floor. Irreparable.

Another week. Mingzhi is glad that in another week he will be gone again, and he can't wait to go. To his Little Hut. Then the city and the exam. And what comes after.

—∾—

The punishment for Mingyuan is no specific punishment. Put simply, he is ignored, excluded, uncared for.

Left alone.

Which is, in fact, the cruellest punishment he could have expected.

As if he is no longer part of the family, invisible, an apparition ambling through the bleak mansion, lurking in the dark. Peering in on the activities from which he is barred: family dinners, festive prayers at the ancestral hall, learning his trade with Uncle Liwei, as Master Chai has instructed that Mingyuan shall not get involved in the family business.

He is not entirely forgotten, though. The sibilant whispers behind him when he passes by, the hands-on-their-mouths sniggering maids and their *looks* that say 'you deserve this' or 'we've been waiting for this for too long'. In them he sees

CONTEMPT, and it swells up inside him like a giant spider, pressing against his stomach, a heavy load that will not go away. It cobwebs in his lung, asphyxiating him, muddling his senses.

He breathes heavily, needing fresh air, needing space, needing to release the weight in his stomach, and he screams inside: *I'll get it all back! Everything that belongs to me! I will!*

—~—

From under the Buddha on her altar, Da Niang retrieves the books Little Mouse entrusted to her protection.

'Be careful, son. You might not always be this lucky.'

Mingzhi nods and takes the books. There is grey ash on the top of the pile, a vague smell of the incense his mother has been burning. He is inside them now, her room, the smoke screen, and the warm, pleasant whiffs of sandalwood.

'But I don't understand . . .' The creases between Da Niang's brows persist. 'Why don't you just concentrate on your studies, your exams?'

Mingzhi lowers his head and answers evasively: 'I know, Mother. Sorry for making you worry.'

I'm sorry, Mother. I can't. I can't leave all this new knowledge behind me.

Mingzhi burns joss sticks and prays with his mother. As he kneels, he looks up at the Buddha, His kindly face indistinct in the drifting smoke.

—~—

Mingzhi has obtained his grandfather's permission to leave three days before the second-level examination for the title of *juren*. A night in Pindong Town, then a day's journey to the Provincial Capital. He and Little Mouse will spend a night there, resting and getting ready. The young servant is as impatient as his master, their luggage neatly packed, stored in a corner, only waiting for their departure tomorrow at daybreak.

Knowing that his master is concerned about the English books, Little Mouse comes out with yet another mousy theory: The most prominent location is the most invisible one. While someone as knowledgeable as Mingzhi begins to scratch his head, Little Mouse pulls a large piece of cotton from the drawer, wraps the *illegal* books in it, ties the bundle to his shoulders. Then he carries the bigger luggage with his hands.

The bundle sits small on Little Mouse's back, almost unnoticeable, with only a tiny strap of cotton running across his chest, while the larger piece in his arms looks weighty, prominent.

Mingzhi now understands, but is still unsure.

'Trust me, Eldest Grand Young Master.' Little Mouse pats his chest, and Mingzhi says no more.

Because Master Chai has a relapse of rheumatism, dinner with the master is cancelled. Because Likang is busy satisfying his appetite with opium, only Liwei, Da Niang and Mingzhi make it to the so-called family farewell dinner. And because of all this, the dinner is held in the north court, Liwei's residence, for the first time. Let me be your host, he says. Da Niang casts her eyes down, nods lightly; Mingzhi smiles and leaves with Uncle Liwei to help him make arrangements. Little Mouse follows.

Taking her time, Da Niang goes to the kitchen and checks the clay pot of bird's nest soup she has kept simmering on a low fire, adds a few pieces of rock sugar to it, estimates the remaining time till it is ready. Reaches for the jar of rock sugar again and adds another piece.

He likes it sweet.

She makes a mental note to remind Mingzhi to leave room in his belly for the nutritious soup, as she stirs the contents once more before leaving for Liwei's quarters.

The south court is quiet, even quieter than the west. So when Liwei proposes a toast, his voice echoes in his living room, loud against the usual silence of a widower's residence. Within seconds the room suddenly comes alive. Mingzhi holds up his wine in response to his uncle's call. Da Niang makes an unsuccessful attempt to refuse the liquor. There is laughter, raised voices and intimate exchanges between mother and son and uncle.

For the first time Mingzhi sees his mother drain a cupful of wine. Her face flushes pink-red in the candlelight. And her eyes gleam, bright, watery.

She is beautiful, my mother. Mingzhi keeps staring, and so doesn't notice another pair of gawking eyes.

Uncle Liwei.

Da Niang has certainly noticed; she blushes further and says: 'Can we have our dinner now?'

The maid brings in the dishes Uncle Liwei has ordered.

Salted-radish omelette! Spotting it, Mingzhi smiles like a child: 'I can't believe my luck! It's my favourite, Uncle Liwei!'

'I . . .' His uncle hesitates. 'Is it? What a coincidence!'

Smiling to himself, his uncle glances up, catches Da Niang's gaze.

—∾—

The west court is certainly quieter than the north tonight, even quieter after the maids have retreated to their residences.

In the darkness, a door creaks open. A shadow darts in, and out later.

—∾—

Red. The couplets, the lanterns, the candles, the fireworks. Smiles on all faces: Master Chai's turns to joyous laughter; Likang's with a wide, upturned mouth, exaggerating his elation; Liwei's amiable, warm, encouraging; Da Niang's diffident, gentle, but Mingzhi also sees contentment in her eyes. The pride of a mother at her son's success.

Why is Mother in the ancestral hall?

Mingzhi's question is left unanswered when the men begin to toast him, again and again. 'It's your day,' they say.

Yes, I'm a juren, *I'm getting my mandarin post!*

Mingzhi drains cup after cup of wine, and he feels the liquid burn all the way through his tongue, his throat, his stomach. There it stirs, boiling, seething, pressing upwards –

Mingzhi wakes at midnight. He curls up and holds his

stomach tight with both hands but the pain does not ease. As if the intestines have twisted, jumbled up, entangled. And his head is cracking open. He moans.

'What's wrong, Eldest Grand Young Master?'

Little Mouse rises from his corner, lights the candle, and is shocked to see Mingzhi's sallow, crumpled face. He pours him a cup of warm water. Mingzhi takes a sip, tries to swallow it, then something forces it up into his throat. Sour, sickening, comes rushing up. He vomits. Little Mouse fumbles for the spittoon under the bed and holds it for Mingzhi.

The pain comes in fits and starts, like washing being wrung, tightening and loosening. Pain and ease. Pain. Ease. Pain. Ease. And in between, he vomits again and again. First the dinner he ate earlier that evening: the yellow, milky mess of salted-radish omelette, a dark pool of braised chicken and Chinese mushrooms; then yellowish fluid, thick and sticky, and later watery.

Never been like this before.

Little Mouse scratches his head: *WhatshouldIdoWhat-canIdoIhavetodosomething!* He puts down the spittoon and rushes out before Mingzhi can stop him. He calls for Da Niang as he hammers on her door, waking not only her but almost the whole mansion.

—

The doctor from Pindong Town feels Mingzhi's pulse and diagnoses: an imbalance of *yin* and *yang* in Mingzhi's intestines and stomach caused by contamination, which in turn caused imbalances in the circulation of *qi* and blood. He concludes that Mingzhi must have been going to bed at odd hours, and is suffering from a lack of sleep.

Master Chai listens closely as the doctor suggests: the patient is to consume a herbal remedy as prescribed, and rest, while taking other nutrition to help restore both *qi* and blood.

So the decision is made: Mingzhi will stay at home for another month.

'No!' Mingzhi struggles to get up. 'I have to go, I have to sit the exam!' In a fluster he grabs the bundle by his bedside.

Plunk!

The bundle falls open. Copies of books scatter across the floor.

'What are these?'

Little Mouse scurries forward but Master Chai has picked one up. Little Mouse closes his eyes; Da Niang, sitting in the corner, turns pale. Mingzhi falls back on his bed. The room swims before him. Master Chai's critical eyes and stern face drift before Mingzhi. He feels weak, a bottomless exhaustion, and he sinks into it.

Outside, as he peers in through the window, Mingyuan smiles. A smirk that has rediscovered its master after a long absence.

This is an unexpected bonus.

Thinking about Mingzhi sipping the bowl of sweet, smooth, tasty bird's nest soup last night, Mingyuan smiles again. The nutritious soup cooked with Da Niang's love, laced with the special ingredients Mingyuan blended in with the loss of his mother and his degraded status in the mansion.

Quietly he retreats. He has got what he hoped for, and more.

—~—

Two days later, when Mingzhi has stopped vomiting, Master Chai makes his grandson swear an oath to their ancestors. The boy will never again touch any foreign books from any foreign devils. The burner for silver paper is conveniently employed to dispose of the forbidden texts. Mingzhi stares at the blazing flames as they gobble up his precious reading. The pages frill, loosen, and their corners roll up in a red glow that spreads fast. They turn black in seconds, crumbling into ashes.

Will they return to their original forms in the netherworld like the silver paper? Will the ancestors collect and consume them? Will they too learn English?

Mingzhi glances around at the many pictures of his ancestors, their snowy beards and stern faces, and suddenly feels absurd. This whole thing. His family.

'HaHaHaHa! HeHeHe!'

His laughter resounds through the hall, shrill, hysterical.

'Stop it! Shut up!'

Master Chai keeps thumping his stick but Mingzhi keeps laughing, as if in a trance. Uncle Liwei steps forward, feels Mingzhi's still feverish forehead and shakes him by the shoulders. Eventually Mingzhi pauses, his bleary eyes catch his uncle's anxious stare, and he bursts into tears, howling as loudly as he'd laughed. His uncle pats his back and leads him away.

—~—

Before dawn on the third day, Mingzhi listens as Mingyuan rises early and leaves his room, the west court, the mansion. He knows his half-brother is setting out for Pindong Town, to sit his first-level examination. Alone. Without an extra night in the town prior to the exam.

Mingzhi sits by the window until the sun rises. Because of his illness, because the provincial-level exam is held only once in three years, it will be another two years before he can sit it.

A long wait, far too long.

Mingzhi's head is aching again.

At the far end of the courtyard, a snail is struggling to climb the wall. Mingzhi squints at the tiny speck, moving so slowly it seems to be motionless.

When life is reduced to only the room, studies and herbal remedies, each day goes by as slowly as the crawling snail. Every inch it moves takes a supreme effort, for one false action, one wrong judgement, may have dreadful consequences.

Yet it moves on.

Late spring, and it's an unusually noisy morning. Mingzhi hears the commotion, and Little Mouse returns with the news: Mingyuan has obtained his *xiucai*.

Mingzhi is pleased for his half-brother; so is Master Chai. A third place, though not first, is good enough for the grandfather to regret his neglect of the boy. He is thrilled, for there is now a better chance of having a mandarin in the family. *Two is always better than one.* As he clears his mind, the master recalls Meifong's death and Mingzhi's recent illness, and knows he shouldn't give up on Mingyuan.

The changes are immediate and dramatic. The thank-you prayer in the ancestral hall marks the milestone, although there was no blessing prayer before the exam. Of course Mingyuan does not object. He happily plants his footsteps on the ground of the clan's most sacred place, standing tall, feeling himself surrounded by the spirits of past generations of the Chai family, to which he belongs.

Then the family dinner of celebration and farewell.

Both Mingzhi and Mingyuan will attend the school in Pindong Town.

—ᴥ—

Master Chai lets Mingyuan lodge in the hostel, while Mingzhi, with Little Mouse tagging along, returns to his Little Hut. Mingzhi is glad to avoid Mingyuan's watchful eyes, to enjoy his little freedom.

'Beware of the real spy,' says Little Mouse, who is meant to be spying on Mingzhi.

—ᴥ—

Mingzhi confers with Scholar Ning. He will only continue editing the journal if he can remain anonymous, and his Head Teacher agrees. It is a secret between them. With other editors leaving the editorial committee, saying they are too busy, Mingzhi remains the Head Teacher's right-hand man, and a thoroughly reliable one. The journal still sells fast; almost everyone in the school reads it.

Including Mingyuan.

Mingzhi has found his half-brother on the bench under the willow tree in the front courtyard of the school, engrossed in the printed pages. Thinking of how the result of his hard work has attracted Mingyuan, Mingzhi quietly smiles to himself. Most of the time he prefers to walk away unnoticed, sparing himself an unfriendly stare. Still, he is happy for Mingyuan when he sees him befriending his fellow students, hanging about in a group. Knows his half-brother is not lonely, and is fitting in well.

The boundary between them is defined; unspoken rules that both know well and abide by. While accidental meetings at school are unavoidable, they keep out of each other's way outside. Have never arranged to meet up, never interfere with one another's business.

Determined to overtake his half-brother, Mingyuan concentrates on his studies, working hard, and paying no attention to Mingzhi's doings. This, in fact, suits Mingzhi well. He is able to steal the occasional Sunday to visit Father Terry, and continue his learning of English and the modern knowledge it brings with it. He is careful now, making his visits irregular, and not bringing home any books.

~

When the summer issue of the journal is ready for printing, Mingzhi is surprised at how quickly time has passed. Surprised, too, at the announcement of an extra exam to be held next year to celebrate Empress Dowager's sixtieth birthday.

Three seasons, just another three seasons. Mingzhi counts on his fingers. *And I must make it this time.*

Ten

Second-Level Examination, Spring 1894

Outside the office of the examination board in the Provincial Capital, a crowd of expectant scholars gathers. Tiptoeing, peering through the open door, exchanging words. Getting more anxious as the two fat strings of firecrackers hanging down the gatepost are ignited, cracking away at once. Amid the ear-shattering clatters, an official sedan is carried out, led by a band of trumpet and gong, a retinue of four officials carrying enormous lotus candles, and a rearguard of armed officials. Showering in the whirling red-paper flakes of firecrackers, swaying in the loud music.

The scholars swarm forward, follow the procession all the way to the government office, their eyes fixed on the chief examiner in the sedan, their minds on the red scroll in his hands.

Which tells their fates.

Behind them, Mingzhi rubs his eyes; already red, they are now getting bleary. Keeping close to Mingzhi, Little Mouse watches his master's every move. In front of Mingzhi the growing mass shuffles along under a tide of noises – voices raised above the shrieking trumpet and rumbling gong – that buzzes in his ears. But Mingzhi hears something more: the pounding of his heart and the beating of his pulse.

The waiting exhausts him more than the exam itself. Time was a tiny worm inside him, wriggling, chewing at the corners of his patience and confidence, bit by bit. Chewing at his sleep, his appetite, his interest in chess, his enjoyment of country walks. As the restless worm twisted on, Mingzhi could bear it no more and steeled himself to ask for Master Chai's permission to leave for the Provincial Capital. To witness the announcement of the results for himself.

Mingzhi walks on, away from the crowd.

The sedan stops in front of the government office, and the chief examiner steps down. He exchanges bows with the waiting Governor, and presents him with the scroll.

The scholars jostle forward as the paper is pasted on the wall, struggling to get a good view of the results: between heads, over shoulders, under armpits. Craning their necks, tiptoeing, jostling. Some cheer, some sigh, some smile, some weep, some laugh hysterically, some burst into howling sobs, some bang their heads against the wall, some are carried off on the shoulders of others, hooraying away to celebrate their success.

Mingzhi retreats to one side, watching. He is eager to find out his results but nervous, too. Prefers to wait a little longer. *When no one is watching.* He stands there for what feels like ages, until people begin to disperse.

Mingzhi rubs his eyes, checks again, and is certain now: he is listed fifth. One of the fifteen thousand new *jurens* nationwide, and ranked fifth among the provincial qualifiers, less than a hundred of them.

He does not see Mingyuan's name.

The public house is full. Successful scholars gather: toasting, congratulating, laughing and chattering.

In a corner Mingyuan throws a slice of braised pig's ear into his mouth, munches noisily and empties his wine. His gang of friends cheer, and the cup is immediately refilled.

'Who cares about the results? Let's enjoy ourselves.'

'That's right. As the proverb says, "Drink now and forget about tomorrow." '

Mingyuan raises his cup and drains it again.

'To hell with the exam!'

Another cup, and he glances around with bleary eyes: the surrounding joyful faces with their laughter seem to be jeering at him. He points his heavy fingers around: 'To hell with them!'

His drink-sodden face flops onto the table, and he mutters: 'To hell with him . . .'

The office of the examination board has been busy since early morning. One after another the freshly qualified *juren*s stream in to pay their respects to the chief examiner. Excitement hangs in the air of the waiting room, in the gossip of the lucky scholars about the exam, the results, even the candidates themselves.

'Look at the young man in the corner, the one in a white gown.'

'What about him?'

'I bet he's the youngest of us all.'

'He does look young. I've never known anyone to get his *juren* before thirty.'

'If he is the youngest, then he must be Chai Mingzhi.'

'The one who's ranked fifth?'

'Must be him!'

'A *juren* at twenty? I'm embarrassed for myself!'

Mingzhi feels his cheeks burning, wishes he had a nook to hide in. He takes up a book and buries himself in its open pages.

It is a long wait and Mingzhi gets his turn at noon to present his two-tael red thank-you envelope.

Imperial Scholar Dai gazes with admiration at the young man before him, and checks the name on the calling note. He smiles, remembering the disqualified paper he salvaged three years ago in Pindong Town.

'I've read your work long before this.'

Mingzhi stares at the kindly scholar, startled, but recalls at once the rumours Little Mouse related to him. *It's him, my saviour, the friend of Old Scholar Yan.*

Mingzhi takes a deep bow: 'Many thanks for taking a liking to my essays.'

Imperial Scholar Dai nods, immediately taking a liking to the writer of the essays, too. He smiles, and his equally well-mannered daughter comes to his mind.

—∞—

'He is home! Our *juren* is home!'

The servant, who has been waiting at the main door, shouts long before Mingzhi enters the mansion. Immediately, there is a clattering of firecrackers, banging of gongs and a fluttering of red-paper flakes. In seconds, all the servants of the mansion have crowded to the door, led by Liwei and Butler Feng, smiling and cheering, welcoming Mingzhi.

The news has whirled around the village in the wake of the messenger, travelling from village to village to deliver results to the qualifiers. This lucky messenger, who was here a day before Mingzhi, left the mansion with a fat red envelope after a substantial meal, and a big grin that never left his face. The best reward he ever had in his years of service, he told the servants, said they were fortunate to work for such a generous master. *A generous master?* The servants could only smile bitterly, and watch the lucky man belch with contentment as he walked away.

Indeed the new *juren*'s grandfather is overwhelmed with pride and joy, pacing the ancestral hall, while Likang celebrates with extra puffs of opium, immersed in the image of his son descending from iridescent clouds. In the west court, Da Niang chants to pay tribute to Buddha for granting her wish.

Walking through the courtyards led by Liwei and Butler Feng, Mingzhi knows what awaits him. His grandfather. The ancestral hall. The ceremony, again. And the insatiable ancestors, waiting for a big feast of braised duck, boiled chicken, whole roast pig with rice and wine. With the smell and smoke of joss sticks and the glow of candlelight.

A sudden flood of exhaustion sweeps over Mingzhi. He needs rest. A long, deep sleep.

—w—

The corridor is dark and Mingzhi keeps walking, imagining the bright, wide mandarin courtroom ahead. There is light at the far end, flickering. *It's there, my destination.* He blunders on for half a mile, then a mile, another, three. Five. First scurrying, then plodding, then dragging his weary feet. But the corridor seems endless, and the walls begin to unfold themselves, narrowing in, cold and damp against his warm body; he is sandwiched, locked tight, unable to move, to scream, to breathe.

A face emerges.

Mingyuan, in a mandarin costume. He closes in –

'Huh!'

Mingzhi wakes in the darkness, panting, his nightgown clammy with sweat. Knees encircled in his folded arms, he sits thinking, realizing he has not seen Mingyuan since coming come.

—w—

As soon as he arrives at the mansion Mingyuan is summoned to the east court. Still thrilled with Mingzhi's success, the grandfather is not unkind. And so Mingyuan is lucky to escape punishment for dawdling in the city, and a reprimand for failing the exam. He is to re-sit, much to his delight.

Another two years by myself in Pindong Town.

Mingyuan's mind moves fast, working out his plan.

—w—

Da Niang rewards Mingzhi with a sandalwood bracelet blessed by a Buddhist monk from a distant temple. Mingzhi slips it on and observes the tiny beads of love, encircling his thin wrist. He wraps his other hand around the bracelet, feels it smooth in his palm. Bringing it close to his nose, he inhales the faint scent of sandalwood.

Da Niang notices that Mingzhi is now a head taller than her. *A grown man now.* She takes a closer look at him, his fine features and bright eyes under thick, clear eyebrows.

Who will be the lucky girl?

A suitable match from the village is impossible. As Likang cares little for anything but his opium, Master Chai will certainly be the one to make the arrangements. And that worries Da Niang.

She sighs, tells herself she will pray for her son.

Lying in bed, Old Scholar Yan stares out from under his heavy lids for some time before he recognizes Mingzhi. Once a proud student of his.

Mingzhi kneels and kowtows, says thank you to his old teacher. Old Scholar Yan draws a hand from under the blanket and waves wearily for him to rise. Mingzhi stays put.

'The great master says, "Being your teacher for a day, he is your teacher for life." And that's what you are to me.' Mingzhi speaks reverently.

Old Scholar Yan nods, grins a toothless grin with his withered lips. His hand droops in the air, a layer of wrinkled bark over shrunken twigs. Abruptly his chest heaves, and he coughs violently, his hand groping for the spittoon under the bed. Mingzhi reaches for it, holds it for his teacher, and the old man coughs out a sticky, yellowish lump of phlegm.

Mingzhi helps Old Scholar Yan to a cup of tea, and watches him take slow sips. The room is dim and stuffy with the smell of books. Aged, tattered books. There is a shelf packed with them and there are heaps on the floor and the desk, coated with dust. Inside the covers, silverfish swim freely through the pages, happily gorging on thousands of years of ancient knowledge. Minute insects with the wisdom of the great sages. Living between the pages in a dim and stuffy room, as contented as their emaciated master.

These are the only possessions of the old scholar, who decided long ago to stay in the village and educate rural children, who refused to take further exams and secure the post of mandarin.

And he has given me the chance to be one.

Mingzhi's eyes turn moist. *I'll visit him whenever I can*, he promises himself, not knowing that this will be his last visit.

—~—

The following week Old Scholar Yan is treated to a funeral procession led by a band of trumpets and gongs. Master Chai orders it, as he suddenly remembered to pay his respects to the respected scholar of Plum Blossom Village.

Mingzhi does not join the procession. He knows his teacher would have preferred a quiet farewell, like the life he lived.

After the salt boat has carried away the spring harvest, Liwei spends more time with Mingzhi. *Before he leaves again.*

Uncle and nephew resume their evening walks. The nephew is keen to give his uncle news from the city, the knowledge he has learned. The construction of rails and roads, the use of foreign machines in modern factories: textiles, steel mills, weapons. He tells his uncle there will be no salt boat soon.

'Times have changed, Uncle Liwei. Even the teachings of Confucius are being reinterpreted!'

Shocked at Mingzhi's last words, Uncle Liwei trips over an exposed root and stumbles.

Days pass, and the letter of appointment does not arrive.

Mingzhi cares less, and starts preparing for the third-level exam as planned. He needs more: needs to attain a *jinshi*, to take the palace examination. To get into the Hanlin Academy and become a member of the imperial think-tank. To advise the Emperor on the administration of the country, the drawing up of laws and policies.

But Master Chai is anxious. All he wants is a mandarin title, regardless of its ranking. He speculates: has the messenger lost his way? Met with an accident? Have the letters or appointments been messed up? He becomes edgier as the days go by, and falls into frequent rages. His targets, needless to say, are the servants. A drop of spilt tea, a crease on the master's gown or a speck of dust on the table incurs a punishment. The servants hold their breath, tiptoeing through the frostily silent east court, fearing that even a sneeze will get them into trouble.

They crane their necks at the doorway for the messenger to come to their rescue.

—⁓—

In Pindong Town the messenger stops by the government office to deliver the list of newly appointed officials under Mandarin Liu's charge. Inside the wax-sealed envelope is a list of five names, neatly written in *kaishu*, the regular script. CHAI MINGZHI stands out, striking the mandarin's eye, together with his title: Reserve Official.

Mandarin Liu sits in his plum-wood official chair, fiddling with his bristly chin, thinking. Moments later, he beckons to his servant and orders a substantial meal for the messenger. With chicken and duck and pork, and a big pot of wine, of course.

Overwhelmed, the lucky messenger enjoys the feast, happy to let the servant of the generous mandarin take care of the letters in his charge.

—⁓—

Finally a letter comes from the Imperial City. Master Chai hastily tears it open and hands it to Liwei. His expression changes in seconds as his son reads it. First a frown, for it is not the long-awaited posting, then a grin: the fourth-ranking Imperial Scholar Dai suggests a marriage between Mingzhi and his seventeen-year-old daughter. Should the Chai family accept this suggestion, a formal proposal including Mingzhi's birth date and time is to be submitted to Imperial Scholar Dai for consideration.

A connection with a fourth-ranking mandarin!

An opportunity too great to be missed! Immediately Master Chai urges Liwei to reply – yes, naturally – and a go-between will be sent at once to present the proposal.

Liwei asks hesitantly: 'Shouldn't Likang or Mingzhi be consulted first?'

'Consulted? For him to say no, like you?' Master Chai raises his voice: 'I'll make no mistakes this time. Mingzhi will do as I say!'

The reply has to be carefully and skilfully drafted. A marriage proposal is for certain but there will be no wedding until Mingzhi takes his place in the office. Until he is in a position to match the bride's. A crafty old scoundrel, Master Chai knows where a fourth-ranking mandarin stands, what his authority is capable of. He knows also that the members of the prestigious gentry seek an equal match. Like the old saying, 'A dragon door pairs with a dragon door.' He realizes that the Imperial Scholar may have foreseen a bright future ahead of Mingzhi, but the marriage will only be possible if their positions are levelled, and with Scholar Dai's authority, Master Chai will see to it.

~

In the midst of the hustle and bustle over Mingzhi's marriage arrangements and the worry over the official appointment, Mingyuan quietly leaves for Pindong Town when the school reopens. With a dark shadow on his face and a heavy cloud in his stomach that refuses to go away.

Determined to cheer him up, his pals drag him to the public house and order him streaky pork, braised pig's ear and chicken feet to accompany the wine. After a few drinks his stomach does lighten, though his face remains gloomy. Loitering in the street afterwards, Mingyuan feels something crawling in his veins, restless, waiting to burst out. He needs to do something. Needs to release that *something* in his veins. Wandering in the darkening evening, he sees light coming through a curtained door in an alley, through which noises filter.

He heads for it.

A gambling den. Shrouded in smoke and noise. Filled with crowded tables. Chain-smoking fortune-seekers throw their cards and dice and strings of cash, shout and cheer and yell and curse and spit. The sounds and actions stir up that *something* inside Mingyuan's veins. It twists and burrows, striving to release itself.

Mingyuan ducks under the curtain, plunging himself into the smoke and noise and excitement he desperately needs.

—∞—

The arrival of professional matchmaker Mama Zhang in the mansion concludes the speculation that has been brewing for days. *There will be good news soon: an engagement, after which a wedding will follow.* Anticipation spices up the dull, bitter life of the servants. They forget about their difficult master, and find excuses to visit the east court to spy for first-hand information.

In the east court.

A hand on her rounded waist, Mama Zhang claps her chest

with her bamboo fan: 'Aiya, don't worry, Master Chai.' She winks at the master. 'I'm at your service. I'll keep everything in order and win you a well-behaved daughter-in-law.'

She flaps her fan at Master Chai's shoulder – oops! – then snatches back as the stern-faced master turns his back on her.

'No messing around here.' Master Chai's serious tone freezes the room. 'Just get the job done, and you'll be well rewarded!'

An expert in the rituals and proceedings of marriage and weddings, this garrulous middle-aged woman has been specially recruited from Pindong Town. With a mission of extreme importance: to present the marriage proposal.

A list is drafted: the proposed bridegroom's exact date and time of birth sealed in a red envelope; a jade bracelet from among the heirlooms of the Chai family as the engagement token, should the proposal be accepted; a finely crafted marble vase for the prospective father-in-law; and for the prospective mother-in-law, a bolt of Suzhou silk. *At least that will show the Imperial Scholar we are level with him in terms of material wealth*, Master Chai thinks proudly. And red pleasing-envelopes for the servants of the prospective in-laws to gladden their hearts and so sweeten their tongues.

Nothing more, nothing less. Just enough to impress the Imperial Scholar. To demonstrate the Chai family's sincerity, prosperity and generosity.

When all is ready, the extremely important mission team, led by Mama Zhang and Butler Feng, leaves for the Imperial City on its extremely important mission. With a bundle filled with red envelopes, the jade bracelet, the marble vase, Suzhou silk and the red envelope. By the time they step out of the main door, the intelligent spies have gathered enough intelligence to set the mansion alight.

—ꝏ—

Mingzhi is reading by the window when Little Mouse rushes in.

'Hey, you're going to be a bridegroom, a New Man!'

Mingzhi ignores Little Mouse's teasing. He lays down his book and stares out into the courtyard.

At the top of the old willow, two tiny, rounded sparrows are capering and chirping incessantly as they preen each other. Wings flapping; pecking busily, as if saying, 'I'm clean, you're not; I'm clean, you're not . . .' After some moments they fly away almost simultaneously in the same direction.

Then comes a pair of dragonflies, one red, the other greenish grey, shuttling between the cascading twigs and leaves, chasing each other. Dashes of red and greenish grey flit here and there. One stops, the other freezes, and moves again only when its partner resumes its flight, before they overlap in the air. Greenish Grey on top of Red. Tail to tail, abdomen to back.

Even a dragonfly makes its own choice.

The morning breeze sends over whiffs of fragrance. Oleander, peony and cockscomb – his grandfather's favourite flowers, found in most of the courtyards – rich and strong, rush into Mingzhi's nostril. He sneezes, loud in the tranquil room.

Little Mouse brings his pale-faced master a kerchief,

a cape to drape round his shoulders and a warm cup of tea. He thinks Mingzhi might have caught a cold in the morning chill. *No wonder scholars have always been associated with feebleness, and are called defenceless bookworms.* Little Mouse watches Mingzhi quietly sipping his tea, does not know it is his heart that is making him weak. That he misses the faint, soothing scent of jasmine, and yearns for a sniff of it.

That long-lost scent of jasmine.

~

As Master Chai had conjectured, Imperial Scholar Dai does wish for a son-in-law with an official position; however, contrary to the master's expectation, the Imperial Scholar also wants more. At least one more exam, at least a *jinshi* if not a Hanlin Academician, before the wedding can take place. *He can do more and he should.* The Imperial Scholar knows the young man's capabilities, trusts him, to such an extent that he will entrust his only daughter's future to him.

The proposal is accepted – for, according to the fortuneteller, the dates and times of the prospective couple are immaculately matched, a god-sent pairing – though on the condition that Mingzhi is to attain his *jinshi* as soon as possible. The happy grandfather keeps his promise, generously rewarding the professional matchmaker for professionally accomplishing this extremely important mission.

When Mama Zhang has delightedly twisted her bulging waist away (bulging not only with excess fat but also abundant taels), Butler Feng is finally given his chance. He relays Imperial Scholar Dai's advice: 'It would be wiser if

Mingzhi did not take up the post offered to him now, but continued with his exams.'

The post? Has Mingzhi been offered one? Where the hell is the letter of appointment then?

Mist gathers in Master Chai's mind, and a vague speck of light glimmers through, indistinct, but clear enough to suggest something, or someone. *Yes, someone.* And he will find out more.

—m—

Mandarin Liu slumps in his chair; in his hand is a letter he has just read, now crumpled in his fist.

It's from the Imperial Court about the recently assigned official posts, questioning Chai Mingzhi's delay with his Reserve Official appointment. Mandarin Liu is reminded also that his negligence of duty has been noted, and that he is to call Mingzhi in with immediate effect.

All right. A Reserve Official can be on reserve forever. Let's see how much patience you have.

Mandarin Liu begins to work out his plan, rubbing at his ears as they itch unceasingly, and wondering who has been talking about him behind his back.

It's Master Chai, his long-term foe.

'Damn the cunning fox! Damn it!' The old man keeps thrusting his stick into the hard soil of the courtyard as he curses Mandarin Liu, but only manages some shallow jabs. He thrusts harder and hurts his wrists. The ground merely sinks a little, not deep enough to match the spikiest thorn that penetrates his insides.

Mandarin Liu. The thorn that stays put in Master Chai's flesh.

But not for very long, Master Chai thinks as he makes his way to the central court and sits down in his dragon chair. He is confident now. A connection with a mandarin of higher ranking has proven useful. He picks up the reply from Imperial Scholar Dai, the result of a simple enquiry to the Imperial Scholar, which confirms his guess: Mandarin Liu has sabotaged Mingzhi's appointment. Master Chai would have been more delighted had he known that with his letter also, the alarm has been raised. Mandarin Liu is now marked, under observation.

Nor does the old man doubt that it won't take long for Mandarin Liu to find out that Master Chai is behind all this.

—ꝏ—

An hour passes, then two. Three. Mingzhi sits in the silence of the empty waiting room, regretting coming, but realizes he has no right to regret. It wasn't his choice to be there in the first place. He glances around for what seems to be the hundredth time. On the wall above him hangs a horizontal board inscribed with *Gongzheng Bu'a*:

Fair and Just

Words of praise for a government official. For Mandarin Liu.

Mingzhi stares at the characters, the strokes that form the characters. Clear gold against a glossy black board: big, bright, shiny. He stares at them so hard and long that they seem to detach themselves, drifting about, making faces at him. Reconstructing themselves into *Bu Gongzheng'a*:

Unfair, Unjust

Bigger, brighter, shinier.

There is a sudden waft of jasmine. A glimpse of silky green flits through the door. Mingzhi rushes out. At one end of the corridor the hem of a long dress disappears round a corner.

From the other end a servant approaches and takes Mingzhi to Mandarin Liu.

—~—

Master Chai rages again: Mingzhi has been sent home without a post. He is to wait until a suitable position arises, according to Mandarin Liu.

Mingzhi quietly retreats as Master Chai hurls his tea to the floor, shouts for the maid to get him a fresh, warm cup, and swears he will ask the Imperial Scholar to see that Mingzhi gets his post.

Mingzhi shuts the door on his grandfather's rage. He steps into the courtyard, into the comfort of the warm afternoon sunlight. Above him, the sky is a clear, soothing blue.

No post for me! He walks swiftly away, with steps as light as his heart, leaving behind him the long wait the day before at the government office in Pindong Town and the sarcasm behind Mandarin Liu's smiling facemask. The fake sigh when the mandarin said that there was no position, and the pretended assurance that Mingzhi would be informed of a future vacancy.

—~—

The night is gradually coming to an end, but not the game. The pieces make slow progress. Between moves there are pauses for talk and thought. And tea to refresh the players' minds.

'You have to be firm.' Uncle Liwei fills Mingzhi's cup. 'And stick to your decision.'

What about you, Uncle? Don't you have a decision to make yourself?

Questions linger in Mingzhi's mind but are unable to find their way to his lips.

Candlelight makes a sharp contrast between Uncle Liwei's black and white hair; casts shadows in the creases on his forehead, between his brows, at the outer edges of his eyes, beneath his cheekbones. Mingzhi realizes these are the shadows of a life in the mansion.

No, I won't spend my life here.

Mingzhi makes a swift move, flying his officer across the enemy's boundary and setting him down with a loud thud. Uncle Liwei darts a surprised glance at Mingzhi. On the beam above a frightened lizard drops its tail as it flits past.

A headless, bodiless tail flaps on the ground. Fast at first, then slow, then motionless. Its master has freed itself, and doesn't turn back for a second look.

That same night in Pindong Town, Mingyuan shouts and cheers and curses in the gambling den. Eyes follow the dice, ears pricked for their rattling.

Red-faced.

Sweat streaming.

Voices hoarse.

Little Mouse opens the door. Everything is as before: the desk, the bookshelf, the wardrobe, the bed. The writing on the wall above the desk:

Little Hut of Leaping Fishes

Mingzhi notices the now yellowish paper, its flapping edges and fading ink. He takes out his four treasures for calligraphic writing: inkstick, inkstone, brushes and paper. Little Mouse grinds a bowl full of ink; Mingzhi smooths out a large scroll of rice paper, picks up the biggest brush and rewrites the name of his home. Bolder, firmer and bigger this time. More prominent against the whitewashed wall.

He is pleased to be back, a result of his future father-in-law's influence on his grandfather, insisting that Mingzhi should concentrate on the third-level exam rather than wasting time waiting for a minor post.

For certain, a scholar is more sympathetic with his own kind. More understanding. Mingzhi is unsure about the marriage, though, the bride-to-be he has never met.

But for the time being, he has only to keep his mind on his studies.

At night, the sounds of splashing fishes soothe him as he immerses himself in his Four Books and Five Classics. And sometimes, whiffs of jasmine too, faint on the evening breeze. Refreshing him, keeping him awake, focused.

Mingyuan feels his pockets. Empty. Gone, his school fees and rent.

I have to win them back! I will win them back!

Peering through the crowd at the busy table, he wishes he had money to place more bets.

'Need some cash, Young Master?' A middle-aged man approaches. Uncle Eagle. Mingyuan recognizes him, a regular here, though he is rarely seen gambling, simply wandering about with his sharp eyes like an eagle targeting his prey. Or conferring quietly with gamblers in dark corners. And now Uncle Eagle fixes his gaze on the piece of jade attached to the tassel hanging from Mingyuan's waist. 'I can get you some.'

Mingyuan follows him to a corner, where Uncle Eagle writes a contract: Mingyuan is to pawn the jade for ten taels.

'It's worth more than that!'

Uncle Eagle holds out ten pieces of silver in his palm: 'Well, do you want it or not?'

Mingyuan stares at the silver.

Come on, Mingyuan, luck is waiting for you! The God of Gambling is calling from the crowded tables. Mingyuan signs the paper and grabs the money, hurries to answer that heavenly call.

—~—

Sunday afternoon and Father Terry's study is cosy. Mingzhi listens as his teacher reads from an outdated *Prince of Wales Island Gazette*. 'Prince of Wales Island' refers to Penang, a small island in the Straits of Malacca, somewhere in the south-east, Father Terry explains. It is one of the Straits Settlements – Penang, Malacca and Singapore – that are under direct control of the British Empire.

The British Empire?

Mingzhi's eyes open wide. In his mind, as in the minds of his fellow-countrymen, there is only one empire: the Qing, and it is the centre of the world.

Eager to know more, he urges Father Terry to read on.

The reports carry nothing else but the arrival of official so-and-so to the Malay states, the setting up of new schools by the British colonists, the activities of missionaries, the trading of pepper, cocoa, rubber and forest produce.

Mingzhi pictures a borderless wooded land, covered in strange trees and plants. Swarthy, naked, short but well-built indigenous people trudging barefoot through the jungle. Running streams, splashing waterfalls. Birdsong under the clear blue sky.

The afternoon passes.

And there are more Sunday afternoons to come, more news awaiting Mingzhi as he waits for spring. The next exam.

—ʍ—

The *Prince of Wales Island Gazette* does not report on the factories mushrooming in the north, in the Land of the Dragon. Nor will it, later, show any interest in covering the trampling of the dwarf ghosts, the Japanese, on the face of the so-called Centre of the World, treading over the Chinese-occupied peninsula of Korea. It ignores, also, the crumbling of the reformation led by the intellectuals, which Mingzhi will soon witness for himself.

Eleven

Third-Level Examination, Spring 1895

In the Chai Mansion, the ancestral hall is warm and smoky. For seven days and nights, candles have been lit and joss sticks burnt on Master Chai's order. Mingzhi, their hopeful descendant, the would-be pride-of-the-Chai, is sitting his exam in the Imperial City.

It is smoky in Da Niang's room, too. Peering in through the window, Liwei finds a smoke-shrouded body kneeling in front of the altar and hears the soft chants of sutra. Eyes closed, Da Niang sees Mingzhi in her mind's eye: writing incessantly, sweating, biting his lip. She keeps her fingers on her sandalwood rosary, trying to count the images away but feeling as if she is counting the words her son is writing. She frowns, bringing the rosary closer to her face. The soothing scent of sandalwood reminds her of the bracelet she gave Mingzhi, made from the same beads, and is now clasped round her son's wrist. She inhales, taking in the smell, and goes on chanting.

At the sound of coughing, Liwei springs back from the window. Likang's asthmatic cough has become a permanent feature of the west court, and is becoming more frequent, more ferocious. Liwei sighs. *If only he would give up opium.* He shakes his head, feeling absurd, as he is just leaving for the fields.

The poppy fields.

—∞—

In another smoke-filled room in Pindong Town, a dispirited Mingyuan puts down a jade pendant from his estranged mother's collection and signs yet another pawn-deal with Uncle Eagle.

The handful of cash he now has straightens Mingyuan's back. The desire to win lurches into the dice, luring him with seductive smiles: *Come get me. Come get me.*

He plunges forward.

Here, I'm all yours.

—∞—

In the examination hall in the Imperial City, papers are collected, counted and checked. The candidates are dismissed. Swarming out of the hall they gather in groups, discussing the questions and their answers; expressing their joy, regrets or doubts.

Mingzhi walks away from their excitement. His head swims in the droning of the crowd. Three tedious rounds of tests in eight days have worn him out: brain racked, eyes strained, fingers stiffened.

Spotting his master, Little Mouse comes running and smiling, takes the calligraphy set from Mingzhi and walks beside him in silence.

Mingzhi wraps his hand over the sandalwood beads

around his wrist, thinking about his mother praying for him at home.

As he walks Mingzhi stares down at the flagstones swimming under him, the ground of the ancient city of the dragon. The fine, smooth surface polished by age, by centuries of footsteps trampling across them. By generations of emperors in their dragon palanquins, their entourages, their soldiers. By mandarins of all grades, scholars and commoners. Merchants and travellers. Trotting or strutting or scurrying, scuffing away the roughness under them with every step.

With each step Mingzhi feels the hard yet smooth surface beneath the thin soles of his shoes, and recalls the proverb Old Scholar Yan passed on: 'With patience, "an iron bar can be ground into a needle".' He knows he has only to wait. A month is just long enough for sightseeing in the Imperial City. This is his first trip and he should make the most of it. His pace lightens and he beckons Little Mouse, knowing that with his mousy wits he must have gathered plenty of information for a tour of the city.

—∿—

Morning, and in his room Mingzhi hears a commotion from the ground floor, the dining area of the public house in which he is staying. There is no sign of Little Mouse. Mingzhi walks out and joins the other guests, leaning against the banister along the corridor, looking down into the dining area below. At the tables, heads shuffle, newspapers are held open, fingers point at lines on the pages. Words are exchanged, faces redden, voices are raised. Veins pulse in straining necks.

It's *Shanghai Sheng Bao*, one of the major newspapers that carry reports from foreign journalists. Mingzhi can barely make out the title, and the headlines are columns of ants slithering with each movement of the hands that hold the newspapers. He cranes his neck, straining his eyes.

'Here you go, Eldest Grand Young Master.'

Acrid smell of ink and oil assaults Mingzhi's nostrils. He sneezes. Under his nose is the *Shanghai Sheng Bao* held out by a frowning Little Mouse.

'They say the Japanese are coming. Are they?' Little Mouse does not smile. 'We won't let those Shorties set their foot on our land, right?'

Mingzhi looks at his servant and is surprised to see worry in his face for the first time. He wishes to find words of comfort but as he reads on, the image of a hundred-thousand-strong Japanese army waiting to invade from Tianjin ties up his tongue. He doesn't wish to tell Little Mouse that the intruders will only retreat if a treaty is signed, and with that Taiwan will be in enemy hands. He quietly folds the newspaper, hands it back to Little Mouse and returns to his room. It's time for his morning routine of calligraphic exercises.

—~—

The first piece of rice paper is scrunched up, tossed in the bin. The second, too, without much writing on it. And the third. Mingzhi tries, again and again, and more papers are discarded. For the regular script, *kaishu*, the strokes join together in one swift movement, so that the intended formal, square effect of the characters is reduced to an unrecognizable mess. Switching to *caoshu*, this supposedly forceful, rapid and cursive style of writing turns languid and weak. Lazy lines lie loosely, squinting up at him with sleepy eyes.

Scrrunch! Another piece of paper is thrown away, another victim of his unsettled heart. And the plate of ink, too, empties in seconds with every quick soak of the fine brush, the same brush that has transcribed his thoughts onto pages of excellent essays. It is now betraying him, resisting his control, as if determined to create words of its own.

Standing to one side, Little Mouse, head lowered, keeps grinding ink and peeping out at his master from under lowered lids. Waiting for his next move.

Outside, the commotion gets louder. This time it comes from the window facing the main road. The high-pitched shouting of slogans is echoed by more shouting. Mingzhi puts down the brush.

In the street dozens of people congregate, mostly scholars. Mingzhi recognizes some of them, *juren*s from all over the country who are here for the exam and now await their results.

'Stop the Japanese! No treaty!'

The scholars, looking feeble in their plain gowns, cry themselves hoarse. Their eyes are red; some are in tears. Mingzhi knows that among them are *juren*s from Taiwan, weeping for the future of their homeland.

What do they plan to do?

Mingzhi peers ahead. In the near distance, the Forbidden City sits quietly within its four walls. High and heavy in thick layers of stone. Keeping all noises at bay.

—~—

The scholars have indeed come up with a plan. A petition, a joint statement from the *jurens*!

Mingzhi is intrigued but excited, too. Intrigued, for 'petition' to him has been just one of the many unfamiliar words, vague and distant, and now it has come alive; excited, for it is said that Liang Qichao, whose social commentaries have deeply impressed Mingzhi and made the author an idol among intellectuals, is penning the petition: A Plea to the Emperor. To be signed by the *jurens* in the city.

What will he write? What can he say to the Son of the Dragon? Will the young Emperor listen to him?

Mingzhi yearns to read the contents, the voice of the respected Liang, of all the scholars and the people.

—~—

At first he wants to find out more, and sits for long hours in the dining area at lunch and dinner, pricking up his ears, listening intently for news about the petition and the peace talks. But only speculation and rumours spew from the spit-spattered mouths. An army that will flood the Imperial City is described. An even bigger and stronger Chinese force comprising heavily equipped naval vessels and well-trained troops seems to be looming, as the ignorant public swear their commitment to the Kingdom of the Dragon. The efforts of the reformers are dismissed. 'With a team of four hundred Hanlin Academicians behind him,' they say, 'do you think the Emperor will listen to those bookworms?'

Disappointed, Mingzhi decides to take his meals in his room, stops listening to hearsay and only scans the *Shanghai Sheng Bao* for the latest development.

At night, when all noises cease, Mingzhi returns to his books, trying to keep up with his scheduled studies. But on the open pages, the ancient wisdoms of the great masters transform themselves into lines of question marks, big-headed hooks with heavy dots. *Is there going to be war? Will I get my results in time? Are the scholars going to cause trouble? Will this affect my plan to become a mandarin?*

He rubs his eyes and shakes his head. Reads the passages aloud but there are cynical faces between the words: 'Yes, you feeble bookworm, get back to your books. It's the only thing you can do.'

Is that so? Mingzhi thinks about the petition. It is said that the initiators are visiting all the scholars to get their endorsement. *How many have signed it? Aren't they worried about being blacklisted? Shall I put my name down, too?*

A big-headed hook with a huge final dot lunges into Mingzhi's dream that night. Black and heavy, pressing against his heart.

The men close in, each with a huge scroll in hand, holding them high and releasing the ties. *Flap!* Giant pages filled with signatures unroll, loud in the silent darkness. Mingzhi shudders, struggling to pull himself away from the four walls of scrolls falling onto him: hands pushing, legs kicking . . .

'They're here, Eldest Grand Young Master!'

Mingzhi wakes, heaving, his heart still pounding from the nightmare.

'They?' He kneads his temples, confused.

'The scholars.' Little Mouse helps Mingzhi dress before

leading the young men in. 'With some papers to show you.'

Mingzhi swiftly smooths his gown as the Guangdong *jurens* enter. He looks at the group of four, at the similar looks of intelligence tinged with worry on their youthful faces, at their identical plain gowns. Mingzhi knows they are not much older than he is. *Yet they are fighting for the nation.*

And me?

He quietly sits down at his desk. The leader smooths out the scrolls: the Plea to the Emperor that Mingzhi has been longing to read, and the signed petition.

Mingzhi takes his time, going through the passages word by word. Admires the skill of Liang's writing, the way he avoids harsh phrases and introduces a long list of suggestions for reformation: rejecting the treaty that demands reparations and secession of territory to the enemy, and, instead, strengthening the armed forces, are among the priorities.

Little Mouse scratches his head, does not understand why his young master is taking so long. He pours another round of warm tea for the visitors, not understanding either why they are being so patient, as he knows they are visiting all the scholars in the city.

The long list of signatures lies tacit before Mingzhi. Different calligraphic styles, different sizes. Unfamiliar names from regions both known and unknown. With the same force against the soft paper, as forceful as their determination: pleading to uphold the nation's dignity.

Will they be able to make a difference? The cynical faces he has seen in the dining area appear between the characters, grimacing, mocking him. Then one stern face emerges to prevail over the rest. His grandfather's. He reads the old man's writhing lips: *This is nothing but a convenient record for the authorities to use if they wish to take action against scapegoats.*

Mingzhi shakes his head and all the faces vanish in a blink. He sits for a long while, staring at the documents. He feels the dampness on his forehead and upper lips, and the itching of his back. Behind him, he knows the men are watching; so is Little Mouse, waiting for his order to grind ink.

It never comes.

Sitting in the open carriage, Mingzhi glances around: shops and stalls, alleys and main streets, government offices and temples, the usual busy traffic and crowds. And no scholars. *Where are they? What are they doing now?* He is curious, but relieved too. After the four *jurens* left yesterday, the sight of long plain gowns has begun to agitate him. He thinks they know: the odd one out, the one who didn't sign.

Maybe they have gathered enough signatures. His heart lightens as the horses trot on, and he is glad of his decision to take the ride, to get away from Little Mouse's silent resentment. Mingzhi can read his servant's mind, his desire to get involved generated more by mob emotion than by patriotism. *What does he know?* Mingzhi shakes his head, determined to leave the matter behind.

The weather is glorious, perfect for a walk in the outskirts. Mingzhi asks the driver to head westwards for Xiangshan, the Fragrant Mountain. Along the way, before they enter the desolate suburbs, new buildings mushroom between older blocks. Fresh golden inscriptions on black signboards gleam in the morning sun. The city has never stopped developing, he notices, as if no serious threat has ever occurred, and will never happen. *Maybe they've been over-worried. Maybe the Japanese aren't so daring. Maybe the matter has been sorted. Maybe* . . .

'Never give up Taiwan! Save our homeland!'

A loud cry pierces through the street noises. The carriage is passing by the House of Minnan, a Taiwanese clan. At the doorstep a young scholar breaks down in tears. He is supported by his companions, about thirty of them. Each wears a long white cotton strip around his waist in mourning, grieving in advance for the death of their homeland.

It's really happening.

Mingzhi sighs. His shameful list of 'maybes' is pushed from his mind. Quietly he orders the driver to turn back and returns to the public house.

Early morning, and Mingzhi is in the street. His eyes are red from a night of tossing in bed.

'Hurry up, there's still time!' Little Mouse, yards ahead of him, calls. Smiling, excited.

At a distance Mingzhi sees the scholars swarming out of the House of Xinhui, a clan of Guangdong. *This is the day!* His heart tightens. Seeing the Guangdong *juren* who approached him with the petition, he hurries forward and waves.

'Wait for me!' Breathless, puffing, he rushes the *juren* back inside and signs on the scroll:

CHAI MINGZHI

Thick black ink seeps through the thin paper. The last name in the long list, in humble script but strangely prominent, standing out. Like an unprepared, fresh recruit going into his first battle.

And the battle is on.

It's the day for receiving public appeals; the government office is already packed with commoners nursing petty grievances. The scholars appear, nearly two hundred strong, heading for the front door.

Mingzhi is tailing the group. Ahead of him, Little Mouse turns back occasionally to wave, grinning. Happy to be part of it, proud of his master.

In the street, curious onlookers gather, exchanging speculations.

Clink-clink!

A passing carriage jerks to a halt. The driver noisily pulls the bell and curses incessantly. More carriages and carts are blocked; more ringing and swearing.

'Hey, what're you up to, blocking the traffic?' a guard shouts from the doorstep of the government house.

The cart bells ring louder, the impatient drivers boo, and the bystanders jeer. Some scholars answer, loud or low, in different voices, tones and accents. All these noises blend into a dull drone, filling the air between the buildings that flank the street, amplifying in Mingzhi's ears. His head begins to feel heavy.

In front of him, the scholars march forward, the hems of their gowns flapping ferociously in the northerly spring wind. A flock of inauspicious white crows.

Mingzhi's brows twitch, and he slows down, unsure if he should continue.

He lags further behind.

The group files towards the government house. Thump! The main door is shut tight in a fluster, and the guards stand in a row of four, blocking the entrance.

'Don't make trouble here! Disperse now and go home!'

One of the scholars shouts: 'We're here to submit a petition!'

The guards remain unmoved. The scholars close in, demanding admission.

'Stay where you are!' More warnings from the anxious guards, yet the crowd ignores them and shows no sign of retreating.

'Yes, keep going!'

'Knock the door down!'

'Teach them a lesson, those arrogant men!'

The onlookers cheer, encouraging the scholars, waiting for a crash. *How exciting!* Already, they are bothered by the rumours about the Japanese invasion, and a wonderful free show like this is just perfect for releasing their frustration.

A scholar at the front is shoved aside, but more move forward to take his place. Angry stares confront four pairs of defensive eyes.

The air of tension hangs low, simmering, waiting to explode –

A side door is pushed open. A man walks out, wearing a gown embroidered with a white roc – a fifth-ranking official.

The noises subside. A scholar steps up, holding out the petition.

'Too late for this, young man,' the official says. 'The treaty is signed.' He goes back inside and closes the door behind him.

Signed?

An outburst of hysterical howls rises from the group of Taiwan *juren*s. Already, some have collapsed on the ground, beating their chests, swearing to protect their homeland. Others console them, helping them up. The onlookers peer and point, but are quiet now, leaving only sighs and whispers and the heart-tearing cries to flood the spring air.

Mingzhi retreats; Little Mouse follows closely. Street after street Mingzhi walks, yet the wails of despair follow him, trembling in his ears. He quickens his pace.

WhatcanIdo?Whatdoyouwantmetodo?

A loud voice rumbles in his head, striving to drown out the cries of sorrow. He breaks into a run.

—∾—

More news is circulated: the Emperor's official seal has not yet been set on the treaty, though the details have been agreed.

There is still hope. The scholars run about, spreading the news. More meetings are called, more *juren*s approached. More petitions are signed, brought to the government offices, and rejected, again and again.

—∾—

Mingzhi moves to a quieter corner of the public house, avoiding other scholars. He spends most of the time in his room, reading and writing. Little Mouse stays with him as he has to, but Mingzhi senses that his servant is half-hearted. That his mind is somewhere else, in a place unknown to Mingzhi. It isn't the amount of inkstick Little Mouse has broken that bothers him, but the way he stares with faraway, anxious eyes.

Mingzhi begins to worry.

The results are due tomorrow. Mingzhi decides to pay a visit to the government office to confirm the announcement. The street leading to the office is busy, and the carriage in which Mingzhi and Little Mouse are riding moves slowly.

There are the rumbling sounds of vehicles and hooves, approaching. Dust rising, horses neighing, people shouting. The way is blocked and Mingzhi's carriage is forced to one side. The first cart passes by. The second follows. The third. One after another horses and carriages jostle past. The street is now at a standstill, packed with people and carriages, with more than a thousand scholars inside them.

From far in front a commotion is heard, travelling swiftly among the scholars. Some speak of a fight, and there are rumours of threats to kill the demonstrators. The scholars become anxious, worried about their leaders and angry with the guards. They shout and hit the sides of the carriages. The horses rear in their traces, struggling to free themselves from the confined space. They kick and neigh and the carriages crash into one another.

The carriage Mingzhi sits in is shoved, jerked to one side, and he stumbles off his seat. The horse goes hysterical: shrieking, twisting, leaping. The carriage overturns and Mingzhi falls to the ground. He is now among the many unsettled hooves, the wheels of carriages, the panic-stricken footsteps of the crowd. Sees only hooves and wheels and pairs of legs from beneath the long gowns that rustle in the mess of yellow dust.

'Eldest Grand Young Master!'

He hears Little Mouse, strives to surface from the sea of people flooding over him and get to his feet.

'Eldest Grand Young Master!'

The call now seems to come from a distance away. Mingzhi pushes against the shoulders and chests and backs that are pushing against him, stands on tiptoe and sees only milling heads, frightened horses and upset carriages. Hears Little Mouse's shouts again, gradually fading.

No, come back, don't leave me!

He elbows and squeezes, freeing himself from the trap of the crowd and dodging into an alley. He climbs up a mound and searches the faces beneath him. Still, there's no sign of Little Mouse. People begin to crowd in. Mingzhi turns and runs.

The hem of his long gown beats against his lean body. There are footsteps behind him, running too, as if in pursuit. Mingzhi speeds up, his heart beating fast, his ears burning. One alley ends, another begins, and there are wider streets. Vertical, horizontal, straight or crooked. Mingzhi has lost his bearings; not knowing where he is, and without destination, he lets his trembling legs take him.

He tilts his head up, gasping for air. The spring sun falls full on his face, into his eyes. White, dazzling, blinding. He feels a throbbing behind his eyes.

Everything goes dark.

—∞—

'Eldest Grand Young Master!'

Little Mouse's voice seems to come from far away, sounding vague, unreal. Mingzhi's shoulders are grasped, shaken, and he opens his heavy lids. A face swims before him, familiar, coming into focus: Little Mouse's worried gaze.

Mingzhi feels a soft mattress under him and knows he is safe. He closes his eyes again, this time for a good, deep sleep.

—∞—

Mingzhi's letter to Uncle Liwei describes a failed demonstration by intellectual reformers. The two hundred thousand painful words of appeal are rejected once again. Scholars from all eighteen districts of the country begin to disperse. Some strike their names from the scroll, and the final list secures less than a thousand signatures.

Including mine.

Mingzhi tosses and turns in bed. The events of the day flash in snatches through his mind: the horses and people, shouting and shoving; the crash, his flight, the disorientation. *What will they do with the petition? What if it really reaches the officials' hands with my name on it?*

He shudders, thinking about the announcement of

results tomorrow, and knowing it's too late to retract his endorsement. He pulls the blanket over his head, his eyes wide under the cover.

—∾—

Early morning, and a loud drumming of gongs brings a clamour to the public house. Mingzhi goes to join other scholars in the ground floor. Two messengers swagger in, holding the list of successful Advanced Scholars who will sit the palace exam in ten days' time, and their official notices in red envelopes.

The scholars crowd towards them, impatient. One of the messengers holds up his papers. Mingzhi keeps his head down. A couple of names are called and there are cheers, calls of congratulation. Mingzhi's head drops lower, and –

'Chai Mingzhi.'

Loud in his ears.

He looks up. Little Mouse waves the envelope he has taken from the messenger. Smiling, whooping, approaching him.

The red colour of the envelope fills Mingzhi's eyes. The world before him swims in the red filter.

—∾—

Late at night. Mingzhi closes his book, thinking about the exam tomorrow. *The last one of all.* He knows that regardless of this final result, as a *jinshi* he'll still be assigned a post. The palace exam will only determine his rank and his eligibility to become a Hanlin Academician.

A Hanlin Academician!

The words nearly leap to his lips, as his heart does out of his chest. With one hand over his mouth and the other on his chest, he presses them all down.

He is unsure, though. *Do I really want to be a Hanlin Academician? Or should I just become a mandarin at a regional office that serves people directly? Maybe I won't have to marry Scholar Dai's daughter if I fail the palace exam? Maybe he would prefer a Hanlin Academician for a son-in-law?*

The questions roll over and over in Mingzhi's sea of sleep.

Or sleeplessness.

The night is short and the first streaks of dawn creep up quietly, lining the horizon. Mingzhi sits by the windowsill, gazing out. Red and orange threads crisscross the faraway black screen, thickening, and gradually nudging away all remaining darkness. The world brightens. *It all begins from a tiny speck of light!*

Mingzhi closes his eyes and thanks the Heavenly God for the answer he has been looking for.

Little Mouse is calling: Mingzhi's washing water is ready.

Foreign books! So many of them!

In a shop in Shanghai, locally translated publications fill a corner. Almost a hundred of them, on various subjects: astronomy, the geography and history of far-off lands, Western art, culture and philosophy, and more. Vastly more variety than in Father Terry's collection. Mingzhi browses the shelves: quivering fingers work along the spines, hungry eyes search for his favourites. He yearns to take them all home.

This first trip to Shanghai has proved unexpectedly fruitful. Mingzhi is glad of his decision to travel to Shanghai on the newly built rail track before heading home. He has decided to leave the Imperial City before the results of the palace exam are announced. To him, the wait is over.

And I'll be a mandarin!

The blood rushes to Mingzhi's head and he hears his heartbeat, drumming in his ears. He hurriedly opens a book, buries his face in it, hiding away his daydream. There are maps, huge and detailed. The first contains a general view of oceans and continents with national boundaries, all clearly marked with strange names. Mingzhi notices that China is in one of the continents – Asia – and Britain and France, where Father Terry comes from, in another: Europe. There are others, too: Africa, Australia, North and South America.

So this is the world, and China is only part of it.

The printed page confirms Father Terry's account. The once vague images in Mingzhi's mind now become concrete. He walks his fingers across the map and explores those foreign destinations he has heard of previously.

China – Yellow Sea – East China Sea – South China Sea – Straits of Malacca – Malacca. Imagines, also, the route Father Terry has taken: *England – North Atlantic Sea – Gulf of Guinea – Mozambique Channel – Arabian Sea – Indian Ocean – Bay of Bengal – Straits of Malacca – South China Sea – China.* Such a long journey!

His mind travels with his fingers, and he sees the tropics, coconut trees and monkeys, the forests and mountains. Hears birds singing, beasts howling, as they fight each other noisily –

'Let go! It wasn't me!'

Little Mouse!

On the doorstep Little Mouse's arms have been pinned behind his back by the shop owner. Little Mouse struggles to free himself, but the shop owner, a strong six-footer, tightens his grip.

'Give him his money!'

'I didn't take it!'

'Who else could it be? You're the only person here!'

'Maybe it really wasn't him.'

An awkward accent, a white man, and Mingzhi can't tell his age from his bearded face. In his limited Mandarin he is trying to persuade the shop owner to free Little Mouse. His tongue gets tied in knots, and English words begin to creep in. The shop owner stares at him in puzzlement, then squeezes Little Mouse harder, thinking his precious white customer is angry. Mingzhi approaches them, speaking slowly, assures them of Little Mouse's innocence, and his willingness to compensate for the loss. The white man anxiously shakes his head and gestures.

'No, no, no, you don't have to!' His red head keeps shaking, his hands sway and flash before Mingzhi's eyes. Mingzhi smiles.

The shop owner reluctantly releases Little Mouse, gives him a glare and is glared at in return. He moves to the counter and steps on something, so that his foot twists and he staggers, banging his head against the display cabinet. Little Mouse smiles a that's-the-result-of-what-you-did-to-me smile, but goes to help him up.

On the floor near the counter lies the cause of the trouble, a bundle the size of a fist wrapped in a kerchief.

'There it is!' The white man picks it up and points to a corner of the kerchief. M GRAY. Embroidered in blue thread.

'My name.' His finger pokes at the M. 'Martin. Martin Gray.'

Mingzhi nods and watches Martin pay for his purchase, a scroll of Chinese painting.

Once outside the shop Mingzhi says quietly, in English: 'Thank you . . . for trusting me.'

He hears his own voice: tremulous, unnatural, and feels his cheeks burning.

'You speak English!' Martin slaps Mingzhi's shoulder. 'I'm glad! I'm so glad!'

He laughs, says he is new in town, and had been trying to learn Mandarin from Chinese sailors on the journey from the West. But most of them were illiterate, former peasants driven aboard by poverty. Their spoken language was tinged with strong local dialects from different regions, and they would only laugh at his pronunciation. Now in

Shanghai he feels lost, though he gets privileges in the British Territory.

He's come from far away, like Father Terry!

Mingzhi remembers the illustrations in Father Terry's book, and the world map he has just studied. He admires Martin: a traveller from across the sea. Mingzhi's earlier excitement about his train trip from Beijing to Shanghai suddenly seems nothing in comparison with Martin's journey on an ocean steamer.

Little Mouse is sent to scout for information about the city. Mingzhi chooses a quiet corner in the teahouse, avoiding conspicuous stares. He shares a pot of *o-long* with his new friend and explains the characteristics and properties of a few common types of tea: *o-long* emulsifies fat, *pu'er* cleans up the digestive channel and *longjing* is simply refreshing. Interested, Martin asks occasional questions, orders a couple to taste the difference.

Determined to practise his English, Mingzhi speaks slowly, selects the right words and phrases, and forms articulate sentences. Martin struggles with his halting Mandarin, mixing it up with his own language from time to time. Soon they are able to understand each other's accents, pronunciation and gestures.

Martin is quickly bored by the tediousness of preparing tea, and impatient with taking small sips from a tiny cup. He beckons over the waiter for a bigger cup and gulps down his tea at will. Mingzhi laughs at Martin's bulging cheeks, but the Englishman is unmoved, savouring his mouthful, the sweet aftertaste of *pu'er*.

They study the painting Martin has bought, a pond with

scattered lotus floating on the surface. Mingzhi reads the title aloud: '*Pingshui Xiangfeng*.'

'Literally, it means the meeting of lotus with the water it lives in,' he explains. 'A chance encounter . . .'

'Like you and I,' Martin laughs. He runs his fingers over the calligraphy, amazed by the meaning contained in only four characters. He holds an imaginary brush between his fingers and draws in the air, imitating the words on the painting. His arm swings in big movements. Every stroke is accomplished with a whizzing sound as of strength. Mingzhi's jaw begins to hurt. *Never have I laughed so much!* Martin sighs, says he wishes he could really write. He urges Mingzhi to be his teacher. Mingzhi can only smile, knowing that this is unlikely: he will return home soon. *And a different life will begin.* For seconds his mind turns blank, unable to imagine what lies ahead.

'Stop frowning! You do it all the time, even when you're laughing.'

Do I? Mingzhi hurriedly feels his brow with his fingers. Martin's wicked laughter rings in his ears. Mingzhi gives his playful friend a stare but bursts into laughter, too.

There are whispers and curious stares directed at this supposed-to-be quiet corner of the teahouse. There a black and a red head sway in unison, dark eyes meeting amber ones, bodies shaking, their laughter, one shy and soft, the other bold and loud, blending into an awkward concoction. Unstoppable. Unstoppable.

Little Mouse returns to their rescue. With a sketch of the city in hand and a few destinations in mind, they set off.

—~—

They trudge through the main streets and side alleys, gardens and temples, the ports and shores of Shanghai. Talking, admiring the views, learning each other's language. Their walks are filled with Martin's careless laughter and blunt questions, and Mingzhi's gentle and in-depth explanations of food and drink, people and clothes, buildings and the craftwork on their eaves, doorposts and the signboards above the doors.

Detailed answers in response to Martin's unquenchable curiosity.

~

Midday, and they are having lunch in a public house. Martin struggles to pick up a piece of braised chicken wing with his chopsticks.

'Why do people here – why do you wear a plait and half-shave your head?'

Mingzhi nearly coughs out his mouthful of rice. He glances around. No stares or whispers. And he sighs with relief, realizing Martin has been speaking in English.

'Do you like wearing your hair this way? It must be unpleasant!'

Mingzhi puts his finger to his lips and *shs* Martin to keep quiet.

'I don't understand. Why do you wear it if you don't like it? Might as well cut it off!' Martin slams down the chopsticks and takes the chicken wing with his hand.

Watching him, Mingzhi thinks about his words and their implicit meaning: *You don't have to do anything against your will.*

Don't I?

Don't we?

Around him, his fellow-countrymen, with plaits hanging down their backs or round their necks, are eating and chatting and laughing. Too busy even to think about the question. Mingzhi's own bundle of hair suddenly feels heavy behind him, dragging at the back of his head like a boulder. Pulling him down.

~

Mingzhi begins to learn about Martin by snatches. That his friend has just arrived. That he works for a British trading company, sourcing merchandise for trade. That his parents – both teachers – want him to be a teacher, too, if not a professor, and resent his choice of career. For travelling so far.

'Yet you came?'

'It's my choice. Whatever I do, they respect my decision.'

Mingzhi gazes at his friend. He imagines his grandfather's response if he were to say no to his arrangements.

'Travel is my aim. Work is only an excuse.' Martin's voice echoes in the narrow alley. 'I like to feel free, to be able to travel to different places. Places I've never been before. This job is good, allows me to do just that.'

Mingzhi is puzzled. Never has he met anyone who is so open about what they feel. *Not Mother, not Uncle Liwei, and certainly not Grandpa.*

'What about you? What're you going to do?'

Mingzhi hesitates, says he wishes to be a mandarin.

'A mandarin? With the feather-tailed hat and heavy gown? Are you sure?'

Am I sure? The question is too sudden and surprising. Mingzhi's mind wanders, as do his legs, treading blindly on the uneven ground.

'Ouch!' He steps in a puddle and loses his footing.

Clink! Clink!

'Look out!'

Martin pulls Mingzhi up to one side, escaping a bicycle that has just blundered past. The rider turns and glares at him, cursing and swearing over his shoulder. His back pinned to the wall, Mingzhi sees Martin's body before him, fencing him from the glare and the curses. And the near accident, of course. Tall and strong and familiar. Like Uncle Liwei's stout leg in Mingzhi's childhood incident with the snake.

—~—

'There's a French Territory, too,' Little Mouse grumbles. 'There're places I'm not allowed in. You, too. Us, Chinese.'

Mingzhi notices a mixture of confusion and anger in Little Mouse's eyes.

'It's our country, our land, isn't it?

For the first time Mingzhi feels tongue-tied in front of his servant.

—~—

A week passes. The new friends say their goodbyes: Martin stays in Shanghai, as he must report to work the next day, while Mingzhi must go back to Plum Blossom Village.

Martin's waving figure, tall and lean, shrinks in the yellow dust as Mingzhi's carriage pulls away. Mingzhi knows it is impossible for them to meet again. He stares at the distant speck of movement, recalls their first meeting, the laughter they shared, the places they visited together, the painting they both admired. Thinks about the lotus and the water, the sentence cut short by Martin: a chance encounter . . . which usually doesn't last long. Eventually, the lotus has to leave the pond, the water it lives in.

Yes, like you and me.

In the yellow dust, he sees also the eyes of his long-lost friend, Little Sparrow: empty, helpless, staring at him.

My friends.

His stomach feels sour, and he knows this journey home will be unbearably long.

—～—

Home. A feast is ready. Strings of firecrackers are hung by the doorpost. More candles and joss sticks are lit in the ancestral hall. And in the central hall, there is a scroll with an imperial stamp laid on a piece of yellow silk on a silver tray, along with the costume that comes with it: silky green, embroidered with a quail in the middle, front and back. The symbol of an eighth-ranking official.

All awaiting the new mandarin.

Twelve

Weeds have grown wild around Old Scholar Yan's grave. Creepers crawl high, declaring their territory over the top of the tombstone. *My teacher.* Mingzhi feels a twinge of guilt. *A man of his qualities shouldn't be left unattended.* He makes a mental note: to arrange for a quarterly clean-up once he is in office.

With bare hands he and Little Mouse struggle to pull off the grass and vines. Hard soil loosens. Earthworms spring up from their broken homes. Ants run wild, disoriented. Mingzhi feels sorry for them, tries to avoid their paths.

Go somewhere else. Find a better place for your new home.

Little Mouse sets out white candles and burns silver paper. Hungry flames gobble up the comfort-money like the money-crazed Cowhead and Horseface guards in the netherworld. Flakes of soot and ash drift languidly in the solemn air. *Hope this will buy you a better afterlife.*

Mingzhi lights joss sticks, pours out a cup full of Old Scholar Yan's favourite *huadiao.*

To my teacher.

He pours the wine over the grave, then kowtows on all fours. On the ground before him, an ant stops at the dark patch of wet soil, as if sipping at it, slowly, gracefully. As though the wine was meant for it and it is enjoying the treat. Mingzhi watches until the little ant has had enough and walks away. He wonders if it is belching, as Old Scholar Yan always did after drinking wine.

Master Chai has more important things to do than visit Old Scholar Yan's grave. He orders Butler Feng to make arrangements: Mingzhi's government office in Lixing Town is to be more comfortable than the district office at Pindong Town, if not bigger, and the signboard more prominent.

Still a rank lower than Mandarin Liu. The old man's chest tightens. He thinks his grandson should have done better, should have secured the provincial post if not become a Hanlin Academician. Should have been a higher-ranking official than Mandarin Liu. He doesn't understand how Mingzhi could have failed his palace exam. *Did I not pray hard enough?* He scratches his head, picks his ears, yet no answer emerges either way.

Anyway, a mandarin is still a mandarin. And the first from Plum Blossom Village! Chin up, back straightened, Master Chai grins, smoothing his goatee. Feeling proud. He thinks about the official authority bestowed on his grandson as he gazes at the flying dragons on the pillars, their bloody, wide-open mouths. So wide, as if they're waiting for something – or someone – to wolf down.

The old brain moves fast, so preoccupied that it loses its usual capacity for detecting even the slightest of changes in the mansion. First a pair of exquisitely crafted ivory chopsticks is gone unnoticed. Then another. And another. Later a jade wine cup. As though they have grown tired of hiding in the cabinet and decided to sneak out. For a walk. A breath of fresh air. And then decided not to return.

~

Da Niang has been busy for hours, deciding on the design, cutting material, sewing the pieces together to make a cotton-filled cushion. She has her eyes on the needlework in her hands; yet her mind is in the east court. The farewell dinner for Mingzhi, with all the Chai men. *My son. He'll be gone tomorrow.* There is *something* wandering inside her. She gulps a mouthful of tea, trying to suppress the strange feeling, but is surprised to find the tea bitter. She shakes the cup lightly and takes a closer look. Light, sodden leaves drift in the pale yellow-green water, like the *something* inside her. Not coming up, not settling down, just hanging there, right in the pit of her stomach.

I should be happy. She shakes her head, dabs at the wet corners of her eyes with her sleeves. Remembers how she has been praying for this day, for her son to escape the dark shadow brooding over the mansion. The shadow that she knows she will never be able to shake off. *But he will, my son.* She stares at the dark blue sky outside the open window, and her mind follows the clump of heavy clouds that is shifting eastwards.

Over to the east court.

The central hall.

The opening toast by the Master of the House breaks the awkward silence. In high spirits, Master Chai downs his wine and asks for more. A mandarin without a wife doesn't seem proper, he says, assuring Mingzhi he will make all the necessary arrangements. Mingzhi keeps his head low and fiddles with the big chicken drumstick in his bowl, deposited there by Likang. Eager to get back to his comforting magic-puffs-for-dessert, Likang wolfs down his food in quick, large bites, and chokes, coughing uncontrollably. Liwei massages his brother's chest, while Master Chai frowns, annoyed at Likang for spoiling the dinner. The familiar awkward silence slips back through the creases between the old man's eyebrows, then sits triumphantly among the Chai men of three generations.

Mingzhi pours a cup of tea for his father, holding it for him as he takes small sips. Uncle Liwei pats Mingzhi's shoulder, a silent approval.

Mingyuan, who has been quiet, seizes his opportunity, proposing a toast to Mingzhi, congratulating him. Surprised, Mingzhi raises his cup, thinking that his half-brother has finally decided to make it up. Mingyuan has been behaving unusually well lately: coming home more often, helping his grandfather and Uncle Liwei with their paperwork. Because Liwei indeed needs a hand, and because Mingyuan is meticulous with numbers, the earlier prohibition is forgotten. They let him. Beginning with simple entries of debt repayments, rental and harvest revenues, Mingyuan works to gain Liwei's appreciation. A relief in his uncle's busy routine.

And now, Mingyuan has helped to light up this evening.

There is a rare smile on Mingzhi's face and his grandfather notices. He smiles, too, admiring the harmonious picture before him. His grandsons: one calm and steady, the other quick-witted. He smooths his goatee, sitting back, feeling pleased. *A night like this should be celebrated with good wine.* He sends the maid for an urn of hundred-year-old wine from the larder.

We'll drink together, grandfather, sons and grandsons.

Under the heavy cloud that shadows the mansion.

In Pindong Town, however, the moon hangs high in the clear sky. Mandarin Liu relaxes in his bed and is surprised at its unusual softness and warmth.

Only an eighth-ranking official, he snorts, *in a town and district smaller than Pindong!* His worries ebb away, and he stacks up his pillows, willing a good night's sleep such as he has not had since the spring exam began. *Not any more.* He smiles in his dreams, where piles of silver come rumbling onto his doorstep. White, flashing. Blinding him to the darkness looming beyond.

—w—

From the moving carriage, Mingzhi turns to the waving crowd in front of the mansion. He cranes his neck and finds his mother among the many heads, knows she is tiptoeing on her bound feet to catch a glimpse of him. Mingzhi notices her pale face, contracted brow, tear-filled eyes. Still, she is smiling. Mother, my only worry. He grasps the sides of his seat and his fingers sink into the soft cushion Da Niang sewed overnight for his long trip to Lixing Town. He remembers his mother's sunken eyes as she pressed the cushion into his hands earlier this morning.

'This will make your journey more comfortable.' Da Niang brushed off stray threads from the patchwork cover, whispered for her son to take care.

'You've packed your chess set to take with you, I suppose.' She hesitated. Mingzhi nodded, watching her tremulous lips. Waiting.

'Remember the proverb?'

'*Yinshui Siyuan*? I know, Mother. I'll never forget my roots.'

'You . . . keep it in mind, son. Keep it in mind, no matter where you are, no matter what happens.'

Thinking back, Mingzhi feels Da Niang had more to tell him. *What about?* The Chai clan, the mansion, his mother and his father. These are his origins. *What else do I miss?* He now regrets not spending more time with her, and promises himself to make it up next time. Mingzhi waves at the now blurred figures and strains his eyes, but Da Niang is no longer in sight.

The mansion keeps shrinking as the horses trot ahead. Mingzhi watches as the crowd withdraws and the main door closes.

Thump.

Like the end of a chapter.

Mingzhi rights his posture, eyes staring straight ahead, his back turned on the confining walls of his early years. Soon the carriage will ride past the fields of poppies he hates, the river that transports the blight to other lands, and then he will be out of the valley.

Out of Plum Blossom Village.

Matchmaker Mama Zhang is sent again to Imperial Scholar Dai, this time to propose a date for the Big Day.

Days pass. Weeks. A month. Mama Zhang returns, head bowed, shamefaced, quiet. An unsuccessful mission, a regrettable blot on her professional life as a go-between: she didn't even get to see Scholar Dai. The Imperial City is boiling with news about the Japanese, she says. The greedy dwarves. Stretching their tentacles out to the Heavenly Son's head, forcing a treaty for the Liaodong peninsula in southern Manchuria and Taiwan. And now, the Taiwanese have declared their independence and sworn to fight the invaders. The Forbidden City is locked in emergency meetings day and night. The Emperor and his ministers and all the Hanlin Academicians, including Scholar Dai.

Finding her scapegoat, Mama Zhang regains her voice, blames the chaos for her failed task. Blames Emperor Meiji from the Land of the Rising Sun, of course, and even Russia, Germany and France, who have intervened, trying to stop the Japanese. This further complicates an already complicated situation.

What bad timing.

Master Chai sits back, thinking.

'Now, can I have my allowance, please?'

Mama Zhang's high-pitched tones pierce Master Chai's thoughts. Master Chai raises his eyes to the flabby face with its fleshy smile. Thump! The brass stick trembles in the old man's hand, and Mama Zhang knows the answer to her question. She pouts, closes her fan and sneaks away.

~

Had Mama Zhang been smart enough, she would have come to the right person for her reward.

Mingzhi.

What perfect timing!

The news about the unsuccessful wedding arrangement comes on Mingzhi's first day in office. *I can now devote my time fully to my job without distractions!* In his room Mingzhi smooths his gown as he gazes at his reflection in the mirror. His fingers linger on the pure silk material, the folds and joints, the collar, sleeves and hems, the embroidery in the middle. *The quail.* He touches the thread lines, the rounded head and body, the feathers, legs and claws. The tip of the beak, where he stops. No cross-threads. No messing-up of colours. A fine piece of workmanship. Impeccable. Impeccable.

And I shall never defile it in any way, Mingzhi promises himself.

Little Mouse brings Mingzhi his hat and helps him put it on. 'They're waiting, Master.'

Mingzhi's heart pounds.

I'm the Master, the Mandarin!

He smooths his gown again, takes a deep breath and walks into *his* office.

Thirteen

At first Mingzhi runs his office like any other government official: takes action in response to complaints filed by the people, serving as a local and district magistrate. Punishes criminals for their misdeeds and compensates the victims. He is scrupulous: listening attentively, collecting statements from both sides, gathering evidence, demanding material proof whenever appropriate. Taking time to digest all the information, thinking it through long and hard before the verdict.

There has been gossip:

'How old do you think he is? Looks no more than twenty to me.'

'A young chick, really, not a bristle on his chin.'

'Is he up to the job?'

'I doubt it. I give him three months. Bet he'll run scared to his darling mummy!'

'That's too long! I'd say a month.'

Mingzhi remains unmoved. *I'll prove you wrong.* He does his job, working long hours, making careful decisions.

In between the scrolls of complaints, counter-complaints and appeals, there are occasional red goodwill-envelopes, sneaked in by the complainers or defendants. Mingzhi pushes them away, and will only receive papers without unlawful attachments. He spells this rule out to his assistants and guards. Offenders will be severely punished.

No more extra income!

His staff grumble, complaining behind his back. The new mandarin hears about their grievances, tells himself to be patient. *Sooner or later they'll know it's to the benefit of all.* He treats his subordinates well, caring not only for them but also their families, especially the weak and aged. Buys them nourishing herbs and tonics, which gradually win their hearts and sweeten their tongues.

There'll be no whipping in his court, Mingzhi decides. Only jail sentences and community labour work: repairing and building embankments and roads, clearing drainage, helping out in the fields.

The people are surprised, unaccustomed to change. But they welcome the new moves, though some express their doubts, wondering if these things can be sustained.

Time will tell. Mingzhi is confident.

Preferring a lively garden to a barren courtyard, Mingzhi gets workers to turn the vacant land outside his room into a luxuriant green space. Little Mouse is given his task: to supervise the builders and gardeners. The instructions he has are simple: a pond is a must, and there must be beds of jasmine and bamboo. *And carp in the water, with lotus and lily for shelter.* Little Mouse knows instantly what's needed.

Soon, an ornamental garden takes shape. Trim and self-contained. With a small yet elegant pavilion in one corner, and in another, a shallow pool where a dense clump of bamboo rustles on windy days. And willows sway, scattering the water and the lawn with slivers of catkin. On one side of the pavilion, stalks of jasmine stand quietly, white blossoms smiling at the blue sky against the green background.

After retreating from the office in the evening, Mingzhi always sits in the pavilion, listening to the tiny movements of the red carp: stirring the water as they dart and flee, chasing and escaping from one another. Blowing bubbles. Pop-pop-pop. Pop-pop-pop. The familiar sounds he enjoyed on his first stay away from home. His first taste of freedom. His Taohua Yuan. *It's back again, my Little Hut of Leaping Fishes.*

The refreshing smell of jasmine soothes him, though Mingzhi sometimes feels a tiny twinge in his chest as he thinks about the person who carries the flower's name. He takes a deep breath. Hold it. Hold it. Before slowly letting it out.

Sometimes Mingzhi prefers the stump by the bamboo clump, sitting there for long hours. Watching the fishes mostly, peeping at the shy ones under the umbrella-leaves of lotus though he never disturbs them. But sometimes, Little Mouse finds his master fiddling with a leaf of bamboo, fashioning it into a flute and then playing it. Strange notes follow: trembling, sad, unfamiliar. And he wonders where his quiet master has learned about the magic and the music.

—~—

There are no major cases to attend to in a small town like Lixing. *What more can I do?* Mingzhi thinks hard, drafts proposals but finds them impractical and scrunches them up. He tries again, and more sheets of paper are tossed away. And he realizes it is impossible to create something out of nothing.

He begins to plan his trips.

—∾—

'The mandarin is coming!'

Peasants in remote villages exchange the news, disbelieve. *Never has a mandarin come this far!* Some dismiss the rumour instantly, thinking it absurd. A pinch of spice to their dawn-to-the-fields-and-dusk-to-bed everyday life.

But the mandarin does come, in his official sedan and with a humble retinue of two, as well as Little Mouse. Meeting the villagers, asking their needs, discussing problems. The image of a friendly mandarin is established: soft-spoken, understanding, polite.

Never before, never before.

The elders smile toothless smiles, their faces crumpled and their eyes stretched into slits, hidden beneath heavy lids. They respect the young mandarin, who respects them, like him and trust him. They take their grandchildren in their arms, whispering hopes for the future. *Better late than never.* They smooth the children's mousy heads with their scrawny fingers, and the young ones giggle and pull themselves away.

They wait.

It isn't a long wait. They cheer when the order comes.

Mingzhi has worked it out: a school for every village. The budget is tight and resources scarce. Mingzhi tries his best, drafting careful, practical plans. Local villagers are organized to work together, to repair and refurbish abandoned outhouses and shacks. The facilities are basic: four walls and a roof for shelter to begin with, and some even without wooden benches. For a start, something is better than nothing.

Literate men from the villages, if there are any, are deployed. A couple of hours' break from working in the field is good enough for the children to learn at least how to write their names. Mingzhi also makes contact with his former classmates at the school in Pindong Town, inviting them to join his teaching force. In his letters Mingzhi explains his long-term plan of improving the life of ordinary people, a silent reformation. And because he has the support of Head Teacher Scholar Ning, the response is overwhelming. Positions are filled immediately. New teachers in crude shacks with barefoot children reciting Confucius and Laozi. Heads swaying, voices raised, spirits high. Outside, the elders squat in the shade and listen, nodding and grinning and swaying their heads, too. And praise their mandarin.

For the towns and villages that already have schools, Mingzhi has other thoughts. The model of the reformist intellectuals' Society for the Study of National Rejuvenation is adopted. Study groups are formed, provided with small collections of texts on various subjects. Through Father Terry's contacts, Mingzhi manages to get a supply of books from the West. There are regular guided discussions led by experienced scholars. Mingzhi tries to tone down these activities, though, to prevent them becoming too conspicuous. As long as there is steady progress, he doesn't mind if it is slow.

~

Hundreds of miles away in Pindong Town, Mandarin Liu is content with his weekly circuit of the main streets in his comfortable official sedan, guarded by a retinue of eight, who hit the gongs and hoo-ha along, shouting for pedestrians and carts and horses to give way.

Mandarin Liu's mind wanders as the sedan sways forward. His brows are knitted tight. Recent pressure from the Governor – who is himself pressured by Central Government – has put him in a predicament. Money. That's their demand. There is a gigantic hole in the treasury of the Forbidden City, dug up by foreign hands. The hands that brought in opium in hundreds of thousands of chests. That drafted and signed the infamous treaties, asking not only for land but also for indemnities. That hole has to be filled. Since the only means of income is taxation, targets are set for the provinces and the districts under the officials' charge.

How am I going to meet my target?

Certainly not from Mandarin Liu's own pocket, bulging with money from other people's pockets. He lays his hands on his paunch, rubbing it in a circular motion, as if trying to lure something out of it. Fat. Or silver. Or a perfect solution.

The team hoo-ha ahead.

At the corner of a street a man is pushed to the ground. A

loud cry. Two burly men rush after him. Slap and punch and kick. More cries follow, and their defenceless target rolls in the road, his scholar's gown now smudged and dusty.

'Clear your debts or you know what you're getting!' one of the men shouts as he spits on his prey.

Gong! Gong! Gong!

The men look up and stop at once. Too late. The parade has turned the corner and the bearers collide with them. The sedan jolts to a sudden halt and inside, Mandarin Liu is flung from his seat; his head strikes the side post.

What's going on? Mandarin Liu clutches his head and shrugs off his pale-faced guards who crowd forward to check their master's condition.

One badly beaten scholar and two surly-looking men, typical bullies.

And they gave me this lump on my head!

'Take those thugs away!' Mandarin Liu roars, angry fingers pointing at the big men.

Still groaning, as he gets to his feet, the victim raises his head and nods gratefully at his saviour.

Mingyuan.

And Mandarin Liu recognizes him.

He glances at Mingyuan, then at his captives, knowing he has some questioning to do when he gets back to his office. He sits back and rubs his stomach again. Wonders if he has indeed rubbed something out of it.

Autumn in the eastern island across the strait is filled with the stink of gunpowder, the trotting of heavy boots, and loud, brutal shouts. And the louder cries of anger, fear and pain that come in response. Red-hot blood spatters onto withering leaves, turning cold, darkening as it coagulates in the September wind. The season ends with the end of a newly independent nation, over which a white flag with a huge spot of fresh blood now flies, high enough for all eyes to see. The evil eyes of the red- or golden-haired or flowery-flagged devils – the British, Russians and Americans.

The walls of the Forbidden City tremble beneath their covetous stares.

Across the strait in the inner mainland, Master Chai is celebrating another bumper harvest. Quietly. And he orders the entire mansion to keep quiet too. No news is to go beyond the walls, he warns, as he knows how risky it will be if word of his prosperity reaches Mandarin Liu. More than once Mandarin Liu has tried to push Master Chai into contributing to his tax target. And more than once the old man has managed to dodge his demands with the excuse of a poor harvest.

Shh, shh. Shh, shh.

Master Chai sips his tea. *I should make good use of the extra money.* He takes another look at the profits, trying to decide if he should hoard them for Mingzhi's wedding or purchase more lands, plant more poppies.

'Yes, definitely more lands!' he blurts out.

Oops. He covers his mouth with one hand and looks around, glad that he is all by himself.

Shh, shh. Shh, shh.

Yet the orders arrive: one official, with a district government seal on it; the other private, words from the messenger. The former demands ten per cent of the opium revenue for tax, with an unspoken understanding that this is in addition to the previously agreed portion for Mandarin Liu. The latter is more of a warning: the mandarin wants no more tricks from Master Chai.

Liwei sneaks out after reading the letter to his father, who snatches it, crumples it up and tosses it away. *A cunning fox he is, and a cold-blooded one.* Master Chai makes a quick mental calculation and works out a rough figure. There is a tic on his face. The servant girl drifts to a hidden corner, promising herself she will re-emerge only in response to a direct order. It doesn't come, as her master is too engrossed in his thoughts. Too busy even to have a sip of tea.

As if he is here, as if he knows exactly what's in my hoard, exactly when to deal me a blow.

Master Chai bangs the armrest, furious that Mandarin Liu has launched his attack before he does.

Your time will come, I swear it.

Master Chai grits his teeth so hard that angry veins squirm under the layer of loose skin on his neck.

—∞—

Mingzhi wakes in the middle of the night. His eyes open on the fine gauze surrounding his bed, streaked with soft moonlight. Blurred, unreal. *Where am I?* The faintly lit chiffon envelops him like a thin layer of smoke. He stares through it at a familiar scene: a smoke-shrouded figure.

Mother.

Mingzhi gets up and paces the room. It has been five months since he took up his appointment. Five months away from the mansion. This is his world now, he knows, and he likes his job. But something is missing. Something.

Restless ants crawl through his sleepless mind, and he longs for a game of chess.

In the south court of Chai Mansion, a chess set is laid out on the table. The pieces have taken their positions, ready for battle. For Liwei to sound the horn and give his commands. Liwei is the commander of both sides: challenger and defender. Playing his lonely game of chess, planning his attacks and counter moves, deciding who shall win. But everything is quiet tonight. There is no sign of Liwei. Not in the hall, his room, or the courtyard.

It is a breezy night and the mansion sleeps soundly. There are occasional hoots of owls from the western hills. Lonely cries break through the monotonous chirping and buzzing of insects, disrupting the seeming tranquillity. Like reminders, that activity never ceases under the amorphous smokescreen of darkness. It brews, surreptitiously, taking full advantage of the night.

Under the smokescreen of darkness, the two-thousand-year-old Confucianism that rules everyday life – pronouncing on what is right and wrong, what may be done and what may not – is forgotten. Eyes are blinded, as are minds, and so the heart takes charge.

Quietly. Quietly.

Likang has been bed-bound for months, by illness this time. His chronic coughing has grown worse. The intervals between bouts of coughing become shorter, and he is breathless, wheezing all day. His room is now a popular visiting place for doctors from Plum Blossom Village to Pindong Town, who have issued numerous prescriptions. It is an unspoken fact among the servants in the mansion that Likang drinks herbal medicine as if he were drinking tea. And that he only drinks half of the dark, bitter, strong-smelling remedies, as he prefers opium, which assuages his pain.

A couple of puffs, then he relaxes, until the next fit begins, and he'll take another sip of herbal remedy. On good days he manages to keep it down, with the help of Da Niang, who rubs his chest or back. On bad days, the dark liquid surges in the pit of his stomach, then rises in his throat, and he coughs ferociously. In the midst of his fit he always asks for his pipe, struggles to take a couple of puffs, then relaxes again.

The pattern repeats itself.

Mingzhi pays occasional visits to remote villages, bringing with him rice and flour and sugar. He never has enough: they are finished long before he reaches the most distant quarters. He can ration the food, he knows, but it is painful for him to see the outstretched hands and desperate eyes. And the disappointment that follows rejection.

Too many mouths to feed, too little to feed them. And the number of mouths keeps increasing, at a rate that far outstrips the paddy harvest. In the fields men with protruding ribs plod on. At home women make watery porridge out of carefully rationed rice. Children with jaundiced faces munch twigs to quench their hunger, murmuring listlessly after their teacher in their shack-for-classroom. Older children are taken from class to help in the fields. An extra pair of hands is more useful than an open mouth.

Mingzhi thinks about his grandfather's lands. Thinks about the old days of planting at least one season of paddy. *If I could only have half of those crops for my people.* He can buy rice brought in by the British from their colonies in the south-east. He has learned about it from his short stay in the Imperial City. *But where can I find the money?*

Mingzhi sits in his pavilion. For the first time he doesn't hear the fishes, their bubble-blowing.

FOURTEEN

The Provincial Capital is as busy as ever. Mingzhi walks out of the Governor's office and enters his carriage, wordless. Little Mouse gestures for the driver to leave. The carriage makes slow progress in the bustling street, much to Little Mouse's delight. *So much to see!* There is a shop displaying square wooden boxes on stands, each with a round glass in front and a piece of black cloth at the back. *What are those for?* He glances up. The characters on the signboard stare blankly back at him like strangers, and at the door, the unbelievably clear black-and-white portraits of some foreign devils in strange suits seem to be laughing at him. Little Mouse turns to his literate and knowledgeable master for help but finds him sitting still, frowning.

Mingzhi came to ask the Governor for funds. He was kept waiting in an empty room. When the Governor finally sent for him, Mingzhi tried to explain about the food shortages. The Governor brushed him away. 'Don't you know how to make money for yourself? All mandarins do!'

And now in his carriage, Mingzhi pictures the *look* that

accompanied those words: *Asking me for money? How stupid you are!* Of course he knows how other mandarins – like Mandarin Liu – make their money. *No, I will never do that.* He squeezes the cushion under him until the cotton turns into sweat-sodden lumps.

The traffic grinds to a halt. There is a commotion in the street, from where angry shouts are heard. The driver prepares to shout for the crowd to 'Give way to the Mandarin!' but Mingzhi stops him. The noises get louder, seething in Mingzhi's troubled mind. Mingzhi stirs in his seat, recalling the proverb: 'Disaster never strikes just once.' *So I'm in a run of bad luck just now and everything is against me.*

There is a familiar voice, strange intonations, cutting across the noise currents.

Martin? Impossible.

Mingzhi shakes his head, until Little Mouse shouts: 'It's him, the red-haired devil!'

Martin touches Mingzhi's gown, feels the material and the embroidered quail, and is amazed.

'Hey! I have a mandarin for a friend!' He pours a cup of tea and bows, holding it up for Mingzhi in pretended reverence: 'Your Excellency.'

His mandarin friend takes the tea. He has been restraining his smile with such an effort that his face turns red and contorts. One touch and it will explode. He glances at Martin's equally awkward expression, the *touch* that ignites the long-awaited burst of laughter from the two friends. One loud and careless, the other a soft chuckle.

Mingzhi instantly covers his mouth with his hand and

looks around. It's a quiet day and the teahouse inside the garden is quiet, too. They are sitting in a pavilion that extends to the lake. A booth reserved exclusively for the guests of dignitaries.

Martin hisses out the remaining laughter bugs and holds up his tea, this time to thank Mingzhi for rescuing him from the angry crowd. He shakes his head and smiles a waggish smile, recalling the episode. Says he had come to source a local speciality, something 'exclusive and exquisite', his boss specified. At the marketplace he was attracted to some porcelain on display: pots, dishes, bowls, vases. Fine craftsmanship, plain or painted with flowers or plants, scenery or people and activities, or simply calligraphy or designs.

'Good God! You really should see it!' Martin's eyes sparkle, his voice rises and he speaks faster. How he had grabbed a vase and approached the vendor. How he had leant across the display table full of the precious porcelain, asking about the factories, the suppliers. How the man had shaken his head and kept retreating. And how Martin, anxious to make himself clear, kept pressing forward, until –

Ping-pang! The pots and dishes and bowls and vases clink-clanged to the ground, save the one in Martin's eager grip.

So came the shouts and cries: the unfortunate vendor pushing and punching and demanding compensation, supported by other stall owners.

Then came Mingzhi the mandarin, who bought the disastrous red-haired devil out of the disaster.

Mingzhi imagines Martin speaking to the vendor in his strange, halting Mandarin, red-faced, sweat-sodden in the southern heat, excited veins green-purple against his translucent skin, hands and fingers flying all over the place. 'The foreign devil is threatening me, he's lunging at me!' must have been the thought in the poor vendor's mind. Mingzhi chuckles.

'Hey, you're laughing at me!'

Martin gives the mandarin a gentle blow.

'Ouch!' Mingzhi rubs his shoulder. He nudges his friend's arm in protest. Martin dodges, his smile as bright as the glittering lake behind him. *Good. Mandarin or not, things are just as they were before.* Mingzhi takes slow sips of tea, lets the bittersweet aftertaste linger on his tongue.

Soft whispers and girlish giggles waft through the afternoon breeze. A light boat ruffles the water. Two figures. Moving, approaching. Gradually becoming clearer.

Jasmine. And the servant girl. Apparently taking a leisure trip in the Provincial Capital.

Mingzhi's heart races. A hand on her forehead shielding the midday glare, she glances around, admiring the scenery, while the other girl rows the boat. Jasmine lets her eyes run from the distant hills and mountains to the temple on a rise. Then the pavilion on the lake.

She sees him.

And he sees puzzlement in her gaze. She doesn't flinch, though, staring straight at him. *The shy young man, now a mandarin.* She drops her hand and smiles, squinting in the sunlight. *Well done.* Mingzhi feels his face burning.

'What is it?' Martin, who has been watching Mingzhi, turns to the lake and sees the girls. The bashful Jasmine. Head down, she hurriedly helps her servant to make a right-about-turn and row the boat away. Mingzhi's gaze follows. He hardly hears Martin.

'Hey, you like her, don't you?'

Mingzhi looks away, busying himself with pouring tea. He spills it and wets his gown, like an inexperienced thief who has been caught on his first outing.

Martin smiles: 'I'm not surprised. She seems like a nice girl. So why wait?'

Mingzhi, face still red, shakes his head and snaps: 'Never mention this again, please!'

'I don't understand. It's perfectly natural –'

'You will never understand.' Mingzhi sinks into his chair. He stares at the vase that Martin salvaged earlier and placed on the table. Court women in the splendid costumes of the Tang Dynasty dance to a house full of guests. Detailed drawing, fine colouring. He imagines how Jasmine would look in those dresses. A celestial goddess drifting in the clouds, on the water, throwing her long flowing sleeves, turning, twisting her tiny waist gracefully.

'My boss will go crazy when he sees this!'

Gone is the goddess, back to the real world.

Mingzhi watches Martin running his fingertips over the outlines: the clothes, the facial expressions of the various characters, the beams, furniture and floor of the court.

'These things would sell like hot cakes back home.'

Porcelain?

A quick movement and the vase is in Mingzhi's hand before his friend can work out what happened. He checks the bottom: Made in Lixing. He looks up and smiles his brightest smile of the day.

—

The old craftsman, already well known for his skill, runs his pottery from home. He is the potter and painter, his wife the kiln keeper, and his son sells whatever they produce. The excellent quality of the products means they fetch a good price in the Provincial Capital, but the family hardly makes ends meet. The porcelain takes time to turn out and there is never much left after paying the hooligans for *protection*.

You can do better, the mandarin tells them. He gets workers to build a bigger kiln, gathers a team of painters and potters, and appoints the craftsman and his wife as trainers and supervisors. They are to ensure high standards of quality are met. Martin is asked to guide the vendor from the marketplace to set up accounts. Old enemies sit side by side, talking with the aid of sketches and gestures.

The first batch is removed from the kiln, loaded into carts, put on a ship.

And there are a second, a third, and many more shipments to come.

While the old craftsman is still wondering who – thousands of miles away – can be using his dishes and bowls, pots and vases, and how they are being used, the supply of rice and flour and sugar begins to reach the distant villages.

—

Mingzhi tries but is unable to get the right pronunciation of MARTIN out of Little Mouse. As if his tongue simply refuses to cooperate, getting twisted in the R of MAR, then tangled with the T that follows. His master gives up, does not understand why Little Mouse has no problem at all saying *er*, goose, and *ting*, pavilion. He thinks Little Mouse's inability to utter Martin's name has shied him into a corner, keeping a distance from the Englishman when he visits.

He tolerates Little Mouse referring to Martin as the red-haired devil.

—∾—

The news arrives in the shrieking December wind: the Society for the Study of National Rejuvenation has been banned. The Forbidden City has forbidden reformist activities by intellectuals under the banner of study groups.

Mingzhi tells his groups to be more careful. He doesn't close them down, though, thinking that they are safe here in small towns. A good distance away, not only from the Imperial City, but also from the Provincial Capital.

Stay quiet, very quiet, he says.

His gentle voice is swept away by the forceful wind of the year's end, howling wildly, disseminating along its path whatever it brings with it. Such as stories about a successful business, about young men learning from foreign books. About Athens and the ancient Greek parliament. About democracy and civil rights.

The wind roars on.

Butler Feng is finally sent. Mingzhi is to go home for the New Year. Letters rare, words scarce, and worst of all, not returning for Mid-Autumn, Mingzhi has infuriated his grandfather. Butler Feng tells Mingzhi not to worry, though, reassuring him that the old man will forget it all when Mingzhi comes home. New Year means happiness, he says, and Master Chai will be delighted to see his mandarin grandson at the reunion dinner.

It is a reunion indeed, but for the wrong reason. Likang lapses into unconsciousness on his bloodstained bed after a fit on the morning of New Year's Eve. He has been coughing up blood lately, despite taking bowl after bowl of herbal remedies.

None of the doctors would visit on this day of the year to risk their luck for the year ahead. Mingzhi persuades, Master Chai rages at first but falls silent when Likang shows no sign of recovery. Father Terry is sent for, arriving late from Pindong Town. It doesn't take him long to make his diagnosis: tuberculosis, final stage. The name sounds strange to the Chai, but not the words that follow, and the head-shaking.

Likang dies the next day.

Mingzhi sits by Likang's bedside, his eyes red from staying awake all night. *This is the longest time I've spent with him. Alone.* He takes a closer look at his father. Drawn cheeks, sharp face. Collarbones, ribs and joints protruding. Chest and abdomen sunken. Like a skeleton.

Is this really my father?

The smell of opium-smoke he has been tolerating mingles with the fishy smell of coagulated vomit to assault him.

Like the most insidious of enemies, they sneak into his every pore, his nostrils, without him noticing. He sneezes with such force that it wets the corners of his eyes.

'It's all right.'

A soft voice, and an equally soft hand on his shoulder.

Mother.

'It's a release for him, in a way.' His mother sounds bitter.

Mingzhi pats the back of her hand, finding it relaxed. Too relaxed. *A release for you, too?*

Then comes a grip on his arm, strong and firm.

Uncle Liwei.

A death on the first day of the New Year. Master Chai shakes his head. He has been in the ancestral hall since dawn. Praying. As though he had known it before the news came. As though he had been waiting for it. And he stays there until Butler Feng has instructed the servants to dismantle the firecrackers and couplets at the doorpost. The red new-year couplets, which say:

Spring returns to the land,

Blessing the people with happiness.

No, not this year. No firecrackers, no couplets. Nothing red should be seen, not even good-luck envelopes for the children. Only white. The solemn, mournful white of a funeral.

Master Chai watches as the servants roll up the last scroll. HAPPINESS and GOOD LUCK disappear into the folds of the fabric. Blindfolded. Trapped. Put away in a dark corner.

—∞—

In the world of the servants, though, a little taste of happiness seeps into their secret New Year get-together. Crude rice wine, tea, roasted groundnuts, pumpkin seeds, and a long night of chatter. Tiredness forgotten, worries put aside. *It's a New Year!*

Now the most widely travelled servant of the lot, Little Mouse gets all the attention he could wish for. Three cups of wine add to his eloquence, and he talks, spittle showering, fingers pointing. About Lixing Town, the government house, the garden. About his master the new mandarin, what he has done and what he is doing. And his audience listens, eyes wide, mouths gaping, can't wait to pass the stories around.

In between the long hours of dull work, the servants whisper among themselves, bits that are worth whispering about: the remote villages, the schools, the pottery, the red-haired devil. And hiss under their breath things that are meant to be secrets. Shh, shh, it's a secret, they say, their mouths hidden behind their sleeves. But they forget the old saying that 'the wind has ears'. So the northerly spring wind, which closes in surreptitiously, takes their hissing with it, whisking it into the eager ears of an insidious spy.

Who has eyes that glow in the dark, a mind that conjures up a powerful weapon from the intelligence collected.

For his own revenge.

Or for somebody else's.

Fifteen

The funeral and the rituals that follow keep Mingzhi in the mansion for a month. He returns to Lixing Town to find that the study groups have been closed down. His precious collection of books is now a heap of dark ashes.

The order came from the Provincial Capital. Apparently, someone somewhere had reported to the Governor. A serious offence against the Forbidden City, the mandarin observed, and responded with an unusually swift action.

He is not unkind, though. As he knows about Mingzhi's connection with Imperial Scholar Dai, he quietly leaves Mingzhi out of his blacklist. 'New and inexperienced,' he comments in his report, an excuse good enough to save the Governor from trouble, either from the unsatisfied informant or any sympathetic party.

The scroll lies open before Mingzhi on his desk. The red seal looks enormous against the carefully constructed official writing. Mingzhi sees it lift itself off the page, swelling in the air, three times, ten, a hundred times bigger. Then it swoops down like an eagle, coming after him. Thump!

Stamping on him, on the hopeful young men, their ideals, the possibility of reinventing the nation.

Thump! Red, striking, like the flames that swallow the books of science, geography, history, arts and humanity. The weapons of self-strengthening.

It keeps burning, the bundle of forbidden knowledge, ablaze in the dark. Fierce fire against black emptiness. Until it collapses into a heap of cinders, blocking the passage to freedom and democracy, smearing the dignity of a nation.

The amber dies out. Black. Cold.

—w—

It is warm and light in the gambling den in Pindong Town, though. Too hot. Mingyuan wipes his sweaty forehead with a handkerchief, then stuffs it into his waistband. His jade-tasselled waistband, which has found its way back to its master.

And it is not alone.

In Mingyuan's silk pouch tied to his waist, his mother's family of jewels – earrings, necklace, pendant, bracelet, rings, hairpins – are clinking and clanking, celebrating a happy reunion. Complaining among themselves about Uncle Eagle's sweaty palms, the smelly, tattered boxes that had kept them apart from one another, and the even darker and smellier safe which kept the boxes that kept them.

Outside their pouch-home, their master gets a treat from Uncle Eagle. A cigarette, carefully lit. An apology. To offend someone with a connection to the most important man in town is far too risky. The man with an eagle's nose and eyes has a mind as shrewd as an eagle's, too. After all, Mingyuan has settled his debts and redeemed the jewels at twice their actual value. *A fat chip he is, again.*

The fat chip moves with his fat pouch to the gambling table. The jewellery siblings clink-clank along.

~

In the mansion, ivory chopsticks, jade cups and porcelain dishes have stopped sneaking out – for the time being. Perhaps they are being cautious. Perhaps it is the rain that has stopped them. The unexpected downpour in late spring that has washed over Plum Blossom Village. The fields. The poppies.

Roots and stalks rot; mature pods droop.

The giant vats in the outbuilding-turned-factory are dry, empty; the air fresh, cleansed of the least favoured smell of the opium favoured by Master Chai. The peasants squat on the thresholds of their homes, watching rainwater cascade from the eaves, smoking the occasional bit of tobacco. Yet they don't seem to be happy, as if they, too, are addicted to it, the opium. As if it has seeped into their veins, their blood, becoming part of them, and now they are unable to shake it off.

'Heavenly God has chosen the wrong time to pee.'

The peasants squint through the rain curtain, seeing only the grey sky sitting heavily above the fields, where the money for rent and rice lies rotting.

Landlord Master Chai slumps on the couch in the central hall, taking long, deep breaths. *At the very least, there's another season to cover the loss.* His body feels heavy, a total exhaustion he has never experienced before. As though it is going to pull him down into a bottomless slough, from which he will never rise. *No, not yet. I have dozens of matters to settle.* He thinks about the lost harvest, Mandarin Liu, Mingzhi's marriage, Mingyuan's exam. The mansion. So much to take care of.

He stares at the pipe on the desk. Likang's. Cleaned and polished, its smoke-blackened mouth shines in the well-lit room. Inside, the dark gum gleams like a seductive eye, winking at him. *Go on, try me and you'll feel better.* Another wink. Long, curly lashes flap down, then roll up like dozens of soft, boneless hands. Beckoning. *One puff, just one.*

He wonders what it tastes like, the black, muddy cake. Why his son was so fond of it. He gestures, and the maid lights it, boiling it up.

Master Chai takes his first puff.

He doesn't choke.

Another order comes from the Governor. A new tax target for Mingzhi, higher this time, of course.

Mingzhi whisks the scroll away, not wishing to lay his eyes on it. Not on the figure, nor on the seal with its square face like a cage, and inside it it's him, Mingzhi the captive.

As though he is equipped with the Thousand-Mile Eyes and Downwind Ears of the Monkey God, the Governor sees and hears everything: the pottery, the connection with a foreign trader. The profits. The connection worries him, but money prevails. He closes one eye, opens the other only to the silver he will receive. White, gleaming silver which, after he painfully cuts out a small portion to satisfy the Forbidden City, will continue to top up his private hoard.

The silver glitters, blinding minds and hearts.

—w—

Martin pays his farewell visit. He has been assigned to company business in the Imperial City. He brings with him a camera and cameraman.

The strange box in the strange shop in the Provincial Capital!

Little Mouse watches closely from a distance while the equipment is being set up in the court-office. Mingzhi tries to help.

'No, leave it to us.' Martin hurries Mingzhi off to put on his mandarin costume.

'Is this necessary?'

Though he grumbles, Mingzhi does not argue. He prepares himself. His official gown and hat are fresh, starched, shiny. His eyes are bright, his beard-for-mature-look clean and tidy. He has his hands on the armrest, his legs spread under the heavy gown. His face is tense, and he stares straight ahead, with a frown between his brows.

Snap! A flash, like an explosion.

In a corner Little Mouse winces, thinking the evil box from the evil land has captured his master's soul. He stares at Mingzhi, smiling and chatting with the red-haired devil, and wonders if Mingzhi's spirit is going to be taken away to foreign parts.

—w—

Master Chai is happy with the picture, now hung on the wall in the central hall. *A real person on paper, not just a painted imitation.* He lies on the couch and squints up at the portrait, hijacked from Da Niang. Taking occasional puffs of opium, studying the details: the exquisite costume that shines in black and white, the quail in the middle of it, Mingzhi's solemn appearance. *My grandson, a mandarin.* He grins and takes another puff, refreshed. *And I will have another mandarin grandson soon.*

The old man suddenly realizes Mingyuan should have been home after the provincial-level exam. After Likang's funeral, Mingyuan drafted a strict, intensive study plan, convinced Master Chai to let him stay in Pindong Town to concentrate on his studies.

He will attain his juren *this time.* Master Chai is confident.

But where is he?

Indeed he has a plan. Mingyuan has spent the past few months moving between the gambling den and the brothel once frequented by his father, studying the subjects that most interest him: the sciences of probability, and of human biology. His servant is warned: never reveal Mingyuan's doings to the mansion, or he will be sent home. He seals the boy's lips with strings of cash, of which he now has plenty in his pouch, courtesy of Mandarin Liu.

News of Mingyuan's special connection with the mandarin circulates fast in the underworld. And so, courtesy of Mandarin Liu, Mingyuan gets first-class treatment in this first-class brothel: getting his choice of girls, the best wine and the most luxurious room.

He has learned something: money is the only thing that is everything. *To hell with the exam, to hell with the mandarin post. To hell with Mingzhi.* Thinking that his half-brother might have been blacklisted and punished, and may lose his post soon, Mingyuan takes a big gulp of *wu jiapi*. Warm, all the way down to his stomach. And beyond. It's burning inside him, somewhere. He pulls his favourite singsong girl – the most sought-after in the brothel – closer to him, gives her a loud kiss on the cheek, pressing for more while his hands grope. She giggles, twisting in his clutch.

'Not here, you little rascal!'

Of course he knows where to go. His luxurious room with a comfortable bed is waiting. So comfortable that he nearly forgets about his father's hundred-day memorial ceremony.

It is smoky and stuffy inside the ancestral hall, with the burning candles, joss sticks and silver papers. Mingzhi tries to control his sneezes.

Kneeling in front of his father's memorial plate, he feels his grandfather's stare on his back. His skin itches, and he can't wait for the ceremony to be over. Huchh! *Stupid nose!* He rubs it with his sleeve and lowers his head against another resentful glare from Master Chai. A kerchief flutters before his face. *Uncle Liwei.* Mingzhi takes it. Immediately a refreshing smell of sandalwood soothes him, and the patches of pink – the peach blossom embroidered on the corners – are pleasant to look at. He nods *thank you* to Uncle Liwei.

Beside Mingzhi, with his eyes closed, Mingyuan has been quiet, as though he is remembering his father with sorrow. Master Chai nods, not knowing that Mingyuan, who came rushing home at dawn, has worn himself out with his favourite girl in Pindong Town. A good son, all the same, respectfully follows in his father's footsteps.

Mingzhi heaves a long sigh as he walks out of the hall, relieved. *It's over.*

He quickens his pace and makes his way to the west court. There are flakes of burnt silver paper on his gown. He whisks them off, and is assailed by an unexpected rush of fetid fumes from his smoke-impregnated sleeves.

Huchh!

'Are you all right, son?' Da Niang calls over from the moon gate. Mingzhi knows she has been waiting for him. Da Niang looks pale in her white mourning dress, paler than the little white lily pinned to her hair near her cheek. As though she were the lily, standing in a garden of gaudy peonies, magnolia and roses. Alone, out of place.

Without him and Mingyuan, without Likang's coughing and groaning, the west court is now quiet and calm. *She must be lonely.* Mingzhi hurries towards her.

Meilian does not come home for the ceremony, nor did she attend her father's funeral. There was a letter of condolence from her father-in-law – the most Mandarin Liu would do. Mingzhi has lost track of when Meilian last come home. Three years ago, five, or more? He gazes at his mother. *She must feel it to be even longer.*

'Let's have some tea.' Da Niang beckons, heading for her room. Mingzhi follows.

—~—

Mingzhi persuades his grandfather: Da Niang has not been to Pindong, the biggest town in the district. She hasn't stepped out of the mansion for more than ten years, only to serve you and my father, he says. And now she deserves a trip; a short one will do. Master Chai relents at last when Mingzhi promises to walk past Mandarin Liu's office in his formal gown, to remind the old enemy that he, Master Chai's grandson, is a mandarin too.

So he can tell lies! Little Mouse laughs quietly at his master's promise. He has packed Mingzhi's luggage and the mandarin costume isn't there.

Once in Pindong Town, Mingzhi broaches his real plan. Little Mouse is to make arrangements for Da Niang to meet Meilian.

Another good story to tell!

Little Mouse is excited; elated at the usefulness of his mousy brain, and the opportunity to further impress his fellow-workers. He is delighted also, that his master is getting *nasty*.

The servant from Mingzhi's previous rented residence has made arrangements. After dark, Da Niang and Mingzhi wait at the back door of the government office. The moon is waning but the sky above the mansion is bright, reflecting the lights behind the high walls. *Something is going on.* Mingzhi can sense the bustle inside: rushing footsteps, the rustling of dresses, the occasional barking of orders.

In the midst of all this, Meilian sidles through the half-open door, then swiftly closes it on the noises behind her.

Da Niang takes Meilian in her arms and holds her tight. They are both breathless and speechless, while tears smear their cheeks. Mingzhi sees his sister almost shrink in Da Niang's embrace. A lean body holding another leaner figure, trembling.

The two women I love. Their lives resemble each other.

Mingzhi feels himself useless, watching their suffering from a distance. Not even able to join in their embrace, to show his love. He grinds his feet into the ground until the gravel crunches under him and the sharp edges of the stones stab his soles. The pain is strangely soothing.

There is a shout from behind the door. Meilian's worried face turns pale in the soft flood of yellow from behind the wall.

'I must leave.' She pulls away from her mother: 'They're preparing for a wedding in there. I have to help.'

Da Niang clasps Meilian's hand, reluctant to let go. Meilian wipes her face, slowly twists free.

'Take care, Eldest Sister.' Mingzhi's voice is dry.

Meilian nods, mouths, 'You take care, too.' She bites hard to stop her lips from quivering. She ducks inside, and the door closes behind her. Light, soundless, like the life she lives. A fragile leaf blown off its mother tree, drifting in the air. Unable to decide its destination.

Mingzhi takes his mother for a trip in the carriage. Relax and enjoy the day, he says. Da Niang nods, her eyes red and swollen from weeping through the night. She tries to smile, manages only an awkward frown. Mingzhi averts his gaze, sees the textile stall piled high with bales of cloth. And the crowd surrounding it, mostly women, young and old, noblewomen and their maids, peasant women, housewives and singsong girls. Everyone is gathered there, except for one.

The one with the blue dress.

Mingzhi looks away.

There are sounds of trumpets and flutes and gongs. A wedding procession is coming their way. The driver steers the carriage to one side.

The band passes. Then the bridegroom on his horse, a mousy-faced man with small, mousy eyes. His mouth is not drawn to the same scale, though. It tilts all the way up, opens as wide as it can, happily boasting its master's happiness.

The onlookers recognize him.

'The son of the richest man in town.'

'The richest and the most powerful. What a convenient connection!'

'Look how happy he is.'

'Of course he is! I would be happy too if I got to marry the most beautiful girl in town.'

The red-curtained sedan passes next. The bride is a shadowy figure behind the thin shield. Still, people crane to catch a glimpse of any movement, any sight of the pair of tiny feet wrapped in embroidered shoes under the flapping curtain.

A new woman.

Mingzhi wonders what she looks like, the girl behind the curtain, heading for an unknown beginning. *Whoever you are, I hope you have a better life than my mother or my sister.*

A sudden gust of wind sweeps the curtain open. The bride is caught with her red veil raised, staring straight at the crowd who are staring at her. Her curious eyes turn shocked on her pale face.

Jasmine.

Mingzhi's heart sinks.

The scarf drops over her face.

The curtain flops down. Closed.

Red. Bright, striking in the morning sun, filling up Mingzhi's vision. He sees nothing but the burning colour. The fierce flame that licks away the last taste of his romantic fantasies.

He closes his eyes.

The sedan passes. The trumpets, flutes and gongs play on. Loud, shrill. Drilling into his heart.

—ꟿ—

Mingyuan's exam result finally reaches his grandfather: another fail.

Master Chai imagines Mandarin Liu sitting in his court-office, laughing and pointing at the list of failures. CHAI. Big and prominent, stooped and shamefaced before the mandarin's elated laughter. Master Chai's breath comes short.

He takes a puff.

What's wrong with Mingyuan? He seems to be bright.

The grandfather reasons, and then decides. Mingyuan,

who has finally returned home, is called to the ancestral hall. The old man makes his grandson light a bunch of joss sticks and kneel before the Chai ancestors. He declares: the dignity of the Chai is to be upheld. Mingyuan is to re-sit the exam. This time he will stay at the mansion whenever he is not at school, and come home every weekend. Study is the only thing he is to concentrate on, which means no more helping with the accounts.

He wants me to be another Mingzhi. Mingyuan darts a grudging glance at his grandfather as the old man busies himself with candles and joss sticks and *yao*. His stooped back, his quivering fingers. Like a stranger. *I am Chai Mingyuan, not anyone else.* Mingyuan clenches his fists and punches the floor.

Clank!

The set of *yao* falls, face down. Master Chai picks the pieces up at once, pretending nothing has happened. He will keep trying until both pieces fall face up, smiling.

With that his wishes will be granted.

And the Chai clan will stand tall before its enemy, on whom calamity will fall.

—~—

Uncle Liwei pays Mingzhi a visit in early autumn, a surprise. Mingzhi has work to finish. He takes his uncle to his court-office, shows him the place where he attends to daily business. Uncle Liwei watches the young man in his mandarin gown, sitting tall and calm, giving instructions to his staff. Reading documents, writing his decisions on them, finishing with a firm seal.

A careful, responsible young man, Uncle Liwei notes, gazing at him long and deep. The boy who sat on the stool with him reciting *Sanzi Jing* seems to have suddenly swelled, hands and legs elongating, turning into an adult. A mandarin.

He has his place in the world now.

Uncle Liwei smiles, feels moisture at the corners of his eyes and wipes it away.

Little Mouse sets their dinner in the pavilion, and the evening passes with chess and tea. Slow moves, small sips, intermittent chatter under the paraffin lamp.

Uncle Liwei's plait hangs grey and thin on his back. His words come out haltingly between breaths. His eyes are red-veined from the long, dusty journey, and tiredness crawls heavily over the lids. He rubs his face occasionally to chase it away and keeps drinking tea to refresh himself.

Mingzhi notices. This is a secret three-day trip before his uncle's rent collecting, and Mingzhi knows Uncle Liwei does not wish to waste it in bed. He sends Little Mouse for a pot of strong *pu're*. Black, very black, he orders. And a plate of groundnuts. The night is prolonged.

In the pond, the red carp express their joy in the visitor's company. Swimming in circles, turning somersaults, splashing water.

The soft light of the paraffin lamp fills the pavilion, an enclosed yellow world within the garden. In it Mingzhi sits with his uncle. He remembers his childhood paradise behind the curtain, and feels something is missing. *Mother.* He wishes Da Niang were here, in his world. *Their* world.

Having tea together, listening to the sound of leaping fishes.

Pop-pop-pop, pop-pop-pop.

Uncle Liwei has left for Mingzhi a packet of bird's nests, carefully cleaned and wrapped by Da Niang in waxed paper. Mingzhi runs his fingers over the neatly tied package, the folds and knots. Thinks about his mother's world in her small, incense-burning room. He winds the string tightly around his finger, until the sides of it turn pale, bloodless against the swollen red-purple at the tip. Numbed.

Da Niang gave a special duty to Little Mouse on the day Mingzhi left for Lixing: to prepare a daily nourishment supplement for his master. The loyal servant takes his responsibility seriously. There is always a bowl of bird's nest soup on the table at night before bed. The sweet taste of the soup reminds Mingzhi not only of his mother, but of the place hundreds of miles away. The mansion. The former he wishes to hold on tightly to; the latter, to pluck out of his mind like hauling off stubborn tendrils of poison ivy. But then, the two are intertwined. Da Niang is a little lily trapped under a poisonous shed of wild ivy. And he stands outside it, watching, enjoying his little freedom.

The soup turns sour. His stomach aches.

An insidious vine quietly extends itself, creeping hundreds of miles into Mingzhi's private garden.

On the island across the strait, bloodstained leaves are now dust buried deep underground, nourishing the soil that produces food – not for the nourishment of the people who produce it, but those who have trampled the land.

The pain and tears are not forgotten, though, and ferment into powerful words that fill the pages of the first reformist newspaper. Which is quickly circulated by means of the many new-laid railway tracks – cobwebbing like the equally new electric cables between and through the cities on the mainland. And some arrive on doorsteps by the hands of uniformed postmen.

—∾—

The newspaper does not reach distant towns like Lixing.

Life has become routine for Mingzhi. Listening to appeals, solving cases, worrying about tax quotas. He is not unhappy, though, knowing that he is serving the people. He goes on making occasional trips to remote villages, taking with him whatever he can. Though the journeys exhaust him, he likes to see the children reciting after their teachers. Green, childish voices ring out under the roofs, bouncing against the crude walls; fresh, smiling faces with curious eyes, asking to be fed with knowledge.

Mingzhi hoards these images in his mind. His treasures. Which he would use, bit by bit, to fill his evenings sitting in the garden. He now prefers the stump by the bamboo clump to the pavilion, keeping his distance from the jasmines. The whiffs of the flowers sent over by the occasional breeze pain him. He contemplates pulling them up, getting them out of his sight. But the idea of trampling on jasmine blossom is too cruel to be thought of. He leaves them there, quietly, in a corner. Keeps his eyes on the ever-active fishes, his ears on the sound of their joy. Pop-pop-pop, pop-pop-pop. And his mind focused on devising better plans to help the people in his care.

Occasionally, he reads about Martin's new adventures in his letters: how he has enjoyed eating rice dumplings in the Mid-Autumn, downing so many that his stomach swelled throughout the following day; and how he now wields chopsticks like a Chinese, able to pick up fishballs with them. *My funny friend.* Mingzhi laughs quietly, as pictures of a white man with a swollen stomach struggling to pick up fishballs with chopsticks come vividly to his mind. Other times, Mingzhi indulges himself by recalling the praises of himself he has overheard from the floor of his court-office, the streets, the villages. Reassuring voices, driving him forward.

He feels as though he will be here forever, in this little corner of the world, and he likes the thought of it. He doesn't need a big space, only a spot where he can stand on his own feet. *Like here, like now.* But with his mother.

In the pond, the red carp are swimming round the edge in a long fleet, one following closely after another, as if there is a leader up front, taking them on a tour. A happy family trip.

As he looks on, Mingzhi promises himself: *One day, Mother will come and live with me.* The fish nod as they dart past: *Pop-pop-pop, I agree; pop-pop-pop, I agree.*

Sixteen

When school reopens in Pindong Town, something puts Mingzhi's plans on permanent hold.

~

Mingyuan can't wait to return to his world. The gambling den. The brothel. His favourite singsong girl.

Who is also favoured by someone else. Someone as stubborn as he is, who challenges him and thinks money – which they both have in handfuls – is the one thing that is everything.

As though Likang has cast his shadow over his son, an immaculate suit of history clings tight to Mingyuan. A row erupts between the girl's admirers. One of them, needless to say, is Mingyuan, who has never budged in his previous fights. Only this time, his rival doesn't budge, either. It is a close fight: kicking, punching, pushing. Their servants, who rush forward to stop them, are kicked and punched and pushed, too, and they all wrestle against each other. In the melee a knife is raised, a frantic stab, and blood spouts from a body that falls onto the shiny white marble floor. Not from the challenger, not from Mingyuan, but his teenage servant, behind whose back Mingyuan dodges to evade the thrust.

The news swims into every household, tearoom, public house, opium and gambling den, the street. Into the steaming rice, the cups of tea and wine, the pipes and dice. Fresh and flavoured with details of the girl in question, the fight, the *loyal* servant, the murderer. More flavours are being stirred into the talks, as though they were all there, the chatters, as though they had all witnessed the act. And they are waiting, wanting to see more, to witness the murderer being punished.

'It never came into my head that he'd do this!'

'Aye, still a new groom!'

'What's the point of fighting over a singsong girl when you have a beautiful wife at home?'

'That's the problem with rich people. They'll never have enough – money or women.'

'A death for a death. Do you think he'll be hanged or beheaded?'

'Who knows? Let's wait and see.'

They wait. And wait.

And nothing happens.

As though nothing has happened.

Mandarin Liu sits in silence in his court-office. On the desk before him, documents pile high. He notices none of them but the one that lies wide open. The report on the brothel murder.

'Stupid idiots!'

Bang!

His angry hand thumps the desk. The papers fall, scattering across the floor.

Those two idiots. One, newly married with his niece, went to look for pleasure at the brothel; the other, with the money he gave, fought against his mousy-headed nephew-in-law.

It is not difficult to deal with Mingyuan. He has sealed Mingyuan's mouth with silver, knowing that he will not want his secret activities disclosed. Not to Master Chai, certainly. Still, the case has to be sorted. Already, he can hear whispers from the streets. The town is watching. People are gathering round the gallows, waiting for the big day.

My stupid nephew-in-law!

Another bang on the desk.

Mandarin Liu squeezes his temples. A wrong move will cost him his position, and he knows it well. There were dozens of witnesses in the brothel that night. The girls and their clients. *A bunch of low-class freaks.* Mandarin Liu snorts, knowing trouble is the last thing they will want. He resolves: he will send his butler, with plenty of silver.

The mandarin sits back, still rigid, anxious fingers knuckling the armrests.

A widely told story is now being revised: the teenager was the attacker, and the other man acted in self-defence. This new version of the insiders' tale races to the ears of the public with the ultimate *truth*: the victim was in fact the villain, the murderer the victim. The so-called eyewitnesses hiss into the ears of the waiters in teahouses and public houses, the most efficient transmitters, who later hiss into the ears of the hawkers and their customers, merchants and traders, gamblers and opium addicts during their tea or meal breaks. Who later hiss into the ears of their women at home. Who then hiss among themselves in the alleys, markets, and while washing by the river.

The first time they hear about it, they shake their heads. Disbelief.

The second time, question marks appear in their eyes. Uncertainty.

The third, more details are asked for, mental images reconstructed.

The fourth.

Heads nod, lips twitch in contempt. Fresh details leap from mouth to mouth, nudging away the older versions. All fingers point at the *delinquent* teenager.

In his court-office, Mandarin Liu stamps his seal on the scroll, endorsing his conclusion: 'Self-defence'. His fingers quiver.

The case is closed.

—∾—

Before Mingyuan has worked out the best way to report his servant's death to his grandfather, the news reaches the mansion. The second version.

The servants shake their heads as they whisper among themselves:

'I bet they're still in the dark, his poor parents in that far-off village.'

'Old and poor, and without their only son to look after them.'

'That's fate. What else can you say? A life like ours is worth nothing.'

'Aye. He was a good kid. I'll believe he launched the attack when the sun starts rising in the west.'

'You know how it is. Justice isn't intended for people like us.'

They are wrong this time.

—∞—

However many versions of the story there may be, it doesn't seem to bother Master Chai. Instead, only one thing occupies his mind:

MANDARIN LIU's nephew-in-law KILLED MY servant.

The notion spreads as quickly as the old man's anger, nudging away the many questions he might otherwise have asked: Where and when and how did it happen? Where was Mingyuan? And where is he now?

A set of nouns with a missing verb come to him:

1. MANDARIN LIU.

2. HIS NEPHEW-IN-LAW.

It doesn't take Master Chai long to work out the connecting word. PROTECTS. A distant light emerges in his old brain, vague, but bright enough for him to find some clues.

There is a long moment of thoughtful silence.

Thud!

The sharp tail of his brass stick strikes the concrete, the

most beautiful note he has heard since the last performance of the Northern Opera Troupe.

'Get Butler Feng!'

Mingyuan is to be sent for. He is to draft a letter of appeal: eloquently and adequately phrased. Although Master Chai would prefer Mingzhi to do it, as no one would be better suited to the task than a *jinshi* – after all, it's for Mingzhi's sake – he is too far off to be reached. It would be too risky to delay this business. Master Chai works it out: the letter will be read by the Provincial Governor, and a crate of silver will enhance its readability. Another copy will be delivered to Imperial Scholar Dai, by hand, without the silver.

He takes a puff of opium, lies back on his couch, and laughs.

Your time has come, my old friend!

'Go and get Butler Feng!' he shouts again, sounding elated rather than impatient, drowned out by echoes of his laughter. The servant girls exchange looks, surprised. Smiles have been absent from their master's face for some time, and laughter even rarer. Their eyes widen when their master orders Butler Feng to arrange a funeral for the unfortunate servant, and compensation for his parents.

What a timely death!

Master Chai takes another puff, feels his head getting lighter, then his body. He is drifting out of the mansion, floating all the way to the government office in Pindong Town. He sees Mandarin Liu trapped between four walls, pacing the room in agitation like an ant on the lip of a hot cauldron: always running, round and round, yet escaping to nowhere. He sees, too, Mingzhi sitting tall in Mandarin

Liu's court-office, in his new seventh-ranking mandarin gown.

The old man laughs: 'I'll see to it. I'll see justice done for my man!'

For himself.

Mingyuan is rushed home that night. Since he is fully occupied with his plan, Master Chai asks no questions and sees nothing of his grandson's pale face or his tremulous hands. Only urges him to write: a miscarriage of justice, a case that needs investigation.

Done. Mingyuan reads his writing in a trembling voice. His grandfather nods, smoothing his goatee. Butler Feng is sent for again. The letters are to be dispatched first thing in the morning.

In the middle of the night, Master Chai re-dreams his daydream. The wordings read by Mingyuan ring like music in his ears, more alluring, more absorbing than a Peking opera. In fact, the opera is in full swing. The villain, who has been caught and chained, turns his head round –

Mandarin Liu!

Master Chai hisses out a sigh of satisfaction, tosses, then settles into the embrace of his soft blanket. The dream continues in the deep darkness where it belongs, along with many other night activities. Such as, the creak of a back door, the ducking out of a shadow.

Mingyuan.

Swift and soundless.

Like a mouse.

The peasants whose day starts at dawn see them: two apparitions, white and lean, drifting through the misty darkness. The eyewitnesses shudder, pale-faced. *Calamity will soon befall us.* They shut their mouths tight, pretending it is an illusion, that they have seen nothing. This way they work the fields throughout the morning: quiet, deep in thought, with heavy clouds in their stomachs. Occasional glances of confusion are exchanged, each waits for the other to broach the subject – lips move, throats are cleared – yet no words are uttered. The clouds accumulate, crowding their guts, and come midday, they burst. Perched on the dike, the peasants keep their voices low, their lips tremble, their eyes flicker with fear, their lunches lie forgotten.

'The Goddesses of Calamity, I'm sure that's who they were.'

'Why here, then?'

'Look at this crop you're working on. Isn't this a good reason for calamities to befall us?'

'No, not us, I'd say. It's the Chai they should go after.'

'Aye, I'd say so. In fact I saw them heading towards the mansion.'

'Are you sure? That would serve Landlord Chai right!'

'Don't be so naive. If anything happens to him, do you think our lives will be any better?'

The peasants sigh, shake their heads and fall silent.

—~—

In the mansion, a different tale is conjured up. The servant who opened the door to Meilian and her daughter, and later hung about in the west court for more news, is delighted with his long-awaited chance to give a show. The busy morning kitchen is his stage, packed with an eager audience, and his news is hotter than the cauldrons: Mandarin Liu has fled with his family and his nephew-in-law, the murderer!

Eyes widen, mouths gape, exclamations and questions are voiced. Eager faces surround the storyteller, urging him to tell more. As if he had been there in Pindong the night before, the servant paints a picture of the panic-stricken Mandarin Liu, who, on receiving certain intelligence, hastily packed and fled in the middle of the night like a stoned dog with its head and tail down.

The messy scene of scattered antique vases and pots, paintings and calligraphic displays, exquisite dresses and gowns comes alive. The servants exchange glances of regret: if they could only get hold of just a piece of those valuables!

The storyteller is elated, though, thinking that he has got his piece from the mess: the attention he longs for, with questions and answers over free tobacco and wine for several days to come. *Too good to be true!* He scratches his head and takes his first free puff, not knowing it will soon be proved that it really is too good to be true.

Da Niang holds Meilian and her fourteen-year-old daughter, Jiaxi, tight in her embrace. Her tears wet the sleeve of the teenage girl.

'Grandma, don't cry. We're here with you now.'

Da Niang glances up at the innocent face. She remembers Meilian as a teenager, how she was married off as young as Jiaxi. She turns to her daughter and sees Meilian's sad eyes, haggard from the overnight journey from Pindong. Da Niang's throat constricts, her words jammed. Her maid brings in ginger tea on her mistress's orders. Da Niang watches Meilian and Jiaxi drink, and is glad to see the colour gradually creep back into their cheeks.

Da Niang smooths Jiaxi's dress, then Meilian's. Their clothes are as white as the lilies pinned to their hair: they are still in mourning after the death of Meilian's husband less than a year ago. Da Niang stares down at her own pale gown. *Her fate resembles mine.* She knows her daughter has been abiding by the Three Rules of Obedience and the Four Virtues. For the former, Meilian was obedient to her husband, and will be obedient to her son, too; for the latter, she is doubtless a woman who leads a life of perfect morality, speaks properly, has modest manners and works with diligence. Yet she has been abandoned by her in-laws, who left her and Jiaxi behind when they fled, taking with them their only grandson. Meilian's son.

Where is he now? Where is my Junwei? An invisible knife cuts deep across Meilian's heart. She bends over, holding her chest. Da Niang hugs her tighter.

The cunning fox has run away!

Master Chai gnashes his teeth. His balled-up fist strikes the armrest. Soundless. The plum-wood feels especially hard for the first time. He kneads his fingers, but doesn't feel the pain. The Governor is yet to announce his action. Master Chai the Informer has been waiting to see his old enemy stumble to his doom.

And now he is gone, with that murderer his nephew-in-law!

The old man's heavy wheezing fills the central hall. The young maid holds her breath; the candle and opium bowl in her hands shake as she prepares the pipe. She peeps occasionally at her master, who is contemplating the prancing dragons on the pillars.

Master Chai's eyes follow the beasts' upstretched tentacles, almost touching the ceiling. *Yes, my Mingzhi will move up the ranks, I'll make sure of that.* He decides instantly, knowing that the Governor will not resist a second chest of silver, the perfect gift for the New Year. He draws his first long breath of the morning and sits back. Tiredness besieges him all of a sudden. He shouts with his remaining strength: 'Where's my pipe?'

Clank!

The clay bowl smashes to pieces on the floor. The death-faced maid fumbles to pick up the debris.

Master Chai glances down at her trembling figure and frowns. *Girls, useless.* Instantly the image of two *girls* in white dresses entering the mansion at dawn sneaks into his mind. An abandoned widow and her daughter, still in mourning. *How inauspicious!* The rain has brought him enough bad luck, which finally began to change with the discovery of Mandarin Liu's wrong-doing. The situation must not be jeopardized. *No, there is no place here for that ominous pair.* He calls for Butler Feng: the servant who let them in – and thinks himself lucky – must be punished.

Giving the order exhausts the old man. The maid brings

him his long-awaited pipe. Master Chai takes a puff, then closes his eyes and feels the warmth travelling deep inside him. He squints up at Mingzhi's portrait on the wall. His handsome grandson is floating on iridescent clouds, as bright and colourful as his young face, and he is parading the hall. *Such a beautiful world.* Master Chai takes another puff and closes his eyes again, this time for a good nap.

An open chest of silver springs into his dream. Glittering white, reflected in the greedy eyes of the Governor, who holds out a scroll. PINDONG TOWN MANDARIN: CHAI MINGZHI. With an official stamp.

Master Chai turns over and heaves a sigh of satisfaction.

~

In the real world, however, the tradition of gift-giving in the Lunar New Year is broken by foreign forces, who, in turn, introduce a new custom: gift-demanding. The gift: the fertile land along Meinam River around Rangoon. A treaty is signed, with conditions as generous as demanded, in time for the red-haired devils to raise their star-flag over the paddy fields in the New Year. A perfect gift for the festive season, indeed.

Traditions keep changing, as the forceful westerly wind sweeps in with it fragments of life from faraway lands. The food, the clothing, the language, the knowledge, and ways of learning and using them. They scatter themselves around, seeping into the earth, melting into the water. Into wells and tanks. Veins and flesh. And so the changes become rightful, indisputable, and are enshrined in the textbooks of the first foreign school in the north.

In a small southern village yet to be reached by the westerly wind, Master Chai prepares his gift chests of silver, happily, willingly.

Seventeen

Pindong Town, 1897

The carriage makes slow progress along the main street. Inside Mingzhi sits upright, his shoulders tense, his ears deafened by the gongs and trumpets at the front of the procession. Before him faces shuffle, curious and staring, pressing forward for a glimpse of their new mandarin. Mingzhi retains his posture, gazing ahead, telling himself to relax. *They are my charges now, my people.* A sudden clattering bursts in on his wandering mind. In the whirling red flakes of the firecrackers, an acrid smell of gunpowder rushes to his nostrils. He sneezes.

The carriage stops.

Mingzhi looks up. The golden strokes of the newly painted horizontal board glow in the morning sun:

PINDONG TOWN GOVERNMENT OFFICE

Underneath, the door is wide open, waiting for its new master. Mingzhi closes his eyes. *Too sudden, too soon!*

For someone with expectations like Master Chai's, it has been a long wait. Anyhow, two full chests of silver given to the Governor have not been wasted. One letter had been conjured up, travelling all the way from the Provincial City to the Forbidden City, another from Mingzhi's future father-in-law, the Imperial Scholar. One would have been good enough; two are irresistible. The Emperor stamped his seal on the scroll. Posted.

Master Chai's laughter hovers beneath the high ceiling of the central hall. He puts down his pipe, lays his head on his jade pillow and stares up. The tentacles of the dragons dance in the echoes of his laughter. He heaves a long sigh of relief, turns and sprawls on the couch, relaxed. Money and connections, the mightiest of weapons, he has them both. A touch of the magic button and the force is released at once. The result:

A sixth-ranking mandarin post for my grandson!

A rank higher than Mandarin Liu. Too good to be true; an auspicious omen for the New Year. Master Chai holds out his hand. The maid passes him the pipe, freshly prepared, froth-bubbling. Master Chai brings the pipe closer. Through the blur before him, the dragons' eyes soften, their faces look tame, their smiles colourful! Master Chai inhales, long and deep. His mind follows Mingzhi as he enters Mandarin Liu's old – oops – *his grandson*'s new office.

Mingzhi steps out of the carriage. The brightness of the clear blue sky falls on his head, shoulders and body, embracing him. He strides forward.

Behind him, slicing through the crowd, a pair of eyes follows, pinned to his back, a glare of hatred, jealousy and anger. Mingyuan stares down from the second floor of the public house. His half-brother's new gown seems too splendid, too shiny. He averts his eyes, gropes for the cup of wine on the table and drains it. Feels the liquid burn his throat, then his heart. He has to put it out, the fire. He empties another cup. And another.

Downstairs, across the road, the new mandarin is hooha'd into the government office. Vague sounds of gongs and trumpets leap over the walls. The onlookers disperse. Slivers of red paper race in the northerly wind, capering high like liberated spirits. But not high enough to reach the banister of the second floor of the public house, and the young man who sits drinking there, so despondent that he loses his usual alertness, his acute sensitivity for sound and movement. Below him, a carriage quietly slips past, entering an alley, approaching a back door where Little Mouse is waiting. For Meilian and Jiaxi.

Inside his new office Mingzhi paces round, pretending to admire the horizontal boards and silk banners hanging on the walls, the congratulations and good wishes painted and embroidered in gold. **All the way up the Mandarin Ladder**. *Have they arrived yet?* Moving steadily up the colourful cloud. *Did anyone see them?* He cracks his knuckles, keeps walking, sees nothing but sweet words about fortune, status and fame. *It's them, my unfortunate sister and niece, who have brought me these.* Meilian and Jiaxi, who came to Mingzhi after Master Chai slammed the door of the mansion in their faces.

Yet they are my lucky stars!

Mingzhi remembers the look of them on their arrival

in Lixing, after days of journeying in an open cart: dust-covered, travel-worn, sick. Like wilting leaves, wrinkled, discoloured, urgently needing water and nourishment. Mingzhi's heart clenched. *I will not let them suffer again*, he promised himself, setting aside the vacant south court for them, assigning Little Mouse to supervise its decoration to the pair's specification. The loyal servant, too, had worked hard to ensure that no news about the occupants should leak to the mansion. He also boiled extra bowls of bird's nest soup for Meilian and Jiaxi. This he did without Mingzhi's instruction.

A clever young man he is. Mingzhi smiles, staring up as he strolls on.

Fair and Just

Only this. Mingzhi stops in front of the board, the highest of them. Four square, honest faces in thick and forceful brushstrokes look down on him. *Only this makes sense.* How he wishes every matter could be settled fairly and justly, every human being treated equally, regardless of class and gender. *Women.* He sighs, thinking about his mother, sisters and niece. How the corrupt fragments of Confucianism and Ritual, the unfair treatments towards women, have thrust themselves into their flesh, invading their veins. Sharp edges pressing against delicate flesh and sinew. Pain. After pain. After pain.

Which he has noticed in them.

The fragments have melted and run into their bloodstream, and they don't feel it any longer, the pain. It has become part of them, the beliefs, the customs, the rituals. They have channelled into their extremities, their bodies, their brains, guarding their everyday life. A majestic voice rings out from inside their bodies, firm and harsh, deciding their place on earth, telling them what to do and what not to. Like how Meilian and Jiaxi kept themselves to their quarters, conscious of their own inauspiciousness, not wishing to cause Mingzhi trouble.

He had given them time, waited.

For the first time Meilian made decisions: about their meals, about lessons for Jiaxi. For the former, she ordered simple, inexpensive dishes. *A good woman should not be a burden on a man*, the voice in her bloodstream sang aloud. And for Jiaxi's lessons, *Sewing and the culinary arts*, the voice said, *will make her a good woman, get her a good husband*. That, she couldn't disagree with. The timetable was set. Cotton spinning, thread twisting in the morning; the afternoon for fine needlework and embroidery; and cookery, baking, and the preparing of wine and sauces in the evening. Discipline, but not exhausting. Along with the cabbage, fresh or salted, the sweet potatoes and fried eggs with salted radishes Meilian asked for, came streaky pork, herbal chicken soup, braised duck or steamed fish specially ordered by her mandarin brother. These she accepted, and they ate, mother and daughter, munching slowly, savouring mouthful after mouthful of their relative's love with gratitude. Let it in, let it in. Let it warm their stomachs, their hearts.

Until their sunken cheeks and limbs had filled out, colour re-emerged, smiles reappeared. Until laughter rang out in the courtyard. Then one evening, the mother and daughter were sent for.

The pair waited at the pavilion. Meilian kept kneading her fingers, twisting about uneasily on her stool. Mingzhi now recalls Meilian's agitation, imagining the questions in her mind: *Has grandpa found out about us? Do we have to leave?*

He shakes his head, *Oh, my sister*, and keeps pacing. On the floor near his desk, a servant is unpacking his books, bundle after bundle. Reaching for one pile, another is knocked over. The tower of books topples, and one of them slides under Mingzhi's foot. He picks it up. It's a collection of poems and verses, the same book he showed Meilian that evening at the pavilion.

Has Little Mouse received them all right? He leafs through it, pauses at the sight of Li Qingzhao's poem 'To the Tune of Drunk in a Yellow Shadow' – one of Meilian's favourites:

> Thin mist and thick clouds dim the everlasting day;
> Camphor incense fades away from the golden animal.
> Once again it is the Double Ninth Festival.
> Through the jade pillow and the gauze bed curtain
> The cold begins to penetrate at midnight.
>
> When I hold up the wine cup by the eastern hedge,
> In the twilight a hidden fragrance fills my sleeves.
> Do not say that one's soul cannot be rapt!
> When the bamboo screen rolls up in the west wind,
> I look thinner than the yellow flower.

He sees a lean figure by the window, alone and pale, shivering in the morning chill. *No, no, my sister will not suffer Li's fate.* He turns the page, seeking out the poem he read for Meilian and Jiaxi, 'To the Tune of a Variation of Rinsing Silk Stream':

Thousands of light flakes of crushed gold for its blossoms,
And of trimmed jade for its layer of leaves;
This flower has the air of scholar Yen Fu.
How brilliant!

Plum flowers are too common;
Lilacs, too coarse, when compared with this.
Yet, its penetrating fragrance
drives away my fond dreams
of faraway places.
How merciful!

Yes, she should drive away the unhappy past and start afresh. He wants Meilian to appreciate every little thing in life as the poet had tried to. He remembers his sister's tearful gaze as she listened to the poem, and knows she understood. He thumps the book closed. A loud echo in the spacious hall frightens the servant into knocking down another pile of books. He glances up at Mingzhi as he hurriedly rearranges them, expecting a roar like he used to get from his old master. Strangely, the mandarin stays silent. The servant gives a sigh of relief, and throws a look of admiration at his new master.

Who notices nothing of all this.

Have they settled down in their new home?

'Of course they have!'

Little Mouse lands a heavy *trust me* pat on his chest, his tone excited, his spirits high. *Another secret I share with my master!*

Mingzhi imagines Meilian and Jiaxi in his Little Hut – now theirs – admiring the pond of fishes, their leaping and the splashing of water. Experiencing the freedom he once experienced in that very same room, that same courtyard.

—∾—

Butler Feng arrives with gifts from home: Master Chai's ivory abacus, elegant, exquisitely crafted; Da Niang's hand-sewn pillowcases, embroidered with plum blossoms; Uncle Liwei's sandalwood chessboard, carefully engraved in his fine writing. At night Mingzhi lies on his pillows, feels the plum blossoms caressing his face, soft against his skin. Through the gauze, he sees the chessboard on the table in the middle of the room, the pieces standing in position, ready for battle. He dreams. A kind smile, a game of chess. Silent, without a starting point, without an ending. From behind a curtain of pink flowers there comes a soft whisper: Do not forget your origins. He wakes with a smile on his face, the voice ringing in his head, and the day is waiting.

Mingzhi keeps the abacus in the display cabinet in his study. Later he lays it away in the drawer of his desk.

—∾—

A bigger town means more work: longer hours spent reading cases, appeals, suggestions. He doesn't grumble, though, immerses himself in the piles of documents on his desk till late at night: focused, prudent, scrupulous. There are no more petty complaints about stolen eggs or goats or unreasonable neighbours, but bullies, traitors, fights and assaults. Notes promising silver in exchange for favours appear more often, the amounts larger, and Mingzhi discards them all as he did in Lixing. *This custom must change, and I must set an example.*

There are grievances, too, noises of discontent and contempt against his age, his inexperience, his new practices. A repeat of his early days in Lixing, though the grumbles are louder this time. More watchful eyes, too, all waiting to witness his failure. He is aware, though not afraid. Promises himself he will be a good mandarin, as he already is. He plans investigations, detailed and meticulous; drafts solutions, fair and just. Firmly holds on to the saying, 'as there are rules governing a family, there are rules too, to govern a state', a principle that has long been imprinted in his mind by Old Scholar Yan. And he is to ensure those rules are followed.

I will, I will, he says quietly, promising his teacher.

~

At night, lying in bed, Mingzhi travels back to his first spring in Pindong: the colours, the sounds, the smells, the air. The people. *A vibrant town.* Yet crime and violence surface from the underworld, lurking in the streets and alleys. Prostitution, gambling, opium addiction, and what comes with them. Mingzhi sighs, staring through the thin gauze at the wall, on which shadows of the willow outside the window are cast. Dark shapes of evil claws spreading, reaching, threatening. *I will not give in.* Mingzhi bites his lip, promises consistency and transparency in his administration. Promises a town of real vibrancy, with a new blueprint of life for its people.

He shuts his eyes against the shadows, pricks his ears for the tiny movement of his fish, the clear, reassuring sound of water. *It will be the same all over again*, he convinces himself. *My little world.* A garden, a pond, some carp. Willows and a pavilion.

No jasmine.

—~—

Now that Mingzhi has settled to his new post, Master Chai has finally got time for Mingyuan. He has begun to rethink Mingyuan's failure in his exam, and the incident involving the unfortunate servant.

Mingzhi is to help to discipline his half-brother and shelters him under the same roof, their grandfather has decided. In his court-office, Mingzhi quietly hands a thank-you envelope to Butler Feng, the messenger, for his long journey from Plum Blossom Village. Later on the same day in Mingyuan's study, the young man turns his back on the faithful butler. No thank-you envelope, not a word. Mingyuan lands his anger on his desk, his fist red and swollen, but he is unaware of the pain.

—~—

A meeting with his half-brother is inevitable, and Mingzhi makes it brief and clear: a courtyard to yourself, your servants, your way. Mingyuan grasps his meaning at once. As in the saying, 'Water from the river shall not run into the well', neither of them is to interfere with the other's business.

Mingyuan nods, his face impassive, then turns and leaves, his tea untouched. Mingzhi stares at his half-brother's receding back, his gown loose and creased at the elbows and hem. There is a sudden grab at his heart, and he blurts out: 'If – when you need anything, anything at all, you know I'm always here!'

Mingyuan pauses – a second or two – then walks on.

Let's see, let's see.

Mingzhi resumes his Sunday outings. Plain-clothed, with Little Mouse for company, of course. Sneaking out of the back door, taking slow walks along the river to Father Terry's church. Where Meilian and Jiaxi are waiting.

Encouraged by Mingzhi, the pair have been attending Sunday Mass, and helping Father Terry prepare lunch and relief for the congregation. Glad to be useful, mother and daughter work together with passion. Smiles exchanged over a steamy cauldron, soft whispers between chopping and frying and stirring.

Father Terry likes his helpers, and is happy to have two extra pairs of hands. In the afternoon when work is done and the congregation have left with full stomachs, bags of rice and sugar, and grins of contentment, Meilian and Jiaxi sit in Father Terry's study, learning English and knowledge as Mingzhi once did. And their mandarin brother always arrives just in time to join them. He darts occasional glances of encouragement at the women as he revises his lessons, listening to Father Terry's gentle words of guidance, and the diffident voices of Meilian and Jiaxi.

A cosy room, a pot of constantly replenished hot tea, a loyal servant waiting to one side. The afternoon passes.

—∞—

Mingyuan counts the money in his kerchief, hearing nothing of the clinking and clattering of dice and blocks, the cheers of joy, the sighs of disappointment, the shouts of anger and fights. He keeps fingering the few pieces of silver and the strings of cash, his reward from Mandarin Liu.

Last of all.

Suddenly, the surrounding noises rise like a surging wave, rumbling towards him from all directions, pounding behind his temples.

Should have asked for more. Should have found out where he has fled to.

He curses. *I saved his life.* He remembers blundering through the darkness, trudging all the way to Pindong, informing the mandarin of his grandfather's letter of appeal. The cuts and bruises, sore toes and aching legs. *And this is all I got.* He stares at the money again. No matter what, he knows that if there were to be an investigation into the murder, his name would certainly crop up. *At least, at least I have these.* He looks around. There is a faint flicker of light from a corner. Uncle Eagle, hawk-eyeing Mingyuan. The young man hurriedly reties the kerchief and tucks the bundle carefully under the inner layer of his gown, near his chest. Without his guardian angel Mandarin Liu, he senses the piercing gaze. A *wait-and-see* stare that says, *How long can you survive?* His spine prickles. He swears he will double his money, maybe triple it. He will.

In front of him at the gambling table there are two familiar figures, strong and burly. Mandarin Liu's former followers, who have been idle since their master left them. They were the hatchet men who made sure the rents and taxes were paid on time. Men with muscles but no brains, who would win everything in a fighting ring but nothing at the gambling table. Like now.

They need a new master.

Mingyuan's mind moves fast, and in seconds a plan has been worked out. He steps forward and taps them on the shoulders.

'Let's have a chat.'

Mingzhi visits his old school, proposing a foundation for needy students, handing out a generous sum to begin with. Head Teacher Scholar Ning thanks his favourite student, praises his achievements. Teacher and student sit talking, taking slow sips of tea between news and plans. The Germans have set foot in Qingdao, a treaty is only a matter of time. There are more railways, more factories, constructed by technical experts from the West, for their own benefit, of course. More opium is imported; higher trade deficits are recorded. A picture of a country in ruins becomes clearer, more visible.

They fall silent, a long interval of tea and thought.

'You will help to stop this. I have faith in you.' Scholar Ning grips Mingzhi's shoulder, his voice firm and persistent. 'You changed him, your brother,' he says, assuring Mingzhi of Mingyuan's recent improved behaviour, and that he has been attending school and making progress. 'And you can do more, I know.'

Mingzhi feels the pressure on his shoulder, the weight of the Forbidden City. I'll try my best, he murmurs.

He does.

In his court-office Mingzhi works his way through piles of documents, burying his head in them, and so he doesn't hear the growing turbulence outside. Over the high walls, from the streets. From the hawkers and shop owners, who, in quivering voices, describe a new gang of thugs who are competing with the local rascals for protection money. While the latter settle for one-off cash for wine and dice, this new gang is different: they keep the details of their victims, their whereabouts, their daily activities, threatening not only them but also their families. A dark shadow that clings onto their life, that they are unable to shrug off. And they are warned to keep their heads down. Shh-shh, shh-shh, no sound is to be heard.

Mingzhi returns late from the Provincial City, his first visit on the Governor's request since taking up his new office. Exhausted, he closes his eyes as the carriage trundles along, yet the Governor's fleshy face with his false smile sways before him. He shakes his head, takes up the invitation and examines his name and title on the envelope.

The title.

Granted by the Emperor, granting a seat level with the Governor, the chance for closed-door discussions. Yet still, tax targets are to be achieved. Still, 'all mandarins know where to get their money from'. Same words, same tone, same expressions.

Nothing changes.

Mingzhi closes his eyes again. Approaching the government office, he hears a commotion. A loud cry, the angry shouts of guards, and louder cries in response. The carriage grinds to a halt. Mingzhi sticks his head out.

'Help us, Your Excellency!'

'Go away!' In front of the carriage, the guards are grappling with two peasants, an elderly couple. The man pushes forward and is quickly pushed back. Seeing the mandarin, the woman drops to the ground and cries: 'Please, Your Excellency!'

Her voice is hoarse, her eyes bloodshot. The man kneels down beside her.

Mingzhi signals to the guards: *Let them in the office.* He prepares his ears and his heart. *I will listen, this is what I'm here for.*

He listens, and takes action. Immediately, without hesitation.

—ʍ—

'This mandarin is different!'

The following day in the streets, the hawkers cheer. There will be a special team of guards patrolling the market area. Local rascals demanding protection money will be seized, severely punished. Cases of extortion and threats are to be reported. A zero-tolerance policy. Shop and stall owners learn the new phrase, relate this hottest story through the town.

'We should thank them, for having the courage to approach the mandarin!'

'What have they got to lose? Their only son had been beaten up so badly.'

'Those hooligans! How much can these poor peasants earn selling sweet potatoes? Where on earth can they find the money for protection?'

'Protection, huh! How dare they ask money for that? You see, now we have a real guardian.'

'I heard he paid a herbalist to treat the poor fellow.'

'Unbelievable!'

They grin. *Never before, never before.*

The new mandarin stands tall in their mind's eye. His face gets confused with that of Bao Gong, the legendary Black-faced Official, the most upright and honest official of all time. An effective, efficient investigator who loathed corruption and embezzlement, righted all wrongs. Saviour of the poor and victims of injustice and discrimination.

'I'm sure he is!' they remark as they pass the word around, nodding, smiling. The reincarnation of Bao Gong is established.

Da Niang's trips to Pindong Town now need no excuse. *To serve my son.* The reason stands tall above the Three Rules of Obedience, strong and indisputable for a widow with an only son to serve. A son of importance, with a position. *Yes, serve him, and serve him well.* Master Chai merely nods and waves her off. The old man lies on his couch, taking occasional puffs as he admires his mandarin grandson's photo on the wall, and imagines a new picture: Mingzhi in his gown that carries the emblem of the eaglet, the symbol of a sixth-ranking official. In his mind's eye the snowy bird lifts its wings and kicks its legs as it dances, white against the iridescent rays of the old man's mental paradise.

Da Niang's mental paradise, however, is built upon the characters 'nǚ' and 'zi', a *daughter* and a *son*, constructing the word 'hǎo', *good*. She is a good woman with a son and daughter, and she feels good. Now. In the Little Hut.

Da Niang admires her small family at the dinner table. Jiaxi pours tea for Meilian. Da Niang stares at the shadows of the pair on the wall behind them, one huge, the other tiny. Sees herself dissolving into the bigger mould, and Meilian the smaller. The moulds of history. Of the past. *How time has flown.* She sighs, but smiles at once when Mingzhi, who has sneaked out of his residence at the government office, proposes a toast to the family. He moves his gaze from his mother to his sister and his niece as he takes small sips, rolling the tea leaves on his tongue, tasting the bitter-sweetness of *pu're*. Smiling. Smiling.

He hears the fishes smiling in the garden, too, and remembers the evening he spent with Uncle Liwei in Lixing. Remembers also the chess set and the new chessboard hibernating in his room. He swallows his tea, the same he drank with his uncle in the pavilion. A tiny leaf escapes from his tongue and sticks in his throat. He chokes, one hand holding his chest, the other reaching for the table. Chopsticks drop, cups overturn, the paraffin lamplight flickers. The room full of smiles turn to laughter. *My mandarin son, he is a child after all.* Da Niang passes him her kerchief. He wipes his mouth and face with it, and the faint scent of sandalwood fills his nostrils. *Where have I smelled that before?* And the peach blossoms embroidered on the piece of silk. All so familiar. Threads of vague memories intertwine in Mingzhi's mind. Too many of them, too messy. He can't make head nor tail of them.

—∾—

In the mansion, Liwei, alone in the south court, works his way through the year-end accounts. Fingers fiddling, wooden pieces of the abacus click-clacking, loud against the quietness, rumpling the calmness between his brows.

—∾—

'Impossible!'

Master Chai hurls the book to the floor. Two harvests a year and the combined figure is less than the first harvest of the very first year. Likang's untimely death has proved inauspicious; but then, things should change from now on, with Mingzhi's new appointment.

Mingzhi.

My lucky star.

Immediately the old man has his next move in mind, something that should have been done long ago. He will see to it this time.

'Call Butler Feng!'

The dowry, the fixing of the date, the gowns and guest list and food. So much to do, yet he can't wait for it. Can't wait to have a glimpse of red, the colour of good fortune.

Red. Candles, curtain, sheets and covers. Cut-outs of *Xi*, Double Happiness, on the wall, the windows. The bright, dazzling colour of a wedding.

Mingzhi stands gazing at the figure by his bedside. Red veil, red gown, red shoes, almost melting into the background. He looks hard, but is unable to tell if she is fat or thin, pretty or ugly.

A stranger. My wife.

The thought scares him. He goes to the table and fills the cups with wine, the drink for their first night. Mama Zhang's lengthy briefing doesn't escape him. He knows he has to call her to him, his bride, remove her headpiece and veil, and they should drink their wine. Instead, he sits. The pair of dragon and phoenix candles are burning fiercely, hot tears of wax cascading down, coagulating into pools of red at the base of the candles.

He sits, watching.

The candles burn low; the pools of red tears accumulate.

There is a sound, faint, muffled. Mingzhi traces the source of it, sees the slight movement: the trembling of her shoulders, the breathing that is getting short. Yet she tries to sit still, struggling to stop herself crying. Mingzhi stares at the patches of dark wet on the veil where the eyes are. *She doesn't have a choice either.* He thinks about Meilian, her wedding, and her tears, which he couldn't understand as a child.

And her, Jasmine. The footpath, the temple, the back garden, the lakeside. Her eyes, her dimples, her giggles.

His heart aches.

Was she happy at her wedding? He remembers her face

under the raised curtain, her curiosity. An active, lively soul.

And a murderer for husband. Mingzhi's heart sinks. The association troubles him. The question he has been suppressing rises in a rush: *Where is she now? Where is she?* He hears the sound of low sobbing, as if Jasmine is responding to him. He turns around.

His bride. She has buried her head in her hands, weeping. Mingzhi's heart melts. He moves forward, sits by her side and removes her headpiece and veil. A clean, innocent face, a glimpse of fear. She blinks, and the tears roll down like drops of pearl. Mingzhi gingerly dabs her cheeks with his sleeves. She glances up, but looks down hastily. Unsure. He holds her hand, gently stroking her soft, delicate skin. A reassurance: *I will treat you well, I promise.* He places his palm on hers, feels the warmth being channelled between them, running through him. A feeling he has never had before. *A woman, mine.* He sees her flush, knows he is blushing, too.

It's time for the wine, Mingzhi whispers to her ears.

Eighteen

Someone has spilt colours on the palette of his life. Everything brightens up. The new groom smiles, reading documents, writing comments, making decisions. Sitting in the carriage, touring the streets. He looks away with his dreamy eyes, a grin on his young face. Shakes his head in a fluster, pulling himself together. The servants exchange looks when their mandarin slips into his happiness, smile too. Happy to see him happy.

The couple like taking evening strolls in the garden, talking: his day in the office, the cases, his worries, solutions and ambitions; the patterns and colours of her embroidery, the clothes and shoes she has sewn, the pastries she has learned to bake. The heaviness of the day melts under her attentive gaze, soft whispers and shy smile. Sometimes they walk in silence, listening to the fishes, watching them. Quiet and content.

This evening, however, husband and wife decide to stay indoors. Sitting at his desk, Mingzhi glances up occasionally at his wife who stands to one side, grinding ink as he writes. A character, two, and more. Verses formed. A poem is taking shape: about her brows, her eyes, her lips. About the tiny mole above her upper lip, like a black pearl that dances when she smiles. And he reads it to her, watching as she blushes, feeling the sudden fullness in his chest. Surprised as the evening passes so quickly.

Little Mouse always knowingly retreats to his corner, allowing space for the couple. Now that he has more time to himself, he spends time with the servants and guards in the court-office, telling stories of his adventures with the mandarin to his new friends. About the Imperial City, Shanghai, the foreign devils. More dramatic, with added details.

~

News from the outside world doesn't seem good, though. In the Imperial City, the intellectual reformers stage yet another failed demonstration. Scraps of the appeal signed by two thousand *juren*s from eight districts swirl in the early breeze of 1898, falling to the ground, rotting fast in the spring rain, seeping deep into the soil. Taking with them the dignity of a nation. It is confirmed: the Germans have a firm grip on Qingdao.

His wife watches as Mingzhi reads the now widely circulated newspaper of the reformers, as he knits his brows tight, then eases: the former for the treaty; the latter the mushrooming of political groups across the country. A determination to fight against corrupt traditions and bureaucracy, to rescue the nation from its invaders.

There's still hope.

Mingzhi drinks the tea his wife brings him. Warm. Like

her smile. He wishes that all the chaos in the north would stop where it is. *Never to reign here; spare my family.* He is immediately ashamed of these thoughts, the cowardice fondly used by the enemies to describe his countrymen.

Hurriedly taking a drink of tea-for-hiding-shameful-thoughts, he chokes and coughs. His wife dabs his mouth and face with her silk kerchief, massages his back, laughing at his clumsiness. Mingzhi feels her soft touch, excuses himself for his cowardice.

—~—

Chaos reigns in the north, and ripples stir in the southern town. More disturbances are reported. The gang of thugs are getting bolder, robbing in daylight sometimes. Their targets are carefully chosen: travelling traders, visiting strangers, men and women in exquisite dresses and gowns. New to the town, less alert, more vulnerable. In quiet paths, side alleys, secluded corners.

Early morning, Mingzhi listens to reports from his chief guard. The townsfolk have been helpful, he is told, but the thugs are cunning. As though they can fathom the office's every move, and they leap a step ahead. The raid on an abandoned temple last week found only empty crates scattered around the dying embers: the men had fled, the goods taken, the ground still warm. Two days later, another raid, another narrow escape. This time silk pouches for jewellery were found. Empty, of course. The trader from the north swore never to return to Pindong.

Mingzhi sits back in his chair. The picture of a gloomy, desolate town looms on the horizon. He shudders, remembering the vibrant scene of his first visit. The colours, the sounds, the people. Their smiling faces.

No!

He sits up straight and drafts his plan. There will be plain-clothes in addition to the existing patrols. Not just double but triple the number of guards. A close relationship must be established with the *dibao*, the local security forces, who know everybody and every nook and cranny in town, getting them to get information. There will be rewards for useful intelligence.

A town map is unrolled in front of Mingzhi. Streets and alleys are marked, and beyond these, the routes leading to the town along which traders and visitors travel. He discusses his plan with the chief guard.

There are noises at the door. Mingzhi frowns but continues with his briefing.

'Second Young Master!' shouts Little Mouse, who is waiting to one side.

Mingzhi glances up.

Uncle Liwei. Ragged, pale-faced, shaking.

'They came from nowhere.' Uncle Liwei takes a sip of tea-for-calming. Fear and anger flicker like unsettled flames in his eyes. 'Everything happened so quickly.'

It was meant to be a surprise trip: to check on Mingzhi and Mingyuan. Master Chai ordered it and Uncle Liwei was delighted with the errand. A bundle was packed: more bird's nests and a new pair of shoes for Mingzhi, from Da Niang, of course. She had also sewn a gown for Mingyuan, with his name embroidered on the inside of the hem. A silent assurance of her care for him, the unfortunate orphan, the son of her deceased husband. A member of the family.

Bundle on his back, Uncle Liwei started early and arrived early. From a rise in the outskirts, the town was in sight: people, stalls, the roofs of buildings. *Mingzhi's residence and court-office.* Uncle Liwei hurried along.

Gravel crunched under feet. Shadows approached. Quick movements. A punch, and Uncle Liwei was knocked to the ground. His bundle was snatched, his shoulder pulled.

Two men, surly and burly, were fleeing.

'Give me back my things!' Uncle Liwei got to his feet and chased after his attackers, with courage he acquired from years of rent-collecting in remote regions, and the limited martial arts he had learned from Butler Feng. He pushed one of the men on his back, was pushed against by both of them. His martial arts turned to water. A kick, another punch, and he was on the ground again.

Mingzhi dabs *baihua* oil onto the cuts and bruises on Uncle Liwei's body. Tells him to relax. Tells him there is no lack of bird's nests, shoes or clothes, and that he shouldn't have given chase.

'They were from your mother.' Uncle Liwei's reason is firm and clear.

He did it for me.

Mingzhi averts his misty eyes and returns to rubbing the patches of blue-black off his uncle's shoulders. The shoulders he once rode on, strong and square.

And now.

Mingzhi feels the sagging flesh under the dull, freckled

skin. His uncle's body grows heavy, a dead weight leaning against him and the bedpost. He has dozed off.

Age has laid siege to him.

Something clenches inside Mingzhi. He doesn't stop massaging, though, enjoying the closeness with his uncle they once enjoyed. Happy for the chance to serve him. Glad to see the healthy colour of red gradually return, clogged blood smoothened.

—w—

Before dusk, before he has come to terms with the loss, Uncle Liwei's bundle is returned.

By Mingyuan.

He says he found it in a quiet alley. He says no one was there. He says he picked it up and saw that it belonged to the family.

He says, he says, he says.

The gang!

Immediately there is a tumult and they are too busy to ask questions: Uncle Liwei checks the bundle for his bird's nests, clothes and shoes; Mingzhi summons his chief guard and sends his men, hoping that the gang has left a trail.

There is no trace of the thugs, yet again.

Uncle Liwei insists and a dinner is arranged. Mingyuan is summoned to Mingzhi's residence: uncle and nephews sitting together at the dinner table for the first time. After a round of tea Uncle Liwei happily distributes the bird's nests, clothes and shoes. Is happier to learn that Mingyuan has earned his first four-tael scholarship. A big leap forward, he nods approvingly. The best report he will bring home to Master Chai.

As for Mingzhi –

Law and order in the town has to be restored. Uncle Liwei's face is stern. The criminals are to be caught and prosecuted. Didn't you promise to serve your people? He looks Mingzhi in the eyes, an expectation rather than a reprimand. But Mingzhi becomes agitated, ashamed. From across the table his half-brother Mingyuan darts a cynical look of *useless*. Mingzhi feels his face burning: *I did do something!* Quickly he broaches his plans: the plain-clothes, the deployment of *dibao*, the scheduling of patrols and the targeted routes. His voice loud in the quiet room to an audience of two: one, exhausted and still in shock, half-listening; the other, young and clear-minded, fully attentive.

Mingyuan.

Sitting still, memorizing every word Mingzhi says, every move he outlines. His eyes flicker, his expression unruffled.

The insidious vine of darkness grows again, stretching its amorphous arms around the high pillars and beams of the government office, under the cement floor of the mandarin's residence.

Quietly, quietly.

—∾—

Two weeks on and the gang has been quiet. As in a game of cat-and-mouse, the cat stays in bright light, the mouse in the dark, observing its predator's every move: sidling away as it glimpses a furry paw, hiding when the enemy presses close. Waiting. For the right moment to strike again.

Morning, and Mingzhi takes a tour of the town, threading between the stalls, the people, the noise of haggling and street buskers. The colours.

The smiling faces.

As though nothing has happened before, and nothing will ever happen again.

Stay vigilant, the mandarin orders.

Shadows, whispers, surreptitious movements. In a dark alley, three figures huddle in a corner: two big, one lean. Low voices of suppressed argument, gradually rising.

'Don't do anything just yet.'

'We're bored to death, and the money's running out!'

'The guards are everywhere. Wait a little longer.'

Mingyuan.

And the former hatchet men of Mandarin Liu, who are eager to launch their strikes again, to indulge themselves with drink and women that only money can buy. Money from vulnerable hawkers and shop owners, tradesmen and travellers, which has also funded Mingyuan's games of cards and dice.

'Wait? For how long?'

'As long as I tell you to.' Mingyuan turns to leave. The two men shift quickly in front of him, blocking his way. He steps back, and the men move forward, two giant shadows looming over him. Mingyuan holds his breath, shells out his money and gives it to them: 'Take this. I'll come up with something soon.'

Mingyuan watches as his hatchet men walk away. There is an uneasy feeling in the pit of his stomach, as if something, some caterpillars, are wriggling inside him. Hundreds of tiny legs march on, bristly hair brushes against the soft lining of his insides. Itchy, eerie.

They are getting out of control.

He shakes his head. The caterpillars coil up, stay motionless. For the time being.

Father Terry is leaving on a month-long errand to the Imperial City. Plain-clothed, Mingzhi goes to the river port to see him off.

Father Terry has been quiet: brows knitted tight, deep in thought. Mingzhi walks with him in silence. A long sigh, and the priest finally speaks. There have been attacks on his missionaries, mostly in the cities: congregations disrupted, churches broken into, property stolen, icons destroyed. Words of abuse painted on the walls of the church, verbal and physical abuse. Meeting after meeting has taken place with local governments, and finally Father Terry is summoned to the headquarters: to help with negotiations, to draft new strategies.

His voice turns low and deep: 'We are here to help them!'

Mingzhi pats Father Terry's shoulder, a silent comfort to his friend: *they will understand, eventually*.

It is a hot afternoon, the sun scorching. The port is busy. People shuffle, seeing someone off or being seen off; goods are piled up, waiting to be shipped or stored or transported straight to the marketplace. Dockers making countless trips in lines up and down the wooden gangplank between the goods, the warehouses and the ships, loading or unloading. A token is given for every trip they make, which will be exchanged for wages at the end of the day.

Stooped under their heavy burdens, they grit their teeth, struggling forward. Beads of sweat roll down their naked upper bodies; their muscles strain, their faces contort. The stronger among them take firm strides, making quicker trips, collecting as many tokens as they can. Most others, though, strive to balance the load on their slender backs and their movements on the shaking gangplank. Underneath them, the water surges, slapping against the pillars, the shore and the sides of the ships. Their legs tremble and they take slow steps, each more careful than the one before, knowing well that one false move could cost them their lives.

Mingzhi notes the signs of hardship: weather-worn faces, shrivelled lips, protruding ribs and collarbones on sunburnt bodies.

These are my people. He feels his scalp itch in the blazing sun.

Flop! An object plunges heavily into the water.

'Help! Someone's fallen!' A loud cry.

Mingzhi turns to the source of the commotion. On the gangplank, the men drop the goods they carry and peer into the river, shouting and pointing. Apparently a docker has lost his footing.

'There, there he is! Quick!'

Flop! Flop! Two figures jump in the pointed direction. At the edge of the pier and on the ships, onlookers congregate, jostling each other aside to get the best view.

The hue and cry intensifies as Mingzhi and Father Terry approach the crowd. A loud hurray, and a man is pulled from the river onto the dock. Lying frail and wet on the ground, the man coughs out water and vomits, gasping for air. Through the gaps between shuffling legs, Mingzhi glimpses the unfortunate man – *it's him!* His heart thumps, and he stares hard. More people press in and the gaps are sealed off. *No!* Mingzhi squeezes through the many sweaty bodies to the front.

And he sees him.
Little Sparrow.

~

Mingzhi gazes at his long-lost friend, lying in bed, muttering, his face contorted as if in pain. A nightmare, perhaps a dreadful experience is haunting him. *What has happened in all these years?* Mingzhi is eager to have a long talk with him, to fill in the blanks between them, the Lost Time. To listen to his friend's stories, and tell him his, as they once did. So much to talk about, so many questions to ask.

Little Sparrow stays in bed for two days, drifting in and out of consciousness, only waking for sips of porridge and herbal soup prepared by Little Mouse on Mingzhi's orders. Exhaustion, the doctor diagnoses. The remedies are food and rest.

Mingzhi sits by his friend's bedside, reading the traces of his life since they parted: his rough, sallow face, drawn cheeks and dark-ringed eyes, calloused knuckles and protruding joints. Hard work, poverty, malnutrition.

There is a sudden tightening in Mingzhi's chest: the delicate, graceful opera singer he knew has long gone.

When Little Sparrow is finally awake, he says: 'Call me Tiansheng.' 'Little Sparrow' is a reminder of his glorious yet painful past. Mingzhi understands: *Tiansheng*, from the sky. From nowhere. *But you'll know where you're heading to, I'll see to that.* Mingzhi is determined.

Tiansheng looks round the room: the exquisite rosewood moon table, and on top of it the porcelain vase with a detailed painting of court women of the Tang Dynasty; then at the mandarin by his bedside: immaculate gown, jade-tasselled waistband, delicately embroidered shoes; and finally, at himself – nothing. Nothing that he has with him now belongs to him. *Difference* swells between them like a green-eyed monster, wielding its powerful weapons of class and status.

What does his friend expect of him, Tiansheng wonders. Descriptions of a life on the streets would be too much for the mandarin. The struggle for each gulp of rice, each sip of water. Fights, quick snatches of food at street corners, thieving in mansions filled with valuables like the one he is in right now. Drifting in and out of odd jobs at the dock, if he is lucky, though he is barely fit for them.

He stares blankly as Mingzhi excitedly lays out his plans: a private tutor for Tiansheng until he is confident enough to go to school; and he will, of course, live under his roof. The Lost Time has to be recaptured, bought back, and Tiansheng will become a member of the gentry. Wasn't that your childhood dream? Mingzhi raises his voice, and he sees his friend sitting beside him in his court-office. Mandarin and assistant working side by side, complementing one another.

Tiansheng shakes his head and closes his eyes.

Mingzhi lets him. *He is tired.* His friend is with him now and there will be plenty of chances to catch up.

Tiansheng has turned to face the wall and seems to have drifted off. *Sleep well.* Mingzhi smiles, closing the door behind him. *A bowl of rice porridge with scallops will help him recuperate.* He makes a mental note to remind Little Mouse about the breakfast preparation.

—∾—

Porridge with scallops, a treat too good for a street rat, perhaps. In the morning, Little Mouse comes to his master's room with the bowl of the untouched delicacy.

'What a waste of my efforts!' the young servant grumbles, staring at the strips of yellowish scallop floating in the steaming white porridge. Can't wait to have a taste of it, the smooth, tender texture and the sweetness.

Tiansheng has left in the middle of the night, without saying goodbye. Taking with him the porcelain vase.

Mingzhi rushes into the empty room. He feels the slight curve in the middle of the bed with his hand, the only evidence that his friend was ever there. It's cold. He fumbles for the pouch tied to his waist, takes out the bamboo-leaf flute. Remembers the music it could give; remembers too the talks, the long nights by the river. All so vivid in his mind's eye.

He tries to play a tune. It is mute. Quietly, his wife comes to him and helps him put the flute back in the pouch. Knowing he will always treasure it as he has done all these years. Mingzhi takes her hands in his, grinding them into his cheeks, feeling the softness against his flesh, a reassuring comfort. He buries his face in them.

Slowly, his wife moves his head down and rests it on her belly. And he hears it, the faint beat of life. He looks up. She nods, smiling, smiling.

A job that serves the people, a wife who listens and cares, occasional secret family gatherings. And a new life, the combined essence of himself and his wife, growing inside her. Life seems to be complete, full. He knows he is already blessed, to expect more would be shameful. Mingzhi quietly thanks his grandfather for the favour he did him: the marriage, that brought him his beloved wife and the soon-to-be child.

Though it doesn't seem so favourable for the old man.

—~—

The wedding has ceased to serve the function Master Chai hoped for. In Plum Blossom Village, the rain has finally stopped. And as though he regrets the earlier downpour, the Heavenly God decides that it's time to turn the pipe off. Click. Not another drop is to be wasted.

In the late spring, Master Chai stands on the hill rise and stares blankly at the fields, the shrunken pods at the tips of the stalks, as wrinkled as his aged and anxious face. Gone is the milk inside them, the juice of his wealth.

What more can I do? He thumps the sharp tail of his dragon stick heavily down as though it is the source of his anger, and he is pounding it away. The stick bounces against the hard, stony ground, jarring his hand, and he loses hold of it.

He watches as it rolls down the slope, as Butler Feng chases clumsily after it.

In the distance, the Plum River glistens in the morning sun, winding round the western hill, slithering across the fields like a band of silver ribbon carelessly dropped on the earth. There are little polka dots on it: smaller spots for rafts, bigger marks for boats.

Salt boats.

Which will leave without the opium.

Master Chai stares at the white sails of the boats, raised high, bulging in the wind, and thinks about the snowy salt stored underneath. The merchants who trade it. The licences they need for trading.

He smiles.

Master Chai waves at Butler Feng who has just climbed up the slope, huffing and puffing. Urging him to hurry. Snatching his stick from him. The old man has a plan to work on, and time is too precious to be wasted.

~

When Father Terry returns to Pindong Town, it is his turn to face a vandalized church. Although the icons are unharmed, a couple of benches-for-pews are broken, and the gold-plated candle holders and the donation box containing the last collection are missing.

Much to Father Terry's relief, though, the new building next to the church is unscathed.

Mingzhi stands alongside Father Terry in front of the whitewashed walls, listening to his priest friend's plans for an orphanage. His determination to serve the community is undeterred by the assault on the church. There have been infants – mostly girls – left abandoned in fields and back alleys, and on a couple of occasions, on his doorstep. They are lucky, though, for the real unfortunates sink quietly into the Plum River, or rot in shallow graves at the back of the western hill. The money to raise them has been saved for a few sacks of rice, or a cow to plough the field – if there is any cash at all.

Father Terry has employed some wet-nurses, and Meilian and Jiaxi have agreed to help run the place.

Mingzhi notes the passion in Father Terry's eyes. He imagines a room full of children, chubby and happy, slowly growing to adulthood, with an abundance of energy and intelligence to offer the country.

A picture of a strong, healthy nation is in view. He will encourage his wife to join Meilian and Jiaxi.

—~—

It's a fine morning for the opening of the orphanage. Mingzhi attends the ceremony as guest of honour in his mandarin gown: a statement of his support for Father Terry, a request for the support of his people.

A crowd has already gathered outside as Mingzhi arrives in his carriage. He is glad at first. *They do appreciate his good deed.* But not for long. From among the onlookers come pointing fingers and looks of suspicion directed at the new building, and complaints, which subside when Mingzhi steps out of his carriage. Then again, pointing fingers resume pointing, looks of suspicion look on. The buzz of discontent rises again like a swarm of humming bees.

'Tuh, you call this a celebration?'

'White? How inauspicious!'

Mingzhi glances around.

At the door of the orphanage, two thin bands of white silk are tied across, the substitutes for ribbon in the opening ceremony. And Father Terry stands by the gate, looking confused. Mingzhi smiles, shaking his head. He pulls Father Terry aside and whispers in his ear.

Midday now, and a long piece of red cloth has replaced the white, which immediately lightens up the atmosphere. With Little Mouse's help, two strings of firecrackers are hung from the doorposts. Plates of buns and mandarin oranges are laid out on a long table.

Joss stick in hand, Mingzhi ignites the firecrackers. *Bang-bang! Bang-bang!* And thunderous cheers and applause break out in response.

Father Terry nods at the people now gathered at the table, enjoying the food. He pats Mingzhi's shoulder, thanking him. In the front courtyard of the orphanage, children shower each other with handfuls of red flakes. Their cheeks bulge with buns and oranges, their faces a healthy glow. Knowing that Meilian and Jiaxi are inside the building, Mingzhi, eager to meet them, turns to enter.

There is a shout, struggling to make itself heard. A man pushes hastily forward through the crowd.

Butler Feng.

He rushes to Mingzhi.

'Eldest Great Grand Master!' he calls breathlessly. 'The master is here to visit. He is waiting at the government office.'

Mingzhi freezes. The laughter and noises fade out.

In the sky far off, a lump of dark cloud begins its journey to Pindong Town. Heavy rain is on its way.

Nineteen

It rains. At first there are only a few drops here and there, then the roof shudders, thunder roars. As if the heavens have cracked open, and the Heavenly God and his Heavenly Palace fall rumbling down, together with his squadron of heavenly guards and servants.

The first rain in Plum Blossom Village in a month.

It is midday and Master Chai isn't there to welcome it, the juice of life he has been yearning for. He left for Pindong Town this morning and is now waiting for Mingzhi in his reception hall.

Da Niang is alone. The smell of heavy air, the damp heat, overwhelms the incense in her room. Needlework still in hand, she stares out of the window at the water cascading from the eaves and wonders if her father-in-law would have stayed had the rain come earlier. Wonders if he would have left Mingzhi alone.

Mingzhi. She sighs.

On the windowsill, a trail of ants hurry across on their way to find a safer home. The rain has caught them unprepared.

Like the old man's visit to Pindong. She wishes she could do something, but she wasn't even in time to send a warning. It was as though the old man decided at the moment he opened his eyes in the morning: calling for Butler Feng, packed and left; leaving Liwei in charge of the household, and both he and Da Niang were barred from travelling to Pindong. Simple, short and clear, obviously after long and careful planning.

He doesn't trust anyone. Da Niang lays down her needlework. On the wall, black ants with fat bottoms scurry away from the windowsill, slithering all the way up to the beam, the S-shape of a moving black line against the whitewash. She lifts her head and follows the dark thread along the beam, remembering the column of ants on Mingzhi's birth. Wishes, again, that his father were there. To help him. Wishes they were all together. A family.

The thought scares her. She hastily picks up the garment she has been sewing, a gown of fine cotton she has spun for days and nights. That will last for a long trip of two months in the country and still look good. She thinks about how *he* would look in his new attire. How *he* would respond on receiving it. With a smile and a long, deep gaze, as *he* always does, perhaps. Her fingers quiver; the needle pokes the pad of her finger. She gasps *Ouch!* lightly, unaware that a drop of blood has dripped onto the sleeve of the half-sewn gown.

Da Niang looks out of the window as she sucks her finger to stop the bleeding. The rain has stopped as quickly as it came, as though the Heavenly God has just made a mistake (*not here, you fool*) and is quick to realize and correct it. Blackness lines the horizon. The lump of dark cloud that has covered the mansion is now moving north-eastwards, slowly, steadily.

To Pindong Town.

Da Niang drops the gown, rushes to the altar, burns some incense and starts chanting.

Naminumemo. Naminumemo.

—w—

In his sedan Mingzhi sees the cloud, dark and heavy, driven by the wind, following him all the way back to the government office. Still accumulating, still pressing down. He feels it crowding his stomach, and wishes he could turn away from it, the gigantic black devil, leaving it behind the way he left the mansion and Plum Blossom Village.

He closes his eyes and leans wearily against the side of the sedan.

The rain pours down, hitting against the thin canopy of the sedan, drumming on Mingzhi's heart.

—w—

The patter on the roof of the government office excites Grandfather Master Chai. He listens to the *dot-dot-dot* that turns to *plop-plop-plop* on the solid green tiles, imagines water filling up the cracked land, seeping through the dried earth. Imagines the peasants, their hoes and rakes on their backs, on their way to plough the fields. Imagines them sowing seeds. He sees blooming red poppies, gradually turning into milky sap. And there comes the next harvest.

The old man smooths his goatee and takes a puff from

his pipe. He is certain he has made the right move, and that the Heavenly God has granted His approval. The rain is the sign. *Mingzhi is still my lucky star.* He regrets that he didn't come earlier.

Taking another puff, he relaxes in his grandson's redwood chair. The chair that the mandarin sits in to receive his guests. That the old man will continue to sit in to receive his guests for days to come.

The cushion is soft, the hall airy and the monotonous rhythm of the rain soothing. *It's comfortable here, like home.* He dozes off.

—ʬ—

Mingyuan would have wished he were in a position as comfortable as his grandfather. The young man is running in the rain. Beads of water hit against his head and body. Every inch of him is bursting with pain, his new gown smudged with dirt, his shoes caked with mud.

Wet cotton sticks to his body like another layer of skin. His long gown slaps against his legs as he strives to lift each in turn, to hurry forward. Each step becomes heavier than the one before it.

Still, he keeps running.

A while ago, Mingyuan had gone to the shack in the east end of town, the gang's hiding place, to meet his men. They were not there, and Mingyuan knew where they had gone. As if they had suddenly regained their missing brains, the two thugs had come up with a brilliant idea: to launch their first strike for a month during the opening of the orphanage, when the townsfolk would be gathered at the ceremony. When the guards would be pulled away from the town centre to accompany the mandarin to the event.

They had selected their target: a new face in the marketplace, a young poultry hawker. Skinny, effeminate, seemingly defenceless.

Their elated laughter shook the shabby shack last night as they broached their plan. Mingyuan had tried to hush them down, 'Not yet, let's wait a little longer!' and was hushed back. He was asked to pay them their allowance instead if he was to stop them.

'Before midday; that's as long as we can wait.' They slammed the door in Mingyuan's face. The hairy caterpillars that had been hibernating stuck up their heads, burrowing their way into the cosy home they had missed for so long. Tender bristles brushing against soft stomach.

Mingyuan's abdomen crumpled.

Strings of cash clanking on his belt, Mingyuan holds them with one hand as he leaps over puddles. Water seeps through his finely embroidered shoes, sharp gravel stabs at the thin soles.

He was listening out for news early this morning, and it was confirmed: the policing of the town was to keep to its usual schedule. The mandarin didn't require extra protection, and had insisted on putting the security of his people before his own.

In his room Mingyuan had emptied his chests and cupboards, searching his pouch and kerchiefs, fumbling under his bed and bedding. The four-tael scholarship, which he won with essays bought for eight taels from a bright but needy student, has long gone. The allowance from Mingzhi is never enough for drink and dice, and for the hatchet men, who are supposed to generate an income for him. Now he has to stuff their mouths with cash.

On the floor the sunlight that slanted through the east-facing window was retreating by the inch, so his heart kept shrinking. When the golden light began to slip out of the window and the thick rain cloud took its place, he grabbed his jade tassel and darted out.

He didn't argue when Uncle Eagle paid him half the price the jade was worth.

Still, he missed the deadline.

Mingyuan glances ahead. Not far away a team of six guards in cloaks and bamboo hats walks out of an alley onto the main street. Mingyuan skids to a halt and watches the guards proceed in the opposite direction. He sighs with relief. Tells himself he will get to the two men before the guards do.

As he stands still he begins to feel the muddy wetness inside his shoes, the sticky itchiness between his toes, like the hairy caterpillars that wriggle inside him. Something is going to happen, he knows it for certain. *But what?* For the first time, a feeling of extreme uneasiness crawls from his tail bone, along his spinal cord to the top of his head. Then comes the cold sweat. *They will hand me over to Mingzhi; I'm sure they will.* He realizes, too late, that the men are unreliable. That they will put the blame on him, the gang-master, if they are caught.

Damn! He spits and resumes running.

He has nearly reached the marketplace when he spots the two figures ahead of him. Vague, distant, fast-moving through the rain. He quickens his pace, gasping for air, but only rainwater flows into his mouth. He chokes and starts coughing.

The gang has now disappeared into a side street. Mingyuan follows.

The marketplace, a square. Canopies, makeshift thatched roofs. Dark and gloomy in the rain. There are no signs of customers, only a few hawkers squat at the stalls, hoping for the chance of a few strings of cash for the day. Mingyuan threads his way between the stalls, stepping over rotten leaves and fruit, decomposing fish guts, heads and feet of chicken and duck, retching at the smell.

There is a shout, coming from the far end of the square. Mingyuan runs to it.

At a poultry stall a young man is pinned face down on the wooden worktop by the two hatchet men. His butcher's knives are shoved to one side. His chickens are hysterical, stepping on each other and knocking against the wicker baskets in which they are caged. Feathers fly loose, falling lifelessly to the ground.

'Stop it!'

'Good timing, Boss! He said he has no money. Do you believe him?'

Immediately there are raised fists, heavy blows and groans.

'You fools!' Mingyuan lunges at them, they all stumble, and the hawker gets loose. The hatchet men grab him. He grabs the knife by his side. Mingyuan rushes to stop his men.

A flash of metal.

A splash of red.

A scream.

Mingyuan falls to the ground, his body in spasm. Blood spouts from the deep wound on his chest; he clutches at it with his hand but the blood keeps flowing. His eyes roll back, then everything stops: the spasms, the rolling eyes, the bleeding.

The hawker drops his knife, standing stock-still. He rubs his face with his blood-stained hand.

Tiansheng, or Little Sparrow from the Lost Time.

There are approaching footsteps and noises. Tiansheng watches as rain-diluted blood is washed into the ditch.

More footsteps and noise. Once more he is pinned against the worktop. He doesn't move this time, doesn't feel the pain in his wrists and arms, the kicks on his calves. Doesn't hear the rain, the shouts, the smashing of his stall.

He thinks about the shed of chicks in his shelter, waiting to be fed. Waiting to grow bigger and fatter, to be sold. To be turned into cash. Then he will reclaim the porcelain vase from the pawn shop and return it to where it came from. He will thank him, his friend, for a chance of the new life. Or maybe he will wait until he is able to write a note himself, and quietly leave it with the vase on the moon table, where it was before. *What if they've got a new vase?* He decides that he will put the vase and the note on the floor next to the table if this should be the case.

The chicks must be hungry. They can never get enough. A couple of them like to peck the toes that stick out from his tattered shoes, seemingly their favourite appetizer. He giggles but lets them, the tingling sensation as pleasant as their chirps.

Maybe I should get some ducks, too. He thinks about those little furry yellow balls rolling about in his palms. The touch of softness.

Quack-quack-quack, quack-quack-quack.

~

Master Chai shakes, his face grey; green veins dance like snakes on his forehead. He curses and spits at Tiansheng, kicks him and hits him with his stick, again and again, until the angry old man is led off to the reception hall on Mingzhi's orders.

Mingzhi sits holding his head. His grandfather's voice and the crushing of ceramic drill into his ears. The familiar rage. The poisonous vines deep-rooted in the old mansion are now snaking triumphantly up the pillars and beams of the court-office, spewing out the memories he has been striving to push away. The nightmares.

He remembers the night when Er Niang was caught. The chaos, the spitting and cursing, and the order to drown her and her lover.

The evening of Meifong's death. The refusal to call a doctor. The order for the rapid disposal of her body.

The moment when his foreign books were found. The shock and humiliation, and the order that he be housebound.

The scene of Master Chai's sixtieth birthday. The broken cup, the opera, Charcoal, the Green Snake. The order for Little Sparrow to be dismissed from the opera troupe.

And now. *What will his order be this time?*

Mingzhi glances at the figure in front of him, face down, tied up and kneeling on the floor, quiet and still. He wonders what is in his friend's mind.

There are patches of blood on Tiansheng's shirt, Mingzhi notices, strikingly red against the worn-out cotton. *Not his, but someone else's. Someone.* Mingzhi tries not to think about it and averts his gaze, and so he sees that *someone*. Mingyuan. Lying in a corner of the hall, eyes wide open. As if he is refusing to acknowledge his death (*too soon, so unexpected*), to be denied his long-awaited revenge against his half-brother. *When was the last time we spoke to each other?* Mingzhi's heart clenches. The boy who joined him in reciting poems on their long walk to school wanders into his mind's eye. He hears his childish voice, his clear laughter, the echoes in the wilderness.

Mingzhi turns to Tiansheng, then back to Mingyuan. Then again. Tiansheng, Mingyuan. Mingyuan, Tiansheng.

My brother.

My friend.

The thugs, kneeling next to Tiansheng, take the silence as an opportunity to plead their innocence: blaming Mingyuan for all their evil deeds, insisting that Tiansheng attacked Mingyuan all of a sudden.

Two tongues against one. One that utters not a word.

Mingzhi watches the men gibber and babble, two bumblebees buzzing busily. His head is bursting. He has to do something, anything. He fumbles on his desk, reaches for the inkwell and hurls it to the floor.

Thump!

Silence. An unprecedented deep, dead silence in response to an unprecedented act from the mandarin.

It doesn't last long, though.

'Chop off the bastard's head, right now! I order you!' Master Chai shouts from the reception hall. *The order!* Mingzhi's body turns rigid. The invisible vines creep into his head, crowding in. He sees himself kneeling in the ancestral hall, shrouded in a thick smoke of incense.

'Your order, sir?' The chief guard's voice rings in his ears. The smoke, the ancestral hall vanish. Mingzhi is back in his court-office.

'Take them down.' Mingzhi's hand drops wearily onto the desk as he watches the captives being dragged away to the detention cells in the dungeon. He needs time to work out a plan. *Little Mouse. Where is Little Mouse*? He needs his loyal servant to help him with this.

—⁓—

It's a delightful surprise, the order from his master. Little Mouse stops grumbling about having only the garden to tend, the fishes to care for, since his once important task of preparing bird's nest soup has been taken over by Mingzhi's wife. Right now he has another chance to prove his usefulness. *And it's my most important job so far!* The excitement overcomes his mousy brain, and he overlooks the consequences that will come with this mission. That will change his life forever.

Little Mouse descends the stairs to the dungeon, a wicker basket in hand. Wine and groundnuts, a set of dice. Perfect companions for the night-watchmen, a treat too good to resist in view of the long hours ahead.

Drinks, snacks, games. Their laughter bounces off the stone walls of the dungeon. Little Mouse keeps losing at both the dice and the finger-guessing games he is good at, and so he keeps pouring wine for the winners, who, overjoyed, drink more than their fair share. By midnight, heads are drooping, loud cheers and sighs of victory or defeat reduced to drunken mutterings. Then, one by one, they flop down on the table.

Next comes the groping for keys.

The click of the cell door.

Another two clicks from the hand and leg cuffs.

One last click from the main entrance.

In the darkness, two shadows duck out of the government office, moving swiftly to the waiting carriage, which sets off at once, heading north.

Little Mouse crouches in his seat, his body swaying to the wobbling of the carriage. Sitting next to him, Tiansheng is quiet. The young servant turns to look back at the building he escaped from, a gloomy silhouette, fast disappearing. Abruptly all the exhilaration of the rescue mission evaporates. He realizes that this is not a game; that he is leaving his master. *Who will wait by his side at the court-office? To grind ink for him, get him what he needs? Who's going to take care of the garden and the fishes?* A sudden emptiness seizes him. His mind goes blank. He wants to shout, to stop the carriage, but his throat feels dry and tight, as though something is stuck in it. He hides his face in his hands and finds it wet with tears.

~

Mingzhi hides his face in his hands and finds it wet with tears. It is pitch black in the garden and he doesn't carry a candle or a paraffin lamp, doesn't wish to wake his wife, already troubled by his worries. A while ago he heard the carriage, clear clatters loud in the empty street, gradually fading away. He wishes he could have left with it, too, but he can only sit and wait.

For tomorrow.

For another outbreak of rage, another roar. More cursing and spitting.

But they never come.

Master Chai lies in bed, too weak to curse and spit, to rage and roar. His head is heavy but he refuses to follow the doctor's advice: to close his eyes and rest. Above him, the vermilion satin lining of the bed-net sways lightly in the occasional gusts of morning breeze from the open window, like the curtain of an opera stage. *Opera?* A far-off memory slowly takes shape. A young face emerges, becoming clearer, blending with the features of the escaped murderer.

His second grandson's murderer. A friend of his eldest grandson.

He feels the urgent need for a boost, a few puffs of opium, enough to keep him up for a while. To give orders.

Order One: Mingzhi will return to Plum Blossom Village to administer his half-brother's funeral, while his grandfather, unfit for travel, stays in Pindong.

Order Two: To ensure that the proceedings of the funeral are observed according to tradition, Mingzhi is to stay for the full *qiqi*, the seven-times-seven-day ritual, before coming back to Pindong.

'Don't forget, he is your brother!' Master Chai expends the last of his borrowed energy on the final word, closes his eyes and slumps in his bed, panting. The word 'brother' drums in Mingzhi's ears, and he knows. That his grandfather knows.

—∾—

Because the elders are forbidden to mourn for the young, because he died unmarried and childless, Mingyuan, in his coffin, lies small and lonely in the central hall. Even smaller and lonelier at night, under the yellowish light of the two giant lanterns that hang high above the altar.

Mingzhi lays the little book of *Sanzi Jing* on top of the bier. On the altar, Mingyuan smiles a bright, innocent smile in his portrait, the work of the finest painter in town, commissioned by Mingzhi. His teeth look dazzlingly white against the carefully coloured lips, as they did when he was a child.

'Men are kind-natured when they are born,' Mingzhi mutters, pacing the room. 'Their natures are similar; their habits become different . . .'

Tears trickle down his cheeks.

Around him, strips of white paper are draped loosely on the wall, where his own shadows loom like trolls as he moves about. The long, dark shapes extend themselves from his feet, standing tall in front of him as if they were devils lurking inside him, his guilt, now lunging at him.

I know, I know, I promised to look after him!

He presses his body hard against the wall, crushing the shadows beneath him. His tears wet the whitewashed walls.

There is a grip from behind; Uncle Liwei takes his nephew in his arms. Mingzhi weeps, his sobbing muffled by his uncle's shoulder.

Mingzhi returns to Pindong Town to a happy, bustling Master Chai. The old man has been enjoying the title of Grandfather of the Mandarin and the privileges that come with it. Since the news that *The mandarin's grandfather is in town!* has broken, visitors – tradesmen, merchants, gentry – have been streaming in with handfuls of gifts and red goodwill-packets. Master Chai has received them all, and their gifts and red envelopes, of course, with a wide smile on his face. Soon, friends and families of the defendants in court cases and convicted criminals join the queue: the mandarin's grandfather will take what the mandarin won't.

And they hope he will, in return, also give them what the mandarin won't.

That, they will find out soon.

Worst of all, the old man has pocketed cash from hopeful merchants desperate for the much sought after salt permits, the assurance of wealth. Four thousand taels each, no more, no less, now lies safely in Master Chai's hoard.

Ten certificates, waiting to be stamped and issued.

Mingzhi pushes away the list his grandfather Chai lays on his desk, and it is pushed back.

Master Chai looks at his grandson with knowing eyes. 'At least,' he says, 'I haven't asked you to track down the murderer.' He takes a puff from his pipe. 'But the Governor will, if he finds out.'

Mingzhi's hands shake.

Thump! He sees the seal stamp on the open page of the Confucian readings, his guide to good moral conduct, already stained by his part in Tiansheng's escape.

Thump! Thump! Thump! Thump!

Thick, stubborn red ink overwrites the black-and-white rules of right and wrong, what to do and what not to do.

~

Mingzhi finds himself in the main hall of the provincial government office, head down, on all fours. The room is spacious and the white, shiny marble on the floor feels cold under his knees and palms. He shivers.

'Chai Mingzhi!'

The Governor sits high in his chair, his face stern. 'You will pay for what you've done.'

He scribbles on a scroll, finishes it off with a seal, then throws it to the floor. Thump! The decree unfolds itself in front of Mingzhi.

Death Sentence

Black characters on white paper, swelling and reeling, gradually dissolve into the sinister faces of the God of Death and his faithful wardens, Cowhead and Horseface. Brandishing their spears, laughing at Mingzhi, reproaching him.

He shrinks back.

'Take him to the block, right now!'

The court guards step forward, one on each side, and pull Mingzhi away.

'No, no!'

He stirs in bed; sweat shines on his forehead. Opening his eyes, the gauzy bed-net surrounds him like a smokescreen, blurring his gaze, and he is unable to see beyond it. *Where am I?* Mingzhi sits up in a fluster.

There is a faint sound of breathing. He turns and sees his wife asleep next to him, her face tranquil.

He heaves a long sigh.

Another nightmare. The same as the one he had last night, and the night before.

Mingzhi leans against the bedpost, staring blankly ahead. On the gauze before him, Peasant Xu's face looms.

It was a simple case. He had only to return the land title to Peasant Xu, the little piece of fertile field bequeathed to the peasant by his ancestors, which was snatched by Landlord Yao.

He didn't.

The landlords are friends, Yao and Master Chai, and some silver has further strengthened their friendship.

The feature of the old peasant in the court-office that day sways before Mingzhi: the look of despair, the deadness in his eyes. And his attendants' stares of surprise, sharp against his shame-filled face.

Peasant Xu hanged himself that night.

In another case, a convicted murderer was set free (*you've already set one free, anyway*), and in another, a gambling house which Mingzhi had closed down was permitted to reopen.

The mandarin no longer tours the streets. The pointing fingers, whispered comments and contemptuous gaze are too much to bear.

'Time has shown him in his true colours, after all.' A voice rings in his ears. He balls his fist and hits his thigh, again and again, and feels the pain deep inside him.

'Another nightmare?' Awake now, his wife sits up and begins to massage his head. Mingzhi takes her in his arms instead, holding her tight. He is careful not to press against her belly, now showing. Gently protecting them, his wife and the new life inside her.

His only hope. That keeps him going.

Twenty

The same unyielding hope boils up an early summer in the Imperial City. Deep inside the Forbidden Palace, the embryo of reformation is now taking shape, a warm, comfortable cradle readily laid out by the young Emperor. A team of devoted progressive intellectuals hovers round, waiting to serve and nurture the new life.

As if regretting the days it has missed for arriving late, the child in the womb grows with astonishing speed. Extending its body and limbs, stretching and kicking. An active, vibrant life, ignorant of the threats soon to come.

Within days, decree after decree is drafted, with a seal from the Emperor: new schools, of defence, science, technology, economics, agriculture; new ministerial departments, of commerce, agricultural geology; new practices, of Western defence, law and legislation.

Old, corrupt customs are scrapped. Gone are the days of foot-binding, of tears and disfigurement. Of wobbling around in pain for the sexual pleasure of men, who toy with women, with the power, authority and status bequeathed to them by their ancestors. Unquestionable norms are questioned, for the well-being of the entire nation, the one and only long-term destination.

Gone also the eight-legged style, the classical writing used in the Imperial civil-service examinations. New literature, new knowledge and plain language prevail in this era of change.

Conservative, old-system-favouring officials are demoted or dismissed; young, forward-thinking intellectuals rule.

Hot, steaming hot. The heat that blurs the eyes and seals the ears; that melts away fear and caution.

And so, eyes are blinded to the discontented faces, ears deafened to the grievances that swell as speedily as the foetus of reformation, and weave their way into the heart of the Garden of Peace and Harmony, where the real power lies. Where the Lady Dragon, her eyes and ears wide open, observes. Every saying, every move. And waits, with the patience of someone nearly a century in age, and the shrewdness of the legendary thousand-year-old fox, counting the days. One, two, three, four, five, six . . .

And autumn comes.

Autumn comes early in Pindong Town, as does the labour. The first contractions begin at midnight. Her eyes small and puffy, the midwife drags her equally sleepy body to the mandarin's residence, and is fully awake when she enters the room. Immediately orders are given: hot water, scissors, towels. More towels! Her voice wavers, her tone conveys nerves: quick, quick, double quick! No time is to be wasted.

Barred from entering the room, Mingzhi paces the garden. Dried, withered leaves crunch under his feet, shadows of tree trunks and branches scatter on the ground. He steps on them, studying the dark shapes distorted in the night breeze, and counts. One, two, three, four, five, six, seven, eight, nine, ten . . .

At nine hundred and fifty, he goes to sit by the pond. There is a *pop* from the water, a sigh of surprise maybe, and then silence. He longs for their company, the fishes, but knows he shouldn't wake them. Next to him the willow is a heavy patch of black. It was yellowish green earlier this evening, he remembers. He plucked a stalk for his wife as they strolled around, their usual evening walk. Told her it would bring her luck. She smiled, her lips curled like a half-moon agate. Full, red, glowing. The tiny mole above them danced, a drop of black pearl somersaulting in clear water. He was tempted to kiss her, but she glided away from him, brushing him lightly with the willow. She blushed a *not here, not now* red, and kept her eyes on the willow sprig in her palm.

Mingzhi remembers now that it was at that moment the idea had come to her.

Willow, that's the name! she said. Perfect for either a boy or a girl. Her voice had a childlike sweetness, raised high at the unexpected discovery, the excitement of it.

Her lovely voice.

He smiles, pulls a branch of willow towards him and studies it, as if studying her, his wife, and the child-to-be. *My family.* His chest feels full, warm.

Then he hears her scream, once, twice. More. Like the

scratching of one metal against another. The branch slips from his hand, swinging away.

His head throbs as he imagines her pain, her suffering. The pushing and breathing. The bleeding. Up and down, up and down. He gets up and begins to pace and count again.

One, two, three, four, five, six . . .

Strangely, he can't get past a hundred this time and doesn't even notice it. One hundred is followed by one, and the counting starts all over again. Like a cycle that never ends and is heading nowhere.

. . . Ninety-seven, ninety-eight, ninety-nine, one hundred, one, two, three, four, five . . .

He keeps counting, between the fits of screams, the shouting of the midwife to push and breathe, to fetch more hot water and towels. Until the first cock-a-doodle-doo breaks the dawn, birds sing, his family of carp raise their heads. Pop-pop-pop, pop-pop-pop.

Then everything stops, the hustle and bustle. The bleeding that wouldn't stop when it should. That flowed like water from a pipe, and eventually, washed out the long-awaited child, as lifeless as its mother.

—~—

Everything stops in the autumn of 1898.

A plot by the reformers to suppress the Lady Dragon is countered before it is launched, with a more drastic, better-calculated coup.

The Emperor, the man behind the plot, is placed under house arrest, the reformers are executed or flee. Previously demoted and dismissed officials resume their positions, new measures are abolished, old rules rule again.

It dies prematurely, the One Hundred Days of Reform, before it can fully stretch its arms and legs, breathe the fresh air of the new world.

Dead.

Lifeless.

Hopeless.

A real mandarin, a real man he is; no tears, nothing out of ordinary. Master Chai is proud of his grandson, despite Mingzhi's pale face, red-veined eyes and empty soul. The physical signs he chooses not to notice, and the inner frailty certainly never occurs to the old man.

That's Chai's man, the grandfather nods. Women are like flowers; when one wilts, more will come. He smooths his goatee, thinking: the recent deaths in the family, two in a row. Of course Mingzhi will get a new wife, or wives. The Chai family will have its scions. He will have great-grandchildren – boys, definitely boys – to continue the family line.

In the reception hall where the bier lies, Mingzhi receives his visitors, the mandarin-flattering mourners. Who come with their silver for the dead and the hope of a future favour from Mingzhi, around whom they crowd like bees around honey. One after another. From morning till night.

Mingzhi stands there, without a sip of water or a bite of rice, watching the many wriggling lips before him but hearing nothing. Surprised at how different one person's lips can be from another's: full shrivelled wide thin wet dry red pink pale grey; and the teeth: big small even uneven loose tight clean dirty white yellow brown black. Flitting past his eyes like vegetables in the marketplace: cabbage Chinese cabbage swamp cabbage tomato carrot dwarf beans broad beans fine beans okra aubergine cucumber spinach spring onions. As though he can just point at them and pick which to have, swamp cabbage or aubergine. Full lips or pink lips. White teeth or yellow teeth. Or choose not to have anything at all.

But he can't. He is a mandarin and he has to say something. He opens his mouth but doesn't know what comes out of it – his voice is indistinct, like that of a stranger shouting from a distance, shielded by layer upon layer of screens. Yet his ears bob, as if under siege by surging waves, again and again. And then, when night falls, they disappear completely, the noises.

The soundless dream of his teenage years resurfaces, the pantomime of a Peking opera, but now it seems real. That the world around him is mute and he is part of a dumb show, playing the role of a mandarin, who doesn't cry, doesn't laugh; always strong, always assumes the right manner for the right occasion.

He feels his body emptying, a hollow wrapped in a mandarin frame, sauntering around with a smile-for-politeness at the corners of its mouth.

A puppet.

The mandarin puppet holds itself up by invisible strings of discipline, family pride and self-respect. Of the social expectations of a culture five thousand years old. Until the day of the funeral. Until the bier is lifted onto the shoulders of the bearers and carried out of the house. Mingzhi fixes his eyes upon it as if he could see through it, the coffin with two lives in it: one big, the other small. The big one, his beloved wife, her face pink with powder, as calm as ever, as though she has just got herself ready for a long journey. The small one, shrouded in silk, is a lump of flesh and blood, with hands and legs and tiny fingers and toes, and a head with eyes and nose and mouth and ears.

His flesh and blood.

The hollowness inside him gradually fills up; the invisible strings detach themselves. Heavy and weary, the mandarin flops to the floor.

Everything turns black.

—ʌʌʌ—

Dead silence. The garden, the court-office, the reception hall. His room, where he hides, day after day, in a corner. Curtains drawn, lamps unlit, food pushed away, visitors rejected. Mingzhi crouches between the wardrobe and the chest of drawers, a screen shielding him from the worried servants and maids waiting to one side.

The first day he sees her face on the wardrobe, a vague figure against the dark rosewood in the dimness of the corner empty of sunlight. But he can read her perfectly: her eyes, her nose, her lips. The tiny mole above her upper lip, the little black pearl that dances as she smiles, that smiles by itself when she doesn't.

You have come to me; I knew you would. He staggers forward, reaching out –

Everything vanishes: her eyes, her nose, her lips. The little dancing black pearl.

Come back, please. Come back!

Mingzhi lurches at the wardrobe, bangs against it, slaps it, scrabbles at it with his fingers. Until he falls flat on it, his hands and body pressed hard against it and he slips, slowly, down to the floor. Two streaks, dark and wet, smear the rosewood.

The second day, he sits. Staring, waiting.

The third.

Master Chai's order comes: Mingzhi is to see him in the reception hall. The young man doesn't budge. He has now turned his gaze on the screen, the fine drawing on silk gauze. Mountains and water, huts and temples, bamboo groves and trees. And peach blossoms. Pink, cluster upon cluster, budding or blossoming, from as tiny as a copper coin to the size of a rice bowl.

A long-buried memory creeps up from the deepest recess of his heart.

Outside, there are footsteps and the thumping of a walking stick.

The screen dissolves into the magic curtain of his childhood, in the mansion in Plum Blossom Village.

'The Grand Master is here!'

His little world of Taohua Yuan.

'Get yourself out of there, you stupid fool!' A thump on the floor.

Where there is *only laughter and smiles*, and everybody

lives happily ever after.

'There are plenty of women for you to choose from,' Master Chai shouts from the other side of the screen.

Mingzhi runs his fingers over the pink flowers. The buds, the petals, the stalks. His eyes turn wet, his stomach sour.

'I've got you one, by the way. Landlord Yao's daughter. Younger and prettier.' The old man's elation fills the room, pressing against Mingzhi's screened corner.

History overlaps. The screen, the curtain. The orders. The same bursting feeling of anger and frustration. Mingzhi holds his breath, waiting for the deflating moment that follows. But it is full, his chest, still swelling –

'No!'

The explosive force gathers in his arms.

A thrust.

A loud bang.

A series of rapid trampling sounds.

The screen breaks into pieces. Mingzhi rises tall from among the debris, his hair unkempt, his eyes bloodshot, fixed on Master Chai, now shrunk back. The dragon stick lies on the floor.

'Grandpa, you're tired.' The mandarin speaks as if there is iron in his throat. 'It's time to go home and rest.'

—∞—

Mingzhi sits firm and sullen in the court-office. *His* court-office. A guarded carriage has taken away the old man, together with the orders and demands Mingzhi loathes.

He doesn't waste time. His previous routine resumes, former standards of practice are observed again: no more red envelopes and gifts for favours, only facts and evidence.

Mishandled cases are revised and reversed, damage made good: compensation is handed out to victims of injustice, honour restored to names that have been smeared.

The townsfolk are confused, unsure if this is just another game, another trap. They look on with watchful eyes, until the season turns, and he is still as just and fair as when he began, still refusing red envelopes and gifts. The townsfolk finally agree that the honest and upright official, the stern-faced Bao Gong, is back.

The stern-faced mandarin steels his heart, his gaze hard, his back rigid. His days are spent at work, evenings at Meilian's, weekends with Father Terry. Grief is nudged away with busyness, and he puts a stop to his evening strolls in the garden. When night falls, though, the past returns, haunting him with memories and dreams. He sits at his desk and focuses his mind on documents and plans, until exhaustion overcomes him and he sleeps, face down, on piles of paper.

Comfort comes from Martin's occasional letters, not so much about himself but more about Tiansheng: that the young man has settled, is learning Martin's trade, and seems to be a natural entrepreneur. *Of course he is!* Remembering Tiansheng's poultry business, Mingzhi smiles, but stops instantly. The memories associated with it are too painful to dwell on.

Strangely, there is no mention of Little Mouse in Martin's letters. *Little Mouse, the eyes and ears and executor of my secret activities.* Mingzhi shakes his head, telling himself not to worry: a little mouse in a big city, his witty servant will burrow through all the holes and drains and dungeons.

Yet still, he is worried.

The Heavenly God has more to worry about, though, such as floods, or a drought. And what if both?

Perhaps she is inspired by the Dragon Lady, or perhaps she is trying to please Her Majesty; in the mountainous north-east the Yellow River – Mother of the Earth – stages a cruel attack on her own children. Drowning them in her angry waves, gobbling up houses and cattle and sorghum. A punishment for the children of the Dragon who have been disrespectful to their mother.

This is just a warning.

The real calamity comes later: the long drought, and what follows.

Without fields to plough, without crops to harvest, idle farm boys saunter on the cracked, barren land. Finding ways to pass the time, searching for food to fill their stomachs.

When stomachs are empty, minds drift, and hallucinations make the impossible seem possible. For instance, possessing extraordinary strength bestowed by unknown spirits, the gods of everything and anything, who grant their followers powerful martial arts, the spirit-boxing.

It is a miracle. Overnight in the summer of 1899, ordinary men, some with limited martial arts and most with none, transform themselves into the almighty Boxers, who can disappear and reappear like the Monkey God, shielding themselves from swords and spears with their naked flesh, fighting enemies with their bare fists.

Or so they believe.

The Righteous Fists of Harmony, they call themselves, shouting out loud their vow to drive all foreign devils from the Land of the Dragon. The devils who are the source of all calamities, who have robbed the nation of its wealth and dignity, leaving the people with only poverty and starvation.

Their movements are rapid, the Boxers. More members are recruited: former soldiers, unemployed men, peasants with no lands to plough. Their goals are simple and their targets clear: foreigners, and those associated with them. Individual Westerners, missionaries, local converts, churches.

Killed, burnt, destroyed.

~

In the quiet southern town of Pindong, Father Terry organizes a performance in his church. It is a Sunday afternoon, and Mingzhi arrives early to find them busy: Father Terry in the church hall hanging a curtain across the makeshift stage; Meilian and Jiaxi in the adjacent room, getting the actors – the children from the orphanage – ready. Dressing them and making them up, giving final instructions.

The children buzz with excitement, comparing costumes, giggling at each other's rouged faces, a rosy blob on each cheek. 'You'll look stunning on stage with those,' Meilian reassures them, and more giggles come in response. Their eyes, which once held only tears and sadness, flicker with anticipation.

Most of them are victims of the drought, these older children. Their parents failed to secure food and left to try their fortunes elsewhere, or died. While the Heavenly God remains immune to the many prayers, skeletal boys and girls are sent to the orphanage, to the hand of the foreign Deity.

Mingzhi looks at the faces around him, far from plump yet, but skeletons no longer. Healthy, smiling, a possible bright future ahead.

Meilian is surrounded by the children, adjusting outfits here and there. Mingzhi offers a helping hand but is ushered out into the hall instead. 'There's no place here for a mandarin.' Meilian tells him off.

A young boy pulls at Meilian's sleeve, pointing at his hair, made messy by scratching. Meilian squats down, unties the band and starts combing, getting stuck where the tangles are. The boy frowns a naughty boy's frown: mouth twisted to one side, eyes narrowed. Blinking, blinking.

Like Junwei.

The combing stops. She hears a loud beat in her heart, surprised at how easily her lost son's name popped into her head. As if he were always there, by her side, and she could just call him round: 'Junwei, come here and have your hair combed.' Then he would reluctantly drag himself over, the naughty boy's frown already on his face. 'Yes, Mother. But promise it won't hurt.' Eyes narrowed, blinking, blinking.

I promise you, my dear.

If only she could.

If only.

Meilian pulls the young boy closer and strokes his head, tender fingers clawing at his hair, spoiling it, and has to tidy it again. She stays squatting long after the boy has walked away, fixing her gaze on him, his tiny shoulders bundled with borrowed love.

Deep breath, deep breath, and she gets up, motherly tears packed away, tucked into a hidden corner.

The play will begin soon. *Without Junwei*.

Mingzhi sits in the front row as guest of honour. Behind him, the townsfolk and villagers are honoured too, thrilled at the chance to be in the same room as The Mandarin. Their excitement is suppressed to sibilant whispers, and they cover their mouths with their hands as they crack pumpkin seeds – shh, shh, no noise is to be made, no disrespect to be shown to their respected mandarin.

Delighted at this unexpected effect, Father Terry pulls back the curtain –

Enter the fairies, the spirits of the forest.

Seven winged fairies glide over the lawn in long pink gowns, singing, dancing. Curious forest creatures peep from behind trees and stones, between branches and leaves. Deer, marmots, weasels, squirrels, frogs and toads, turtles, butterflies and dragonflies, cockatoos and peacocks. Admiring the beautiful fairies as they praise this beautiful world.

Foreign fairies in Chinese costumes! Mingzhi nods approvingly at Father Terry, remembering the incident at the opening of the orphanage.

The song changes. The tunes get low and gloomy. The fairy sisters are unhappy. Their Fairy Mother has forbidden them to venture beyond the forest. They are the fairy weavers, and they need to carry out their duty, to spin silk for their fellow fairies.

Mingzhi now knows that his priest friend has done more

than just play with the costumes. He has cleverly adapted the folk story of Niulang and Zhinu, the Herdsman and the Weaver Lady, and combined it with Western fairy tales: forest spirits have slipped into the bodies of Heavenly fairies, the Fairy Mother has replaced the Heavenly Mother. *With Meilian's help*, Mingzhi is certain.

'How boring!' The youngest fairy sister swirls round and round, whipping up leaves and flowers, letting her anger whirl in the air.

'Let's go out for once, just the once, please!' she pleads, describing the human world she has always peeped at from the top of the highest mountain: green fields, silvery rivers; hot, steaming, tasty human food; and the beautiful huts dotted round the hills.

Her sisters finally relent, and they set off.

The fairy sisters wander through human lands. Happy tunes return, happy dancing brightens up the air. Then a stream of clear water in a secluded bamboo grove catches their eyes, just perfect for tired legs. They wade into the water, swimming, splashing at each other, laughing and screaming.

Until they hear a sound. A human sound. Panicked, they rush to the shore and hurry away. She is too slow, the youngest of the fairies. 'Wait for me!' Panicked, she trips over a tree trunk and falls.

How life has changed without their little sister. The weaver fairies sing a sad song as they observe how their sister has been made the wife to the young herdsman who rescued her, hiding away her fairy wings so she can't return home. But she seems happy, deeply in love with her human husband, enjoying her human food; tolerating the crude shack she lives in; continuing to spin, not silk but rough cotton, just as easy.

Like Martin, appreciating his life here in this foreign land. Mingzhi knows what is going to happen next. The Fairy Mother will intervene and the couple will be separated, only to meet once a year on the Seventh Day of the Seventh Month. That will spell out the difficulties faced by the foreigners in this country. Foreigners like Martin and Father Terry.

He is wrong.

Instead the Mother Fairy, after listening to her fairy daughter's plea, understands and agrees to let the couple live happily ever after. The fairy sisters sing in celebration of the happiness of their beloved sister.

A Chinese story with a twist of Western optimism. The ending that Father Terry longs for. Understanding and acceptance. But do they, the people, understand?

Mingzhi looks round, sees the fast dispersing crowd and hears their comments: on the costumes (*beautiful*), the stage (*well, a little better than Chinese opera*), the singing and dancing (*Chinese opera is still the best*), the story (*not bad, but where are the magpies? They are supposed to meet once a year, bridged by the magpies*). Walking, talking, frowning. Not rude, no angry faces, a good start for certain.

Mingzhi goes to Father Terry, seizes his hand in a firm *trust me* grasp, shakes and shakes and shakes. It's only a matter of time, he says.

—∾—

Time does matter. It wheels past the seasons and turns the year round. It makes even the strongest lion aged, its body feeble, its limbs atrophied, emaciated by illness. A once strong and loud and agile lion like Master Chai.

Another drought descends on Plum Blossom Village in the spring of 1900. This time, Master Chai is too weak to leave the house to inspect the fields. He had a relapse of his illness after being sent back from Pindong Town, and has never fully recovered since.

But he sees them in his mind's eye as he lies in bed, the fields and the poppies: the cracked earth and dried stalks.

His lost harvest.

His cash.

A full, bursting feeling clogs his chest, and he needs to let it out. Chest heaving, he shouts: 'Get me my pipe!'

Silence.

It has been quiet in the mansion lately. Fewer footsteps, less movement, as some of the maids and servants have been dismissed. So there are fewer mouths to feed, less money to be spent. Liwei did the accounts, worked out the budget and solution, and the old man could only agree. Reluctantly.

Things changed overnight when he was sent back. He sees the invisible eyes of his ancestors peering from corners, their fingers pointing through the darkness; hears their contemptuous sniggers from behind walls, and knows why. The ancestral book of hierarchy has been rewritten, his name repositioned – or scratched out altogether, perhaps. Too much shame on the Chai clan, a laughing-stock among the eighteen generations of ancestors in the netherworld.

He can hear their laughter, tinged with anger and disbelief: 'The rightful giver of orders is being ordered around!'

He has tried to stage a comeback, messages have been sent to Mingzhi. But 'Home, Urgent, Grandfather' are no longer the force they once were. He does return, his grandson, on Likang's anniversary, for the New Year family reunion. Grandfather, uncle, mother and grandson sit at the dinner table, still getting together, still a family. And Mingzhi plays his part: tea for the elders, incense for the ancestors.

A dutiful young man, as polite as always.

But there is something in his eyes. Something. The old man tries to think but his mind is blurred, confused. He needs a boost.

'Where is it? Where's my pipe?'

Master Chai waits and listens. There is no sign of his maid. *Oh no, they can't have sent her away!* He shouts again, louder, and hears his broken voice tearing through the tranquillity. Then Da Niang comes rushing in.

The old man's heart sinks.

Da Niang keeps her head and eyes low, preparing the pipe and handing it to her father-in-law, who snatches it from her and hurls it against the wall. The clay bowl inside it smashes to pieces; black opium stains the floor, as dark as the cloud in Master Chai's stomach. He gasps for air.

Outside, Liwei stands by the window, watching Da Niang clear the mess, making slow jabs with a bamboo broom, a thin figure weighing down by Master Chai's heavy breathing. Liwei grips the window frame, fighting back the urge to rush in, to take her in his arms. To protect her.

In the room, Da Niang squats to sweep the debris into a dustpan. Without turning, she senses *his* gaze at her back, and feels protected, as she always does when he is around. Like that night, years ago, when Likang came home drunk and beat her with a candle holder. Alerted by his maid, Liwei hurried over and stopped his brother, throwing a loud slap on his face. Humiliated, Likang did not set foot in the mansion for a month after that.

Liwei began his habit of checking on Da Niang, to make sure she was well, and that Likang did not hurt her again.

Da Niang smiles quietly. She remembers those times when they sat in silence, drinking tea, a moon table between them.

Yet still, his caring gaze, his gentle words leaped over, warm and soothing. At first, accidental meetings of eyes set her pulsating, her face flushed. Later, their gazes locked together, long, wordless, and her heart felt full. When she began to long for his visits, she stopped him from coming. One day, two. She locked herself in her room, and paced about. Sleepless nights, tear-sodden pillows, unsettled heart.

On the third night, when the lights were out, when the mansion was asleep, she heard a knock on the door and did not hesitate this time. The Confucian codes crumpled in the soft whispers that soothed a fragile heart, in the firm, strong shoulders that embraced a thin, pitiable soul.

Their world, just two of them, on nights when no one was watching.

Until Likang came home, having spent his allowance. And inside her, a new life grew.

The best thing that's ever happened to me.

Da Niang rises and turns to the window, a smile on her face.

It's a Saturday morning and Mingzhi decides to take a tour around the town. Not wearing his official gown, taking slow steps, as casual as can be.

His recent circuits of the town have pointed to a significant finding: the place is getting quieter. There is no lack of shops or stalls, and the marketplace is operating as usual. But merchandise is scarce, people fewer. The mounds of rice and corn once piled high in abundance are now reduced to just a few sacks hidden under counters: only for those who can afford them; the prices are as high as the demand.

Mingzhi makes his way along the main street, noting that the crowd has dwindled yet again. He walks past the shops and stalls, where starving flies gorge on whatever they manage to find. Traces of dried anchovies. The remains of salted fish. A drop of coagulated lard. A fresh green lump of chicken dung. Swarming black dots seal up the stains and crumbs and droppings, humming, climbing on each other's backs, fighting for their delicious meals. And at the counters, shopkeepers doze, waking only to make occasional flaps with their flyswatters. One flap, and the flies disperse, before they return again, the food too good to resist.

At least they still have scraps to fight over. Mingzhi thinks of the equally starving peasants, and the dockers at the now much idle port. His head feels heavy, already burdened with the governor's unrealistic tax targets. He sighs. Only if a miracle arises could he achieve his target. A miracle like –

Martin!

Mingzhi remembers the pottery business in Lixing Town. Perhaps his friend can come up with an equally miraculous idea. He should have thought of consulting him much sooner. Martin's letters have been infrequent lately. Maybe it's time to pay his friend a visit, and to check on Tiansheng as well. Maybe he should take Meilian and Jiaxi with him, a reward for their hard work at the orphanage.

The thought excites him and his pace lightens.

There's a crowd ahead, a rare sight. At the centre of it a banner hangs down from a bamboo pole:

Job Opportunities

Big, bright red letters. Like delicious pieces of rice cake. And more people are being drawn towards it; people hungry for a mouthful of the cake, sweet and tasty and filling.

Gravitated to it, Mingzhi moves closer and hears a strange accent, like Father Terry's: 'Good jobs, good money!' He is pushed forward by the throng.

'Good food, nice place!'

At the front, a Westerner sitting at a table is taking down the particulars of a peasant, who is then asked to ink his thumb and press it onto the sheet of paper. A finger print for a seal. Stamped. The promise of a job hundreds of miles away in the south-east. A dream of abundant food and better lives for his wife and children.

A life is sold, to the land of vast rubber estates, mine works, coconut trees. Never to return, never to see his home again.

Another peasant takes his turn. And another.

Jobs, promises, dreams.

The South China Sea laughs its slyest laugh, waiting eagerly for the countless boatloads of cheap labour, the ocean's offerings. For the chance to show his mighty power.

His roar is the surging waves, his sneeze the thunderstorm, his hiccup the whirlpool. And he will have fresh food to feed his family of sea creatures. Some days his mood is good, however, and he will relent, will let them sail all the way to the Straits of Malacca, where other creatures are waiting. Creatures such as bloodsucking mine owners, secret societies with their open fights against one another, and the unbearable tropical heat in which malaria lurks.

These are not described in the contracts.

Mingzhi walks away with a frown, uncertain. The banner flutters in the morning breeze, the characters shout aloud in the air. Big, bright, red. Too seductive, impossible to resist.

Twenty-One

Imperial City, June 1900

They are having tea, Mingzhi and Martin, in a secluded corner of a teahouse in Beijing. Meilian and Jiaxi have gone to explore the surrounding area, with Tiansheng as their guide. Since arriving this morning, mother and daughter have been fascinated by the many shops with merchandise they have never seen before: fabrics from across the country and abroad, exquisite headpieces, paintings and ornamental displays, clocks and fob-watches. And there are occasional glimpses of Western women in bulging frocks, delicate hats and umbrellas. All too luring for a first-timer in the Imperial City.

Mingzhi is content to have tea with his old friend, sharing a pot of *pu'er*. But this time, Martin prepares it: discarding the first brew, rinsing the cups, getting the second brew ready just in time for the right taste. Focused, without hesitation, in perfect measurements.

Although he still laughs (as he recalls the misunderstanding with the porcelain vendor) and jokes (about finding Mingzhi a *girlfriend*), Martin is obviously much quieter than before. Mingzhi sips his tea, lets the sweet aftertaste of *pu'er* linger on his tongue, wondering how to explain the main reason for visiting his friend. Then he hears noises from outside.

'Down with the foreign devils!'

'Boycott foreign goods!'

Mingzhi peers through the window. In the street, people hold placards carrying the same slogans. They shout, and angry veins dance in their necks. Then come louder cries and hurried footsteps.

'Police! Run!'

The protesters flee. But not quickly enough. A team of uniformed men rushes into the crowd, batons in hand. Lunging forward, striking fast. Screams and curses come in response, followed by running and chasing. Placards are trampled, displays and stalls knocked over.

And they are gone. The street returns to normality, seemingly.

'Welcome to Beijing,' Martin smiles bitterly.

Trade has been difficult lately. Martin tells of chaotic scenes of attacks against shops and warehouses storing foreign merchandise. And in a few instances, Westerners have been assaulted. These are random raids carried out by individual groups. A greater threat comes from the more organized Boxers in the north, and rumour has it that they are advancing southwards.

Mingzhi reads fear in his friend's tone, tries to find comforting words but his tongue is stiff.

'Maybe they won't come here,' he mutters.

Martin smiles, gestures to the waiter for more hot water.

They will come, he knows. But now he will prepare a pot of *longjing*, a fine green tea, light, refreshing. To share it with his friend. Hot tea, old stories, new dreams. A cosy afternoon to remember.

They will come soon, the Boxers, so the foreign diplomats and ministers believe, telegraphing their coded nerves across the oceans: HELP. TROOPS NEEDED. NOW. To Great Britain, Austria, Italy, Germany, France, Japan and Russia. They, too, will come soon.

Mingzhi finds out from Tiansheng that Little Mouse had left him and Martin just a few days after arriving in the Imperial City. That he said he'd go anywhere, so long as he didn't have to live under the roof of a foreign devil.

As he owes his life to Mingzhi, Tiansheng takes every opportunity to repay his friend: making sure Mingzhi's meals are served on time, preparing the carriage for every outing, getting everything he needs ready for him. He is making himself a replacement for Little Mouse.

Mingzhi understands, knows that rejection will be hurtful, so he quietly accepts Tiansheng's help.

He is as adept as Little Mouse, too, a surprising discovery. The former opera singer is now a shrewd trader, Martin's right-hand man. Accurate, meticulous, good at negotiations. Despair and deprivation are the stories of yesterday, though still painful to recall.

The two friends work together, complementing one

another, and Mingzhi is happy for them, unexpected outcome of a tragedy.

~

It's their last day in the Imperial City, and Martin hosts a dinner for his guests at a restaurant in the British Territory. Martin orders a pot of tea while they wait for Tiansheng, unusually late.

After two rounds of tea, Martin gestures for the waiter to bring out the dishes. Mingzhi watches as Martin carefully picks bones out of the steamed fish for Meilian and Jiaxi, who, unaccustomed, push back Martin's serving in a fluster.

'We should serve you,' says Meilian in the fluent English she learned from Father Terry, and spoons food into Martin's bowl instead.

Martin holds her wrist, stopping her: 'Forget it. You're my guest, and men are supposed to serve the ladies.'

Meilian freezes, still held by Martin. *A man, holding my hand!* She blushes. Mingzhi captures his sister's shyness, her sudden beauty, and he sees that Martin notices it, too, keeping his eyes on her. The hands – one yellowish tan; the other pale and pink – are momentarily locked in the air, then retreat. The face that is already red gets redder.

Mingzhi looks at Martin and then Meilian. *My friend, my sister.* He smiles. A secret plan creeps into his mind.

'Look!' Jiaxi, who has been quietly admiring the view from the second floor, points towards the east, where the evening sky burns red. There are occasional showers of sparks, accompanied by crackling sounds, similar to those of the fireworks. 'Is there some kind of celebration?' Turning back to the table, Jiaxi sees only the pale faces of the adults around her.

Martin rises to his feet. 'The churches! They are in the East City!'

Parts of the sky are black with smoke, thickening, hovering over the Heavenly Roof of the Imperial City.

There is a commotion, seemingly a distance away, gradually drawing nearer. Mingzhi can recognize the noises now: the shouting of a crowd, mixed with the banging of gongs and drums.

Martin follows some of the other diners, rushing to the terrace to observe the situation; while Mingzhi keeps himself close to Meilian and Jiaxi, both shaking.

In the streets, dark shadows loom, running, jostling. Martin can make out the silhouettes of several approaching squads of men in black, scurrying towards the British Territory from every direction. Lean and light, darting fast, chanting slogans:

'Heavenly God protects us! Down with the foreign devils!

'Heavenly God protects us! Down with the foreign devils!'

Like the guards of the God of Death from the netherworld, humming the tunes of death as they corner their targets, as they cancel out their names from the Book of Life. Martin shivers.

Peering down at the entrance of the restaurant, he sees a familiar figure burst in. Tiansheng. He blunders up the stairs, knocking against tables and chairs along the way, stepping over cups and bowls and plates that crash to the floor, and hurrying towards them.

'Quick, we have to leave!' Tiansheng shouts, his face full

of fear. The Boxers are all over the city, he says, and are laying siege to the foreign quarters, targeting the churches in the East City. 'They have burnt the foreign temples, and have killed the local converts, too!' The groups are attacking foreign legations, missionaries and individual Westerners, too. 'And anyone connected with the Westerners!' Tiansheng glances at Mingzhi.

Panic stirs in the restaurant; the customers, mostly Westerners, begin their race to the exits. More tables, more chairs are knocked over, more cups and bowls and plates smashed on the floor. Anxious footsteps thump the ground, fearful cries tear the ears. The most eager among them jump down from the upper-floor terrace to the street, but there are more crushing their ways through the narrow exit of the main door.

Mingzhi, Martin and Tiansheng stay close to Meilian and Jiaxi. Mother and daughter are almost crying now. The fleeing crowd presses against them, pushing them down the stairs, towards the exit, and then they are jammed at the door. Elbows and fists fall hard on their heads and bodies as the people squeeze to get out. Cries, screams, curses. More pushing, more shoving, and they are in the street.

Outside, there are even more people, knocking against each other as they run in all directions. More cries, more screams, more curses. Abandoned carriages are scattered in the streets, blocking the way; the drivers are long gone, the horses neigh hysterically as they gallop, brushing by the old and young, men and women in their panicked fleeing.

Mingzhi and his group huddle together, avoiding the men and women and horses that dart past them.

'Heavenly God protects us! Down with the foreign devils!

'Heavenly God protects us! Down with the foreign devils!'

The sound of gongs and drums and chanting is getting nearer, rumbling in their ears.

Martin shouts: 'We have to get out of here!' And they begin to run, too.

'Come on, faster!' Tiansheng urges. Lifting their long gowns, Meilian and Jiaxi grit their teeth as they struggle on their tiny feet.

But not fast enough.

They are waylaid. A team of Boxers stands before them, angry eyes staring at Martin.

'I am Chai Mingzhi, the mandarin of Pindong Town, a sixth-grade official.' Mingzhi goes to stand in front of Martin. 'This is my friend.'

'To hell with the mandarin!' One of the Boxers pushes Mingzhi to one side and points his sword at Martin. Mingzhi immediately steps up to Martin again, drawing himself closer to the enemies.

'What the hell!' The group surges forward, knocking both Mingzhi and Martin to the ground.

Mingzhi hears a light *Ah!* among the group as he falls. Familiar. He searches. In the dimness of evening, among the shuffling black figures, he sees him. Little Mouse. A sword on his back, stout and strong. Mingzhi captures a flicker of pain in his former servant's eyes. He opens his mouth, but holds back his words on seeing Little Mouse's muted *shoo*.

Unaware of all these, Tiansheng goes to whisk away the sword that points at Mingzhi. 'Let them go!' He is immediately pressed down, made to kneel on all fours under the sharp edge of a sword. Meilian and Jiaxi hug each other tightly together, crying.

'How about we send them all to the Western Paradise?' The young man who is aiming his sword at Martin turns to Little Mouse, apparently the leader of this squad.

'No! Please, let them go! Please!' Meilian flops down on the ground, pulling Jiaxi with her, and kowtows to the group. Her forehead knocks hard against the gravel, each thump falls heavily on Mingzhi's heart. He steals another look at Little Mouse, who glances away instantly.

Taking their leader's silence as an answer, the group starts chanting, preparing for the execution.

'Heavenly God protects us! Down with the foreign devils!

'Heavenly God protects us! Down with the foreign devils!'

Their voices get louder, thundering in their captives' ears. The captives. Heads bowed, feelings and senses voided. Everything stops, only waiting for *the moment*.

'Hey, that lot is trying to get away!' Little Mouse shouts, pointing at some fleeting figures in a distance. 'Go and get them! I'll take care here.' A loud 'Yes!' comes in reply, and the Boxers retract their swords and run after their new targets.

At the far end of the street, there are more identical groups of men in black, waylaying foreigners, crashing open doors and windows, pulling out those hiding indoors: push, kick, punch; and furniture: exquisite rosewood bedposts, dining tables and chairs burst into splendid flames.

Little Mouse hurriedly ushers Mingzhi and the rest to a secluded alley. 'Go now. Leave the city!' Little Mouse keeps his eyes on his former master, his voice low and firm.

'Come with me, please. Stay with me, like in the old days.' Mingzhi's heart clenches.

Little Mouse shakes his head. 'It can never be the same. And it's not over here yet, not till the last foreign devil is gone.' He glances at Martin. 'Leave now, please. Go back to where you come from. I can only save you once.'

Martin nods *thank you*. Little Mouse takes another look at Mingzhi, then turns and dashes away.

Something sticks in Mingzhi's throat. He fixes his gaze at the black shape that is swiftly dissolving into the distant darkness. As though Little Mouse has simply disappeared into the air, now thick with smoke.

Mingzhi remembers his former servant's indignation against the Japanese occupation of Taiwan, and the existence of the foreign territories in Shanghai. Knows now why Little Mouse couldn't pronounce Martin's name: he simply refused to do so. The acrid smell of smoke tickles Mingzhi's throat; tears squeeze from the corners of his eyes as he chokes and coughs.

They manage to find a carriage and rush to Tianjin. Tiansheng secures places for them in a salt boat and they set off, sailing downstream along the Grand Canal.

It is fully loaded with people, this boat. They all sit squashed against each other on the deck. Fear hovers in the night air, intensified by the frightened eyes, the suppressed sobs. Opposite Mingzhi, Meilian and Jiaxi, exhausted from their flight, have fallen asleep hugging each other, their dresses tattered, their faces covered in soot. He feels a twinge of guilt, and hides his face between his knees.

Someone grasps his arm. Martin. Sitting next to him, he pats his shoulder lightly: *It's all right, it's all right.*

There are whispers in the darkness, talk of travelling across the sea, southwards to the tropics. Of sun and beaches and coconut trees, of exotic fruits and colourful fishes. Martin listens attentively, and Mingzhi notes the embers of longing in his friend's eyes. Martin looks back at him, smiling, a knowing nod. A decision is made.

'Are you coming?' Martin whispers. 'You want to see the world, don't you? Let's do it together, then.'

Silence. The government office, the townsfolk of Pindong, Da Niang, Uncle Liwei, and the articles in the *Prince of Wales Island Gazette* flash before Mingzhi. The building, the faces and the lines of black print sway like the waves underneath and around the boat. His head spins, his eyelids feel heavy, and he dozes off.

A string of young coconuts falls into Mingzhi's dream. Green, juicy, sweet.

—~—

Things have changed in just a few days.

They return to Pindong. Mingzhi asks Tiansheng to crouch inside their carriage, aware of the danger of him being recognized.

But trouble persists.

The news of the Boxers' siege of Tianjin and the Imperial City has whipped up anti-foreigner sentiment. At first there are only stares – angry, hateful – at Martin, who sits at the open front of the carriage. Then comes the abuse and the stones, aimed at Mingzhi, too, the foreign devil's friend. *And I have done so much for them.* Mingzhi feels the pain not on his skin but inside him.

What will they do next? Suddenly Mingzhi's heart sinks. He directs the driver to head for the church.

There are only a few pillars left, still smoking, a slant on the rubble where the church once stood. Before Mingzhi can stop them, Meilian and Jiaxi have rushed to the building next to the ruin, the orphanage, which is unscathed. The door and windows are shut tight, and there are placards on the walls, *Down with the foreigners*. The mother and daughter hammer on the door, calling for Father Terry. A reply comes from behind the door, a foreign accent.

Mingzhi sighs, relieved. Meilian and Jiaxi cling tight to each other and cry with joy.

Despite their lengthy pleas, Father Terry is determined to stay with the children, to rebuild the church when the situation is under control.

'They need me here, and it's my mission.' The priest stands firm and confident at the doorstep, persuading Meilian and Jiaxi to leave instead.

'Go now, all of you. They know you are friends of mine.' Father Terry shuts the door.

A click, and they are two worlds apart.

Mingzhi drags his sister and his niece away, in tears.

It's safer there in the village, Mingzhi suggests, and they head for Plum Blossom Village instead of the government office.

~

There will be a ship tomorrow and they decide to shelter overnight in Plum Blossom Village.

Mingzhi looks around the dinner table: Da Niang, Uncle Liwei, Meilian, Jiaxi, Martin and Tiansheng. *My friends and family.* The perfect dinner he has always dreamed of, though with one person missing. He thinks of her, his wife, sitting beside him, and he would pour tea, spoon dishes for her, not the other way round.

If only he could.

But for now, he will do what he still can. He pours a round of *wu jiapi* for the table, and proposes a toast: 'To better luck and the future!'

'To better luck and the future!'

Drinks, food, an evening of chatter, of warmth and togetherness.

In his room, Master Chai hears their noise wafting through the empty courtyards. Earlier in the evening Mingzhi brought him his dinner, feeding him rice porridge, carefully wiping away the excess from the corners of his mouth and beard.

My grandson.

The old man's anger melted away with the spoonfuls of gruel. He wanted to say something but his voice clattered at his throat. He wanted to tell his grandson that the ancestors would always be proud of him, but his head drooped before he had finished his dinner. Drifting off, he heard the sound of footsteps, drifting too. Away.

Now that he is awake again, Master Chai thinks of the dragons in the central hall. He sees them slide off the pillars and begin to somersault across the empty hall, their mouths spurting fire, their claws sharp and glistening. Then they lunge at him, their faces turn to Mandarin Liu's, laughing hysterically, swooping down –

Master Chai closes his eyes tight, puffing, and everything stops. He drifts off again; this time a sea of poppies billow in his dream. Red, beautiful, waving at him.

In the west court, the party continues.

Da Niang spills her wine. She hurriedly pulls out her kerchief, but a soft piece of silk is already dabbing at the back of her hand.

'Are you all right?' Uncle Liwei, sitting next to her, wipes her sleeve.

Da Niang pulls way, flustered, triggering the same reaction from Uncle Liwei, now aware of the presence of the others in the room. Not fast enough, though, not to Mingzhi's sensitive eyes. He has captured them all: Uncle Liwei's caring gaze and Da Niang's shyness, and the flickers of uneasiness in their eyes that ensued. He reads the quick exchange of gestures between them: Da Niang frowns *Be careful*, while Uncle Liwei nods *I am sorry*.

Mingzhi stares at the kerchiefs in their hands: the identical peach blossoms embroidered in the corners, the familiar smell of sandalwood. The kerchief Liwei used to stop him from sneezing on Likang's hundred-day memorial ceremony, another given by Da Niang to wipe his face at the dinner with Meilian and Jiaxi in the Little Hut. Distant memories resurface: the soft whispers at night, Liwei's refusal to remarry and his decision not to leave the mansion.

Mingzhi stares up at his mother's blushing face, the same shyness he saw in Meilian just a few days before.

He feels dizzy, and everything, everybody seems to be receding into the distance. He sees their smiling faces, but in his ears, Er Niang and Golden Swallow's frivolous voices bob, loudly. Their faces dissolve into those of his mother's and his uncle's.

An outburst of laughter brings Mingzhi back to the dinner table. They are playing a game with chopsticks, his friends and family, passing a meatball from one to another. Martin, who is keen to show his chopstick-wielding skills, has just dropped it. Uncle Liwei's turn now. Next to him, Da Niang raises her chopsticks, ready to take the meatball over from him.

Mingzhi watches, as if there is an invisible line in the air, a line drawn by the book of The Analects of Confucius, the two-thousand-year-old code of conduct that is ingrained in him, that defines the roles and rules in a family, society and nation. Lines that are not to be crossed. Yet as he watches, the two pairs of chopsticks cross the line, intertwine in the air.

Mingzhi notices how Da Niang and Uncle Liwei work in accordance, the passing and the taking over. A seamless effort, as smooth as the evening, a harmonious family gathering. He wishes he had noticed nothing, nothing did happen, and he is just enjoying his time with his family. But he can't, curious eyes keep looking, searching for clues to prove himself wrong.

Another attempt to pass the meatball, and Uncle Liwei frowns as he tries to stay focused, his usual expression at the numerous chess games they had. The games. And the evening walks, his caring words, and the long journey to Lixing, just to see him! *Why did Uncle Liwei spend so much time with me, and not with Mingyuan?* A sudden spell of cold sweat washes over Mingzhi, his face ashen. He has an immediate urge to leave the table, walk out of the room, the mansion, the village, and never return.

'Hey, it's your turn now!' Martin taps on Mingzhi's shoulder: 'Show me how good you are at this!' But the young man sits still.

'Son?' Da Niang puts her hand on Mingzhi's, and he pulls away at once, but slowly places it back where it was before. Eyes cast low, body rigid, lips wriggle. Around the table, smiles freeze, noises cease, all eyes on Mingzhi. He wishes he could simply sneak away, unnoticed, but knows he has to say it out loud – the decision he has just made. He clears his throat.

Mingzhi sits alone in a quiet corner of the ship's deck. The morning breeze sends over the fresh, muddy smell of the river. Not far away, Jiaxi is holding Meilian's hand, admiring her mother's engagement ring, a token Martin inherited from his grandmother.

Last night Mingzhi delivered Martin's proposal to his sister, and Meilian did not hesitate for long, encouraged by her brother. Days of adventure on the road together have allowed Meilian to learn more about Martin: the way he takes care of her and Jiaxi, his tenderness, his laughter, his optimism. She missed out on much in the earlier part of her life, and doesn't wish to let happiness slip away.

Mingzhi is proud of his sister, her brave decision. She will have a second chance, of her own choice: a man who will serve her, and serve her well.

The morning sun falls on the smiling faces of Meilian and Jiaxi. Bright and luminous, like the future they envisage. Next to them, Martin and Tiansheng are involved in a discussion, working out plans for their arrival in the new world, perhaps. *My practical and efficient friends*, Mingzhi nods.

He feels the contents of the bundle in his lap, the chess set Da Niang insisted he took with him. *Remember,* yinshui siyuan, *never forget your origins*. And a letter. *My origins.* Mingzhi smiles bitterly. He had steeled himself against his mother's tears. The announcement at the dinner table that he would leave with the others was too sudden for her. Uncle Liwei had tried to dissuade him, too. We are a family; we should stay together, his uncle said. Mingzhi kept his head down. Said he would write to them. Later that night, he drafted a letter, leaving the mansion and everything associated to it to Uncle Liwei. There will be no more opium poppies, he is certain: Uncle Liwei will see to it.

What do they expect me to say? He shakes his head. *And what are they going to say to me?* He holds the letter up against the sun and wind, squints, and sees a thin sheet of paper inside the envelope, the soft corners flutter in the gusts. He is afraid. Uncertain if he should open it, if it contains the truth he is running away from.

He puts it back in the bundle and goes to stand at the front of the deck. The ship cuts through the waves like scissors, white foam bubbling along the sides of the hull. He wishes it were the books of Confucius he has read that are lying on the surface of the water, being cut open, torn to pieces, turned into foam and bubbles. Pop, pop, pop. Vanishing into the air. And that he would happily stay with his family, a real family, a new beginning in the old mansion.

But they are inside him, the black and white of the dos and don'ts. Of what is moral and what is not. The two-thousand-year-old rules that have made men stand as men.

Mingzhi takes out the letter again, holds it in his hand, then lets it go.

The thin sheets of paper swirl in the air, before falling into the river and floating on the surface like a withered lily on a pond. Then they sink, disappearing into the frothing water.

Tomorrow the ship will enter the sea, across which the naval fleets of the Eight-Nation Allied Powers – Britain, France, Italy, America, Austria, Japan, Germany, Russia – will soon sail, bringing with them tens of thousands of troops. All ready for a bite of the cake they have been hungry for, sweet and soft and creamy.

A cake called China.

Standing on the deck, Mingzhi lets the hem of his gown flutter in the wind. He stares ahead at the horizon, where flocks of seagulls hover, where the water turns a deeper blue and the river widens into the sea.

Acknowledgements

To Xinran and Toby Eady – thanks greatly for making me feel warm in this cold country, and making this book possible; also to my editors Laetitia Rutherford and Sam Humphreys for their generous support.

Thanks to Willy Maley for always being there. To Alasdair Gray and Susan Castillo for their kind words that moved me on in the early days of writing this book, and to James Kelman, Tom Leonard and Liz Lochhead for their critical comments; also to my other readers, Rob Maslen, Andrew Radford and Rory Watson.

To my family, especially my brother, Ping Sui, and my sister, Chew Peng, for believing in me; my sister-in-law, Sow Yeng, for taking care of the family when I was writing this book, thousands of miles away; and most importantly, my mother, who never understands my choices in life, but loves me enough to let me go.

To my friends: Seng Wee, Teresa Kok, Siew Kook, Chew Fong, Roland Lee, Dorothy Alexander, Eunice Buchanan, Tara McKevitt, Jackie Killeen and Richard Bull, for standing by me; and to Margaret and Michael Welsh for their cosy kitchen and warm tea. To R.S., who sent me her book, which inspired me to write mine.

I am grateful to the Scottish Arts Council for the bursary that eased my worries, and to Jamie Coleman and Samar Hammand for their hard work and their enthusiasm for my writing.

I share this book with you.